THE ANDERSON LINE
Book 1 The Seas of Fortune

Edward Anderson was the youngest captain in Driscoll's fleet, a hardened self-made sailor who had spent half his life before the mast. Penelope was the pampered and cherished only daughter of a plantation millionaire, a Southern society belle groomed for marriage to a man she loathed. The captain and the heiress had nothing in common—except a headstrong desire to break every rule, to risk all they had in the storm of love and fortune.

The Anderson Line
The Seas of Fortune

by
Simon McKay

MAGNA PRINT BOOKS
Long Preston, North Yorkshire,
England.

British Library Cataloguing in Publication Data.

McKay, Simon, *1930*
  The Anderson Line.
  Bk. 1 : The seas of fortune
  Rn: Christopher Nicole   I. Title
  823'.914(F)

  ISBN 1-85057-430-8
  ISBN 1-85057-431-6 Pbk

First Published in Great Britain by Sphere Books Ltd. 1983

Published in Large Print 1988 by arrangement with Sphere Books Ltd. London and Berkley Publishing Group New York.

Printed and bound in Great Britain by
Redwood Burn Limited, Trowbridge, Wiltshire.

CHAPTER 1

'Careful there, careful.' Edward Anderson leaned on the rail of the barquentine *Regina*, watching the crate being lifted from the Bordeaux dock, trembling and swaying as the stevedores tugged and pulled on the ropes, which in turn creaked through their blocks and pulleys as if about to find the weight too much for them. 'Easy…oh, you talk to them, monsieur.'

Monsieur Decazes, the shipping agent, broke into a stream of French, which was quite beyond Edward's understanding. Foreign languages did not come easily to him. He was what he appeared to be, and not only from his blue jacket and peaked cap: a sailor, who had spent the last eleven of his twenty-five years almost continuously at sea. His profession and confidence was reflected in his every movement, as well as his tall, powerful physique, his mop of unruly fair hair, his piercing pale blue eyes, the wind tan which coated his somewhat aquiline features a deep and permanent brown. Monsieur Decazes no doubt thought him uncommonly young to command a Driscoll Line ship, but that was the Driscoll way. Old James Driscoll, whatever his faults—and he possessed

7

a great number—could recognise a seaman when he saw one. He had been responsible for launching the careers of several famous skippers in his time. Besides, he took no risks. A Driscoll skipper was always a half partner, in his ship and his cargo. Thus a successful, and lucky, master could soon be a wealthy man. An unsuccessful, and unlucky one, could equally soon be back on the lower deck, owing his employer a fortune, dependent on his goodwill to keep from starving. That was Driscoll's way.

Edward went to the taffrail to look at the fast flowing River Garonne bubbling under the *Regina*'s stern, causing her to tug on her mooring warps, swirling around the piles which supported the wormeaten docks, as it hurried upstream, deep into the heart of southern France. His fingers tapped the rail, impatiently. The flood was slackening. When the tide turned, in not more than an hour, he estimated, he would need to cast off. It was over a hundred miles from Bordeaux down to the sea, but with a fair east wind that immense distance could be covered on a single fast running tide—and today the wind was out of the east. But by the same token, if the tide was missed, it was a matter of anchoring for the next six hours. There was no way of breasting the Garonne, and even less its larger sister, the Gironde, formed by the confluence of the Garonne with the Dordogne, just twenty miles downstream.

But there was no means of hurrying the

stevedores, either. In the early summer of 1845 all France, all Europe, indeed, seemed to be in the grip of a revolutionary individuality, a growing disregard for both wealth and authority. And the French, having begun the revolutionary cycle fifty years ago, were the least disciplined of the lot.

Yet the loading was going well. He estimated they *would* be underway in about an hour, at ten o'clock. Which would just about do it. He was loading the most precious cargo in all the world: best quality claret to grace the tables of the Carolina gentry. Bordeaux was the very centre of the largest wine growing area in France and there was no finer wine in the world than that which was now being stowed in his hold.

A wild, irresponsible gamble, the experts had said. Even old Driscoll thought so. And had said so, as well. But he would not attempt to dissuade his most youthful commander. He let men cut their own throats.

Edward regarded the situation without bitterness. This was his third voyage as master of the *Regina*, and the first two had both lost money. Driscoll never accepted more than three losses in a row. So then, make or break. But this wine would sell for a fortune in Charleston. If he could get it there.

Edward Anderson never doubted that he could. He could do anything with a ship, and the barquentine was a superb sailing vessel. He would have her moored up in Charleston within three weeks of leaving the river mouth, and even claret wine, the worst travelling cargo in the world, would stay at its best for twenty-one days. At least, that was his belief. Because it had to happen. He no longer had just himself to think of. There was also Amanda.

'Ready forward.' Casimir Malewski was an enormous man; he possessed Edward's height, and was twice his breadth, moving slowly and ponderously, but with determined exactitude. As much as any man, Edward thought, a Malewski was a representative of revolutionary Europe, although it had been fifteen years since *he* had been forced to flee his native Warsaw to escape arrest by the Russians. Then he had been a Baltic sailor, pure and simple, although he had skippered his own ship. Learning the ways of the sea had not come easily to him; he had had to start at the very bottom, as an ordinary seaman. But Edward had quickly recognised his ability, as well as early forming a personal attachment for the huge, soft featured Pole and had been delighted to be able to promote him to First Officer for this voyage. He was deeply satisfied with the way his friend had turned out.

He nodded. 'Then let go, Mr Malewski.'

The Mate saluted, and hurried forward to supervise the releasing of the bow warps.

'With *his* weight up there, it'll be a miracle

if she comes round at all,' remarked Henry Driscoll, who, as Second Mate, was in charge of the stern lines.

Edward ignored the jibe. Having young Driscoll on board at all was a nuisance. Yet the toffee-nosed university graduate, small, slight and dark, like all his family, could not be dismised as a mere misfortune of nepotism. He possessed a good deal of determination and a self confident certainty as to his own best interests. Nephew of the Old Man, and, as James Driscoll was childless, obviously destined to succeed his uncle as head of the firm, Henry had decided to learn all there was to know about seafaring. On his return from his post-graduate European Grand Tour, he had shipped out as Second Mate to a man scarcely older than himself and distinctly socially inferior; where the Driscolls were old Carolina gentry —there had been a Driscoll at the side of Lord Baltimore when the colony had been founded, two hundred years before—the Andersons were New Englanders, men who had always earned their livings with their hands, who knew the sea and nothing more. Hard as young Driscoll tried, he could not let this fact escape his mind, and if he could not fault Edward's seamanship, he equally could not resist regarding Malewski with contempt. 'You'll keep those lines hard, Mr Driscoll,' Edward said, as the bows were released and immediately began to swing away from the dock on the

11

current; with the stern still made fast *Regina* would soon be pointing downstream. 'Set the foresail,' he commanded the boatswain.

The sailors heaved on the halliards, and the square foresail—a barquentine, the *Regina* was square rigged only on her foremast, the other two being rigged fore and aft—slowly climbed the mast.

'Sheet her in,' Edward said, and the ropes attached to the foot of the sail to control its angle to the wind were hauled to the required tautness. 'Let go aft, Mr Driscoll. Steady as she goes, cox.'

The stern lines were released, and the ship, all two hundred feet of her, began to drift sideways on the current. Immediately the wind filled the foresail, and she gathered way through the water, enabling the helmsman to take control.

'We'll have one jib, Mr Malewski,' Edward shouted, as the First Mate came aft. 'And set the mizzen, Mr Driscoll,' he said quietly. Lightly canvassed, but with a balanced sail area, the ship would be best able to make her way down the river. The Gironde was broad and well marked, but was also littered with sandbanks to ensnare any vessel which allowed itself to be carried out of the channel. More than one good ship had been left stranded, to dwindle into a rotting hulk and Edward well knew that he had a long afternoon ahead of him before the *Regina* would be securely anchored

12

for the night off the seaport of Royan, at the mouth of the river.

'All shipshape, Captain,' Malewski said, climbing the ladder to join him.

'Thank you, Cas,' Edward said, dropping formality now that they were standing beside each other. 'An east wind. There's fortune for you, eh? I've a notion this one is going to be a lucky voyage.'

'Home in a fortnight, eh, skipper?' Driscoll asked.

'There'd be a dream,' Edward said. 'The Atlantic in a fortnight!' It could be done, of course—if the wind held steady throughout. But that *was* a dream. 'But home inside a month, you can bet on that.' He moved to the taffrail in the stern of the ship, looked back at the dwindling spires of the third largest city in all France—the huge bridges, the busy wharves, and then forward, at the green trees which filled the banks, the eddying patches of light brown water denoting sandbanks and the line of great buoys which marked the channel. The Gironde, he supposed, was the most difficult part of the entire voyage. With a foul wind, his passage downriver might take three days. Whereas today...'Oh, aye,' he said. 'Home in a month.'

Malewski made no reply. Unlike either Edward or Driscoll, he *had* no real home. Driscoll had been born and bred in Charleston. Following the search for employment and advance-

13

ment in his chosen profession and lured by the magic of the Driscoll name and the opportunities it offered, Edward had made the southern seaport his base, and now, in marrying Amanda Dart he had done more than that—even his crisp Yankee accent had almost been softened into a Carolina drawl. But Malewski's heart remained in Warsaw, and however often he had written, there had been no word from *his* wife and family since he had left; he could hardly doubt that they were in some Siberian prison.

'Home,' Edward said, and threw his arm round his friend's shoulder. 'Amanda will have apple pie on the table, the day we come in. Three weeks tomorrow.'

Edward chewed a cold chicken bone for a belated dinner, prepared for him by his fretting Negro servant, Jehu, who would have preferred him to come below and eat in a civilised fashion for all his determination not to leave the deck for an instant. Cooking, he thought, was only one of his wife's accomplishments. On the short side of medium, and inclined to plumpness, Amanda Dart *attacked* life, with a tremendous and apparently inexhaustible fund of energy, her small, compact features often taut with concentration, her whole being consumed in the immediacy of her task, however small or large, careless of any destruction involved, whether it be to her fingernails or her gown, or the tight ringlets in which she wore her pale yellow hair.

Her parents, of course—her father was a solid, respectable Carolina merchant—had not been pleased with her decision to marry a too young Yankee sea captain, even one who, it was widely accepted, had his feet firmly on the ladder of success. He thought she had doubted the wisdom of it herself, in the beginning of their courtship. The Darts knew nothing of the sea, had no association with it; Edward Anderson, who had taken his first berth at the age of thirteen, knew nothing else. Since the death of his parents, the sea had been mother and father to him, as it was at once hobby and profession. Amanda had introduced him to a world of music and art, of balls and horse rides in the park, of the political conversation—that always abounded in Charleston—and the discreet flirtation...and had watched his unavailing efforts to appreciate that world, and to fit himself into it, with sad resignation.

Yet had she eventually been won over by the determination of his fidelity, no less than the passion which she had discovered in him and which he had seemed able to arouse in her. From the moment when she had allowed him to take her in his arms, one night just before his last voyage, and had responded to his embrace with all the intensity of her nature, the matter had been settled. And yet she had retained the self possession, even when they were lying together on her parents' sofa, clothes sufficiently disordered to prohibit any further modest protection on either side, to check him gently but firmly. 'Do you go to sea, dear Edward,' she had said. 'I shall be waiting for you when you return, to be your wife.'

Since that moment he had drifted from cloud to cloud. Even the very real financial disaster of that voyage had seemed no more than an irrelevant indication by Fate that no man was intended to be quite so happy. They had had but two months together, to set up home, to explore each others' delights, to consider the future as well as the present. And it had been Amanda, used to assisting her father with his accounts, who had looked at the *Regina*'s trading figures, her pointed chin resting on her palm, her hazel eyes remote with concentration, and had said, 'You must take care to make a profit, on your next voyage, Edward. Whatever the risks.'

When he had mentioned French wine, instead of more prosaic cargoes like manufactured goods or even lace, she had clapped her hands with delight. The daring of it had attracted the adventure in her soul. And when James Driscoll, on the quayside to see his ship off, as ever, had remarked, 'Your husband is a madman, Mrs Anderson. Three in every four shipments of Bordeaux wine perishes long before it can be landed,' she had merely smiled, and replied, 'But he has the madness of suc

16

cess, Mr Driscoll, as you will see.'

With such support, he thought, tossing the chicken bone over the side, how could a man fail? And indeed, how could this voyage fail, having begun so well? For the wind still blew out of the east, as the river widened and became dotted with islands, and they hurried past the little village of Pauillac, on the slopes behind which most of the wine in his hold had been grown. He studied the sky, as he watched the sun drooping into the western horizon. The weather was set fair, and the barometer high; in these latitudes that meant a continuation of the easterlies for at least another few days. Long enough for him to get out of the Bay— often a hard beat against a west wind—and make south for Madeira, there to pick up the trade winds which would rush him across the Atlantic. Conditions were so perfect, indeed, he begrudged the necessity to stop even for the night. But it would be dark in an hour, and the mouth of the Gironde was littered with sandbanks which required the services of a pilot to be successfully negotiated; none would take him out tonight. But they had made splendid time in any event—the lights of the little seaport of Royan were twinkling on his starboard bow, while before him he could see the surf breaking on the sand; even on a calm night the Bay of Biscay contained a swell.

'Ready for anchoring, Captain.' Henry Driscoll had appeared on the bridge. Malewski

17

was already waiting forward.

'Very good, Mr Driscoll. You'll hand that foresail. Starboard three points, coxswain.'

The orders were given, the squaresail came clouding down and under jib and mizzen alone, speed already cut by two thirds so that she merely ghosted through the calm water, the *Regina* left the main channel and swung into the anchorage.

'For God's sake,' Driscoll remarked. 'Look at smoking Joe.'

He was, Edward supposed, attempting to capture all the traditional sailorman's contempt for a steamer. And yet, he thought, there *was* something incredibly ugly, incredibly hermaphrodite, about the ship, also flying the Stars and Stripes, which was already waiting at anchor. Only about half the length of the *Regina*, her hull seemed to be built too high out of the water; that was no doubt to accommodate the two huge paddlewheels which disfigured her sides. While the three masts seemed absurd in such dimensions, especially as into their midst there poked the smoke-stained chimney for her boiler.

He had, in fact noticed her loading in Bordeaux during the preceding week, and had watched her leave yesterday. Why she had got only this far was a mystery. He had not attempted to fraternise up river; he had been too busy loading his ship, and besides, what could he possibly have to say to the master of a steamer?

18

But now the work was done, and he had the feeling of well-being that invariably followed the navigation of the river on a single tide, and for the next three weeks at least he and his crew would be alone with the ocean. He gave the people on the quarterdeck of the *Mohawk* a cheery wave as his anchor plunged into the sand, and the *Regina* came gently to a halt.

'Ahoy, there, *Regina*,' came the call across the water. 'You've made good time.'

'I had a fair wind,' Edward replied.

'Then you'll wish to celebrate. Will you and your officers dine on board a steamer?'

Edward looked at Driscoll, who winked. 'There's a skirt on board that boat.'

Trust him to have noticed that. But indeed there were two women to be seen, their gowns fluttering in the breeze. 'Why not?' he asked, and cupped his hands to shout back his acceptance.

'John Able.' The captain of the *Mohawk* was a busy little man with a bristling moustache. 'My First Mate, Mr Larkein, and my Engineer, Mr Harrison.'

Edward shook hands, introduced Driscoll and Malewski. But the three seamen could not prevent themselves from glancing curiously about their strange surroundings, and indeed from regarding the scuppers and even the deck with consternation; in contrast to the snowy cleanliness of the *Regina*, there was coal dust everywhere.

Able observed their expressions, gave a shrug. 'Well, what would you do, gentleman? With an Atlantic crossing ahead of us, we need every lump of coal that can be squeezed aboard. While I was in such a hurry to catch the tide yesterday, I didn't give my people time to hose down properly. And what would you...' he laughed. 'One of my paddles touched a sand-bank, swung us round, and there we sat for six hours. Damned annoying. Ah, well, what's a day at this stage? My schedule doesn't start until tomorrow. As for this dirt, a shower of rain will clear that up. You'll come aft, gentle-men.'

Once again the three officers from the *Regina* exchanged glances as they were escorted aft. Here was an insouciance they had not previous-ly encountered in a seaman.

'I'd have you meet my passengers,' Able said, mounting the ladder to the quarterdeck. 'You'll know Mr Meigs, of course.'

'I have not had the pleasure, sir,' Edward said. 'But I have heard of you.'

The millionaire, tall and bluffly handsome, the grey wings to his hair only adding to his air of utter confidence, smiled his pleasure at having his name recognised, and shook hands. 'My wife, and my daughter Penny.'

Edward introduced his officers, Malewski shyly stumbling over his greeting, Henry coolly confident, even as he glanced at his captain, his expression easy to read: one too old and the other too young. Yet even at what Edward estimated could not be much over sixteen years of age, Penelope Meigs gave every promise of one day being a beauty, from her height, which already very nearly matched her father's, through the deep brown glowing texture of her undressed straight hair hanging from her bonnet past her shoulders, to the obvious health and vigour of the as yet immature body.

Fortunately, Driscoll's implied criticism had not been noticed, at least by the girl's mother. 'Henry Driscoll?' she asked. 'You're not related to Jim Driscoll?'

'His nephew, ma'am,' Henry admitted.

'I told you, my dear,' Titus Meigs said, 'that was a Driscoll Line ship. Recognised your flag, Captain Anderson.'

'A fine looking vessel,' Captain Able acknowledged, gesturing his steward to come forward with a tray laden with glasses of claret.

'Coals to Newcastle,' Driscoll said, raising his glass to the ladies.

'Eh?' Able was clearly mystified.

'This is our cargo. A man could get drunk just by sniffing through the main hatch.'

'You're shipping wine by the barrel?'

'By the bottle,' Driscoll smiled.

'By the...isn't that highly risky?'

'Worth it,' Driscoll explained, as if he had been responsible for the entire concept. 'The

21

Charleston gentry will pay a fortune for chateau bottled wine.' He laughed. 'I should know. I'm one of them.'

'We've been touring Europe,' Priscilla Meigs confided, seating herself on one of the canvas chairs arranged by the taffrail, and beckoning her daughter to join her. 'Such a lovely country. Now Titus says he must get home.'

'I'm kind of interested to see what sort of a mess that son of mine has made of the cotton crop,' Meigs said. 'I've known your father for years, young Driscoll.'

'My uncle, sir,' Henry said.

Meigs ignored the interruption. 'If I'd have known one of his ships was in Bordeaux, why, I'd have sought passage with you. You take pasengers?'

'Only if the captain were to say so, Mr Meigs,' Driscoll said.

Meigs looked at Edward.

'I could hardly steal another man's customers, Mr Meigs,' Edward said.

'Anyway, sir,' Able put in. 'You said you had to be back in Charleston on June seventeenth. That's four weeks and three days. Can you get back to the States in that time, Anderson?'

'We'll be home June seventh,' Driscoll declared.

'Three weeks? Why sir...'

'That is if we happened to have a fair wind the whole way,' Malewski pointed out. 'At least

22

until we're out of the Bay.'

Driscoll gave him a disgusted glance.

'Three weeks,' Meigs commented. 'Say, that sounds pretty quick.'

'As Mr Malewski says,' Able remarked. 'Only if the wind holds fair, which is asking a lot of Providence. By the same reasoning, the voyage *could* take six weeks.'

'Well, Captain Anderson?' asked Penelope Meigs. '*Will* you do it, in three weeks?'

Her interruption took him by surprise. And for all her youth she spoke with total confidence. No doubt being the daughter of the man reputed to be the wealthiest planter in South Carolina helped.

'I'm optimistic, Miss Meigs,' he said. 'But as Mr Malewski says, it all depends on the wind.'

'About which no man can be certain,' Able repeated. 'Whereas I'll have you home on June fourteenth. Not a day before, and not a day after.'

'Well, sir, I guess there's no answer to that,' Meigs agreed. 'You care to have a little wager on it, Captain Anderson? Five hundred dollars says we'll be tied up before you.'

'You'd lose,' Driscoll said.

'Captain?' Meigs continued to study Edward's face.

'I don't have five hundred dollars, Mr Meigs,' Edward said. 'And I don't gamble money on the sea. I'll have to be content with wishing you a good voyage.'

'Even if we have to risk a little coal dust with our soup,' Penelope said with a bright smile. 'But *I'll* hope to see you tied up alongside when we get there, Captain Anderson.'

Edward sipped his after dinner brandy. 'I'm interested to know how you can hope to be so exact, Able, about your time of passage.'

'Mathematics,' the little man said expansively. 'It is three thousand seven hundred nautical miles to Charleston from where we now lie, give or take a mile or two. Would you agree?'

'As the crow flies,' Edwards said. 'Not as a ship sails.'

'Ah, but, I don't have to go looking for the wind, you see. So you may regard the *Mohawk* as a crow. Now, sir, we make six knots. We can make more, but six is our best economical cruising speed. Well, sir, if you divide three thousand seven hundred by six, you obtain six hundred and sixteen and two thirds hours. Divide that by twenty four, and you obtain twenty five and two thirds days. Well, I reckon it'll take us at least a third of a day to get out of here and drop our pilot, and we might just have an accident on the voyage to use up a day. If not...' he leaned over to whisper, 'I play safe with my estimates. If we are ahead of schedule, I can easily reduce speed by a knot or two over the last week, to arrive dead on schedule. Schedules, which can be kept, and which must

24

be kept, Anderson. That's what steam is all about.'

'And you'll maintain your six knots, no matter what the weather?' Malewski asked.

'Within reason, sir. Those paddles out there are driven by two-cylinder, side lever, Watt piston engines, each developing one hundred and twenty horsepower. There's no argument about that.'

'Then you'll use steam all the way?' Malewski pursued the subject.

'No, sir. That I will not. Because I cannot. My engines burn six pounds of coal per horsepower per hour. To obtain my cruising speed I must develop a hundred horsepower on each engine. That means twelve hundred pounds of coal an hour, or something more than fourteen tons a day. Well, sir, my capacity is two hundred and fifty tons, which means no more than seventeen days continuous steaming. On the other hand, I reckon I can count on some wind assistance most days, so I can reduce my engine speed and save coal, and on three or four days, at least, we should have enough wind abaft the beam to push us along at my six knots when I can shut down the boilers altogether.'

'But you will not use the wind to go faster than six knots, if you can?'

'No, sir, I will not. If the wind freshens so we find ourselves going faster, then I reduce sail.' He smiled. 'Mind you, with her draft, and those paddles, it takes a full gale to get *Mohawk*

25

moving at more than seven, anyway. And of course, as the wind drops, or heads us, or if there's a calm, I stoke up my boilers. Schedules, sir, that's...'

'What it's all about,' Driscoll said, winking at Penelope Meigs. He had had more than enough to drink, Edward decided.

But he was too interested in this entirely strange world to which he was being introduced to consider reprimanding his officer. 'But how do you manage to control the speed, so accurately?' he asked.

'I trail a log. Don't you?'

'Indeed I do. But it has to be reeled in for reading. Unless the wind is very steady, I can't judge within a knot of how fast I'm going until she's streamed again.'

'With engines, Anderson, that's no problem. I *know* I'm making a certain speed, according to my revolutions.'

Meigs was smiling at Edward, happy to see the sailors, with whom he would obviously have rather been travelling, discomforted by the expertise of their rival. 'All mathematics, as he says, Captain Anderson. And as much Greek to me as it is to you.'

'But why,' Malewski asked, still interested, 'do you not carry more coal, Mr Able, and thus eliminate any risk to your schedule at all by steaming the whole way?'

Able gave him a pitying smile. 'Where would I put my passengers and cargo, Mr Malewski?

26

Steamers is a science; everything worked out to the last detail. There's not an inch of wasted space on board this ship, sir. A science, that's what it is.'

'Science,' Driscoll remarked. 'Look at him puff.'

The two ships had made the passage out of the estuary of the Gironde in company, the *Regina*, under shortened sail, following the steamer, which had set no sail at all thus far but emitted huge clouds of black smoke. Now the barquentine was hove to, watching the little pilot cutter, having already picked up the *Mohawk*'s pilot, dancing towards them over the waves, and watching too, with professional interest, their rivals setting their sails, while the boilers blew off steam; the offshore breeze was fresh enough to push even that handicapped hull along at Able's required six knots.

'What do you think, Ned?' Malewski asked. 'Do we take him down?'

'I reckon,' Edward agreed, shaking hands with the pilot as he escorted him to the gangway. 'See you in the autumn, monsieur.'

'And a successful voyage to you, Captain,' the Frenchman agreed. 'Don't forget, if you encounter bad weather, drink your cargo, eh?' He winked. 'It would be a shame to waste it.'

'There's a happy thought,' Driscoll commented.

'Let's get to it,' Edward decided. 'We'll set

everything we have, Cas. Topgallants as well. Let's show those engineers who rules this ocean.'

'Yippee,' Driscoll shouted, hurrying forward to chase the men into the rigging.

'He has enthusiasm, all right,' Malewski observed, a trifle sadly.

'And why shouldn't he?' Edward asked. 'The whole world is right there at his feet. So he can enjoy every moment of it. Let's try doing the same. Bring her up a point, cox.'

The helmsman spun the wheel to turn the barquentine somewhat more before the wind. Now the great sailing ship bore down directly on the steamer, bounding over the shallow waves where the *Mohawk* seemed to lumber up them with immense effort. Edward reckoned his ship was already making ten knots, and she would do eleven, once the breeze freshened; if it could be possible for *him* to sail as the crow flies, sure always of a wind, he could make the passage in just over two weeks, he thought ruefully.

'Two points to port, now,' he said quietly. 'We don't want to run her down.'

'But pass her close by, Ned,' Driscoll said, returning aft again. 'I want them to have a good look. And I want to have a good look at them.'

Edward smiled good naturedly. But his own spirits rose to the brief race. And undoubtedly the *Regina* must be presenting a magnificent sight, three jibs billowing, one atop the other;

square foresail surmounted by fore topsail and fore topgallant sail, also square; huge, gaffrigged mainsail boomed out to port, surmounted in turn by her topsail; and smaller mizzen sail, also gaff rigged—its upper edge as well as its lower supported and controlled by a wooden boom—carried out to starboard, so as to extract every bit of propulsion from the wind.

They were already within a hundred yards of the steamer. 'I'll take her,' Edward said, and closed his hands on the spokes. Immediately the ship came alive, transmitting all of her own energy from her rudder up into his own arms.

'Hurrah!' Driscoll shouted. 'Hurrah!' as the long bowsprit drew abeam of the steamer's quarterdeck. Now they could see the Meigs family quite clearly, standing at the rail to watch them, while they could see too that Able had emulated Edward and himself taken the wheel to coax the last ounce of speed from his hull.

But nothing could stop the onward rush of the barquentine, sending a huge white bone away from her bows, and leaving a deep bubbling wake astern, almost to the fast disappearing land. Within a few minutes they were quarterdeck to quarterdeck, and barely fifty yards apart.

'See you in Charleston, Captain Anderson,' Penelope Meigs shouted, waving her hat.

'We'll have unloaded and sailed again,' Driscoll bellowed. 'By the time you get there.

Hurrah! Hurrah!'

The steamer fell astern. Ahead of them were only the white-capped waters of the bay. Edward relinquished the wheel to the coxswain and looked up at the sails. They were all filling perfectly.

'Science,' Malewski said.

'They need it, I reckon, to get that tub moving at all,' Driscoll remarked. 'I'll bet those Meigs are wishing they were aboard us. Say, that would be sport, eh? That pretty little girl could just grow on me, on an ocean crossing.'

'Then it's a good thing she's over there,' Edward said. 'We have work to do.' He went below to write up his Log, and sat at his desk, the pen tapping against his teeth, as he wondered why she had shouted her farewell to him rather than Driscoll.

'Now, look at that.' Henry Driscoll stood on the poop deck with his hands on his hips to look up at the sails, flapping noisily against their booms. 'Of all the luck.'

'Mustn't complain,' Malewski said. 'We've not done too bad. And the wind will be back again.'

Edward frowned at the sky. Indeed they had not done too badly, for the past week. Unlike the steamship, which they had dropped astern that first day, the *Regina* could not sail as a crow might fly. She needed to make a parabola,

30

getting out of the bay and then sweeping near a thousand miles to the south west, to the latitude of the island of Madeira, to pick up the trade winds which would hurry her across the Atlantic and then up through one of the various Bahama passages to the Gulf Stream and home. With fortune, the fortune he was counting on, the trades would blow every day and all day, varying between fifteen and thirty miles an hour, sufficient for him to maintain a speed of between six and ten knots and thus be well within *his* schedule. And indeed, for the first three days after Madeira they had performed according to expectations. But today the wind had fallen to a light air, and now, even as he watched, it died away altogether; the *Regina* rolling gently in a surprisingly deep swell, which was arising, amazingly, out of the south west—exactly opposite to the direction of the wind.

He went below to his desk and noted the change in the Log, gazing past the miniature of Amanda which had been her wedding present, to the barometer hanging on the wall, his frown deepening as he glanced through the Log, noting the pressure levels he had entered every two hours throughout the voyage. Over the preceding twenty-four hours, while the wind had steadily dropped, the glass had fluctuated, now falling a fraction, now rising again. Of course it was only just in June, and early for those devastating revolving tropical storms called hurricanes to develop—but they had been known to occur even at this time of the year.

'Here it comes again,' came the shout from above his head.

'Hello,' Driscoll commented. 'That's not right. You'd best fetch the captain.'

Edward was already on his way up the companion ladder to find the wind blowing into his face as he emerged on deck.

'South-westerly,' Driscoll said. 'What do you make of that, Ned? Doesn't seem right to me, in these latitudes.'

Edward examined the sky again. Now he could see the wisps of white cloud, high above him. There was a lot of wind coming. But still a good way off. The new breeze remained light, yet the *Regina*, now close hauled—her fore and aft sails sheeted hard in, and her square yards turned as much as possible so that they too could pick up some of the wind coming across the port bow—and heeling, was still making good time, and taking the short seas quite comfortably.

'What do you think, Ned?' Malewski had also come on deck. 'A head wind will slow us up, eh?'

'That's the least of our worries,' Edward muttered, reaching back into his brain for all the lore he had picked up in his years at sea. He faced the wind, and then turned ninety degrees to his right, pointed over the starboard bow. 'There's a hurricane out there.'

32

'Where?' Driscoll peered into the empty horizon.

'You won't see it for a while,' Edward said. 'But it's coming. Or rather, we're sailing into it.'

'How can you be sure?' Malewski said.

'Four things,' Edward told him. 'First, the glass has been fluctuating, this past twenty-four hours. That's a bad sign. It'll start to drop, hard, sometime soon. Second, this swell. Third, those mares' tails up in the sky. And fourth, this south westerly breeze.'

'Okay,' Driscoll said. 'So there's a storm about. What makes you so sure it's ahead of us?'

'Because of a law worked out by a Dutchman, named Buys Ballot,' Edward explained. 'He studied weather all his life, and he deduced that in this hemisphere, if you face the wind, the centre of low pressure is on your right hand. There.' He pointed again.

Driscoll scratched his head. He might never have been in a hurricane, but he had heard all about them. 'So what do you aim to do?'

'The safe thing is to turn away from it, put the wind on our right hand,' Edward said thoughtfully. 'That way we know we're moving into high pressure.'

'That'll mean steering south east, just about,' Malewski said. 'Virtually back on our tracks. It'll add at least a week to our voyage.'

33

'Maybe,' Driscoll said. 'But it'll be better than getting mixed up in a hurricane.'

'It could add a month to our voyage,' Edward said. 'Depending on the size of the storm, the area it covers. If we have to run south for a week we might find ourselves below the trade winds, and in the doldrums. Once in *them*, it'll take us a long time to come back out.'

'Which won't do the cargo any good,' Malewski said.

'Looks as if we may have to drink it ourselves, after all,' Driscoll grinned.

'So we'll stand on,' Edward decided.

'*What* did you say?' Driscoll demanded.

'We'll maintain course,' Edward said. He smiled in turn. 'We'll get there in a hurry, all right.'

'But...that's foolhardy,' Driscoll cried. 'It's crazy. And utterly wrong, for the sake of a few bottles of wine. My uncle...'

'Put *me* in command of this ship, Mr Driscoll,' Edward said. 'It is not foolhardy in the least. You may call it a calculated risk.'

'Yeah? How do you figure that?'

'It's early in the season,' Edward told him. 'The odds are very much against this developing into a bad storm. So we may catch a gale of wind. This ship will take a gale. And so will this crew.' He looked Driscoll up and down. 'Properly commanded.'

'And there's the cargo to think of,' Driscoll sneered.

'Why, yes, Mr Driscoll,' Edward said coolly. 'There is the cargo to be thought of. We're in the business of shipping cargoes, in case you've forgotten. Not running from a cupful of wind. But I will record your objections in the Log. Now get busy. I want the topsails handed, and the topmasts struck and secured. Then I want all the hatches checked, as well as the cargo. Then I want deadeyes in every port. Meanwhile, keep her as close to the wind as she'll sail.'

He went below, leaving Driscoll muttering at Malewski. Not that he would get much sympathy from the big Pole. Malewski might never have been in a hurricane, either, but he'd known enough bad weather in the Baltic.

He wondered what either of his two officers would say if they knew that he had never been in a hurricane either? But he had been in sufficient gales, and he had the utmost confidence in his ship, and in his ability to take her through anything she was likely to encounter. He smiled at Amanda, smiling at him. 'We'll be there,' he said to the portrait. 'And with an intact cargo.'

Malewski stood in the cabin doorway. 'All secured, Ned,' he said. 'But the wind's freshened. Shall I take a reef?'

Edward was lying on his bunk, reading a book on weather lore. This he now closed and sat up. He had known the wind had freshened from the increased motion of the ship. But so far she was still taking the waves easily enough. He looked at his chronometer; it was half past four in the afternoon. The glass had by now fallen, but as yet not dramatically. 'I'll come up,' he decided.

He had made himself rest since taking his noon sextant sight; it was very important to be absolutely sure of his position before the storm struck, as he might well have several days of cloud cover ahead of him. Now he felt completely at ease, and ready for anything the night might bring.

'You going wrap up, Mr Edward,' Jehu suggested.

'There's time for that,' Edward said, and put on his cap before following Malewski up the ladder.

Immediately he was aware of the wind, which was stronger than he had supposed; the sea had not yet had the time to get up commensurately. But the wind was starting to howl, and to whip the tops off the rising waves; it was not less than twenty knots, he was sure of that.

Driscoll was also on deck. 'Look there,' he said in an awed tone.

Edward looked due west, where the sun was slowly sinking into a huge band of black cloud, tinting the edges crimson, suggesting an enormous fire burning on the horizon.

'There's trouble, Ned,' Driscoll said. 'We've still time to miss it.'

'Forget it,' Edward said, and went down the ladder into the waist himself to inspect the battens on the hatches, the deadeyes—wooden plates which exactly covered the vulnerable glass—being screwed into place over the portholes. 'We'll need lifelines,' he said. 'Rigged the length of the waist. You fellows turn in and get some rest,' he said to the offwatch members of the crew, who were clustered in an anxious group on the forecastle, also watching the western sky. 'We'll need every man later.'

He returned to the poop, chased by a rattle of spray tossed over the bows. 'All right, Cas,' he said. 'Take a reef.'

'Aye-aye, sir,' Malewski said thankfully, and called the watch to release the huge mainsail and bring it several feet down the mast before making it secure again and tying up the loose canvas at the foot. The foresail was taken right off and stowed and so was the number two jib. Under reduced canvas the *Regina* hardly seemed to lose any speed, but she was moving easier and less water was coming on board.

'Those waves are ten foot high,' Driscoll complained, holding on to a shroud.

'Yes,' Edward agreed. But it was still mainly swell, and only occasionally breaking, to send a shudder the length of the ship. 'You're off watch, Mr Driscoll. Turn in and get some rest. Call me if she freshens any further, Cas.'

He went below again, entered the latest situation and his preparations in the Log, resumed his reading, but he was scarcely taking in the words now, as he listened to the slaps of the waves against the hull. He tensed his muscles to each surge of the ship, heard the howl of the wind in the rigging, thought of everything he had done and tried to remember if he had done everything he should have.

And sat bolt upright as he suddenly heard a noise like that made by a fast train passing through a station, hurtling straight at him.

Edward reached the main cabin at the same time as both Driscoll and Jehu, and the train-like noise. With a crash the *Regina* was knocked over, rolling through ninety degrees so that her starboard side hit the water with the sound of a large cannon exploding. But it was the lesser reverberations which alarmed Edward, as he found himself on the settee berth against the starboard bulkhead, Jehu sitting in his lap, Driscoll sprawled at his feet.

'Ow, me God,' said the little Negro. 'But you done lost them sticks, Mr Edward.'

They had sailed together for only two voyages, but Jehu knew at least as much about the sea as his master.

Driscoll seemed incapable of saying anything; his face was white with fright.

'Yeah,' Edward muttered, and as the ship came upright again, he pulled himself up and climbed the companion ladder, pausing in the hatch to survey the situation.

The *Regina* had not lost any of her masts; she had been too sturdily built. But the mainsail had been torn away, and now flapped in shreds, her gaff boom banging dolefully against the mast. The force of the blow had turned the ship away from the wind, so that she was careering forward, each huge wave picking up her stern to give her a shove as though by a giant hand, each shove burying her bowsprit and her entire bow in the back of the preceding wave, so that it seemed she was certain to keep on going, down and down and down, to the very bottom of the ocean a thousand fathoms beneath her.

Always she came up again, tossing clouds of spray over her shoulder, buoyantly determined to challenge the seas. But what seas! Aft Edward looked at towering monsters, twenty five and thirty feet in height, he estimated, and not less than a quarter of a mile in breadth, each topped by a foaming white mass of breaking water some six or eight feet high; forward there was nothing but mountainous precipices, great holes in the ocean waiting to swallow the suddenly tiny ship; and everywhere the surface of the sea was white, long streaks of foaming spume, like knife cuts made by the wind across the surface.

Because the wind was now a live thing, a gigantic howling, whistling monster, travelling at sixty miles an hour and more, impossible to move against, or even to stand against, unless braced. While the evening sky was utterly dark, covered from horizon to horizon by an enormous mass of black cloud, although even as he blinked Edward was blinded by a horrendous flash of lightning, followed almost instantly by a brain-numbing crash of thunder.

He gasped, clung to a shroud and pulled himself towards the wheel, where Malewski and the coxswain were fighting the rudder in an attempt to keep the ship before the wind, and prevent her getting broadside to any more waves, to suffer perhaps another knockdown, which might stove in one of her timbers or even roll her right over, so big had the seas become.

'I'm sorry, Ned,' Malewski shouted. 'I was slow. I should have taken sail off her when I saw the squall coming. But I had no idea it would be so strong.'

Edward ignored the apology. Now was not the time for recriminations. He grasped the wheel himself. 'That boom must come down,' he bawled. 'Use axes.'

Malewski hesitated, then nodded. 'You will heave her to?'

Edward chewed his lip, irresolute for a moment. Heaving to was the traditional way of combating a severe storm. By using the smallest possible sails, and sheeting one in to starboard and the other to port, and then lashing the helm, it was possible to leave a ship to herself. Turned to face the wind, she would gather way on one tack, but immediately fall away again as the opposing canvas filled, thus in effect she would almost stand still, taking the seas on her strongest section, the bows, and not requiring any men permanently on deck, at risk of life and limb. On the other hand, the motion, as her bows rose to each wave and then crashed down into the following trough, would be extreme. The ship would take it—but what of the several thousand bottles of wine in his hold?

To run before the storm was a much more risky operation. There was no danger of hitting anything, as they were well out into the empty ocean, but there was the constant possibility of losing control of the ship as she was picked up by each wave, and then of broaching —turning broadside to the seas—and losing everything, ship and lives as well as cargo. But running, the movement was much easier. The *Regina* cut the waves rather than slamming into them. It would all depend on the quality of the helming.

And the wind had backed until it was almost due south. Edward's reading of the tendencies of tropical storms convinced him that it would continue to do so for a while, moving anticlockwise round the compass. Thus by running he would at least be travelling roughly in the direction he wished to go. While when it commenced to veer and resumed its more normal clockwise tendency, he would be sure the weather was improving, and he might even be able to set sail and beat into it.

'No,' he said. 'Just bring down what's left of that mainsail. We'll run before the storm, under mizzen and jib.'

Driscoll and Jehu had also reached the deck, Jehu bearing his master's oilskins and sou'-wester, into which he inserted Edward even as he stood at the helm.

Driscoll clung to a shroud and gazed at the scene around him in horror, giving a wail as another vivid flash of lightning showed the night in all its magnificent terror. 'Mad,' he shouted. 'We're lost.'

'Get down there,' Edward shouted. 'Help Malewski. Get down there.' He pointed. 'You too, cox. Haste with that sail. I'll keep the helm.'

Malewski stood beside Edward. The mate had not had the time to don oilskins, and was soaked to the skin; he had lost his cap and water ran out from his har. 'All secured,' he gasped.

Edward could not spare the time to look at him, as he fought the helm. Each huge wave lifted the stern and threw the rudder out of the water as the ship was hurled forward. In those few seconds lay the greatest danger. He had to sense which way the ship was going, and counter it immediately, so that as he regained control he was already heading away from the following wave; to make a mistake, or be too slow, and allow the ship to follow the direction

42

in which the bow was already slewing, would bring about the broach he dreaded.

But a quick glance the length of the deck convinced him that Malewski had done a good job, just as the sight of a wave coming in from the side and filling the waist with five feet of foaming water equally convinced him that it was too dangerous for men down there, even with the lifelines he had had strung for them to hold on to.

'Get everyone below,' he said.

'But you?'

'I'll stay with the helm. Check with me every ten minutes.'

Malewski hesitated, then obeyed, and a moment later the deck was cleared. Edward chose the next flash of lightning to look up at the masts, at the Stars and Stripes still flying up there whipping savagely—he should have taken the flag down, in the interests of economy, but now he was glad he hadn't. If the sea wanted to fight, he was prepared to do battle. A tremendous exhilaration filled his mind and his body. Here was his true love, his true métier. A stout ship and a howling gale. Here was meat and drink and all the joy he had ever known. Before Amanda, he reminded himself. But in the strangest fashion even Amanda seemed to be a part of the battle, because the conflict contained every element of human emotion, even a sexual one, as the sea, hugely and overpoweringly feminine in the immense softness of its embrace, clearly desired him and wanted him and would do all it could to suck him into its eternal kingdom.

How strange, therefore, and disturbing, to realise that he was not actually seeing Amanda in his mind's eye, but instead the willowy figure of the Meigs girl, dark hair fluttering in the breeze as she had waved her bonnet farewell.

A tremendous roaring sound recalled him to his situation, made him realise the dangers of losing concentration. But there was nothing he could have done about this wave, anyway. Larger and faster than anything he had previously encountered, it broke on the very stern. Instantly Edward was standing in water up to his neck, thrown against the wheel with a force which left him breathless. The sea was gone in a moment, flooding the main deck before flowing overboard through the scuppers, but the waves were clearly growing all the time as the wind rose. Now the howl was continuous, where earlier it had from time to time died. The speed of the ship was also increasing, and she was flying off the crests of the waves and hurling herself at the next blue wall as if determined to smash her bows in.

He looked at the after hatchway and saw Malewski's face. 'She is tearing herself to pieces, Ned,' the Pole shouted.

Obviously the noise would sound much more dangerous below decks. Edward could tell, from the exuberant life still beneath his hands, that the *Regina* remained as buoyantly strong and therefore undamaged as she had always been. But that did not mean he could continue to risk these seas, or this speed indefinitely. 'We must slow her down,' he shouted back. 'Get all sail off her.'

Malewski summoned the watch, and the jib was hauled in, the oilskin clad sailors working up to their waists in water and utter darkness, before they came aft to hand the mizzen as well. But even under bare poles, the *Regina*'s speed was hardly reduced.

'She'll never take it,' Driscoll yelled. 'She'll founder. We're lost.'

'Oh, get below,' Edward snapped. 'Warps, Cas! Bend all the rope you have together, and pay it out astern.'

Malewski and Reynolds the boatswain got to work, securing ropes one to another until they had accumulated a length of several hundred feet on the after deck. Now they made each end fast to a mooring bit, and then paid out the bight, allowing the rope to trail behind the ship. The effect was instantaneous; not only did the weight of the hemp slow the barqentine down, but the rope also cut into the crests, causing them to break astern of the vessel, and so removing the risk of another pooping.

'Good work, Cas,' Edward said. 'Now get your people below again.'

'You got for drink this, Mr Edward.' Jehu was beside him, holding a mug of soup to his lips. The liquid was scalding hot, but most of it blew away on the wind in any event. 'You shouldn't be up here,' Edward said. 'What will I tell the mistress if you get washed overboard?'

Jehu grinned. 'That I done swim all the way back to Africa,' he suggested.

He was more than a servant. In the two voyages he had shared with Edward he had become a friend. Edward had never had a personal servant before. He had never been able to afford one, and the idea of owning a slave had always been abhorrent to a New England Yankee. When he had gone south to seek a berth with James Driscoll, and had found himself living in a slave owning community, he had accepted the situation without considering the matter very deeply, but without considering partaking in it himself either. Amanda had changed all of that. Being a merchant rather than a planter, her father had possessed only domestics, but it would never have occurred to either him or his daughter to exist without slave labour. And in the Dart household it had been the most civilised and mutually acceptable form of slavery that could exist, Edward supposed. If John Dart owned his people, he also regarded them as very much his responsibility, to feed and clothe and maintain in health, and even to educate and amuse. Amanda had adopted all of her father's principles towards those of her slaves she had taken to her new home. It had been the most natural thing in the world for her to present Jehu to her husband as a wedding gift. Just as he, remarkably, had found it the most natural thing in the world to accept it.

And suddenly he wished he had a whole crew of Jehus, anxious only to do his bidding. Then would life be much simpler.

He clapped his hand on the black man's shoulder. 'Now get below.'

'And you staying up, by yourself, all night?'

Edward winked at him. 'I'm enjoying myself, Jehu. This is what sailing is all about.'

'Wind's veering,' Casimir Malewski said.

Edward's eyes opened, and his head jerked in alarm. He had been sleeping the sleep of utter exhaustion, after spending twelve hours on the helm. By then the wind had dropped, only a fraction perhaps, and the seas had remained mountainous but he had felt able to hand over the helm to the coxswain, and snatch some rest. He looked at the chronometer; he had been sleeping for twelve hours as well.

'By God!' He leapt out of bed, reached for his hat and oilskins.

'All's well,' Malewski reassured him. 'Look.' He tapped the glass. It had ceased its dizzy fall and levelled out at nine hundred and forty-six millibars and was actually starting to rise again. Edward made himself think. They had certainly not passed through the eye of the storm; the wind had never dropped and they had seen no blue sky. But if the glass was trying to rise, then they had certainly reached the other side of the depression, which meant that they had bypassed the eye and had indeed skirted the edge of the storm. Certainly he had been right in his estimation that it would not be a severe one.

He accompanied Malewski on deck, where Driscoll was on watch. It was nearly dawn. And there was blue sky above; he could see the stars. The barquentine still hurtled onwards at what, three days ago, he would have considered too fast for safety, but the waves were breaking regularly and were still restrained by the trailing warps. On the other hand, they were now steering north east, or approximately back to Bordeaux.

But not for long. Every indication was that soon the wind, and the sea, would have subsided sufficiently to set sail and beat their way back into the trades.

'We've licked it, by God,' Driscoll said. 'Licked it.' He had entirely regained his composure now that the danger was past. Nor did he seem in the least abashed by any recollection of his panic.

'Aye,' Edward said. At the cost of one mainsail torn to shreds, and a few cuts and bruises amongst the crew. And what else? 'You'll bend on a new mainsail, Cas,' he said. 'And have those warps brought in and stowed. Prepare to make sail.'

'Aye-*aye*,' Malewski said.

'Mr Driscoll, come with me,' Edward went on. 'Get those hatches off.'

'Is that safe?' Driscoll demanded.

'It's safe enough,' Edward said. 'And it's time to know the worst.'

The crew held lanterns while he climbed down into the hold. They had taken on only a little water, despite the long buffeting they had suffered, and the wine crates had been so securely stowed they did not seem to have shifted. But it was the bottles inside that mattered. Edward got down on his hands and knees and crawled the entire length of the hold, listening to the still boisterous waves, slapping the planking of the hull only inches from his head, shining his lantern between each crate, looking for telltale drips or discolourations and finding none. He could not believe it. A lucky voyage, he thought. Oh, a lucky voyage.

He returned to the deck and had the hatches replaced. It was daylight now, the sun just peeping over the eastern horizon to shine across the still spray-strewn sea, but the waves were down to ten feet, and the wind had dropped to perhaps thirty knots.

'How many broken?' Malewski asked.

'Not one,' Edward said. He ran up the ladder. 'Not a single one. By God, I feel as if I was walking on air. Now, if we can just find ourselves a fair wind...'

'Smoke on the starboard bow,' came the call from forward.

Driscoll levelled his telescope. 'Well, glory be,' he said. 'Who'd have believed it?'

Edward joined him at the rail, watched the *Mohawk* approach from the east, paddlewheels churning the sea; true to her intentions she carried no sail, as the wind was westerly, but merely chugged straight into it, altering course just a fraction to pass close to the barquentine.

'Ahoy there,' came the call through the speaking trumpet. 'Do you require assistance?'

Edward looked up at his bare masts, realised they must present a peculiar sight. 'No thank you,' he called back. 'Have you had weather?'

'Nothing worse than this,' Able called back. 'Well, God damn,' Driscoll said, as together they gazed at the ladies on the afterdeck, sitting in deckchairs, and waving their kerchiefs. 'They don't have a clue what nearly hit them.'

'Lucky them,' Edward said. 'Let's get sail on this ship, Mr Malewski. We've a cargo to deliver.'

But by the time the *Regina* was again underway, the *Mohawk* was just a cloud of smoke on the horizon.

'Hand your mainsail,' Edward called. The *Regina* was slipping gently between James Island and Fort Sumter, and ahead of them were the houses of Charleston.

The sails came clouding down. 'Home,' Henry Driscoll said. 'My God, there's a pretty sight.'

50

'Aye,' Edward agreed. He bore no grudge for the other young man's terror during the gale. A first storm at sea is fairly unnerving at any time, and to have it a hurricane...but he was determined not to have him as mate again. Old Jim Driscoll would have to see his point there. He was slowly but surely licking a good crew into shape, and, for all his error at the beginning of the storm, which could have been catastrophic, Cas was learning fast. But he could not be expected to put up with Henry's gibes or his habit of questioning every order for another voyage.

As if it truly mattered, now. He was home; Mr Drayton the harbour pilot had taken command of the ship, and his responsibility was over. They were ten days late, to be sure, but it had taken them longer than they had expected to beat their way back into the trades. The important thing was that his cargo was intact.

Home! Because in the strangest fashion this city *was* home. It had a great deal to do with Amanda, of course. But he had come to regard it as home before he had ever met her. In the beginning he had been rather taken aback, and not only by the excesses of a slave-owning society. He had contrasted the leisurely way of life in South Carolina with the hustle and bustle of New York, and the gentle manners of Carolingians with the brusque rudeness of New Englanders, just as he had been offended by the arrogant independence of their minds. As he had got to know the people better, however, he had found much to admire. The politeness covered deep emotions, and where an offended New Yorker put up his fists, an offended Carolingian took out his pistol. While their arrogance, their concept that the United States existed for the good of Carolina rather than the other way around, was surely but a logical development of the original idea of Confederation in an era when the Washington bureaucrats more and more sought to interfere with States' rights.

Certainly he had no regrets about settling here, could not see himself ever returning to the north. Even without Amanda. Because there she was, standing on the quay beside old James Driscoll, waving her parasol. He squinted into the afternoon sun, made out the *Mohawk*, securely moored up three docks away. One up for the steamer. And thank God he hadn't been foolish enough to take Titus Meigs' bet.

The *Regina* had now lost way, as her bow warps were being passed down to the steam tugs which would put her against the dock. They fussed around her like so many chicks looking after the mother hen. But they knew their job. Even as Drayton returned the command to him, there was little to be done.

'Damned fireboxes,' Henry Driscoll grumbled. 'That's all they're good for, pushing and pulling.' He too had spotted the *Mohawk*, and appeared to be annoyed at having lost the race. Supposing there had ever been a race.

'Edward! Oh, Edward,' Amanda shouted as the barquentine came alongside. 'We heard there was a storm.'

'A hurricane,' Henry Driscoll shouted. 'You should have seen it. Waves as tall as the mast-heads.'

'Well,' Edward smiled. 'As high as the deck, anyway.' The gangway was run out, and a moment later Amanda was in his arms, bonnet tossed backwards to hang around her neck by its ribbon, opened-mouth, showering kisses on his cheek.

'We were so worried.'

'I told you he'd bring her safe home, Mrs Anderson,' James Driscoll said, shaking hands. Like his nephew, he was only just medium height, and slightly-built, but every fibre of his body seemed to quiver with suppressed energy, and his still black hair was cut short and crisp while his grip was as firm as that of a man half his age. 'Welcome home, Edward. A hurricane, you say?'

'It was quite frightful, Uncle,' Henry said. 'The wind, why, it must have been blowing at over a hundred miles an hour.'

'And no damage?' Driscoll's eye swept over the ship.

'We lost our number one mainsail, Mr Driscoll,' Edward said.

'Nothing else? That sounds like some good seamanship, boy.'

'Jehu, you old rascal,' Amanda cried in delight, as she walked aft, still arm in arm with her husband. 'Did you look after the master?'

'Oh, yes, Miss Amanda. Well, as best he would let me.'

'But I suppose the cargo took a beating,' James Driscoll remarked.

Edward grinned at him. 'Not a single bottle broken, Mr Driscoll.'

Driscoll frowned. 'I don't believe it.'

'See for yourself.' Edward pointed; the hatches were already being unbattened.

'I intend to,' Driscoll said. 'A hurricane, and no breakages? That *would* be a miracle.' He went to the main hatch.

'You'd better let me go first,' Edward said and kissed Amanda on the cheek before swinging himself down into the hold. 'Pass me down that lantern, Cas,' he said.

Malewski handed down the lantern, while Driscoll slowy descended the ladder into the hold. 'Good stowing,' he said. 'You supervised this yourself?'

'My First Mate, Mr Malewski, is in charge of cargo stowage,' Edward said.

Driscoll gazed at him for several seconds. He had not approved Edward's decision to appoint the Pole as First Officer.

'Well,' he said at last. 'Everything seems to have turned up trumps for you, boy. Mind you,

I always knew it would. You've guts, and determination, and talent...all a man needs to add to those is a little bit of luck and he's bound to go far. Tell you what, I'll buy the first case off you, and we'll have the first bottle, here and now. Open one up, and we'll drink a toast.'

'Pass me down a marlinspike,' Edward shouted, and opened the nearest case of wine, while Driscoll returned on deck. Edward soon joined him, carrying a bottle, while Jehu had already produced a corkscrew and a tray of glasses. Edward and Amanda stood with the Driscolls and Malewski, while Jehu uncorked the bottle, filled the glasses.

James Driscoll held up his glass to the light, looked at the rich ruby colour. 'Here's to the *Regina*,' he said. 'And all who sail in her.' He held the glass to his lips, sniffed, frowned, and took a cautious mouthful. The he spat the red liquid on to the deck. 'Vinegar, by God. Red vinegar!'

CHAPTER 2

Mr Skipton cleared his throat, set his notes carefully in front of him, looked up and down the polished mahogany table, left, to where James Driscoll sat, his nephew on one side of him, a secretary on the other, and then right, to Edward and Malewski; these apart, the boardroom of the Driscoll Line was empty, save for the paintings of past Driscolls looking down on them from the walls.

'I have now sampled a dozen bottles,' Skipton said. 'Taken entirely at random. And I am sorry to say that not one would be acceptable to a connoisseur. Or even an occasional drinker.' Skipton, with his red face and hoarse voice, was clearly not an occasional drinker. But his expression was suitably solemn, to match the enormity of the disaster which had required his presence.

'You mean we were swindled, in Bordeaux?' Edward demanded. 'I cannot believe that.'

'No, sir, Captain Anderson. I would estimate that the wine was in perfect condition when it was loaded aboard your ship.'

'And you mean that a ten day delay in docking caused it to go off? *All* of it?' Malewski asked.

'No, Mr Malewski. I do not think the length of passage had anything to do with the deterioration in the quality of the wine, save in a most general way. The damage was caused, I would say, by the amount of shaking up each bottle received during the passage. I understand you had several days of bad weather.'

'Three or four,' Edward said.

'Enough, sir. Try to imagine. You have bought yourself a bottle of best quality wine.

Would you really take it home, and then for three or four days continuously shake it violently, as if making yourself a gin swizzle, before uncorking it? This is the risk in transporting quality wine by sea. It is lessened by shipping in barrels, of course, but once the wine has been bottled...obviously you were unlucky, to encounter such a storm. Had you sailed in reasonably calm seas the whole way, with just a regular, gentle motion being transmitted through the hull, then you would probably have got away with it, or at least, with a very low percentage of loss. But as it is...' he shrugged.

'So the wine was shaken up,' Edward said, determined not to allow the panic which was clawing at his mind to gain control. 'And we only docked yesterday. Now when the wine has settled down, won't it be all right again?'

Mr Skipton gave a pitying smile. 'Wine is not water, Captain Anderson. Once it had been ruined, it has been ruined. I am not saying you may not be able to find a few dozen drinkable bottles in your cargo, but this will only be ascertainable by opening each bottle. I cannot see anyone being willing to buy, on those terms.'

Edward gazed at Driscoll, but his employer's face remained expressionless. 'Thank you, Mr Skipton,' he said. 'You'll submit your account in due course, I have no doubt.'

Skipton collected his notes, stood up, glanced

right and left again, and left the room.

'Bad *luck*?' Henry Driscoll remarked, as the door closed. 'It was that foolhardy course you took, in sailing right through that hurricane.'

'I did what I thought was best,' Edward said quietly.

'And then, Malewski's carelessness in letting us be knocked down by that squall. That probably ruined more bottles than anything else.'

'Perhaps someone will explain to me exactly what happened,' James Driscoll said, also speaking quietly, but looking at Edward.

'Nothing *happened*,' Edward said. 'I elected to come home by the fastest possible route. It was a calculated decision, taken with the wind in mind. It seems I made a mistake.'

'Nevertheless,' Malewski put in. 'The knock down was my fault.' He gazed at Driscoll. 'I had never been in a hurricane before, Mr Driscoll. I knew there was a squall coming, but I could not believe it would hit us so quickly, or with such force.'

'Whereas,' James Driscoll said, perhaps to himself, 'a more experienced officer would have reacted more readily.'

'I doubt there are many men sufficiently experienced at combating hurricanes, always to do the right thing,' Edward said. 'In any event, it is necessary to *gain* such experience. No damage was occasioned by the knockdown, save to the mainsail as has already been reported, and Mr Malewski is now fully experienced. We all are.' He looked at Henry. 'Even your nephew.'

'I warned him against bucking that storm, Uncle Jim,' Henry said. 'It's in the Log. I told him it was foolhardy.'

Driscoll continued to look at Edward.

'It is in the Log, Mr Driscoll,' Edward said. 'You are welcome to study that whenever you wish, and take note of *all* my entries. However, I was in command, and it was my decision to stand on. I may say that Second Officer Driscoll was even less experienced than Mr Malewski, at such weather. And revealed it during the storm.'

'Why, you...' Henry Drisoll shouted.

His uncle tapped the table. 'I see no reason to descend to personalities,' he remarked. 'You have summed up the situation with admirable succinctness, Edward. You were the master. You made the decision. And, as you yourself have said, it has turned out to be the wrong one. Although I suspect the truly wrong decision was in attempting to ship bottled wine in the first place.' He allowed himself the ghost of a smile. 'It seems we in America must survive without the finer pleasures of life until some quicker and smoother means is found of crossing the ocean.' His smile died. 'But that is by the by. Each of your three voyages has now lost money, Edward. This last one is quite catastrophic. It has not merely lost money, it is not going to earn back a cent. It was a gamble,

59

which failed. And gamblers who fail usually lose their shirts. I am not going to take your shirt, Edward. I recognise your enthusiasm and your talent. But you have this unfortunate habit of attempting more than you can accomplish.'

Edward's stomach churned with despair. But with anger as well, and not only at the whims of Fate. 'Shipping wine to Charleston, even bottled wine, *could* work,' he insisted. 'A steamship would get it here in good time, and the profits would be enormous. God knows it goes against the grain to suggest it, but if you'd build a steamship, Mr Driscoll, or buy one...'

'And put you in command, I suppose?' Henry Driscoll inquired.

'Given the opportunity, yes,' Edward said. 'I'd deliver on time then.'

'Steamships are a passing and irrelevant fad,' James Driscoll declared. 'The wind has served mankind all of the thousands of years this earth has existed. Had the Almighty not been satisfied with that, He would have shown us the way earlier. As I was saying, I sympathise with you. But I am sure you will agree that your record indicates you are still a trifle immature for command. On her next voyage, the *Regina* will have a new master, and you will sail as First Mate.'

Edward's head came up. He could not believe what he was hearing.

'Your share of the vessel's cost will be transferred to your successor,' Driscoll continued. 'Your share of the accumulated loss of these three cargoes will of course be set against your pay, at a moderate rate of interest.' He glanced at Malewski. 'I think you had better return to the lower deck, Malewksi,' he said. 'At least until you have gained some *more* experience.'

'No,' Edward said.

Driscoll looked at him.

'You will not find a better first officer than Malewksi in your entire fleet.' He was talking, defending Cas, not only because they were friends, but to stop himself from thinking. Stop himself realising that his entire life had just crashed in ruins about his head. Amanda had married a ship's master. Not a First Mate. All of their dreams were based upon that simple fact. But now...suddenly his anger seemed to have sharpened, from a general feeling of ill luck into a crystallised emotion of distaste for this man who could sit in the security of his office, and control men's lives with the careless ruthlessness of the wind itself.

'I will note your opinion in Mr Malewski's record.' Driscoll stood up. 'This meeting is at an end.'

Edward also stood up. 'I trained your crew for you,' he said. 'I brought your ship through a hurricane. Without losing a man or a mast. But you give me no credit for that.'

'I have no doubt you were lucky. Besides, it was *your* decision to risk the hurricane.'

61

Edward could suppress his anger no longer. 'I am the best master, the best helmsman, the best *seaman*, in your entire fleet,' he shouted. 'And you treat me as if I were dirt.'

'I am treating you as what you are, an over confident boy with an inflated sense of his own importance,' Driscoll said. 'Good day to you, Edward.'

'Then you'll find someone else to be mate of the *Regina*,' Edward said.

Driscoll, already on his way through the door, stopped, and turned. 'Don't act the fool, boy. You either sail for me, or you sail for no one on this coast. I'll black you with every firm that flies the United States flag.'

'You do that,' Edward set his cap on his head. 'I'd not sail for you again if I were starving in a gutter.'

'Edward.' Malewski hurried down the stairs behind him. 'I am sorry. So very sorry.'

'So am I, Cas,' Edward said. 'About everything.'

'If you had not tried to defend me...'

'It would have come to the same thing.' They walked together down Market Street, towards the docks.

'But what will you do now?'

Edward shrugged. 'Look for another berth, I suppose.'

'Driscoll is a man of his word,' Malewksi said. 'You'll not find it easy.'

'Yeah,' Edward said.

'I...' they had arrived before the *Regina*, still being unloaded, the precious cases of wine still being handled like the liquid gold they should have been. 'Do you think I should have resigned as well?' the Pole asked. 'Would you like me to do that?'

'For God's sake, no,' Edward said. 'That would be utterly pointless.' He slapped his friend on the shoulder. 'You'll fight your way back up. You'll soon be an officer again.'

'And you?'

Edward forced a grin, for all the sickness in his belly. 'I'll fight my way back up again too,' he said. 'And when I do, when I'm master of my own ship again, you'll sail as my first officer, Cas. There's a promise. Jehu,' he shouted, unwilling to return on board the vessel he no longer commanded, 'fetch my gear ashore. We're going home. All of it, now.'

'Coming at you, Mr Edward.'

'I'll have my list of stores ready by tomorrow morning, Captain Anderson,' said Reynolds, the boatswain, leaning out of the gangway.

Now the sickness had become almost a pain. 'You'll give it to the new master, Mr Reynolds, whenever he arrives.'

'The *new* master?'

'I've been dismissed,' Edward said, quietly. 'Call over the lads.'

The sailors crowded round to shake hands,

and voice their disapproval of what had happened.

'We'll not sail with anyone else, Captain Anderson.'

'We'll form a deputation, Captain.'

'Aye, we'll go see Mr Driscoll.'

'We'll tell him it's you or nothing, Captain.'

Edward held up his hands for quiet. 'It'll be nothing, and you know it,' he told them. 'There's too many sailormen waiting around these docks for berth, and Jim Driscoll is a hard man, as you all know as well. Believe me, I'm grateful for your loyalty. More grateful than I can say. But you'll not help me by losing *your* jobs. And you'll not help yourselves either. God bless you all.'

He walked away, quickly, so that they would not be able to notice the sudden brightness of his eyes.

Jehu hurried behind him with the sea chest. 'Man, this is a business, Mr Edward,' the Negro said. 'But what you going do?'

'I have no idea.'

'You ain't going sell me, Mr Edward? Say you ain't going do that?'

'No,' Edward said. 'I won't sell you, Jehu. Although maybe you'll have to do a bit of starving, from time to time.'

'Captain Anderson!'

He stopped, and turned, and looked at Penelope Meigs. She was driving a phaeton, herself handling the reins, although a liveried

Negro driver sat beside her. She wore orange silk, with a matching bonnet, and looked utterly delightful. Edward raised his cap as she drew rein beside him.

'May I offer you a ride home?' she asked.

Edward hesitated, then nodded. 'That would be very civil of you, Miss Meigs.'

The black man got down, to walk beside Jehu; Edward sat beside the girl.

'I heard the *Regina* had arrived yesterday,' she said. 'And thought I'd come down to see how you made out.' A faint flush crept into her pale cheeks. 'I could not help overhearing what you were saying to those men. Have you really been dismissed by Mr Driscoll?'

'Yes,' Edward said, angry that this chit of a girl should share so unhappy a secret. And angry too with the mere presence of her, the careless wealth she represented, the fact that her father could hardly be different to James Driscoll in his attitude to those he employed—and more than anything angry because he could not fault *her*. She had none of the arrogance of Henry Driscoll, for example. Her huge amber eyes were filled with a genuine concern. Just as her youthful body suggested a hardness which would make her totally unlike the average well-to-do Southern Belle in that it indicated she might even occasionally take some exercise, as exemplified by the way she drove her own trap.

'But why?' she asked.

'My cargo is ruined.'

'But that's monstrous.' She concentrated on the road, gloved fingers tight on the reins. 'It wasn't your fault.'

'I'm afraid it was,' he said 'I was the Captain. Anything that happened on board that ship was my responsibility. You need to turn down here.'

'Oh!' Her nose wrinkled as she guided the phaeton down the side street, looking in distaste at the small, neat houses. 'You live down here?'

'I'm a sea captain, Miss Meigs. Not a planter. Correction: I'm an *ex*-sea captain. This is my house.'

She reined the horse before the cottage. 'You'll obtain another berth, Captain Anderson. Won't you?'

'I shall try,' he agreed. 'Does it matter to you?'

Now the colour flared in her cheeks. 'I...I do not like to think of so talented a man being unemployed.'

'But you do not know I am talented, Miss Meigs. You are acting on information. Or is it instinct?' He was being hateful. But he felt in a hateful mood, to all mankind. And particularly to the daughters of millionaires who possessed everything he would have liked to be able to offer Amanda—and now had no hope of doing.

'I wished to be sympathetic,' she said. But

66

some of the softness had left her tone; she *had* been offended. 'I supposed it might be worth your while to come out to Greenacres, perhaps for tea. Father might be able to help. To offer you employment.'

'Does your father own a ship?'

'Good lord, no.'

'And I am a seaman, Miss Meigs. I know nothing else. I am also not accustomed to accepting charity. And, Miss Meigs, I am *also* a married man, and thus hardly suitable to be the protégé of a sixteen-year-old girl.'

Now he had, at last, succeeded in angering her. 'Then you had best get down, sir,' she snapped. 'No doubt your wife is overseeing us now, and will have a rolling pin for your head. Good day to you, *Mister* Anderson.'

'Who was your friend?' Amanda asked.

'The Meigs girl. We met in Bordeaux, briefly.'

Amanda poured coffee. 'And how did your meeting go?'

'I've been dismissed.'

Her head came up, sharply.

'Well...I was offered a position as first mate. On my own ship. I suppose I should have touched my cap and said, yes, sir. It is Company policy, after all, and I knew that. Instead, I lost my temper. The Driscolls are such insufferably *smug* people. Are you very angry with me?'

She got up, came round the table to sit on his lap. 'I'd not have it any other way. As you say, the man's name is Driscoll, not God.' She kissed him on the mouth. 'Will you find another berth?'

'I doubt that, my love. At least, not immediately. He has sworn to blackball me the length of the coast.'

'Can he *do* that?'

'I'm afraid he probably can. He's a powerful man. I think my best bet is to volunteer for the Army.'

'To do *what*?'

'Well, the Government is calling for Volunteers, I'm told, because of this trouble with Mexico, down in Texas. The Army is one thing old Driscoll can't dictate to.'

'You'll do no such thing, Edward Anderson. Volunteer for the Army, indeed. You're a sailor, not a soldier. It's so *unfair*,' she said, resting her head on his shoulder. 'If you'd had a steamship, you'd have brought that cargo home in perfect condition.'

'Jim Driscoll doesn't believe in steam,' Edward said. And smiled into her hair. 'Neither did I, until yesterday.'

She raised her head. 'But you believe in it now?'

'I believe it is the way of the future. It has to be. Oh, not ships like the *Mohawk*. She was neither one nor the other, and thus failed to be either. Yet she got home before the *Regina*,

68

and we could leave her standing in a fair breeze. If there was some way they could get more speed out of those paddle-wheels...'

'Why don't you apply for a berth on a steamship?'

He kissed her on the nose. 'I'm a seaman, remember? I'm no more an engineer than I am a soldier. It would mean starting from scratch. Supposing anyone would have me.'

'Well, then.' She stood up. 'We must be practical.'

He caught her hand. 'Mandy, I'm sorry. So terribly, terribly sorry. There was so much we were going to do...'

'And we'll still do it all,' she declared. 'We have the time. For Heaven's sake, this can only be a temporary setback. But as I said, we must be practical. There are the mortgage and the servants to be thought of. We won't starve. Father will give you a job...' she checked herself, staring into her husband's face. And sighed. 'No,' she said. 'I don't suppose you could stand behind a haberdashery counter without going mad. We'll think of something.' She held out her hands. 'But there's always you and me. We'll manage, lover. We'll manage.'

To lie with Mandy in his arms was indeed to put all the cares of the world behind him. Her flesh had the texture of velvet, and the quality of a superbly ripe pomegranate, a sexual readiness which emanated from her brain as much as her groin. She loved with the same intensity she brought to everything else in life, moving her sweat-wet body against his, imprisoning him between her powerful, anxious thighs, forcing him to accompany her through the threshold of ecstacy however much his brain might be sagging with misery, his belly rolling with the burden of catastrophe. And as she had said, he had been away for ten weeks, and therefore chaste for that time; he was not the sort of man to sample the dubious delights of a Bordeaux brothel.

If only it were possible to lie here forever, knowing only her soft comfort, dependent only upon her formidable strength. If only he could stop his mind wandering, to all the things they should have had, had been going to have. A house, like Titus Meigs' Greenacres, perhaps. He had never been there, but he had heard of it. Several hundred acres of rolling parkland, with an extensive river frontage, great colonial pillars, each room bigger than this entire cottage, servants and horses at a moment's call... and a bed big enough to wallow in, as opposed to the narrow cot in which they now lay.

And for Mandy, all the frills and furbelows so carelessly displayed by Penelope Meigs. And all the jewellery worn by her mother.

Instead of a long, poverty-stricken haul, back to prosperity. If it was ever to be accomplished. He did know nothing but the sea, and his future could only be taken from those rolling blue waters. But at the same time he was well aware that ships and seamen formed a small, inverted community. Reputations once lost were not easily to be regained. He thought he had proved his seamanship in combating the storm. But Driscoll had been right; he had been foolhardy to accept the storm in the first place. Shipowners certainly wanted their masters to be men who could handle any weather which might be forced on them; but they also wanted them to be men who would avoid bad weather when they could. They did not look for gamblers.

He would have to have something more to offer them than just the ability to sail a ship. But what was there, more than that, for a sailor? Thus he would have to accomplish something quite out of the ordinary. Such as crossing the Atlantic in a week. The record was just over twelve days, held by the British paddle steamer *Great Western*, and she had made it under power alone just ten years before. But that had been on the shortest of Atlantic routes, Bristol to New York, where by using the Great Circle Route and taking advantage of the curvature of the earth's surface to follow a shortened parallel of latitude the whole way as opposed to sailing direct from one point to another, the journey could be reduced to scarce three thousand miles; the *Great Western* had never achieved more than ten knots. And most skippers, like Able, were content to meander along at six knots, simply because they dared not go any

71

faster without using up their precious coal too quickly. There had to be something wrong with that reasoning. Every logical train of thought convinced Edward that a ship which could use the best of the wind and yet have the power to move when there was no wind had to be able to travel faster than a sailing ship pure and simple.

But not while she was as clumsily designed as the *Mohawk*, as handicapped by those high topsides and ghastly paddle-wheels. Yet that was what steam required. And he did not really know sufficient to have any idea of how it could be changed. He knew nothing of engines and ratios, of the mathematics of being an engineer. He had had no formal eduaction at all; reading and writing were the sum of his intellectual accomplishments, and sufficient arithmetic to be able to make the necessary simple calculations involved in navigation.

Amanda moved in his arms, suddenly, raised her head. 'The ferry,' she said.

He looked down the long curve of her naked beauty. 'Eh?'

'The Locock Ferry. You know, up the river. Locock wants to sell it. He's too old.' She sat up, turned on her knees above him. 'I'm not quite sure how it works. I think it's a system of chains and pulleys and things. But he does quite well at it. I know Father would lend us the money to buy it.'

'A chain ferry? You mean a floating bridge.'

She laughed, a delicious deep contralto. 'Didn't you tell me that was how your grandfather started? In New York?'

'He was a ferryman, sure. But it was at least a boat.'

She leaned forward to kiss him, her heavy breasts scraping up his chest. 'You'll be on the water. And you'll be your own man. James Driscoll can't trouble you up the river. It'll give you time to think.' She settled herself on top of him. 'Jehu can be your crew.'

'Easy there. Easy.' Edward stood on the flat wooden deck of the ferry, beckoned the stage coach forward. The heavy vehicle came sliding down the bank of the river, rendered soft by the recent wet weather, brakes squealing as the driver strained on his reins to keep the four horses under control. The first two animals gained the ferry deck, and the flat-bottomed craft dipped and swayed as they were followed by their mates and the additional weight of the coach. Yet its basic stability—it was as wide as it was long—enabled it to absorb the load, and when Edward had the coach firmly in the centre of the platform it might have been a feather for all the difference it made to the ferry's draft.

'Tie those wheels down, Jehu,' he said, 'and put in the chocks. You're responsible for your animals, Mr Dentry,' he said. As he always did. Dentry the coachman grinned good naturedly, got down from his box to attach the nosebags

73

to his horses' heads.

Edward went to the shore side, replaced the planking which acted as a gangway, raised his hat. 'You may come aboard, ladies. Fare's four bits a head.'

There were three ladies, and three gentlemen, who now came cautiously down the bank, the women holding their skirts free of the mud, the gentlemen gallantly sacrificing boots and even trouser hems to give their fair companions an arm to lean on.

'Edward Anderson, by Heaven,' remarked one of the men.

Edward raised his head, stared at the slight young man. He wore the dark blue jacket and pale blue trousers, the peaked cap and the yellow facings of a dragoon volunteer, the badges of a captain, the wispy moustache of the man who fancied himself. He carried himself with an even greater air of arrogance than Edward remembered.

'Henry Driscoll,' he said.

Driscoll looked him up and down, taking in the open-necked shirt, the rough trousers, the well-worn boots, and the faded blue peaked cap with the tarnished braid and then laughed. 'So this is where you've go to. Do you know, I wondered? How long have you been at it?' He glanced at his travelling companions. 'This chap used to work for my uncle,' he explained. 'Some time ago.'

'I've been at it, as you put it, Mr Driscoll,

74

for near two years,' Edward said. 'It's no secret.'

'Two years? My word. But I've been away, you see, old fellow. Licking the Mexicans.'

'Then I congratulate you, sir,' Edward said. 'On having survived, as usual, unscathed.' He crossed the raft. 'Let her go, Walt,' he shouted at the boy who drove the horses.

'Aye-aye,' Walt shouted, and cracked his whip. The two horses started forward, yoked together, round the huge drum, the chain clanked into its toothed wheel, and the ferry slowly moved away from the bank.

Driscoll came to stand beside Edward. 'And now you're skippering a ferry,' he said. 'Well, well. I'll wager with all the discipline you maintained on the old *Regina*, eh?'

'Yes,' Edward said. He had always known this sort of meeting was likely to occur. He might operate well up-river from Charleston, and only a country ferry, but the world was too small for him never to meet a Driscoll again. So there was absolutely no point in being angry about it. It was only a short journey to the other side.

'Of course you do,' Driscoll said. 'Once command gets in the blood, it's there forever. I'm going to be given a command, as soon as I get back. Uncle Jim promised it to me, before I volunteered for the army. I'm quite excited about it.'

'I'm sure you are,' Edward agreed.

75

'You know, Ned, I could probably get you a berth on her. I know Uncle Jim doesn't forget, but...' he grinned. 'I'm his favourite nephew. Hell, I'm his only nephew. What do you say, Second Mate on the newest ship in the Driscoll Line fleet?'

Edward looked him in the eye. '*Second Mate?*'

'Well, hell, man, you have to begin again somewhere.'

'Under you as master. I'm happy here, thank you, Mr Driscoll.'

'Do you really expect me to believe that? You, Edward Anderson, skippering a raft in some backwater? You'd be a fool to let your pride keep you down for the rest of your life.'

'You know what I don't understand,' remarked one of the young ladies, who had come to stand beside them, 'is how it takes four horses to pull that stage coach, and yet there are only two horses dragging this entire ferry, which has the stage coach on it. That doesn't make sense. Do you know about that, Captain Driscoll?'

'I think I do, dear lady,' Henry Driscoll said. 'But perhaps we should ask Captain Anderson, as it is his ferry.'

'I'm sure you're an expert in these matters, Henry,' Edward said.

Driscoll frowned at the careless use of his Christian name, then smiled at the girl. 'It is all to do with matters like torque, of which you have never heard, my dear. But the important fact is that this raft is flat bottomed. It presents no resistance whatsoever to the surface over which it is travelling, the water. It glides. Unlike a ship, you see, which has to possess a deep keel to keep it from turning over, and which therefore would require quite a few horses, more than a hundred, perhaps, to move *it*. The same applies to our coach, you see. We have two wheels, and their axles are greased to make them turn with the maximum facility, yet do we find that even our wheels are resisted by the ruts and the puddles, the soft earth and the stones, and thus it takes all the strength of four horses to drag it along. We cannot glide. We merely bounce.' He smiled at Edward as the ferry came in to the far bank. 'Is that an accurate analysis of the situation, Ned?'

'An admirable one, Henry,' Edward agreed.

'Yes,' Driscoll said. 'Well, you may be sure I will tell Uncle James that I encountered you. Who knows, he may wish to buy you out, and send you once again on your travels. I do remember his saying that you would never work on water again, so long as he lived. I do not suppose he meant only salt water. Good day to you.'

Edward watched the coach lumbering up the slope, the passengers get in. Henry Driscoll. Pursuing his preordained passage through life, ever onwards and upwards. While he...nearly two years of working this ferry had produced barely enough income to keep Amanda and himself from starving, and to meet the interest payments on the loan from John Dart. It was a job, and nothing more, with no end or accomplishment in sight. Amanda was happy enough; he came home every evening, instead of disappearing for months at a time. And he allowed her to suppose that he was similarly content.

But in fact, being always on water made his present existence more difficult to stomach than if he *had* been a clerk in Dart's haberdashery store. It made him dream, all the time. He sat on the upturned box which acted as his chair in between loads and took the crumpled envelope from his pocket, straightening it on his knee. Licking the point of his pencil, he stared at the rough sketches he had made there. The theory of hull design, as so briefly expounded by Henry Driscoll, had become an obsession with him. He spent several hours a week in the Public Library in Charleston, seeking answers to the questions which roamed his brain. And finding none. Obviously the less draft a ship possessed, the less resistance she would meet from the water, and thus the faster she would go, before the wind. She would not of course sail to windward at all; the windward motion of a ship was produced by the wind pushing against the hulls and the sails, and *being resisted*. It was rather the same series of events as that produced by a man holding an orange pip—

the ship—between thumb—the wind—and forefinger—the sea. As the man squeezed with his thumb, the orange pip, unable to move sideways because of the forefinger, was instead propelled forward. Without a keel, the ship would merely drift sideways, in the direction the wind was blowing.

But windward work would be academic, if one had an engine as well, because once the wind headed the ship, or even came abeam, the engine would do the work. But a keel would still be necessary to prevent the wind, as soon as it rose above six knots or so, from again pushing the ship sideways, or even backwards, especially with those great paddle wheels acting as sails. The only solution was speed. If the ship could travel fast enough, then she could hold her own against the wind, even with a shallow draft. Always back to speed. But no design he had been able to find, and no steamer crew he had been able to talk to, had been able to think of a way of driving a paddle steamer at more than nine knots, and even that speed could only be achieved by a prohibitive comsumption of coal. Of course there were stern paddlewheelers as well, with but a single engine. But these were even less efficient than sidewheelers, as they had to be much larger, and thus required a larger and consequently more expensive engine, as regards fuel consumption as well as initial cost, and in addition they were at once a drag and a weakness when the ship was under sail before the wind; a stern sea such as the one which had pooped the *Regina* would have torn a paddle wheel right off.

He smiled wearily and looked up at Jehu, who had come to stand beside him.

'You ain't letting that Driscoll man go worrying you, Mr Edward?' the Negro asked.

Edward shook his head. 'He ain't bothering me, Jehu,' he lied.

'Well, we got custom.'

A wagon this time, again heavily laden and drawn by four horses, accompanied by an armed guard as well as an armed driver.

'What have you got in there?' Edward asked. 'Gold?' Because there was a rumour of gold having been found somewhere in the west of the country.

'Better'n gold, young fellow,' said the guard.

'It's a secret,' said the driver.

'Aw, hell, Willie, everybody knows about it.'

'Forget it,' Edward said. 'I don't want to learn your secret.'

'We're for Norfolk, Virginia,' the guard said chattily, offering Edward a chaw of tobacco. 'You know Norfolk?'

'Never been there,' Edward confessed, refusing the offer with a shake of his head. 'They build warships up there.'

'That's right,' the man said. 'That's what we've got here.'

'A warship? In the wagon? That *would*

be a secret.'

The man guffawed. 'You're a witty lad. But something *for* a warship now, eh? You ever been to sea?'

'Some,' Edward said.

'Now look here, Lewis,' Willie the driver said. 'That there propeller is a secret.'

'Look who's talking,' Lewis said. 'I knew you was a sailor, son, the moment I clapped eyes on you. Yeah, that's a propeller in there.' He raised the flap on the back of the wagon, and Edward stared at the huge, four-bladed bronze fan, as it appeared.

'What's it for?'

'What's it for? What's it for?' Lewis gave another guffaw. 'To drive the steamships, that's what it's for. You can't have steam warships with paddlewheels, son. They'd get shot off too quick. So that's the answer. An Ericsson screw propeller. It's the latest thing.'

The orchestra struck up, *See the Conquering Hero Comes*, and heads turned as conversation ceased. Then the Mayor hurried across the flag draped ballroom of the Charleston Assembly Rooms, arms outstretched. 'Henry Driscoll! Welcome home, son. Welcome home.'

Dancing was forgotten as people crowded round to shake Henry's hand, slap him on the back.

'Tell us about the greasers, Henry.'

'Were they really as murdering as they say?'

81

'What about the senoritas, Henry?'

'Was that desert real hot, Henry?'

'But Henry, the war isn't over yet.'

'Henry Driscoll! Remember me?'

Henry, laughingly passing from hand to hand and from cheek to cheek, making the necessary answers, accepting the plaudits as his due and gazing at the young woman in admiration. Tall, slender, with a wealth of glorious dark brown hair which was really spoiled by being dressed in the fashionable ringlets, magnificent creamy complexion, and huge amber eyes to bring life to the somewhat solemn heart-shaped face with its straight nose and pointed chin and wide mouth, white poplin evening gown cut in a daring décolletage which exposed her shoulders and the tops of her breasts, added up to a superb picture of a lady.

'Penny Meigs,' he said. 'By all that's wonderful.' His eyes dropped, to glance at her left hand—but the fingers were concealed beneath the white kid glove.

'You flatter me, Henry,' she said.

'Not as much as I mean to,' he told her. 'You have become quite a beauty.' He imprisoned her arm beneath his to lead her away from the throng, while the other young women accepted his choice, as their defeat, in a flurry of whispered comments behind their fans. 'I mean, you always were a beauty, Penny. But now...'

'You have spent too much time with the

senoritas,' she said, but allowed herself to be swept into his arms as the band struck up a waltz, having to look down on him from her superiority in height of at least two inches.

'I think you may be right,' he said. 'But I'm home now...'

'And off to sea,' she said. 'So I hear.'

'Well, I've been given a command,' he said importantly. 'It is necessary, you see, for me to have the experience of mastering a ship before I succeed poor dear Uncle James. He's not well, you know. That's why I've come home early. Went against the grain, of course, to leave my dear comrades, but Uncle insisted. He wrote to President Polk himself, demanding my discharge. So what could a fellow do?'

'What you have done, Henry,' she said. 'Come home.'

The music stopped, but he did not release her, obtained some fruit cup from a passing waiter, and escorted her on to the balcony, whence they looked down on the twinkling lights of King Street, and beyond, the harbour. 'Yes,' he said. 'And I'll have to confess that I really am looking forward to being at sea again. Do you know, the last time I was on a ship was that race we had with you, across the Atlantic. Which you won.'

'Was it a race?' she asked.

'Well...we thought of it as one. But then there was that storm. You missed it, of course, by being so far north of us. We sailed right through the middle of it. Poor Anderson...do you remember Anderson?'

'Yes,' she said, turning her head away from him.

'Well, he wanted to turn tail and run away from it. I ask you. I had virtually to take command. I spent twelve hours on watch, at the height of the gale. It was quite exhausting.'

'Oh,' she said. 'I understood that your uncle dismissed Captain Anderson because he lost the cargo by sailing through the storm. But if it was your decision...'

'Well,' Henry said. 'There was more to it than that, of course. I'm afraid Anderson just didn't measure up to being the sort of man my uncle, my firm, needs as a ship-master. Ah, well, he's found his true level now, eh?'

'I have no idea what he's doing now, Henry,' Penelope said. 'I haven't seen him in ages.'

'Well, of course, you wouldn't have. Believe it or not, he's operating the old ferry, up river. Not far from Greenacres, really. But Uncle James blacked him for sea work, so I suppose that was all he could find. And in fact he seems quite happy.'

'I think we should dance again,' Penelope said, leading him back into the ballroom as the music restarted. 'I really have no desire to spend the evening discussing Edward Anderson.'

Penelope slept fitfully, was reluctant to awaken,

pretending to be still dozing when Harriet, her maid, drew the blinds and placed the tray of chocolate beside her bed.

Indigestion, of course. She had never been able to stomach too much rich food. And thus she had had the oddest dreams. And these, being night dreams, had been uncontrollable, chaotic affairs—and not always pleasant.

Harriet closed the door softly as she left the room, and Penelope was able to roll on to her back, throwing her arms wide and spreading her legs, wishing the banging in her head would stop.

She had dreamed of Edward Anderson. That was really quite absurd. Certainly she could remember him as if she had seen him yesterday, for all that nearly two years had elapsed since the day he had sat beside her in her phaeton. She had had a crush on him. She could admit that to herself, now. One of those wild, irrational passions to which sixteen year old girls are prone, she thought with contempt. The fact was that her imagination had been hopelessly titillated by Venice, and Naples and Rome, and then Vienna and Berlin and Paris... and yet it had been so *boring*, seeing all of those magnificent places with Mama and Papa. To her they had been *alive*. She had been able to sense the brooding presence of the spirit of Joanna of Naples, who had fought and killed to maintain herself in that gloomy castle overlooking Naples Bay, who had been the most beautiful woman of her time and who at last had been brought to book and strangled by her enemies. What did it feel like to be strangled, to know that the last breath was being squeezed from your body, that there was to be no escape... what would it feel like for anyone, much less someone who had been a queen, mistress of all she had surveyed?

Naples, huddled beneath the brooding immensity of Vesuvius, had been the high spot of the tour for her. But there had been others, almost as dramatic. She had imagined Lord Byron at her side as she had walked through St Mark's Square and had been dazzled by the white clad army officers who had asked her to dance in Vienna, every one a past master at the art of waltzing. She had stood above the newly carved tomb of the Emperor Napoleon, to house the body the French had at last succeeded in bringing home from St Helena, with tears in her eyes.

And Mama had said, 'Oh, my, isn't it gloomy in here.' She had made the same remark about the castle in Naples.

And Papa had said, 'Say, you have any idea what all this marble must have cost?'

Penelope had never felt terribly close to her parents; she was a good deal younger than her brother Jonathan, and had in fact been something of an afterthought; Mama, having had her daughter at the late age of thirty-five, had been content, even more than other

86

Carolina matrons, to leave the child's up-bringing in the care of governesses and Negro nannies. But by the time they had reached Bordeaux to take ship for home, Penelope had felt she was travelling with total strangers. And she had still found her pleasure in dreaming. Of a long, slow voyage home, with handsome officers to stand beside her on moonlit nights... instead of which there had been John Able and his elderly assistants, their fingernails stained with engine grease. Her heart had plunged at the prospect that all of that romance was behind her, gone forever, until the beautiful barquentine had dropped anchor beside them, and that so handsome, dashing, utterly confident young captain had sat next to her at supper.

He had not actually appeared to notice her at all, had seemed if anything rather put out when she had interrupted the conversation from time to time. But that had not been relevant to her dreams. He just did not know her, that was all. Had they been travelling on the same ship, and the ship struck a rock or something and gone down, leaving just the pair of them adrift in a lifeboat...it would have been hard lines on Mama and Papa, and the other sailors, of course, but they could not really expect to be given a place in her dreams, especially Henry Driscoll.

And then to see Edward again, or at least, not him, really, but only his ship, battered but still ruling the waves, emerging from the grip of the hurricane...

She rolled on her stomach, pillow clutched tightly against her chest. What a *child* she had been. And yet...she could still remember him on that last day, just after his dismissal by James Driscoll, his face so stiffly determined not to show any emotion. He had been aware of her then, as he had brusquely reminded her of the facts of life.

She wondered what *would* have happened had he been less upset, if he had accepted her invitation to come out and speak with Papa? Certainly Papa would have offered him a job. And certainly the job would have had to be better than operating a ferry which wasn't even a proper boat.

Instead he had so annoyed her she had even refused to dream of him any more. An important loss. She still dreamed, every night, daydreams, in the space between turning down her lamp and actually falling asleep. They were still romantically active dreams, in which she was invariably the only female survivor of some holocaust or other, and in which she would be rescued and loved by some heroic figure. The problem was, she didn't know many heroic figures. She had formed a tremendous attachment to Mama's physician, just before leaving for Europe, but in Italy, his dignified face and somewhat portly physique had seemed utterly inadequate to her needs. That had been the trouble with Europe. She had been so anxious to dream, and there had been no one to dream of. And that, she supposed, was why Edward Anderson had seemed so attractive when she had met him in Bordeaux. The fact that he was married had been no more relevant than that any other of her dream men—certainly the doctor—had been married. She didn't know their wives, and wives, like parents, had no place in dreams, anyway.

But actually, of course, in reality Anderson could hardly be any more romantic a figure than Dr Simpson; there was nothing heroic in allowing himself to be brought down by James Driscoll, so that he was reduced to operating a floating bridge.

'Penny!' The door opened with Mama's usual vigour. 'Still abed? All of that fruit punch. But wasn't it a splendid party?'

'I suppose so, Mama.'

'Suppose so?' Priscilla Meigs stood by the bed and looked down on her daughter. 'Oh, Penny, you *are* the limit. Don't you think young Henry Driscoll has turned out well? So handsome, in his uniform.'

'Oh, really, Mama. He is the most utter little squit.'

'Penny. I am *angry* with you. And you will have to change your mind about him. He is coming for lunch.'

Penelope sat up, still clutching the pillow. 'Here? Whatever for?'

'I invited him. And he accepted. I think he

fancies you. Because I think...' Priscilla Meigs' voice became a conspiratorial whisper. 'That we could do a lot worse.'

'Do...Mother, you are insane.'

'You really must learn to control your choice of words, Penelope,' Priscilla said, stiffly. 'Just as you must one day accept the fact that you are no longer a little girl. It is time for you to grow up, and stop this silly daydreaming, and realise that it is high time you were married.'

Penelope stared at her with her mouth open. She had not realised Mama knew anything about the dreaming.

'And Henry is a very nice, and very wealthy young man. In the not too distant future he is going to be the President of the Driscoll Line. Now you may not think this is important, but it is impossible to have too much money available. And I *know* he is greatly taken with you...'

'Mother,' Penelope shouted. 'He is two inches *shorter* than me.'

'For Heaven's sake, how can that be important? Penelope? Whatever are you doing?'

Penelope had leapt out of bed and was throwing her nightgown on the floor. She opened the door to shout for Harriet. 'I am going for a ride,' she said. She glanced at her mother over her shoulder. 'I am going to *exhaust* myself. That way I may just be too tired to be rude to Henry Driscoll.'

She knew *where* she was going, of course,

long before she actually left the Meigs estate. Greenacres was not actually a part of Titus Meigs' plantation—it was twenty miles away from the cotton fields. Meigs had liked the site, and had bought it as a retreat for himself and his family, away from the hordes of Negroes he owned, the constant hustle and bustle of plantation life. But it still covered fifty acres, along the river bank, and there was still an enormous number of grooms and gardeners to be negotiated, every one anxious to raise his hat or wave to the young mistress, before she could reach the high road. And then leave it again, taking the side lane which led down to Locock's Ferry, as she had always known it. Although now, she supposed, it should be called Anderson's Ferry.

How odd that Edward Anderson should have been working there, not five miles from her home, all of this time—and it had never occurred to her to go and look.

She slowed her horse to a walk, principally because here the trees crowded the lane and occasionally dipped over it, and more than once her silk hat came close to being dislodged by a drooping branch. But also to give herself time to change her mind. Because there could be no doubt that she was going to be disappointed. There could not possibly be anything the least bit romantic or heroic about someone operating a floating bridge.

But she had dreamed of him, involuntarily.

91

She had never done that before about any of her mental heroes.

And then, seeing him might clarify her mind, make her understand what she had to do. Because she understood her mother very well. Once Priscilla Meigs got an idea into her head, it stayed, and was generally implemented. So, marry Penny to Henry Driscoll. He was young, but still ten years older than she—just the right difference in age—he was rich and due to become richer...and he was of seafaring interests, in which Titus Meigs had no stake at all. Did that mean that Papa was considering going into shipping?

Which would mean that both her parents would be in alliance on this project, which did not often happen, and which would therefore also mean she was really up against it. Because the fact the Henry Driscoll was a stuck-up little prig who suffered from a quite unbelievable over-estimate of his own importance did not of course enter *their* calculations at all.

So what was she going to do about it? Because, she supposed, she *was* about the right age for marriage. It was not something that had previously entered *her* calculations at all. She had no real female friends; she had suffered from malaria fever as a girl, and had been brought up very much in seclusion, while her education had been entirely in the hands of her governesses. The European holiday two years ago had, in fact, been a sort of reward to her for at last apparently throwing off the continuous agues which had made her childhood such a misery and had prevented her from enjoying life as she should have done. But she had never been involved in the excitement of other people's engagements or their marriages. She had never even been a bridesmaid. The fact was that Papa, who was a self-made man, had never really fitted into the Carolina aristocracy—rumour had it that not all of his amazingly successful business deals had been entirely honest. Which would equally explain why his daughter —for all her undoubted beauty—had never actually been taken up by Charleston society, and why Mama was so anxious to have her marry into that society.

But marrying Henry Driscoll was not something she could contemplate. In fact, she could think of nothing more dreadful. When she married she wanted it to be someone like her brother Jonathan, who had all of Father's drive and slightly ruthless determination, and who was obviously much like Father must have been as a young man. Or like Edward Anderson, another young man with drive and determination and no weight of family behind him, obviously destined to make his own way. Save that in his case the way had been brief and stormy. She almost smiled. Quite literally, stormy.

She drew rein on the bluff overlooking the river and looked down on the ferry. It was still very early in the morning and the floating bridge had not yet apparently commenced work. The horses were still being yoked to their load and a black man was applying grease from a large can to the chains. And Edward Anderson was standing on the bank, just bending his head to kiss a yellow-haired woman on the mouth. Penelope felt a pang of almost real pain, even as she realised that the woman had to be his wife, who must, with true domestic fidelity, have ridden out here with him to see the start of the day's work; the pony and trap waited beside her, in the back seat a basket which would undoubtedly contain his lunch. A role she had dreamed herself into, so often. But no doubt that was all she would ever do, dream.

Suddenly obsessed with a desire to see what this woman who possessed the most attractive man she had ever met actually looked like, she kicked her pony forward, urged it into a gallop as she charged down the slope, determined to arrive with all the panache that was the prerogative of the daughter of Titus Meigs. She realised that she was going far too fast and leaned back in the saddle even as she tightened her fingers on the rein, and with a feeling of helpless horror felt the leather strap suddenly come free in her hands.

CHAPTER 3

Edward heard the drumming of hooves and the cry of the girl at the same moment and looked up to see an unidentified horsewoman careering towards him, black silk hat falling from her head, dark brown hair trailing behind her, mingling as it did so with her crimson scarf, deep green riding habit a flurry of white underskirts as her left boot came out of the stirrup and she was maintained in the saddle only by her right knee curled round the pommel.

Amanda's fingers bit into his arm. 'My God!' she screamed. 'She's going in!'

The filly scattered up to them, swerved as it saw the people, the strange machinery and then the two stallions, and plunged into the river. Penelope Meigs gave a despairing wail, which was drowned in the splash as she rolled out of the saddle.

'Ow, me God,' Jehu bawled, dropping his grease can to run to the bank.

Walter stood with his mouth open.

Edward pulled himself free of Amanda's grasp, ran down the slope and across the ferry and hurled himself off the outer edge, for the river flowed at several knots, and the girl was already being swept past the landing stage. And very obviously she could not swim as she struck the water with her hands, vainly attempting to keep from sinking, but was hampered and being dragged down by the weight of her habit.

Edward had forgotten how cold the March water had to be; it took his breath away. But he reached her in a few powerful strokes. She struck at him as well, and he had to get behind her, thrusting his hands under her armpits and locking his fingers together over her breasts, while swimming backwards with vigorous kicks of his legs, not attempting to challenge the current, but drifting with it, directing himself towards the bank. 'Easy, Miss Meigs,' he said, having realised who he was grasping. 'Easy.'

'Oh,' she gasped. 'Oh...'

Edward's feet struck mud, and he was able to stand up, the water swirling about his thighs, while he brought her against him. Her eyes opened as she stared at him, panting for breath, wet hair plastered to her neck and shoulders. 'Oh, Edward,' she said, and fainted.

'Let me help you, Mr Edward.' Jehu splashed into the water beside him, helped him carry her ashore.

'Here,' Amanda had driven the trap along the bank, and now spread one of the seat blankets on the grass. 'Lay her here. Why...isn't it Penelope Meigs?'

'Yes,' Edward said, and laid Penelope on the blanket. 'She seems to have fainted.'

'I'm not surprised,' Amanda remarked,

kneeling beside the girl. 'What an experience. Thank you, Jehu. Go and get Walter, and find that pony. Edward, help me get these sodden clothes off her.'

'Me?' he asked in alarm.

'She'll catch her death otherwise.' She glanced at him, and smiled at his embarrassment. 'For Heaven's sake, Ned, she's only a girl.' She tossed him another of the blankets. 'You'd better get your own off. Wrap yourself in that.'

Edward stripped, encased himself in the blanket, watched his wife unbuttoning Penelope's habit and carefully peeling it from her body, then scoop the sodden petticoat to her waist. Penelope's eyes opened. 'Oh,' she said.

'Ah,' Amanda said. 'Come along now, Miss Meigs. Sit up and we'll get these clothes off.'

Penelope sat up, looked at Amanda, then past her at the crimson-faced Edward. 'But...' she looked down at her exposed legs; her sodden drawers were clinging to her almost like a second skin.

Amanda gave another smile. 'I do assure you, Miss Meigs, he knows what a woman's linen looks like. He's an old married man. But I think you had better take the trap back to the ferry stage, Edward, until we are ready. Instruct Jehu in what to do for the next couple of hours. You and I will have to take Miss Meigs home.'

Titus Meigs bustled into the book-lined

study, rubbing his hands together. 'She's going to be all right,' he said. 'Yes, indeed. Just a nasty shock. When I find the scoundrel who saddled that horse...by God, I'll take the skin from his back.' He surveyed Edward, who, wrapped in one of his own dressing gowns, sat in a comfortable armchair before the desk, a glass of brandy at his elbow. 'Your clothes will be dry in half an hour,' he said, and refilled the glass, pouring one for himself. 'She'll be eternally grateful to you, of course, Captain Anderson. As will we all. Yes, indeed.' He made an expansive gesture. 'You have but to ask...I mean to say, she might have been drowned.'

The door burst open and another man came in. Edward could tell at a glance that he was Meigs' son, Jonathan; he had the same height and breadth, the same florid face, the same air of almost hoping someone would attempt to stop his headlong progress through life.

'Pa,' he shouted. 'I heard there was an accident.'

'There was,' Titus Meigs agreed. 'Penny's horse ran off with her, and she got dunked in the river.'

'The river? But she can't swim.'

'She's all right,' Titus Meigs said reassuringly. 'She'll be down in a little while. This young fellow went in and got her out, and he and his wife very kindly brought her home. You've not met my son, Anderson. Edward Anderson,

98

Jonathan Meigs.'

Edward got up to shake hands.

'Edward Anderson,' Jonathan Meigs said. 'Of course. You used to sail for the Driscoll Line.'

'I did,' Edward said.

'And got dismissed rather shabbily, I've heard.'

'I opposed Company policy,' Edward said.

'Spoken like a man,' Titus Meigs said, pouring his son a glass of brandy. 'And now you operate the old Locock Ferry, eh? Must be interesting work.' He looked at his son and raised his eyebrows.

'I've heard you were the best skipper out of Charleston,' Jonathan declared.

'The best skippers, Mr Meigs, are those who bring home intact cargoes,' Edward said, and sat down again to finish his brandy. In fact the two brandies, so early in the day—it was still not lunch time—added to the excitement and the shock of the icy water, had him feeling quite heady. He supposed the house was not helping matters, as he gazed around him at the panelled walls, the leather-bound books, the carved ivory chess sets, the glass cases filled with exquisite porcelain…all of the beautiful things he had always dreamed of possessing and never had.

'Aye, well…' Meigs refilled his glass. 'Shipping's not something I know a lot about. But like I said, young fellow, you saved the life of

99

my daughter. You have but to ask, and if I can get it for you, it's yours.'

Edward gave a wry smile. 'I'm a seaman, Mr Meigs,' he said. 'And not even you can get me a ship.'

'Well now...' Meigs looked up as there was a knock on the door.

'Mr Driscoll is here, sir,' said the Negro majordomo.

'Henry Driscoll! I remember you.' Titus Meigs hurried forward to shake the young soldier's hand. 'I was tickled pink when Prissy said you were coming out to lunch. Mind you, I can't say what time lunch will be, in view of all the excitement. You know my son...and say, I guess you know Edward Anderson as well. Last time we met you were one of his crew.'

Henry stared at Edward from beneath arched eyebrows. 'I heard there'd been an accident,' he said.

'A runaway,' Jonathan explained. 'Penny would have been drowned, but for Captain Anderson here.'

'Indeed,' Henry observed. 'I trust Miss Penelope is all right?'

'Oh, she'll be fine, fine,' Titus Meigs said. 'Say, you know what, young Driscoll, you've turned up at just the right moment. Captain Anderson has done a mighty proud thing, jumping into that river after my little girl. And he won't accept a thing for it. So, sir, I'd take it as right friendly if you were to ask that

100

uncle of yours to put him back in command of a ship. I think it's real shameful that a fine fellow like Captain Anderson should be stuck ashore when he wants to be afloat.'

'Now, really, Mr Meigs,' Edward protested, flushing with embarrassment.

Henry was flushed with anger. '*Mister* Anderson contravened Company rules, Mr Meigs,' he said. 'And he was not dismissed. My uncle considered that he lacked the sense of responsibility required in a shipmaster, but he offered him a berth. Anderson refused it and he was downright rude about it. Perhaps, were he to apologise...'

'I *am* a shipmaster,' Edward said. 'Not a mate.'

'And what rules did he contravene?' Jonathan Meigs demanded 'Refusing to run away from a hurricane?'

Henry's flush deepened. 'He endangered the cargo,' he said. 'And as a result, it was lost.'

'Now boys,' Titus Meigs said anxiously. 'Don't let's have any quarrelling. It's all in the past.' He refilled Edward's glass, poured one for Henry. 'Although I think it's a darned shame one slip-up like that should ruin a man's career. I'll bet if you'd have had a steamship, Anderson, you'd have brought that cargo home, eh?'

'Steam,' Henry sneered. 'Six knots.'

'It got you home, Mr Meigs,' Edward agreed. 'As you say, if I'd had a steamship, or

101

if I had one now, a proper steamship, I'd take on any sailing ship afloat.'

'Now there's a turn up for the book,' Jonathan said. 'A sailorman declaring for steam?'

'It's the future,' Edward said, now definitely feeling a little tight, and quite unable to restrain the ideas which were tumbling over themselves to escape his brain. 'If the ship is properly designed.'

Jonathan glanced at his father, and then frowned at Edward. 'You know, you strike me as being a man who has an idea knocking about in there.'

'Steam,' Henry said. 'There is no way any great ugly paddle steamer is going to beat a sailing vessel, except by accident of weather.'

'You're entirely right, Henry,' Edward said. 'I was not thinking of paddles. I was thinking of a screw propeller.'

'Say now, I've been reading about propellers,' Jonathan Meigs said. 'I didn't know they've been properly tried.'

'They haven't,' Henry Driscoll said. 'And where they have been they've proved no more successful than paddlewheels.'

'Do you know, I thought so too,' Edward said. 'Until I started looking into it. They've been the subject of some considerable experiment in Great Britain. With tremendous results.'

'The *Rattler*,' Henry sneered.

'It proved a point,' Edward insisted.

102

'What's this *Rattler*?' Titus Meigs wanted to know.

'Well, sir, to compare the relative merits of paddlewheels and propellers, the British Navy a few years back built one of each. Two ships, exactly the same size and displacement, but one, the *Alecto*, had paddlewheels, and the other, the *Rattler*, had a screw propeller. First of all they raced, over a hundred mile course, and the *Rattler* won comfortably. Then, sir, the real proof of the matter, they were set stern to stern and attached by powerful cables, and instructed to steam in opposite directions as fast as they could. Believe it or not, sir, the *Rattler* towed the *Alecto* at a rate of two and a half knots.'

'Holy smoke,' Titus Meigs said, and looked at Henry. 'There's no answer to that.'

'An experiment,' Henry sneered. 'What does it prove? I still say a sailing ship is twice as fast.'

Titus Meigs looked at Edward.

'Well, sir,' Edward said. 'The British thought so much of it that they built a steamship, the *Great Britain*, with a screw propeller, and sent her across the Atlantic. She did the crossing in fifteen days. Okay, so that's not a record time. But it's pretty quick. And she did it time after time.'

'For a year,' Henry pointed out. 'Then she was wrecked.'

'Any ship can be wrecked,' Edward said,

refusing to lose his temper. 'My point is that she was a proven fast ship, maintaining a steady ten or eleven knots regardless of the weather. And she was just a ship. In my opinion she wasn't properly designed for the job she had to do.'

'And you would design a ship differently,' Henry said.

'I've done a lot of thinking about it,' Edward said. 'And reading.' He grinned. 'I don't have much else to do, on that floating bridge, but think.'

'So tell us,' Jonathan invited.

Edward glanced at Henry, then at Titus Meigs. 'You don't want to hear my theories.'

Titus looked at his son, who nodded. 'Sure we do, Captain Anderson,' the millionaire said. 'Always willing to learn.'

'Well...' Edward got up, holding the fold of the dressing gown in front of him, rather like a toga, took his place in the centre of the room. 'As I once told you, Mr Meigs, with the old *Regina*, if I could have carried a fair wind all the way from Bordeaux to Charleston, I could have done the crossing in fifteen days.'

'*Fifteen days?*' Jonathan cried. 'But...isn't that what the *Great Western* did the journey from Bristol to New York in, in thirty-eight, and that's only two thirds the distance.' He frowned. 'She was using coal and sail, too.'

'Yes, but as you point out, the Great Circle route from Bristol to New York is hardly three thousand miles, compared with nearly four thousand from Bordeaux to Charleston. But that was the record. The *Great Western* maintained just over eight knots. Then she got her speed up to ten, and made the journey in just over twelve days. No one has ever done it faster. But I'm talking about *eleven* knots, minimum.'

'But as you *can't* carry a fair wind from Biscay to America, that's so much bunkum,' Henry said. 'It's even more bunkum from Bristol to New York, where you have head winds nearly the whole way. A sailing ship has to go looking for fair winds, and adding a thousand and more miles to her journey. There's no way round that.'

'Sure there is,' Edward insisted. 'By steaming when the wind is foul.'

'For Heaven's sake, back to square one.'

'I reckon the lad should be let speak his piece,' Titus Meigs said, seating himself behind his desk and resting his chin on his hand. 'No interruptions, now. Shoot, Captain Anderson.'

'Well, sir...'

Edward drew a long breath. 'My contention is that all that has so far happened is that shipbuilders have taken existing ships, and existing designs, and added paddlewheels to them. Or in the case of that British ship, the *Great Britain*, propellers. In fact, in several cases, they've made existing designs worse by having to build higher topsides to accommodate the

105

wheels, thus creating more windage and necessitating more draft. Now, sir, in my opinion, there are already faults in sailing design. Take the *Regina*, for example. She's one hundred and ninety-eight feet long, and forty-eight feet wide. That's totally unnecessary. Wouldn't she go faster, by reason of moving less weight through the water, if she was say thirty-three feet in the beam? That is, one in six instead of one in four, length to beam ratio.'

'She'd turn over,' Henry Driscoll said.

'Not properly handled. The *Great Britain* had a ratio of six-to-one.'

'And she didn't last a year,' Henry reminded him.

'She ran aground, Henry,' Edward said, patiently. 'She didn't roll over. And then, the *Regina* draws twenty-five feet. Can you imagine, Mr Meigs, the amount of hull she has in the water, that has to be pushed *through* the water to get our eleven knots?'

'I can probably work it out,' Meigs said. 'But by narrowing her down, won't you lose a lot of cargo space?'

'Some,' Edward agreed. 'And of course there will always be a reason for the high, square ship. But I am positive there is also room for the low, sleek one, which will transport certain cargoes, those cargoes which need to be got someplace more quickly than others, at twice the normal speed. Such cargoes would of course attract higher freight charges, so your profit would be the same.'

'The whole idea is quite nonsensical,' Henry said. 'With less draft she'd certainly roll over. Think of that squall which knocked us down in mid-Atlantic? If her hull design had been narrow and shallow as you suggest, the *Regina* would have turned turtle quicker than you could spit. Anyway, how'd she work to windward?'

'The whole point of my argument, Henry, is that she would never *need* to work to windward, under sail.'

They stared at him.

'What did Captain Able do, with the *Mohawk*, Mr Meigs?' Edward asked. 'When the wind headed him, he dropped sails and put on his engine. But because he was commanding a sailing ship with a couple of paddles stuck on his sides, and displacing, relative to her length, just as much hull through the water as the *Regina* does, he could only manage six knots, or nine by burning his fuel at a prohibitive rate. But suppose, sir, he had had a custom built ship, intended to sail like a sailing ship, when the wind was right, and motor like a steam pinnace, when the wind was wrong? Suppose she was two hundred feet long, and only thirty-three feet in the beam, and carried only a fifteen foot draft? And suppose in addition, instead of twenty foot high topsides she was only ten feet out of the water. What then?'

'You'd have a floating coffin,' Henry declared.

'You'd have the fastest thing afloat, and the safest, if the men who were sailing her knew what they were about. You'd have a custom built steamship, which would move like a bat out of hell, before the wind. But the very moment the wind shifted from abaft the beam, down would come the sails, and on would go the engine. No paddlewheels, but a screw propeller, getting the maximum torque, and pushing a hull that would have been designed especially for the purpose.'

'How fast would it go?' Titus Meigs inquired.

'Under sail, sir, I would bet fifteen knots. And under steam, well, it would depend on the size of the engine, the amount of steam we could raise. But I don't see why she wouldn't do the same.'

'My God,' Jonathan said. 'Then she'd do Bristol to New York in nine days.'

'A floating coffin,' Henry asserted again.

'A damned interesting project,' Titus Meigs said, and got up. 'I hear the ladies coming down. Let's go and see if we can find you some clothes, Captain Anderson.'

Edward heard the hoofbeats coming down the lane towards the ferry and looked up in embarrassment. Obviously he had known that she would have to come, eventually. But it would be certain to embarrass her as much as himself; he had supposed, and hoped, that as a week had now elapsed since the accident, she might have decided it wasn't necessary after all.

And at least, he realised, looking past her, she had brought her father as well. There was a relief.

He walked up the sloping ramp, stood at the head of the lane. She was riding the same pony. 'You've checked your leather, I hope,' he said. 'I'm not sure I feel like a swim today.'

She came up to him, freed her boot from the stirrup and slid forward. He caught her under the armpits and set her down, remembering the previous time he had grasped her there, and what had followed...she was only the second woman he had ever seen in quite such deshabille—the odd prostitute he had encountered in his youthful days as a sailor had hardly done more than remove her drawers—and the slender muscularity of her body, so different from Amanda's soft curves, was difficult to forget. But no doubt she was sharing the same memory in reverse—there were little pink spots in her cheeks. 'I never had the time to thank you properly,' she said. 'Last week. At lunch. There was so much going on.'

'So forget it,' he suggested.

'But I owe you my life,' she insisted. 'And Mrs Anderson...' She looked left and right.

'She's not here today,' Edward said. 'She doesn't come out every day. It was pure chance she was here last week. Although it's just as well...' he flushed, and she did the same. What a silly thing to say. 'She'll be pleased to know you're out and about,' he added, speaking quickly to hide his embarrassment. He stepped back, as she had not moved, had remained standing almost against him. 'Good morning to you, Mr Meigs.' The planter was just catching up with his daughter.

'And to you, Captain Anderson,' Meigs said.

'Father has the most tremendous news,' Penelope said.

'Sir?'

Meigs dismounted, shook Edward's hand. 'That ship of yours.'

'Ship? Oh...' again Edward flushed. 'I'd had a bit too much to drink, Mr Meigs. All of that brandy...'

'But you *had* thought about it?' Meigs asked anxiously.

'Well, of course, sir, but...'

'Jonathan liked the sound of it. Has a good memory, Jonathan has. He could remember most of what you said. He wrote it all down, after lunch. And I was able, therefore, to discuss the project with one or two people.'

'To discuss...not with James Driscoll?'

Meigs smiled. 'No, Captain Anderson. I didn't reckon you'd take kindly to that. I have to tell you, though, that opinion regards the project as mad. Informed opinion. Steamship men. Leastways, most of them. There were one

110

or two suggested it might work. But only with a skipper who knew what he was about, and a crew, too.' His smile widened. 'I reckon I might have the skipper.'

Edward frowned at him. 'I'm not sure I understand you, sir.'

'There are various details which you didn't mention last week, so I guess you hadn't really considered them. Like this propeller and its shaft. You realise that means driving the shaft through the hull of the ship?'

'Well, of course, sir. But the problem has been solved. There are various packings which will render it watertight.'

'Sure. I've been finding out about them. But the fact is, no screw propeller has been so far designed to give more than twelve knots. You want fifteen. That means a bigger engine than any yet put in a ship. People tell me there just won't be room for anything else.'

'I would say that is an exaggeration, sir. It would all depend upon the interior design.'

'I reckon you're right. But I wanted to be sure you were aware of it. I've a man coming to see me, tomorrow afternoon. He's an engineer, mainly to do with ships. I'd like you to be there to talk with him. Bring your wife and stay to dinner. I'd also like you to work out how much this dream ship might cost. Have those figures ready by tomorrow afternoon too.' He looked past the dumbfounded Edward at the ferry. 'I don't reckon you're going to have the time to continue with this operation. I'd better buy you out and install someone else. Have a price on that ready for me tomorrow, too.'

'But...do you mean you're considering building such a ship, Mr Meigs?' He had to be dreaming.

'Considering, Captain Anderson. Considering. If the price is right, and we can find a shipyard and then a crew. And if old Jim Driscoll doesn't fight us too hard.' He winked. 'But I reckon I know how we can tackle that one.'

Penelope put out her tongue at him, then squeezed Edward's arm. 'It's going to happen, Captain Anderson, I know it is. You're going to have your ship.' She stood on tip-toe, kissed him on the cheek. 'The fastest ship in the world.'

Mark Trethowan made brief dabs with his pencil on the sheet of paper on Titus Meigs desk. His quick, jerky movements were typical of the man, tall and angular, convulsed, it seemed, by an unquenchable burning energy; his Cornish brogue was spoken unusually quickly and mingled oddly with the Canadian accent he had accumulated over his years in Nova Scotia.

'What you need is two engines, Captain Anderson,' he said. 'And we'd place them as low down as possible in the hull, in view of the design you have in mind. They'd each have four cylinders, each with a bore of eighty-eight inches and a stroke of seventy-two.' He allowed himself a smile at the utter bewilderment on the three faces in front of him. 'By that, gentlemen, I mean that the size of the piston, the diameter of the hole into which it will fit, the *cylinder*, will be eighty-eight inches. That's a big piece of metal. And it will be driven, or stroked, a length of seventy-two inches. Six feet. That's a lot of power. You'll need three boilers. If they each have eight furnaces, they should produce steam at fifteen pounds per square inch above atmospheric pressure, and develop something like one thousand five hundred horse-power each. That will give your engine eighteen revolutions per minute.'

Jonathan Meigs frowned. 'A propeller turning at eighteen revolutions a minute isn't going to push a ship very fast.'

'No, sir. But that's where the gearing I was telling you about comes in. The engines will drive a large sprocket wheel at, as I say, eighteen revolutions per minute. But if we attach a set of chains, I reckon four, to a sprocket wheel only a third as large as the master, that smaller wheel will be turned three times as fast, near enough. So you've got, say, fifty-three revolutions per minute. And *that's* the speed at which your shaft and therefore your propeller will turn. I wouldn't like to swear what speed you'd get. But you'd get eleven knots, for sure. Eleven is the speed the British got out of their

113

Great Britain, with a similar set-up. But she's more conventional in hull design than Captain Anderson's concept. So it's possible you'd get more.'

Edward scratched his head. 'Two engines. That sounds an expensive installation.'

'Well, it ain't cheap,' Trethowan agreed. 'But it's the only way you'll get the power you want inside a ship the size you're aiming at. More important, if I may say so, Mr Meigs, is the space it will take up. And then you have to carry sufficient coal. Those engines will burn a lot of coal. Sure I know the *Great Western*, when she set the record, arrived in New York with two hundred tons still in her bunkers. But she was lucky with the weather. The *Sirius*, which tried to beat her to it, only got there by burning all her furniture and some of her superstructure as well, because she ran into a storm. That sort of thing scares the passengers. Now the *Great Western*, as you gentlemen will know, before she went out of service last year, got her time down to just over twelve days, that's an average speed of ten knots for the Bristol—New York run. But she cut her coal supply pretty low. The *Great Britain*, well, she maintained eleven knots, as I said, but then she was a big ship, over three hundred and fifty feet long, and fifty in the beam. I don't suppose...' he looked at Titus Meigs.

Who shook his head. 'Our financing isn't going to run to anything over two hundred feet,

114

Mr Trethowan,' he said. 'As in Captain Anderson's original design.'

Trethowan nodded. 'Well, what I'm saying, gentlemen, is that if you aim to use your ship on the trans-Atlantic run, out of Charleston, you won't be able to carry sufficient coal to steam the whole way, in my opinion.'

Titus Meigs gazed at Edward.

'The New York to Europe run is what we should aim at, Mr Meigs,' Edward said. 'That's where the real money is. Freight and passengers.'

'It's where the worst weather is, too,' Trethowan pointed out. 'Taken year round. Well, then, to maintain, say twelve knots plus for two hundred and fifty hours I reckon you'll need something like a thousand tons of coal on board. That's going to take up a lot of room, too.'

'But there *will* be room for passengers?' Jonathan Meigs asked anxiously.

'Sure. But I don't reckon we'll manage more than a dozen staterooms. Not if you want to carry freight as well. I understood you were aiming at an elite service, the fastest in the world. Well, if you achieve that, a little bit of competition for space on board isn't going to harm.'

'That is the idea,' Titus Meigs agreed. 'But these twelve staterooms have to be the very best. No expense should be spared on the cabins or in the lounges. If we are going to have the fastest ship in the world, then we must also have the most comfortable ship in the world.'

'That will cut into space even more,' Trethowan said. 'But if that's what you want, Captain Anderson, I'll provide those engines. There are two other points you have to consider. First of all, the rig. Most steamships use the barquentine rig, which gives them at least some windward capability under sail.'

Edward shook his head. 'Square rig on all three masts, Mr Trethowan. We are going for the ultimate, so there is no point in compromising. When the wind is abaft the beam, we sail; when it heads us, we steam. So when we sail we want the maximum effect, just as when we steam we want the maximum horsepower.'

Trethowan shrugged. 'She's your ship. The last point is iron. The *Great Britain* was, I should say, is, wood sheathed in iron. This was decided because it was felt that to drive a ship that hard would inevitably weaken her timbers and maybe open them up. And they were talking about twelve knots, not fifteen. You can't deny they built a strong ship. She's been stranded off the coast of Ireland for upwards of a year, yet the hull remains in such good condition that they're refloating her with the idea of putting her into commission again.'

'That may be so, Mr Trethowan,' Edward said. 'But if I may say so, I cannot see the point of building a ship in order that she may survive a stranding. The object is not to get her

116

stranded in the first place. Iron means weight, and weight means less speed. We'll build in Burma teak and Canadian rock elm. I cannot believe a well founded ship will not stand up to any sea.'

'Right you are. Well, I reckon that's the limit of my knowledge. I build the things, I don't take them to sea. I am bound to say that in my opinion what you are planning is a very large river steamer, which you're planning to take across the North Atlantic. *You* are planning to take?'

'Nobody else,' Edward said.

'Will you get a crew to sail with you?'

'I'll get a crew,' Edward said. He glanced at Meigs. 'We might have to pay them a bit over the odds at first, but once they realise it's safe...'

'There's the point, Captain. Will it be safe?'

'I reckon it is, properly handled,' Edward said. 'How about it, Mr Trethowan? Will you sail with me as engineer? At least on her maiden voyage?'

The Canadian gazed at him for several seconds, then grinned. 'I might, at that.'

'She'll be built here in Charleston,' Titus Meigs said. 'My...ah...associates will want to have the credit here.'

'I've already made arrangements for that,' Jonathan said. 'Bartell will do it.' He met their astonished stares. 'Sure he's only built coastal schooners up to now. He's got the slip space

117

to handle a bigger vessel, and the shipwrights, certainly if there's no iron sheathing involved. And frankly, no one else around here will touch it, because of James Driscoll. Say the word, and the keel can be laid tomorrow.'

'You've got it,' his father said. 'But there will be just one change in your plans, gentlemen. I agree that we must aim for the New York-England traffic. But her maiden voyage will be Charleston-Bordeaux.'

Trethowan frowned. 'You'll have a serious fuel problem.'

'Surely you won't have to steam every day. Edward? Can you do it? We want, we have to have, maximum publicity. In the North Atlantic you're just one more ship. Down here, with a much longer distance, if you can make the round trip, say in a month, including loading time in Bordeaux, we'll really hit the headlines. How about it?'

'A month,' Edward said. 'Ten days out, ten days back, ten days in Bordeaux. Maybe a shade less. But we're talking about fifteen knots constant.'

'Well?'

'You said you could give me ten days fuel, Trethowan,' Edward said.

'Just. You won't have a shovelful to spare.'

Edward grinned. 'We'll do it, Mr Meigs.'

'I thought you would,' Titus Meigs came round the desk to stand by him. 'I'll find the money to match your brains and your seamanship. And your guts, come to think of it. I reckon that's worth a seventy-five twenty-five split. What do you say?'

Edward shook his hand. 'I'm overwhelmed, Mr Meigs. I can't believe it. I don't see why you should stick your neck out like this, for me.'

'For you, boy? For all of us. Let's say I'm a gambler. I'm sitting at a table and an ace suddenly falls into my hand. You don't reckon I should bet on it? Let's get the girls in.' Titus Meigs opened the door, smiled at his wife and Amanda and Penelope. 'Looks like we may have ourselves a ship.' He beckoned his butler, who was waiting with a laden tray, took a glass from it, raised it high. 'Here's to...well, what do you know? What are we going to call her?'

Everyone turned their heads to look at Edward. 'Well,' he said. 'I suppose...' he looked at Amanda, received a quick shake of the head. 'I think she should be called, the *Penelope*.'

'The *Penelope*,' Henry Driscoll said in disgust. 'I really am confounded that you should have lent your name to such a ham-handed scheme, Penny. That ship will be the laughing stock of the coast. Of the entire world. It already is the laughing stock of the entire world. Having it built by a one-horse outfit like Bartell's. And putting an untried chap like Anderson in command. It's incredible.'

They were sitting on the upstairs verandah
119

at Greenacres and drinking mint juleps. He had become quite a regular caller, encouraged by Mama. And nothing she could do, neither her obvious dislike of him nor this constant annoyance of Papa by his objections to the new ship, could put him off.

Still, she thought, she must keep trying. 'Jealousy suits you,' she remarked. 'It goes with your personality.'

'Oh, really, Penny. Jealousy? I'm just distressed to see your father pouring so much money down the drain, and at a time like this. I've heard he's already put twenty thousand dollars into the scheme.'

'At a time like what?' she inquired.

'Oh, well, that doesn't matter. The fact is...'

'Oh...' she got up in sudden irritation. 'For God's sake go away. Go home, Henry Driscoll. Go home, and leave me in peace.'

He stared at her with his mouth open. Then he got up without a word, placed his glass on the table, and went into the house. A moment later she saw him riding down the drive. He did not look back.

As if *he* mattered. It was the things he said, the innuendoes he constantly let drop, the suggestions...at a time like this? What time? And yet she could not deny the evidence of her own eyes that Papa had been looking worried from time to time recently. She had too often caught him in a brown study, a letter drooping from his hand. But that had been before any talk of

120

building a ship, so it could have nothing to do with it. While, as he *had* decided to invest in this ship, there really could not be much the matter with his finances at this moment.

But it was all just another irritant to add to those she already suffered. She went to the verandah rail, looked down at the slaves weeding beneath her. Her every instinct called on her to have her pony and trap harnessed up, and ride into Charleston to Bartell's shipyard, where the *Penelope* was slowly taking shape. Why, it was almost her second self, as it bore her name. But she didn't dare.

She had never anticipated one of her dreams actually becoming a breathing, talking reality—and yet remain a dream. So most of the men she had dreamed of in the past had sooner or later come face to face with her—but always it had been a time to stop dreaming, as she had discovered on every occasion that a man's exterior seldom bore any proper relation to his character, and that he never seemed to possess any of the qualities she had hoped to find in him. Even Anderson had seemed like that, two years ago. He had fallen so naturally into the pattern of every other man, in his apparent acceptance of the misfortunes of fate, his reluctance or his inability to fight against them, that it had been perfectly simple to stop dreaming about him.

But that had been before he had dived into an icy river to save her life. That alone would have made him different, a true dream figure, quite apart from the utter intimacy of those minutes on the river bank, the drive back to the house, both of them wrapped only in blankets. But when in addition she had discovered that he had not meekly accepted fate after all, had instead gone away and dreamed himself, and more than that, had made plans and calculations...

Now she dreamed of him every night. And hated herself for doing so. Because she dreamed of Amanda as well. She had never met a more charming and unaffected woman, a more friendly one...and not too many who were prettier, either. And she was Anderson's wife. She shared his bed, every night. Penelope gave a little shiver. She had no proper idea what sharing a bed with a man entailed. There again, her lack of female friends was proving a tremendous handicap. She knew the feelings of her own body. She had even, on occasion, assisted them to develop, abandoning herself to waves of sensuous delight. But she had no idea what a man might want, or require. Even a man like Henry Driscoll, much less a *man* like Edward Anderson. Her dreams always stopped when she found herself in his arms.

And he liked her, too. Well, she merely had to look in the mirror to know that he must. She could still remember the feeling of having his hands clasped across her breasts, through all the cold and the shock. She hadn't really fainted when he had carried her ashore; she just had not been able to look either him or his wife in the face.

And then Amanda had undressed her. How much had he seen? She could not really remember. But certainly her breasts had been exposed, and her calves. If she had not sat up, but had lain still, Amanda would have stripped her naked—and it would not have occurred to the woman to send her husband away. If only she had lain still.

Another hateful thought. The woman had been assisting in saving her life. And she was Edward's wife. He must love *her*, no matter how he might be capable of admiring other women. The point was, she was sure he could love her, too. Back to the desert island theme. A world where there were no Amandas, no wedding rings, nothing, except two people, and passion, and opportunity. A world where right and wrong was absorbed in the necessity to survive, and love.

Back to the dreams.

But she was surely entitled to go and see her namesake being built. She ran downstairs, called for her phaeton.

'She does look awfully narrow.' Amanda Anderson stood beside her husband on the platform above the ship slowly taking shape beneath them. 'Are you *sure* she's safe?'

Edward squeezed her against him; it was the

first time she had visited the yard, and the hull was all but complete. 'Of course she's safe. This is the shape of the future. In fact, it is not as narrow as ships will be in the future. Six-to-one will be nothing. As ships get longer and longer, ratios of seven-and-eight-to-one, or even nine-and-ten, will be used.'

'It seems incredible.'

'Not incredible, logical. It stands to reason. If you built a four hundred foot ship on a four-to-one basis you'd have a hundred foot beam. Think of the sail area you'd need to push *her* along. And what about finding a harbour to put her in? It really is just a matter of getting used to the increased dimensions. Do you know that five and six hundred years ago, when they were first using sailing ships as opposed to galleys, they worked on a two-to-one ratio? Now, can you imagine anything more absurd than a ship which is half as wide as it's long? But they were sure, then, that anything narrower would immediately turn upside down.'

'I suppose...will they *ever* build a four hundred foot long ship, Ned?'

'Within ten years.' He winked at her. 'If I make a success of the *Penelope*, I'll persuade old Meigs to build her for me.'

'Oh, Ned...' she nuzzled his neck, oblivious of the shipwrights who were laying down their tools to watch them. 'I'm so happy. So very, very happy. If only you had a crew...'

'But I have got a crew, my darling. Who do

you suppose that is down there?'

Amanda leaned over the rail. 'Cas? Cas Malewski? Is that really you?' she shouted.

'Nobody else, Mrs Anderson.'

'And there's Reynolds, the boatswain from the *Regina*, over there, and another half dozen Driscoll men, come to us.'

'But...Driscoll?'

Malewski laughed as he came up the steps to shake her hand. 'Jim Driscoll ain't pleased, Mrs Anderson. But we always said once Captain Anderson got another ship we'd sail with him and none other. We told Driscoll that, too.'

'Well, glory be,' she said. 'It *is* all going to work. Isn't it, Edward? It is all going to work?'

'Yeah,' he said. 'It is all going to work. Do you know, sometimes I have to ask myself if I'm dreaming? The way this has worked out... the way it began. You know, just a chance meeting off Royan, really, and then that disaster with the wine, and the ferry...the way old Meigs has just taken us over, settled our debts...'

'Our debts were peanuts to him,' she said. 'And things always work out, for those who want them badly enough, and are prepared to try. Nothing would have happened if you hadn't spent these two years dreaming, and studying, and planning.' She squeezed his arm. 'She *will* be as fast as you say? So you won't be away from us for so long at a time?'

'I'll never be gone more than a month,' he said. 'And that includes loading at the far end. Mind you, if she's a success you may have to move up to New York. Would you like that?'

'New York?'

'It's where we'll have to sail from, to get the best cargoes. And the best passenger list.'

'But...it's full of damn Yankees.'

He made a mock bow. 'Of which I have the honour to be one myself.'

'Oh, you're almost a naturalised Carolingian.' She blew him a kiss. 'I'd go to the South Pole, to be with you, Ned. And I suppose Baby would too. But I want him educated here in Charleston.'

'The South Pole,' he said dreamily. 'Who knows...*what* did you say?'

Her cheeks were pink. 'I came down here especially to tell you. But I didn't know how, you were so wrapped up in your ship.'

He swept her into his arms. 'Oh, my darling. Do you know...'

'Yes,' she said. 'After three years I was beginning to wonder too. But I guess maybe I wasn't happy enough until now.'

He held her away from him, looked at her stomach. 'But...when?'

'Oh, not for seven months. When are you launching?'

'At the end of next month, I hope. Seven months...we'll have made our first voyage, by then.'

'Well, just mind you're here for the birth.'

'Seven months,' he said. He walked to the rail, looked down on the ship. 'I'm to be a father,' he shouted.

The shipwrights put down their tools to stare at him. Mark Trethowan's head appeared from the main hatchway.

'A father, Mark,' Edward shouted. 'I'm to be a father. A father!' He hurled his cap into the air. 'A father!' He gazed at the door to the huge shed, through which Penelope Meigs was at that moment walking. 'Penny,' he shouted. 'Penny. I'm to be a father.'

The girl stared at him, then at Amanda at his side, then turned and walked out again.

Penelope Meigs drew the longest breath of her life, glanced left, at her father, then right, at her mother, then up at the bows of the ship towering above her. 'I name this ship, *Penelope*,' she shouted. 'And may God bless her, and all who sail in her.'

The bottle of champagne sliced through the air and shattered on the ship's stem; immediately the chocks were knocked away, and the *Penelope* slid gracefully and effortlessly backwards into the calm waters of the river. Trumpets blared, drums banged, and people cheered. Everyone was here today, from Father, smoking a cigar, to Mother, all smiles, to Jonathan, red face beaming—to James Driscoll, standing with Henry. And even he looked

127

at least interested. And of course, already on the ship, Edward and his crew. But this was the ship's day. Her ship. Because it was she, by the very fact of her being, who had given it life.

'Come along,' Titus Meigs was saying. 'You'll want to go aboard. The launch is waiting.' He ushered his guests along the dock to the gangway, their wives leading the throng.

'Come along, sis,' Jonathan said, as Penelope lagged behind. 'Don't you want to go aboard?'

She drew her coat tighter round her shoulders, allowed him to escort her on board the launch, smiled mechanically at the complimentary, and not so complimentary, things which were being said about the vessel, hardly hearing any of them.

She had not been back to the shipyard since the day she had heard of Amanda Anderson's pregnancy. She would not have come today, if she had not had to perform the naming ceremony. Thus she had not seen Edward in that time. Five weeks. Partly this had been caused by shame. She had behaved very badly, in storming away like that, at his moment of joy. Worse, she feared that she might have betrayed herself. What she thought about Edward Anderson was her secret, and no one else's.

But more than any of these, she had been angry. Wildly, unreasonably, disconcertingly angry. Because somehow the fact of the pregnancy put an end to all her dreams. It made them seem dirty. Up to that day it had been possible to suppose all manner of events taking place to throw them together—because such events would only have involved three lives, and in the realm of dreams wives, even pretty, charming, and unsuspecting wives like Amanda Anderson, had to take their chances. But now there were four lives involved. Besides, a man *might* fall out of love with his wife, at least for a while; men did not often fall out of love with their children. And when Edward Anderson came to her, even in her dreams, she wanted all of him, without a single reservation.

She had, in fact, realised that she was in love, with a man who was not only her social inferior, but who was married, and about to become a father, and who had never given her the slightest indication of feeling anything similar for her. And who was therefore, on every count, quite beyond her reach. It was not a situation she was used to. As Titus Meigs daughter, she had always in the past only to indicate her preference and it had appeared. But then, she had never actually wanted a man before.

How handsome he was, in his new blue uniform, with its gold braid, his new cap, similarly braided, with his officers, Casimir Malewski and Mark Trethowan at his elbow, as he greeted the distinguished guests, one after the other, not changing his expression at all as he shook hands with James Driscoll.

'You've done well, young Anderson,' Driscoll said. 'Well. I always knew you would, mind. Now all you have to do is sail this floating cigar.'

'That's my intention, Mr Driscoll,' Edward said, and passed on to the next guest. She was the last. 'Why, Penny,' he said. 'I thought you'd gone off ships and sailors.'

'Yes,' she said. 'Yes, I have.'

He raised his eyebrows, but was immediately called away by Titus Meigs to take his guests on a tour of inspection.

'She's too narrow, and she's not enough freeboard,' James Driscoll said. 'That's my opinion, anyway, Meigs. I think you're a fool.'

Titus Meigs merely smiled at his rival. 'The proof of the pudding, Driscoll, is in the eating. This ship sails on April seventh, that is exactly one year after her keel was laid. She's bound for Bordeaux and back, and she'll make the round trip in one month exactly. Thirty days. And that is allowing nine days for loading and unloading in Bordeaux.'

There was a chorus of derisive protest.

Meigs held up his hand. 'Anyone care to bet on it?' he asked.

'Oh, she's fast, maybe,' Henry Driscoll said. 'But I'll bet you she's uncomfortable. What happens when you hit big seas with this low freeboard? How are your first class passengers

130

going to enjoy that, promenading up to their knees in water?'

'Our first class passengers won't *be* promenading, if we hit big seas, Henry,' Jonathan Meigs said. 'They'll be below, in that lounge which made your eyes pop. And this ship will be so fast she'll drive through any bad weather in six hours.'

Another chorus of protest, which the Meigs met with continued aplomb.

'Why don't you come along for the ride, Henry?' Jonathan asked. 'We're fully booked, but I'm sure Captain Anderson would be able to squeeze you in. It'll be the experience of a lifetime.'

'Not me,' Henry said. 'I aim to live to be ninety.'

It was wearying. When at last the guests departed, Titus Meigs took out his handkerchief and wiped his brow. 'God damned pessimists,' he said. 'By God, I hope they're not right.'

'They're not right, Mr Meigs,' Edward said. 'And I'll prove that to them in April. Let them croak. As you say, we've fifty fare paying passengers says they're wrong.'

Jonathan Meigs sighed. 'I wish there were. I wish there was one.'

'Eh? But you said...'

'Sure I did. That's legitimate business tactics.'

'There have been no takers at all, Edward,'

Titus Meigs said. 'Not one. All this damned publicity about her narrow guttedness, and her low freeboard, and then, what happened to the *Great Britain* hasn't helped. Do you know, I haven't even been able to get an insurance quote?'

'They'll change their minds when we make that record passage, Mr Meigs,' Edward said.

'They'd better. I don't mind telling you, son, but only you, that everything I have is riding on this ship.'

Edward frowned at him, then looked at Jonathan, who shrugged. 'Everything?'

'Every damned cent, and a lot of cents I don't have. To do it I've even mortgaged the plantation. Even Greenacres.' He smiled at Edward's consternation. 'Everybody has his ups and downs, Edward. Cotton has been going through a slump and...well, maybe I made a few bad investments. Maybe I can't resist a gamble. So I'm gambling on you, and this ship. If you break all records, lad, and bring her home in one piece, then, as you say, they'll be clamouring to get in on the act. I'll be able to form a company, get things moving again, build more ships...' His smile became twisted. 'Even my creditors will get off my back. At least for a while. Right now, they're just holding their horses, because they don't understand what's happening. They don't understand me, you see. My motto is, when things are going wrong, you convince everybody

132

they're actually going right by doubling your spending. It's always worked in the past. It's working now. But you're the man who must *make* it work. So don't fail me, son, or we're both on the beach.'

Edward clasped his hand. 'I won't fail you, Mr Meigs. You've my word on that.'

Meigs gazed at him for several seconds, and then nodded. 'If I'd ever felt for a moment you *would* fail me, son, I'd have blown my brains out long ago. But remember, this is strictly between the three of us. Now where are the girls? Gone ashore, eh? We'd best be after them, Jonny. I'm real sorry Mrs Anderson couldn't be here tonight, Edward. You give her my best wishes.'

'I'll do that, Mr Meigs. It's nothing more than a colic. But with the babe...'

'Of course,' Meigs said. 'She mustn't take any chances. Good night, Edward. I'll be down in the morning.'

Edward watched them descend the ladder to the waiting launch. The stewards were packing away the wine, and only the watchmen remained on board. The river was quiet, no more than a whisper of slow moving water, and the *Penelope* surged lazily to her mooring. But even on a mooring she transmitted a feeling of life, of energy, of anxiety to be up and doing. His ship. Far more so than any ship he had commanded before. Because she was his design and his dream. And his gamble. Titus Meigs might

133

be risking his fortune—*he* was risking his life, and the lives of all those he had persuaded to sail with him.

He took a last glass of champagne from the tray of the last steward as the man headed for the gangway, slowly walked aft, towards the great companionway down to the drawing room. Of course the ship was a gamble, in every way. She was a gamble in her predicted speed, on which everything depended. She was a gamble in her passengers' comfort. He had no doubt they would *be* more comfortable, down here where the motion would be felt less than anywhere else on the ship. But would they *feel* more comfortable, in the occasional storm, where they could not see out?

As if it mattered, at present, when he had no passengers, anyway?

But she was also a gamble in not being iron-sheathed. And most of all, she was a gamble in her stability. Yet he knew that he at least would be able to sail her, and sail her well, and make her work. He had no doubts about that.

He went down the wide, deep carpeted staircase and stood in the lounge, looking up at the chandelier, the candles still glowing, left and right at the mirrored bulkheads, the freshly painted pictures, scenes of Charleston, one of Fort Sumter, and then he strolled down the corridor between the staterooms, again on deep pile carpet, with scarce a suggestion that he was not inside a luxury hotel instead of on board an ocean going ship.

'The king, surveying his kingdom,' said Penelope Meigs.

He had been so busy before, so preoccupied, so excited, indeed, that he had not properly noticed her. Now he could take her in at his leisure. She was a blaze of colour in a printed woollen dress in red, green and mauve stripes, with green braid at her collar and sleeves and white frills at her neck and wrists. On deck she had been wearing a dark blue velvet cloak with a pale blue bonnet, but these had now been discarded and thrown on the bed in the state-room out of which she was emerging. She had been drinking champagne, and there were pink spots in her cheeks. It occurred to him that she might be drunk.

Edward also had been drinking champagne. He thought he had never seen a more beautiful object in his entire life. But he was not drunk.

'Your father and brother have just left for the shore,' he said. 'If we hurry , we can call them back.'

She took a deep breath. 'Do we wish to call them back, Edward?'

He frowned at her. Her face wore a some-what defiant expression, but he did not suppose she was directing it at him. Rather did he suspect she had just won a battle with herself.

'I thought,' she said, 'that we might share a moment or two, as this is our ship. *Our* ship,

Edward. Yours because you dreamed of her, made all the calculations. Mine because I gave your dream life.'

'That's true enough.' He held out the glass. 'So drink a toast to her.'

She did not take the glass from his fingers, but carried his entire hand to her mouth, drank with her lips touching his flesh, waited while he did the same.

'I love you, Edward,' she said.

His frown returned. Yet he was aware of a complete absence of surprise, or even alarm. The champagne was having a dulling effect on his nerves, of course. But had he not always known that she loved him? Had she not made that plain from the very beginning? Even that day he had been dismissed by James Driscoll, he had suspected at least her girlish adoration. And over the past year, as she had just reminded him, they had been yoked together, in their mutual dream, mutual ambition.

'I know,' he said.

She stood against him. 'And you love me, too.'

The champagne had had the effect of removing inhibition, fear, of enabling him to consider things logically and accurately. 'I think I desire you,' he said. 'That is not the same thing.'

'It is sufficient,' she said.

He shook his head. 'It is wrong. I love Amanda. She is going to be a mother for me, and we are married. To allow myself to love you would be a crime. Even to desire you is a crime.' He half smiled. 'Especially now that you know of it.'

He attempted to step past her, to pick up her coat and hat, but he was checked by her body, by her arms going round his neck. 'It is only a crime, Edward,' she said. 'If it harms anyone. It cannot harm Amanda, if she never knows of it. And it cannot harm me. I promise you that. It is not having you that is harming me. That is driving me mad.'

Now warning signals were flashing in his brain. He held her wrists, allowing the glass to drop to the carpet, and disentangled himself. 'We have both been drinking champagne,' he said. 'Now, I shall summon a boat for you and send you on home.' He gazed into her eyes.

'You would love me,' she said. 'If you could. If you dared.'

'I *could* love you,' he said. 'You are the most beautiful, and probably the most exciting woman I have ever known. But as you say, I cannot, and I dare not.'

'And thus you will not,' she challenged.

'That's right.' He released her wrists. 'Perhaps, if we had met at a different time, in different circumstances...perhaps if we had met even now, but you were not Penelope Meigs, I might have at least been tempted to take what you offer. But, quite apart from Amanda, you are the daughter of my benefactor. What sort

137

of a cur do you take me for?'

She seized the bodice of her gown and with a single movement tore it open. 'It is the man I am interested in,' she said. 'Not the cur. You touched me here once, Edward. Hold me again. I remember your touch. They are yours. Everything is yours. For God's sake, Edward...'

He stepped past her. 'You'd best put on your coat,' he said. 'And I will fetch a boat, to carry us ashore.'

CHAPTER 4

'I'm sure you should see Mr Driscoll,' Priscilla Meigs said. 'It's the fifth time he's called. He really has been most solicitous.' She gazed at the row of cards on the table by the bed. Seven of them were from Henry Driscoll. One was from Edward Anderson—signed jointly with his wife.

Penelope made no reply to her mother, nestled more snugly into the bedclothes. She wondered what Mama really thought of it all. What Papa thought of it. Or Jonathan. She had been left behind on the ship, quite inadvertently, obviously, when they had all gone home. And she had been brought home, very properly, by Father's protégé, who was also *her* protégé. And she had then gone to bed, and stayed there, giving herself up to a transport of utter humiliation and despair. Dr Simpson had come and peered into her mouth and eyes and had taken her temperature, and he had made her sit up and thumped her back—and had clucked his tongue and taken Mama into the corner. Of course she had heard what he had said perfectly clearly; she rather thought she had been intended to.

'There is nothing actually the matter with her, Mrs Meigs,' he had said in a loud whisper.

'What absolute nonsense,' Mama had declared, having a mind of her own when it came to medicine. 'Anyone can see she is ill. She has spent the entire night weeping. It's her malaria returned. I know it is.'

'Tears are not necessarily a symptom of malaria,' Dr Simpson had pointed out. 'Or any other illness. She has no temperature, there is no rash, there is no evidence of any blockage in the lungs...'

'She has not eaten in twenty-four hours.'

'Quite,' Dr Simpson had agreed. 'The fact is, Mrs Meigs, Penelope is suffering from what can best be described as a brainstorm.'

'A what?' Mama was properly outraged. 'Are you accusing my daughter...'

'Of being under a great emotional stress.'

'Oh, for Heaven's sake. What great emotional stress?'

Dr Simpson had considered the matter, and

then decided not to offer a further opinion. 'That I cannot say, Mrs Meigs. I can only say that she will undoubtedly recover her health, probably in a surprisingly short time. I recommend that she be left in bed, offered food at every opportunity, and perhaps some stimulating company from time to time. But it is to time that we must look in this matter.'

Dear Dr Simpson. He knew exactly what was the matter with her. Even if he did not know the name of the man, or what had actually happened. Only she knew that. Only she knew the madness which had swept over her, and the depths of misery into which she had plunged. Only she knew how utterly impossible it was for her even to contemplate ever seeing Edward Anderson again. Someone she had to see again, over and over and over, as he commanded her father's ship. Her ship. Her namesake.

She became aware that Henry Driscoll was seated by her bed. No man other than Father or Jonathan or Dr Simpson had ever been in her bedroom before. It was just her fate that the first intruder should be Henry Driscoll—and now that he had officially been discharged from the Army and wore the blue uniform of a sea captain he looked more ridiculous than ever.

'It's been an upsetting time for all of us,' he was saying. 'Even those of us not directly involved, to watch your father pursuing this madcap scheme, being led by the nose by a lunatic

140

like Anderson...' he discovered she was looking at him, and flushed. 'We must hope that all will be well. But you, my dear Penny, you have no cause to be upset. This I swear. No matter what happens...Penny, I shall not be here when the *Penelope* leaves on her maiden voyage. I am due to sail in command of the *Regina*—my old ship, you know—just the week before. But I shall of course be back long before the *Penelope* returns. If she returns at all. And when I do return, I shall be offically installed as Commodore of the Driscoll Fleet.' He gave a contemptuous smile. 'Uncle Jim has this idea that I should not become Commodore until I have commanded at least one Atlantic crossing, you see. And then, my dear, dear Penny, I should be the happiest man in all the world, if you would consent to be my wife.'

She stared at him. You, she thought, Commodore of the Driscoll Line? And now you want to marry *me*? After all the things I have said to you, the contempt with which I have always treated you? You? You want me to get into bed with *you*?

He leaned forward, picked up her hand, kissed the knuckles. 'I shall take your silence as acquiescence, my dearest Penny. And I shall visit you again tomorrow, when I hope to find you recovered. Adieu, my own dear Penny. You have made me the happiest man in the world.'

Henry Driscoll, she thought. My God! But

what was the alternative? If only she could dissolve the raging tumult in her brain, analyse her true feelings, understand what she had done and what she must do now.

She was in love. Madly, passionately, consumingly, dangerously in love. With a man she *knew* was very close to being in love with her. But who was forever lost to her, because Amanda Dart had a prior claim. How unjust it was.

And how wrong of her, how wicked, even to think like that. But it was herself thinking, about herself. Surely she could be honest with herself. She loved, and she wanted to be loved back. Not by Henry Driscoll. Not by anyone else in the world. Only by Edward Anderson. She really didn't want to hurt Amanda, or the baby. She didn't want to hurt anyone. She only wanted Edward to take her in his arms, at least once. Why, oh why, could he not have been a Muslim? She would cheerfully have gone to him as his second wife.

Or why could he not have been as drunk as she, that night last week? If he could have brought himself to love her, as he had so obviously wanted to, just once—then she felt she could contemplate life without him, even contemplate marriage to Henry Driscoll. Because she would have known ecstacy, once. But to go to Henry, to belong to him, without ever having known anything better, without ever having been able to *love*...

She sat up, chewing her lip. That was all she wanted, all she asked from life. Gradually the concept crystallised in her brain. Almost she prayed, but then changed her mind; this was not a matter for God. Then should she become a female Faust? But those concepts were absurd. She wanted. Surely she could have, at least briefly, without harming anyone? Surely she and Edward could share something, one hour, just the pair of them, develop a secret which would be theirs alone. Something sufficient to carry her through the rest of her life, while he returned to his wife and his child and the happiness and prosperity which was bound to be his. Surely.

She got out of bed, heart pounding with the audacity as well as the wickedness of her resolution, but determined not to allow conscience to interfere. Now she was sober, and more desperate than ever. Only Henry Driscoll loomed in front of her. That surely could not be what Fate intended as the greatest achievement of her life.

The alternative would be to go mad.

She wrapped herself in her dressing gown, went downstairs, praying she would not encounter Mother and that Father would be at home. He was always at home, nowadays; the ship filled a much larger place in his life than cotton planting. It was like a new toy.

She paused at the study door, then took a long breath and opened it, very softly. For a

143

moment neither her father nor her brother seemed aware of her presence.

'So there it is,' Titus Meigs was saying, staring gloomily at various sheets of paper spread on the desk in front of him. 'We can't hoodwink people any more, Jonny. She's due to sail in three weeks' time. There can be no question any longer about pretending she's full. Of either freight or passengers. But at least there is *some* freight.'

'What gets me,' Jonathan said, 'is that there's no way we're going to *convince* people she's safe, and comfortable, until someone actually sails on her and says so. And if they won't sail on her, how'll they ever be able to say so?'

A great light seemed to explode in Penelope's brain. She had come down here prepared to beg and plead, if necessary to throw a scene. But suddenly Fate was again working on her side, giving her its blessing, however nefarious her scheme. 'Ahem,' she said.

The men looked up in alarm.

'My God,' Titus Meigs said. 'How much did you hear?'

'Enough,' she said. 'You can't get any passengers to sail on the *Penelope*. You've been telling lies about how booked up she is.'

'You're not to repeat that,' Jonathan said. 'To anyone.'

'And especially not to your mother,' Titus Meigs said. 'It would upset her.' He frowned

144

at his daughter. 'What are you doing up, anyway? I thought you had malaria?'

'I'm feeling much better.' Penelope crossed the room to stand in front of his desk. 'I can tell you why you've no passengers for the *Penelope*. It's because you won't sail in her yourself.'

'Eh?'

'Well,' she said. 'It stands to reason. If *you* won't sail in her, it's because you yourself are unsure about her safety.'

Her father frowned at her.

'Do you know, she might just have a point,' Jonathan said.

'Whereas,' Penelope said, leaning over the desk. 'If we were to go with Edward on her maiden voyage, if you were to announce that now, I bet you'll have lots of applications for staterooms.'

'By God,' Titus Meigs said. 'By God.' He looked at Jonathan. 'But I can't. You know I can't. My commitments here, especially right now...'

'Yeah,' Jonathan said. 'They'd take a dim view of that. You mightn't ever come back.'

Penelope had no idea what they were talking about. But she could hardly believe her ears; the situation was getting better and better. 'But that's even better,' she said. 'So you can't go. But if you were to send Mother and me, or even me alone...' she paused, hopefully. But that was asking a shade too much of Fate.

'By God,' Titus Meigs said. '*Would* she?'

'We'll ask her,' Jonathan said. He came round the corner to kiss his sister on the cheek. 'You've quite a brain in there.'

'She'll come,' she said. 'She'll come.' She wanted to scream her joy.

'Sail on the *Penelope*?' Henry Driscoll was aghast. 'That is absolutely out of the question. I forbid it.'

'*You* forbid it, Henry?' Penelope inquired, her voice dangerously soft.

'Well...' he flushed. 'We are all but betrothed. I have certain rights.'

'We are *not* betrothed, as yet, and you have no rights at all.'

'I shall have to speak with your mother.'

'By all means do so. Mother understands the situation perfectly. If you must know, I am sailing with...sailing on the *Penelope* just so that I can properly consider the matter, make up my mind what I wish to do. Mother knows this, and is entirely in sympathy with it. I shall answer your request for my hand when I return. I shall certainly refuse it if I do not go. But I *am* going. And there's an end to it.'

'Penelope and Mrs Meigs sail on the *Penelope*?' Edward was aghast. 'But...that's impossible.'

'Of course it's not impossible, Edward,' Titus Meigs said. 'In fact, it's essential. Don't you see? We have to convince people that we know the ship is all she's cracked up to be. Well, hell, if the word was to get around, as I believe it has got around, that my family are afraid to travel on my own ship...it'll make one whale of a difference, you'll see. I'm going to give it the maximum publicity. I only wish I could come too. But business commitments... and I need Jonathan here as well. But that means I'm putting an even greater trust in you, and your ship, boy.'

'I think it's a splendid idea,' Amanda said. She was very obviously pregnant now; he had had to rig a special basket to swing her from the lighters on to the deck of the ship. But now that *Penelope* was actually launched, and actually fitting out for her maiden voyage, she refused to keep away. 'I wish I could come too. I think it's going to be a marvellous trip.'

'You don't understand,' Edward said. 'They can't come, Mr Meigs. They simply must not.'

Titus Meigs frowned at him. 'You're not uncertain of her, yourself, boy?'

Edward flushed. 'Of course not, sir, But...'

'Oh, I see what's eating you. Believe me, they'll be passengers, and nothing more. I give you my word on that. If they utter the slightest criticism, make the slightest suggestion as to how the boat should be run, act the owners in any way, you've my permission to clap them in irons. That's the right nautical term, eh? Ha, ha! That's it. You clap them in irons, boy.'

Edward looked along the long, low, sleek
147

lines of his ship, to where Malewski was supervising the loading of the scanty cargo they were actually going to carry, and then up past the funnel at the masts and spars. The *Penelope* was everything he had ever dreamed of commanding. And now she would be carrying everything he had ever dreamed of possessing, in his darkest midnight hours.

He had supposed, that night, that she had been too drunk to understand what she was doing. Well, no doubt she had been. But now he realised that her drunkenness had not really affected what had happened. The little vixen. Behind that eager, innocent, and utterly lovely face there was the heart of a succubus, who, having set her sights on a target, would not let go. And not a soul on the face of the earth, not even Amanda, suspected. Because Amanda had never had the slightest cause to doubt his love.

Well, he thought, he could not stop Penelope from sailing with him, as she was the owner's daughter. And why had he *not* taken her, there and then? Had he not wanted to? Did he not want to now? Did he not know that was what was certain to happen on this voyage? Because he desired her more than he had ever desired any woman in his life. Not even Amanda had ever aroused such a powerful sexual urge within him. As he obviously did in Penelope, as well. They were two people bound on a collision course, but a course which he had felt had to be resisted, because of the dictates of honour and society and even self preservation.

But why? If she was hell bent on breaking all of those rules, why should he worry about her virginity or her relationship to his benefactor? As she had so truly said, he could not hurt her, in her eyes. Nor could he hurt anyone else—supposing no one else ever found out.

And as Titus Meigs had just reminded him, once they put to sea he was in sole command.

He smiled at his partner. 'Perhaps it would be a good idea if you were to put that in writing, Mr Meigs,' he said.

The band played, and the considerable crowd cheered and waved flags. Slowly the steam tugs pulled the *Penelope* away from the dock. Edward opened the speaking tube to the engine room. 'All ready, Mr Trethowan?'

'Steam's up, Captain Anderson.'

'Then stand by.'

He moved to the helm, stood beside Reynolds. Malewski came to the other side. The Meigs stood in a cluster, Amanda with them, coats held close against the spring breeze. Edward felt his heart swelling with sheer pride. His ship. His very own creation, going out to do battle with the Atlantic. He had not been beyond Fort Sumter for three years, since he had brought the *Regina* back out of the hurricane. Three years.

He wanted to throw back his head and shout his joy to the sky. Whatever the problems that lay ahead on this voyage, and he did not suppose Penelope Meigs was going to be the greatest of them, by any means, nothing could compare with the sheer magic of once again being afloat, and in command.

But, as he *was* in command, dignity and quiet confidence must be the only emotions he could permit himself. He crossed the deck to stand by the official party. 'We shall be under our own power in fifteen seconds, Mr Meigs,' he said.

'Attaboy,' Titus Meigs shouted.

'Oh, Edward,' Amanda breathed.

Penelope said nothing. She just stared at him, her expression a curious mixture of defiance and joy. They had not been alone together since the night of the launching. Neither of them had wanted it, had been prepared to risk it. And when they had met, they had preserved an absolute formality. All a sham, a lie, an act of deceit, as they both knew what the other was thinking. He had been more than usually loving to Amanda these past few weeks because he *knew* he was about to betray her. And because of her condition he had been unable to love her as he had wished, as it was the only way in which he might have been able to resist the temptation which was about to be thrown at his feet.

He felt like a man on a treadmill, quite unable to stop it turning, forced to continue setting one foot in front of the other. His greatest triumph, and his greatest crime, all at the same moment. He returned to the helm. 'Drop those tow lines, Mr Malewski,' he said, and opened the speaking tube again. 'Slow ahead, Mr Trethowan,' he said, at the same time moving the jangling lever to confirm his command.

There was a rumble from below, a sudden tremor running the length of the ship, a sudden bubble of water at the stern, a sudden puff of black smoke from the funnel. The *Penelope* came to life, and slipped forward through the water. One of the sailors on the foredeck gave a cheer, which was instantly taken up by the rest of the crew, by the tugmen, by the crews of the other ships in the harbour; critics and prospective clients alike might be sceptical, but here was a new ship putting to sea for the first time. That was all that mattered to the seagoing men of Charleston.

'Edward,' Amanda cried, and threw her arms round his neck for a hug.

'I'll wish you a good voyage, Captain Anderson,' said Drayton, the pilot.

'She'll do,' Bartell the builder said. 'She'll do.'

'We'll expect you back, one month today, Edward.' Titus Meigs clasped his hand. 'One month exactly, boy.'

'One month today, Mr Meigs,' Edward said, and rang the levers to stop. The ship lost way, rested on the still water, rolling only slightly. Edward stood at the gangway to see the guests

151

down the ladders and on to the waiting pilot cutter.

'You'd better be sure it's a month,' Amanda said. 'I'm due in six weeks. Now you take care of Mr Edward, Jehu.' Now she was openly weeping.

'Oh, I must be going to do that, Miss Amanda. I going do that.' Jehu was as happy as his master at being at sea again.

'And you take care of *your*self, my love,' Edward said, kissing her a last time, and hating himself for his hypocrisy, for the surging happiness in his heart, and most of all for the insidious thoughts which kept seeping through his mind—because if she never knew, she could never be hurt.

'One month, Edward,' Jonathan shouted.

'One month.' He returned to the bridge, rang for slow ahead once again. Another puff of black smoke issued from the funnel, and the ship moved forward.

'One month,' Penelope Meigs said, coming to stand beside him. 'One month!'

'Do you *ever* sleep, Edward?' Priscilla Meigs inquired.

They were four to dinner, the two ladies, Edward and Trethowan—Malewski was on watch —and as they had sailed with a full complement of twelve stewards, apart from Jehu, they were considerably outnumbered by their white-jacketed attendants.

'I snatch an hour from time to time,' Edward said. He smiled at her. 'I suppose I'm much too excited to sleep.'

He gazed at Penelope, who gazed at him. They had been at sea three days, had eaten together and walked together and talked together; both the ladies were intensely interested in the operation of the ship, wanting to learn everything about her, and had made the descent into the coal and grease coated bowels of the engine room to inspect the machinery. Throughout those three days they had actually exchanged nothing but the occasional glance. Because he realised, as she also undoubtedly realised, the deed was already done, in their minds. They were like two people who, having arranged a sumptuous feast, and seeing it spread on the table in front of them, could now afford to sit back and sip an aperitif, feeling the hunger building, knowing that it could be satisfied whenever they were ready, but knowing it would taste even better for the waiting.

Because, as they had both known from the beginning, nothing could prevent it, now. At sea they were in a special world, and it was a world which he commanded. His world.

He had not even consciously been avoiding his cabin at night. The fact was that there was a great deal to be done, all the time. There had been the inevitable teething troubles of a new ship, and now there were other problems as well. For the first two days the wind had been light and variable, and the *Penelope* had used her engines, driving through the calm seas at a steady fifteen knots, a phenomenal speed, slicing the waves, hardly rolling at all because of the impetus of her forward thrust, leaving a wide, bubbling wake which stretched out of sight to the distant horizon. Fuel consumption had been somewhat higher than he or Trethowan had expected; indeed, Trethowan's calculations had indicated that if they had to steam the whole way they would run out of coal while still five hundred miles west of the Gironde Estuary. He blamed it on the newness of the engines, feeling that they would do better on subsequent voyages.

That had not, in Edward's opinion, been a serious matter for concern; he could not conceive of an Atlantic crossing where they would not obtain at least two days of fair wind, and two days was all they needed. This very morning the wind had sprung up out of the west, and had steadily increased to a good Force Five on the Beaufort Wind Scale, or twenty plus knots. He had ordered the sails set immediately and this afternoon had instructed Trethowan to shut down his boilers. Now the ship travelled silently, save for the sounds of the waves slapping the hull and the hiss of the water racing away from the stern.

'It is so marvellous,' Priscilla Meigs had said, 'when the engines can be stopped. So peaceful.'

154

Their fuel problems were therefore already nearly at an end. Yet a far greater problem had immediately arisen. There could be no doubt that the *Penelope* was too tender under sail. Trethowan of course was not aware of it, and neither were either of the ladies. Not even Malewski, was entirely aware of it, Edward thought. But he was all too aware of it himself. The meal over, he returned once again on deck, stood by the helm, looking back at the wake over which the setting sun sent the sparkle of hundreds of miniature rainbows. The seas were about five feet high, he estimated; to a ship like the *Penelope* that should hardly be very different to a flat calm. Yet the helmsman was working hard to keep the vessel dead before the wind; her shallow draft was causing her to threaten a yaw every time one of even these slight waves picked up her stern. Clearly, running before a hurricane, as he had done with the *Regina*, would be a vastly more hazardous operation with this vessel, if it could be done at all.

He was not, of course, concerned at the moment, nor did his faith in the ship or in his ability to command it dwindle for a second. With the alternative power under his hand he should be able either to avoid a hurricane altogether, or, if the worse came to the worst, heave to under engines; that is, steam slowly into the waves until they abated. Yet it was a design fault. His design. Because he had made a basic mistake, he realised. The theory that a lower freeboard would compensate for a shallower draft was perfectly sound; but, of course, once all her sails were set the *Penelope* was a full rigged ship. There was no danger, he kept reminding himself, as the sails were only intended to be used in these ideal conditions, with the wind dead astern. But the wind was seldom settled in one direction for very long, and he had not anticipated having constantly to watch it for any sign of a veering, or a backing, movement, especially in what was no more than a fresh breeze.

Yet it went against the grain to reef, to shorten sail, at this stage. Nor could he really afford to, if he was going to maintain that fifteen knots.

Something to be solved, when he got back to Charleston. But certainly, he was not going to leave the deck for more than a few minutes at a time as long as they were running under full canvas. Much as he valued Malewski's friendship and loyalty, and much as he knew the big Pole had learned about the ways of the ocean, he could not forget that first squall of the hurricane, three years ago, to which Cas had been so slow to react. He could not run the risk of anything like that happening to the *Penelope*.

So, he thought, smiling wryly to himself, you *were* a bit rash, and, in careless hands, she could be something of a floating coffin. But nobody else must suspect that. And the basic ideas were sound. It was just a matter of getting them all in the right proportions. That could only be done by building yet another ship. And *that* could only be done by making this one such a success that people would start to believe in him. It was the sort of challenge he relished.

'Sail ho,' came the cry from forward.

Edward picked up his telescope, levelled it, handed it to Penelope as she hurried on deck. 'The *Regina*,' he said. 'I thought we might catch her up; she must've been just about standing still during those light airs.'

'Then take her down, Edward,' Penelope said. 'Oh, please take her down.'

The *Regina* was also under full working canvas, topsails as well as her big sails, and was moving well—about eleven knots, Edward estimated. So there could be no question that he *would* take her down if he maintained his present rig. Not even after the barquentine had increased sail—as he watched through the telescope he saw men swarming aloft to set the topgallant sails as well.

'They've spotted us,' Malewski observed.

'Oh, set more sail, Captin Anderson,' Priscilla Meigs had also come on deck. 'Please set more sail.'

'Not necessary, ma'am,' Edward said. 'We're faster than anything she can do, as we are.'

Penelope clapped her hands in excitement.

The *Penelope* gave a slight yaw, instantly corrected by the helmsman. Edward exchanged glances with Malewski; the wind had freshened and was now approaching thirty knots, he estimated. And the mate was asking a question with his eyes; he *had* noticed the tenderness. But to reef now would be an admission of defeat, and not only in terms of this little race. It would be telling the world that he doubted the seaworthiness of his own ship.

'I'll take the helm, cox,' he said.

'Now we'll show them,' Penelope shouted.

Even the watch below, together with the stokers and engineers, headed by Trethowan, were now on deck. And they were overhauling their quarry at a tremendous rate; although it was by now quite dark both ships were a blaze of light and Edward could make out the knot of people on the *Regina*'s quarterdeck with his naked eye. Henry would be there.

And only *he* knew that the *Penelope* was leaping and heaving under his hands, seeming to wish to leave the sea altogether and fly, skimming through the water, while the seas started to foam and break, and the rising wind sent the spray whipping through the night air.

'Perhaps you ladies would rather go below,' Edward suggested over his shoulder. 'We'll call you when we're abeam.'

'Not on your life,' Priscilla Meigs declared.

And possibly, he thought, they were safer on deck. But what an admission to have to make.

Because now the race was not between the two ships: it was between his taking a sufficiently substantial lead, and thus being able to shorten sail, and the wind reaching a strength which would make the *Penelope* unmanageable. But that race too he would win. Despite the occasional tremor of real alarm which ran through his mind as the ship answered her helm only slowly, he was getting the hang of her, beginning his corrective movements earlier, and certainly she was the fastest thing he had ever sailed, of any size. She was careering along at better than fifteen knots, he suspected, leaping from wave to wave, the wind thrumming loudly in her rigging, the whole ship straining and almost panting. And already they were abeam of the barquentine. Penelope was waving a lantern. 'Henry,' she shouted, 'Henry? Hurry up, slowcoach.'

The lights began to fall astern. And the wind was still rising. Now, Edward thought. Now, I have to reef.

But he thought he could hold her for a little while longer, although by now he was as exhausted as after the twelve hours of the hurricane. He looked over his shoulder. The *Regina* was half a mile astern. That was far enough. And the wind was up to near gale force. As the waves were also getting bigger. As he turned back to the helm the *Penelope* was suddenly picked up and thrown off course. For a terrible, trembling moment she all but broached, slid sideways across the surface of the seas, masts creaking and sails screaming, starboard gunwale buried in flying foam as Edward fought the helm, and Malewski leapt to help him. Between them they brought the ship back straight.

'Wheeee,' Penelope shouted.

'Wheeee,' Malewski muttered. 'Do you know, Edward...'

'Yes,' Edward said. 'I thought she might go over, too. We've done our stuff, Cas. Reduce sail. Reef her right down. We'll still be out of their sight by morning.'

'Aye-*aye*,' Malewski said thankfully, and hurried forward. Edward watched the sails being clewed up, felt the tension and the uncertainty leaving the helm. 'She's all yours, cox,' he said, and turned towards the stern.

'That's enough racing for one night,' he said.

Penelope put both arms round his neck and kissed him on the mouth. 'But you did it,' she said. 'You beat him, fair and square, under sail alone. You did it, Edward.'

He remained awake, because this night he knew she would come, so complete was the mental rapport they shared.

But perhaps he would have remained awake in any event, brooding on what he had learned today, considering possible remedies. Was he, then, more in love with a ship than a woman?

The cabin door opened, and she stepped inside, closed it behind her, stood against it for a moment. She wore an undressing robe, but her feet were bare, and her hair was loosed and brushed free of its ringlets; he supposed no woman could convey a greater sense of intimacy to a man.

He sat up in the bunk. 'Are you sure that you know what you're doing?' he asked.

She crossed the cabin towards him, quickly, to hold on to the bunk; the wind remained strong, and although under triple-reefed sails the *Penelope*'s motion was much easier, she was still bounding along at not less than twelve knots, the entire ship a *whine* of concentrated energy. 'I have never been more sure of anything in my life.' She sat beside him.

'You are a virgin,' he reminded her. 'You will go to your husband incomplete. And you must understand that I will not leave Amanda for you, no matter what happens.'

'I would not expect you to, Edward,' she said.

'But you want *me*?' He shook his head in bewilderment. 'I wish I could understand why.'

'Because I love you,' she said, and leaned forward to kiss his lips. Her dressing gown sagged open; she wore no nightgown, and he saw, and then touched, her breasts, and felt a shiver go right through her body. He had held them before, that day they had, no doubt, fallen in love. They were not large, like Amanda's, and

161

not as soft. They were a girl's breasts, only just becoming a woman's breasts, and the touch of their hard-nippled firmness sent a thrill down his body as well. Then he was on his back, and she was lying on him, kissing him, and his hands were sliding down her back to her buttocks, carrying the shrugged-away dressing gown with them.

She raised her head, to dispel the very last of his doubts. 'I want you to touch me,' she said. '*Everywhere.* I want to belong to you as I can never belong to any man, ever again. Love me, Edward. Love me. I have dreamed of this moment for three years.'

As had he, perhaps. As perhaps he had never allowed himself properly to love Amanda, fearing rejection from her serious intensity. Lovemaking for Amanda had always been a business of haste and concentration, never of gently stroking, of soft investigations of all her damp secrets, of sifting the down at armpit no less than at groin, of total possession.

But suddenly there was no more time. He waited for a cry of pain, a jerk away of horror and disgust, as he then waited for an explosion of recrimination and disappointment. Instead she lay quite still.

'You'll observe,' he said. 'That it is an overrated pastime. At least for the woman.'

She found his lips and kissed them again. 'Only,' she said. 'If the first time is also the last.'

Edward lowered the sextant, made a note on his pad and handed both pad and sextant to Malewski. 'By my reckoning,' he said, 'We are six hundred and twenty-five miles due east of Charleston.'

'My word,' said Mr Thomas Dutton. 'I have no idea how you do it.'

The Englishman was their very first passenger, a railway engineer who was in a desperate hurry to reach Central America. 'Nicaragua,' he would explain to anyone who would listen. And even to those who were obviously not interested. 'I'm to manage the railroad there. Oh, yes, they have a railroad in Nicaragua. Well, not a very big one. But a good one. My firm built it, you know. It's not complete, but you can travel pretty near right across the isthmus by train. And still they can't make it pay. Would you believe it? No savvy, you see. They don't understand simple economics. Or simple engineering. You get me there in a hurry, Captain Anderson. I've a job to do.' And certainly he appeared well pleased at the progress they were making.

As was Priscilla Meigs. She looked at the bubbling white wake. They had sailed for the first week of the return journey, and thus had hardly used any coal at all. Now that the wind had at last gone westerly they were still tramping along, the engines throbbing beneath them, a huge trail of black smoke hovering astern.

'But,' she said. 'Did you not say that we are making better than three hundred miles a day?'

'About three hundred and fifty,' Edward said.

'That means we'll be home in two days. But we're not due in for four.'

'Ah,' Edward said. 'We have been phenomenally lucky with the weather, with that easterly breeze all last week. And of course we picked up that day and a half in Bordeaux.'

'But you're still going to break all records for speed,' Priscilla said. 'I am so proud of you, Edward. Of the ship. Of the crew. Titus will be absolutely delighted.'

Penelope said nothing. She was amazed that her mother seemed unaware of what had happened on this voyage, did not even suspect. Mother was not the most observant of people, of course, and as she supposed her daughter's betrothal to Henry Driscoll was a *fait accompli*, there was no reason for her to suspect anything. And yet...Penelope stood by the rail, watching the leaping blue water, and watching Edward, too. Her mother probably just thought her daughter shared her pride. How could anyone be less than proud of such a skipper, such a man. And such a lover. She did not know how she could avoid revealing it. But now it was coming to an end.

At least...

She remembered the day, three weeks ago now, when they had overtaken the *Regina*. It

164

had been the most exhilarating day of her life, as the *Penelope* had seemed to fly over the waves, hardly touching them at all. Had Edward not been so obviously confident she might even have been scared at travelling so fast, faster surely than any ship had ever been intended to. She had, in fact, been quite relieved when he had taken the helm himself.

Up to that moment, that day, it had all remained a dream, from which she knew she could awake, at will. The desire to be possessed, to be loved, by a man like Edward Anderson, actually bore no relationship to the act of surrender of her body to the hands and penis of an alien being, no matter who he might be. She had always been peculiarly selfish about her body. She had guarded it and cared for it, exercised it and pampered it, and even on occasion loved it. The man who eventually claimed it, in her dreams, would do nothing more to her than she had ever done to herself, with the exception of the ultimate. But could there be a real man in all the world who could possibly know what *she* wanted, and when?

Yet it had to happen, and with Edward. Or it would happen with someone else, like Henry Driscoll, and that would be that. The fact of her virginity had not entered into her calculations. She was the daughter of Titus Meigs. Her husband, and especially *if* his name was to be Henry Driscoll, would have to take her as he found her. It was the act of surrender,

165

even to Edward, the yielding up of that last most private possession, even to Edward, and most of all the fear of being disappointed, even by Edward, that had kept her standing outside his cabin door for nearly half an hour before she had dared enter.

Before she had dared open the gates to Paradise. But to Purgatory as well. She had never considered *afterwards*. She had sought one hour of bliss, without realising that she had organised things so well there would have to be several hours of bliss. And without realising, either, that it would get better and better. The first time had been less painful than she had expected, but at the same time less consuming, the fact of his entry of less importance than the feel of his fingers, too soon suspended. The second time he had been able to be more patient, and she had been less afraid. And since then she had hovered on the very brink of ecstacy. Perhaps she had even gone over the brink once or twice. She could not be sure. But one day it would happen in a way which would leave no room for doubt. She would *know* that she had enjoyed the greatest happiness a woman could expect.

Save that the days were now down to two at the outside.

This awareness had been growing on her throughout the return voyage. At first, ten days had not seemed much less than three weeks. But then the ten days had become one week, and then…she had even considered abandoning all her usual precautions, her douches and her calisthenics, in favour of allowing herself to become pregnant. But that would have been a betrayal, of him. He had outlined his terms to her, and she had accepted them. Therefore by those terms on the day after tomorrow she must walk out of his life. She had asked of Fate, or the Devil, one hour in his arms. She had been granted thirty hours. To seek more would be criminal.

But would *he* be able just to let her walk away from him?

He was standing beside her. 'Mind you,' he said, and pointed to the bank of black cloud which clung to the horizon in front of them. 'It may not be so early after all. And we may even be glad to have those two days in hand. I thought we had been just a little lucky with the weather.'

'Oh, pray we're unlucky for two days,' she said. 'Pray it.'

Pray it, Edward thought, and recorded the falling barometer in his Log. The glass was indeed plunging sharply, far too sharply he would have thought, for a hurricane. What was approaching might be a severe storm, but it was also going to be a very brief one. He was sure of that.

Therefore it could and should be avoided. The same rules would apply to it as to the hurricane. As the wind was dead ahead, by altering course to port he would probably be able to skirt the storm. And he had very nearly forty-eight hours in hand. But only forty-eight hours. He had promised Titus Meigs to be back in Charleston on May the seventh, and to be certain of fulfilling that promise he had driven his ship harder than she had really been designed for. Her seams had begun to give before the constant pounding, and the pumps were going several hours a day to control the constant seepage into her bilges. But that was not relevant to his purpose now. He was prepared to arrive on the sixth of the month, but not the eighth. When he had maintained his schedule, had shown what he and the ship could do, then perhaps he could afford to be a day late through stress of weather. Not on the maiden voyage.

Besides, he *wanted* to steam the *Penelope* into a storm. If he was going to improve upon the design, it was essential that he discover how she would behave in a blow under engines—especially now that he knew for sure he could not risk *sailing* her under extreme conditions. If only the ladies weren't on board…and if only there wasn't the insidious thought that another couple of nights at sea would mean another couple of nights of the most utter bliss.

But there was the most important reason of all for driving straight on, for regaining Charleston at the earliest possible moment. Because with every day he remained at sea, waiting only for the night when she would come to his arms, the thought that once they tied up in Charleston they would say goodbye forever in the sense of their love daily grew more intolerable. And yet it had to be. Amanda would be waiting for him, and on the verge of giving birth to his child. Amanda was his wife, the woman he had sworn to love, or at least to protect and never to hurt, for the rest of his life. If he had betrayed her nightly for the past three weeks, if the residual puritanism of his New England ancestors had left him daily expecting a catastrophe as a just reward for his infidelity, he certainly could not risk compounding his crimes by protracting it.

'Yes,' he said in reply to Malewski's knock. 'Come in, Cas. I doubt it will be a prolonged blow, and I'm a bit reluctant to give away any of our time advantage. We'll stand on.'

'That's fine by me,' Malewski agreed. 'There's a man of war signalling us.'

'Eh?' Edward put down his pen, picked up his cap and hurried on deck. The craft was a small steam cutter clearly in the coastguard service, and still some half a mile distant, but he could see through his glass that she was flying the yellow-halved-with-blue signal flag which denoted: 'I wish to communicate with you.'

'She must think we're a pirate,' Edward said with a smile, and rang down for reduced speed. There could be no question of stopping altogether or of sending a boat across; the wind had already freshened and was spuming spray away from the tops of the waves to send it clouding over the *Penelope*'s bows. Indeed, the motion was much more satisfactory at this slower speed.

'Whatever can she want?' Penelope asked, standing beside him.

'I hope nothing's happened to that railroad,' Dutton said anxiously. And added, to reassure himself, 'But they don't even know I'm aboard.'

'We'll have to wait and see,' Edward watched the pinnace slowly approaching them, and watched too the huge black clouds rolling out of the west. 'I hope she gets to us before that squall.'

'Ahoy, the *Penelope*,' came the call from across the water. 'I have a personal message for Captain Anderson.'

Edward waved. 'Let's have it,' he bellowed through his own speaking trumpet.

'Captain Anderson...' the coastguard's words were lost in the howl of the wind, the lashing of the rain as the squall broke. It struck the *Penelope* when she was almost stopped in the water, driving her sideways, and throwing her over almost on to her beam ends. From below there came an enormous crash and bang of cutlery and crockery where the stewards had been laying the table for supper, and a rush of sea came surging up the deck.

'She's rolling over,' Penelope screamed, clutching at a shroud.

Edward leapt for the engine controls, thrust them down for full speed ahead. Slowly the ship came upright, but almost immediately, and before she was again on an even keel, she was struck by another huge wave, which once again threw her over, and this time tearing one of the pinnaces from its chocks on the main deck and hurling it over the side, carrying several feet of rail with it. Dutton had to throw both arms around Penelope to stop them both from being swept across the deck.

'Christalmighty,' Malewski gasped, helping the coxswain to spin the almost useless wheel. 'Another of those and we're done.'

Edward himself seized the helm, again worked the engine telegraph, his mind seething as he wondered what might have happened below. But now came the reassuring *thump* of the engine gathering power, and the ship surged forward, seeming to slip away from the next beam sea which threatened to overwhelm her. Yet the wave broke on the stern, again knocked them over, although not quite so dramatically as before; waist-high water swirled around them and, as she had been released by the embarrassed Englishman, plucked Penelope from the rail and washed her across the deck. Edward caught her with one arm while spinning the helm with the other, hearing the cries of alarm from below as some of the sea certainly found its way down the main staircase.

But now the ship was answering the helm and turning, and the next wave was taken on the bows, throwing an enormous cloud of spray as high as the mastheads before it descended on them like an extra downpour of rain. The *Penelope* shot off the crest of the wave and hurled herself into the following sea like a torpedo. Water foamed over the bows and surged along the main deck and broke at the foot of the bridge. 'Get below,' Edward bawled, releasing Penelope to ring down for a reduction to half speed before the ship tore herself apart.

Dutton was glad to take the advice, but Penelope laughed and shook herself to scatter water from her hair. 'I'll stay with you,' she shouted. 'Oh, I'll stay with you.'

Edward looked down at her, then up at the seas again, left and right. The engines still growled reassuringly, and at half speed the *Penelope* was taking the waves quite easily now, with only the occasional hard slam to send spray whistling aft. But the coastguard cutter had disappeared.

Trethowan came on deck. 'We've a bearing overheating down there,' he said. 'Those seas damn near tore everything loose. I'm going to have to shut down the starboard engine for a while.'

'All right,' Edward said. 'But be as quick as you can.'

'I'll be quick. But if you steam into the waves

on one engine, nice and slow, there shouldn't be any problem. For God's sake take it easy, though; if we were to lose the other one...'

'I'll take it nice and slow,' Edward agreed. 'But you'll have to accept some more buffeting. We'll be circling.'

'Circling? In the name of God, why?'

'I think the coastguard cutter may have been overwhelmed. We have to see what we can do.'

The engineer raised his eyes to heaven, but departed back to his engine room. Edward retained the helm himself, for he knew the coming hours were going to take every ounce of his skill. The seas were now very big, as the wind howled across the surface of the ocean to send great clouds of spray arcing the full length of the ship, while visibility was further limited by the heavy rain, blowing almost horizontally by the wind. He could steam slowly into the waves without too much difficulty, but to turn meant accepting a broadside blow, and had to be completed as quickly as possible. So, a surge of speed as he gave full right rudder, then a hasty reduction again, accepting the following wave which broke on the stern and flooded the quarterdeck. But by now everything had been stowed and there was less uproar from below, while to his relief he discovered that the ship was much easier to handle downwind under power than she had been under sail.

'I think she's doing splendidly,' Penelope shouted. Although she was soaked to the skin and clearly very cold, she still refused to leave the deck, remained beside him, clinging to the rail, supported by Malewski. 'What do you suppose that coastguard wanted?'

'He was probably waiting to congratulate us on our fast passage,' Edward grunted. 'We'll find out for sure when we find him.'

'Will we find him, Edward?'

'If he's there,' Edward said grimly. So, he had two days in hand. But finding the coastguard was more important than his schedule. Even *his* schedule.

Darkness fell, and the waves became even more boisterous. The storm was more severe than he had supposed it would be. Malewski went below to check the hold, and reported three feet of water. It was necessary to summon the weary watch and set them to pumping, and pray that she would not suffer any structural damage.

At dawn Trethowan reported that he had done all he could with the starboard engine, but that it was impossible to obtain full power. Edward accepted the inevitable. The seas were still wild, although he thought the wind had somewhat abated, and there was still no sign of the coastguard vessel, or even of any wreckage, although they had steamed back and forth over the same area all night. If she had foundered, then she had gone straight down and carried everything and every man with her.

Sadly, Edward handed the helm over to

Reynolds and set course for Charleston, steaming slowly into the wind.

Then he could go below to change into warm and dry clothing, and join Penelope, who was also changing for breakfast; Priscilla Meigs had retired to her bunk and clearly intended to stay there, as had Dutton, while Trethowan remained in the engine room.

'When will we get in now?' Penelope asked.

'Tomorrow morning. Is your mother all right?'

'She'll survive,' Penelope said. 'But that's still on schedule, tomorrow morning. Despite everything that's happened, you'll still be on schedule.'

'Yes,' he said.

She gazed at him. 'Do tragedies like that often happen at sea?'

'Too often.'

She sighed. 'Well, I guess our voyage had to end some time. *Our* voyage. I'd sort of hoped it might have waited to end until we were actually inside Charleston. But maybe it's better this way.' She leaned across the table to hold his hand. 'I guess you know you've made me happier this last month than I have ever been in my life before. That I'm prouder of you than I have ever been of any man, or will ever be, of any man?'

He gazed at her in turn. And how happy have you made me, he thought, poor little rich girl, spoiled and pampered but with the power

175

of bestowing everything this man could ever want.

'And you've broken the record,' she said. 'We'll get Papa to build you other ships. An entire line, like Driscoll. The Meigs Line. No, I'll make him call it the Meigs-Anderson Line.'

'There'll have to be some modifications in design,' he said.

'But you can do that, Edward. I want to watch you grow, *big*. And feel that I had just a little to do with it.'

'A lot,' he said.

But she was right. No matter what had happened, he *had* broken the record. As every man on board was aware. They were all on deck the following morning as they hove to off Fort Sumter and signalled for the pilot. Mr Drayton came on board with total bemusement written across his features. 'But...we heard you'd been lost,' he said.

Edward frowned at him. 'You heard? How could you have heard that?'

'The coastguard cutter got in last night. She said you were both hit by the devil of a squall while you were speaking, and that you rolled right over.'

'By God,' Edward said.

'And when they managed to get steam up again, because they were hit pretty hard too, they searched for an hour or two, and then gave up and returned here. But you...'

'*We* were searching for *him*.' Edward gave

a shout of laughter. 'And then we had a problem in the engine room and had to cruise at reduced speed. And you mean he's been snug in harbour since last night? Well, thank God for that.'

'And everyone thinks we were lost?' Priscilla Meigs asked. 'Oh,they must have been so upset.'

'Then they'll be the more pleased to see us,' Penelope said. 'And bang on time. That'll make old man Driscoll suck his teeth.'

'And Titus jump for joy,' Priscilla said. 'Oh, he'll jump for joy.'

Edward was frowning at the pilot; Drayton's face continued very long and grim. But he could not ask about the coastguard's message now, while the pilot was conning the ship. Already the harbour was opening out before them, and the steam tugs were hurrying to assist in the berthing. People were crowding the wharves to watch them, but there were none of the cheers and flag waving he had anticipated.

He went to the rail as the *Penelope* came alongside, his stomach seeming to fill with lead as his brain became obsessed with a nameless dread. Because there on the quayside were Jonathan Meigs, and, surprisingly, James Driscoll. But no Amanda. Well, she would hardly be here with her babe due any day now. But there was no Titus Meigs, either.

The gangplank was run out, and Jonathan

177

hurried up, followed more slowly by James Driscoll.

'You could at least look pleased to see us,' Penelope said, kissing her brother on the cheek.

'We heard you were lost,' Jonathan said, his normally ruddy face ashen.

'So we've been told,' Priscilla said. 'You don't want to go believing every rumour you hear. As if this ship could be lost. Where's Titus? He's not all upset, is he?'

Jonathan stared at his mother, his mouth opening and shutting again. Then he looked at Driscoll.

'Where is he?' Priscilla Meigs' voice rose an octave. 'Where is he? What's happened to Titus?'

Jonathan clearly could not speak. James Driscoll drew a long breath. 'He thought as we did, Mrs Meigs,' he said. 'That the *Penelope* had been lost at sea, with all hands. Including you and...and Miss Penelope. Last night he shot himself.'

Priscilla Meigs stared at him for a moment, then gave a great shriek and fell to the deck. Edward stooped to pick her up, gazed at Penelope. Her huge eyes were utterly stark with horror. She had sinned. *They* had sinned. And she had been visited with the most terrible retribution.

'I'll take her,' Jonathan said, and held his mother up. 'Have you any brandy?'

178

Edward nodded, and snapped his fingers for Jehu. But Mandy...she'd be worried as well. 'You'll excuse me,' he said, and looked at the gangway—and at John Dart, who had come quietly on board behind the shipowners. 'Mandy?' His own voice rose. 'For God's sake, Father, tell me *she*'s all right.'

John Dart's cheeks seemed to have sunk, and his shoulders slumped. 'Mandy died in a premature delivery, two weeks ago, Edward,' he said. 'The coastguard was waiting to give you the message before you docked. But I guess he didn't make it.'

CHAPTER 5

Edward replaced his cap, stood straight, turned away from the graveside. He had not wept. It had been impossible to do so. There was too much guilt, too much remorse. And now, too much emptiness. Life had offered him too much, and in his foolish greed he had attempted to grasp it all.

Logic kept whispering that she would have died anyway, whether he had ever laid a finger on Penelope Meigs or not. But logic had nothing to do with sin, and crime, and punishment.

John Dart waited for him at the little cottage.

179

As he had lost his only daughter, after losing his wife several years earlier, he was even more bereft than his son-in-law. And yet sought for some prospect of happiness, perhaps for them both.

'For a child nearly a month premature,' he said, 'I think he is doing marvellously well. I know Dr Samuels was very doubtful as to whether or not he would survive either. But of course, we were very fortunate in locating Miss Udal as a wet nurse, and Miss Pike, and...will you not look at him?'

Edward was frowning. 'Was there any decision to be made?' he asked. 'The child or the mother?'

John Dart hesitated.

'Tell me,' Edward shouted.

John Dart drew a long breath. 'No, Edward,' he said. 'There was no decision to be made. Amanda suffered a haemorrhage. There was nothing could be done, for her.'

Edward turned away, stared out of the window.

'He is your son,' John Dart said. 'Will you not go in to him?'

'In time, perhaps,' Edward said.

'Well, he must have a name. No doubt you and...and Mandy discussed names?'

'No,' Edward said. 'We did not discuss names.'

'Well, then...what about Edward?'

'No,' Edward said. 'Not Edward.'

180

'Ah. Well, then...what was your father's name?'

'Robert,' Edward said. 'His name was Robert Anderson.'

'Well, then, we shall name your son Robert as well. I am sure Mandy would have liked that. Do you agree?'

'Call him whatever you like,' Edward said, and went to the door, to encounter Jehu. The slave was as crushed by what had happened as he was. And *he* carried no burden of guilt.

'Mr Malewski is here, Mr Edward,' he said. 'And Mr Trethowan. They asking about the ship.'

Of course, the ship. The ship which had been the cause of all this. But also the ship which had broken every record for speed on the ocean, and which was in desperate need of repair. The ship which was his responsibility.

The ship which was the millstone Fate had hung around his neck to remind him always of where his greed and his lust had taken him.

But the ship which had been Mandy's dream as much as his. And the ship, at least, was innocent of any wrongdoing.

'Tell them I'll be right down,' he said.

They rode to the dock in silence. His two friends had offered him their condolences yesterday. There was nothing more to be said, and they would not speak of other matters until he gave them the permission.

181

He sighed, gazed at the *Penelope* and the crowd of people gathered there; the pumps still clacked and a steady stream of water flowed over the side; he realised with a pang of conscience that Reynolds and his faithful crew had kept working all night and that this morning they had carefully set both the national ensign and the South Carolina flag at half mast.

'Has Bartell been down?' he asked.

'He is waiting on board,' Malewski said.

'Will you now sheath in iron?' Trethowan asked. 'If you are going to cross the North Atlantic regularly it might be wiser to sacrifice a knot or two of speed. It won't be more than that, I'm sure. And you've proved your point.'

Edward dismounted. 'Will we ever cross the North Atlantic again, Mark?'

'Captain Anderson!' The reporter was well known to him, from the Charleston *Star*. 'You'll forgive this intrusion, sir. I appreciate your grief. But you must understand that the entire world is anxious to learn the details of your remarkable exploit. I am told that down to the storm of two days ago you were averaging sixteen knots. Frankly, sir, I find that difficult to believe.'

'You are welcome to peruse my Log Book, Mr Evett,' Edward said.

'Anderson!' Dutton waited at the head of the gangway. Now he held out his hand. 'There's not much to say. I'm sorry.'

'Thank you, Mr Dutton,' Edward said.

'Your gear been taken off?'

'Oh, indeed. Now it seems that I must find some schooner or other to get down to Nicaragua. Do you know, sir, that I have been informed that it will take me a further fortnight? That is to say, nearly half as long again to travel from here to El Bluff as it did to reach here from Bordeaux in the first place, thanks to your fine ship. I find the discrepancy quite amazing.' Once again he squeezed Edward's fingers. 'I will never forget that crossing, sir. Never. I but wish it could have had a happier ending.'

He disappeared into the crowd, and Edward went on board, where Bartell was already making notes. They shook hands, silently.

'You've a report?' Edward asked.

'Some. She'll have to be slipped to have those seams caulked. Man, she must have been hitting those waves.'

'She was,' Edward said. 'Any other damage?'

'Well, there's that section of starboard rail carried away...' he pointed. 'And of course a pinnace to be replaced. But everything else seems secure enough. That starboard engine will need some work, though. Have you any idea how soon you sail again?'

'Do I sail again, Bartell?' Edward asked.

The shipbuilder pulled his nose. 'Well, there are all manner of rumours, you know. But dammit, man, Meigs was a millionaire.' He peered at Edward. 'Wasn't he? You had his wife

183

and child aboard. The thought that they might have been lost would have been sufficient...'

'And she wasn't insured,' Edward said, and went aft.

'Permission to come aboard, Captain Anderson.'

He glanced at the gangplank, at the man wearing a shipmaster's uniform who stood there, a big, bluff fellow with the weather-beaten face of a lifelong sailorman.

'John Gregory, master of the *Unicorn*.' Gregory pointed, and Edward looked across the harbour at the four-masted sailing vessel, one of the new class being built further north and described as clipper ships because of their great speed and deeply-raked bows.

'A fine looking craft, Captain Gregory,' he said. 'Welcome aboard.'

'Thank you, Captain Anderson. Aye, she's a fine ship. And up to last night I thought she was a fast one, cruising at twelve knots with a fair wind. But I've been hearing all manner of wild talk about sixteen knots and the like.'

'We were lucky with the weather.' Edward continued to study the clipper ship, the seething crowd of people on her decks. 'You've a big crew.'

'That I have. But those are my passengers, Captain Anderson. They're all my freight.'

'Passengers?' Edward was incredulous. 'Where are you taking such an emigration? And from where, indeed?'

Gregory chuckled. 'We're out of New York, sir, bound for San Francisco and the goldfields of California. And would you believe it, in that blow three days back I sprung my bowsprit? I went to Mr Bartell here, seeing as how I'd heard he built this greyhound of yours, and he tells me he'll have it put right in twenty-four hours. Well, I hope he's right, or I'll have a riot on my hands. Those fellows count every day in port as costing them a thousand dollars.'

Edward scatched his head in mystification, interested despite his misery. 'You sir, are transporting men from New York to California to look for gold?'

'Yes, sir,' Gregory said. 'Seems it's lying about there in chunks big as a man's fist, just waiting to be picked up. I've an idea I might even get me a nugget or two for myself before I come home.'

'But...you will have to sail all the way round Cape Horn,' Edward said.

'That's right. But they're prepared to put up with a bit of weather. And that ship can take it, too. Oh, aye. Leastways, I thought so until three days ago.'

'But,' Edward said. 'Wouldn't it be simpler, and quicker, for those prospectors to go across the continent, by wagon train?'

Gregory gave a bellow of laughter. 'You'd think so, Anderson, looking at the map, now wouldn't you? It's three thousand miles across America, and thirty thousand round by Cape

185

Horn. But the fact is, sir, no wagon train can make much more than twelve miles a day, if that. So you're talking about eight months' trekking. *And* the people are risking dying of hunger and thirst and attacks by savage Indians every day of the journey, supposing they don't get froze up in the mountains. The *Unicorn*, sir, will make the voyage in one hundred and twenty days, at an average speed of two hundred and fifty miles a day. Half the time, sir. That's mathematics, that is.' He lowered his voice. 'And I can tell you, sir, that those people are each paying a fortune to get there. One thousand dollars a head, New York to San Francisco, is the going rate. And I've seventy of them on board, a few women too, mind. I'm not going to pretend they're all sleeping on feather beds. Or any of them, come to think of it. They're packed tighter than any slaver. But they're happy. They reckon they'll be able to buy the entire ship when they're ready to come home. And it sure beats ordinary freight, every time.' He looked up at the masts towering above him. 'This vessel seems a little light for the seas off Cape Horn. Otherwise, with her speed she'd make you and your principals into wealthy men, Captain Anderson. Well, sir, I'll wish you a good day. It's been a real pleasure to tread the deck of the fastest ship afloat.'

He went down the gangplank, and Edward watched him threading his way through the crowd of interested spectators. All manner of

186

thoughts, of ideas, were roaming through his mind. Of possibilities. Of things to take Mandy's death, his own guilt, from his conscience.

But there were far more immediate matters to be dealt with first. He watched Jonathan Meigs coming towards him along the wharf, went to the gangway, and frowned as he saw that his partner, as Jonathan would now have to be considered, he supposed, had James Driscoll at his side. Driscoll would have to be discouraged, for a start. He seemed to have adopted an almost proprietary attitude towards the stricken Meigs family. Which was no doubt very decent of him. But he remained a rival shipowner.

'Jonathan,' he said, and shook hands. 'I didn't have a chance, yesterday...'

'We both had a lot on our minds. May we go below? There's a deal to discuss.'

'Of course.' Edwards hesitated, glanced at Driscoll.

Driscoll merely smiled. 'You suffered some damage, I gather. In that storm.' He nodded to Bartell, ignoring Malewski altogether.

'Nothing serious,' Edward said.

'That's good news. I'm making arrangements to have a space cleared at my yard now, and she can go up on the slip first thing tomorrow morning. I'll have her shipshape in a week. You can rely on that, Ned.'

'*You'll* have her shipshape?' Edward demanded, and looked at Jonathan.

187

Who flushed, and glanced at Bartell, and Malewski and Trethowan, and Reynolds, who were all endeavouring to overhear. 'We'd best go below,' he said.

Edward led them down to his cabin, indicated chairs. 'Perhaps you'll explain,' he suggested.

Jehu poured coffee, and Driscoll looked at Jonathan.

Who cleared his throat, his face redder than ever. 'The fact is, Edward, that Mr Driscoll has made what, in all the circumstances, is a very fair offer for the *Penelope*.'

For a moment Edward was too surprised to reply; he could not believe what he had just heard.

'I'll admit I'm a conservative,' Driscoll said. 'I couldn't see any future in steam, and hell, while these bone-shakers were making no more than six knots I was damned right. I'll be frank with you, boy: I underestimated both its possibilities, and you. But I'm a man who can admit his mistakes. You left three days after the *Regina*, and you came back, bang on schedule, even with bad weather and engine trouble, a week before she's due. There's no answer to that save praise. Now you hear me out, Ned. I'm not a man to let bygones hang around. You and I have had our differences. But you dreamed up this ship, and you skippered her, and as far as I'm concerned that's good enough. You'll stay in command. There

188

will have to be one or two changes in the crew, of course. Malewski and Reynolds will have to go. They walked out on me, just like that. Well, hell, no man can be expected to put up with that. But I'll not penalise the other Driscoll men you have sailing with you; I reckon they were led astray by Malewski and Reynolds. And of course you can keep Trethowan as your engineer. Now, I have a paper drawn up, which will transfer ownership to me, so if you'd like to sign it as an equal partner with Jonathan here...'

Thoughts tumbled through Edward's mind. Driscoll had no idea that anything was wrong with the *Penelope*'s design—he was a man who went entirely by results. Nor would he ever know that anything was wrong, with Edward to skipper her for him. But...sail for Driscoll, even if it did not entail abandoning Malewski and Reynolds?

Then why not merely resign? Let Driscoll have the ship and discover her problems for himself? Because that might be to condemn good men to their deaths, merely because they would try to match his speed. While to confess her faults would be to halve her value.

Besides, she was still his dream, the dream for which Titus Meigs, and perhaps it could be said even Amanda, had died, the dream on which he would one day build, to reach the fastest, and safest, ship in the world. Even at this moment he had no idea how that would be funded, or even where the *Penelope* could safely be traded. He only knew that she could not be handed over to James Driscoll.

He looked at Jonathan. 'You agreed to this?'

'The price offered is sixty thousand dollars, Edward. That seems very fair to me. And I think it's the best you'll get.'

'But we don't want any price at all,' Edward said. 'This ship is our future.'

'Well...' Jonathan glanced at Driscoll.

Who smiled, sympathetically. 'I know how you must feel, Edward. By God I do. But that's life. I guess old Titus never told you how strapped he was.'

'I knew he was cutting things close to the bone,' Edward said.

'Close to the bone? I guess that's one way of putting it. He was broke, boy. Absolutely skint. And he borrowed the money for this ship from a financial consortium of which I happen to be chairman. Hell, Edward, I'm not just being sympathetic, I'm being downright generous. I could *take* your ship, by foreclosing on that mortgage. But I'm offering to *buy* it from you, so as not to leave the Meigs women with nothing at all. And you're quibbling?'

'This mortgage you hold,' Edward said. 'Is it on the ship?'

'Hell, no,' Driscoll said. 'He couldn't get any insurance cover. Suppose she'd gone down? The mortgage is on Greenacres.'

'Then you can't touch the ship,' Edward said.

They stared at him.

'Greenacres is our home,' Jonathan said.

'And the *Penelope* is all the hope you have for the future. Your father said that if we made this voyage on schedule there'd be people queueing up to sail in her and send freight in her. Well, we've made the voyage on schedule. What good is sixty thousand dollars going to do you? Will you live off three per cent interest? It's a short price in any event, as she's worth a hundred thousand at the lowest possible estimate. But I'd say you have a ship worth three, four times that, as of our return yesterday. *We*'ve got a ship, Jonathan. Your father made me part owner. I'm sorry, Mr Driscoll, but we're not selling.'

Driscoll, his face slowly suffusing, looked at Jonathan.

'You'd better let me discuss things with him, Mr Driscoll,' Jonathan said.

Driscoll stood up. 'Discuss all you like,' he said. 'But you want to bear one thing in mind. Either this ship is mine by noon tomorrow, or I'll have your mother and sister out in the street so damn quick they won't know what hit them.' He pointed at Edward. 'And you can forget about continuing as master, Anderson. You've riled me for the last time.'

'You'd best come in.' Jonathan himself was at

the door. Edward removed his cap, stepped into the great hallway of Greenacres House.

'He's in the dining room,' Jonathan explained. 'We'll be burying him this afternoon. Just a small funeral, of course, in all the circumstances. But we'd appreciate if you'd attend.'

'Of course I shall be there,' Edward agreed. 'Have you discussed the situation with your mother?'

'I thought it would be best to wait until you arrived. Peter Renseller is here as well. Father's attorney. He has all the facts and figures. You understand, well...they're not likely to appreciate your point of view.'

'Then I'll have to persuade them,' Edward said.

'Yes,' Jonathan said doubtfully. 'And me, as well, I'm afraid.' He smiled. 'But come in.'

Edward stepped into the study, hesitated. He had not expected Penelope to be present, for some reason. He had been hoping for time, to think, before having to see her again.

No doubt she had been hoping the same. She glanced at him, looked away, got up and went to the window.

'Peter Renseller, Edward Anderson,' Jonathan was saying.

Edward shook hands; the lawyer was small and precise, running to stomach but, that apart, everything a lawyer should be.

'Edward!' Priscilla Meigs came forward to embrace him. 'My dear, dear boy. Did you manage to sleep?'

'Some,' Edward said.

'It seems so dreadful, having to get down to business, so soon,' she said. 'With poor Titus still lying there...' she sighed. 'But it seems we are in financial difficulties. Or did you know that?'

'A little,' Edward said.

'I think we should all sit down,' Jonathan suggested, and himself took his father's chair, behind the desk. Priscilla Meigs sat next to him, and Renseller on his other side. Penelope slowly returned, hesitated, then sat in front of the desk, next to Edward, but half-turned away from him. He wondered what she did feel. It was here, in this very room, that the concept of the *Penelope* had come to life, and that their love, too, had started to grow. So then, what did *he* feel? Merely sick. But also angry, again, at the whims of Fate. No doubt he had deserved punishment, as did she. But that the actual punishment should have been inflicted upon Mandy, and Titus Meigs...

'Perhaps you'd state the situation, Peter,' Jonathan said.

'If you wish me to.' Renseller looked at Edward.

'Captain Anderson is totally involved,' Priscilla Meigs said. 'He is part owner of the ship.'

'Yes,' Renseller agreed, drily. 'Well, we should be able to salvage something from the

193

wreckage. I am not going to bother you with detail, but very approximately, your assets add up to just over two million dollars. To break this down, again very roughly, I have valued the cotton plantation, with its horses and equipment and houses and slaves, of course, at one point five million dollars, the value of the unsold cotton crop at three hundred thousand, the value of this estate, Greenacres, at two hundred thousand, the value of the contents at fifty thousand. There is cash in hand amounting to seven thousand dollars, and the value of the ship *Penelope*, I would place at fifty thousand. I know that she cost twice that to build, but we're talking of what we might realise in a quick sale.'

'Two million dollars,' Priscilla Meigs said. 'I cannot see why everyone is looking so long faced. Surely we can exist on two million dollars.'

'There are, unfortunately, certain liabilities,' the lawyer said. 'And you will observe that the actual cash position is virtually nil. Now then, the plantation is mortgaged for its full value, one point five million dollars. Payment of this mortgage is now being requested, in full. The crop value was also realised in advance, and has been spent. This I may say was your husband's regular practice. And there is also an outstanding mortgage of one hundred thousand dollars on Greenacres. This was incurred due to the shipbuilding enterprise your husband undertook over the last year.' Renseller's frosty gaze played over Edward. He obviously had not approved of Titus Meigs' final gamble. 'This is the item with which we have to concern ourselves, at this moment. The plantation is gone. There can be no argument about that. However...'

'But where did all the money *go*?' Priscilla Meigs cried. 'All that money. Two *million* dollars?'

'Ah...well, Mrs Meigs, your husband was not the best businessman in the world. He adopted a rather paternal attitude to his slaves, as you are probably aware. Of course this is most laudable, where it can be afforded. But he would never break up a family, or sell any of his people, no matter how aged and infirm they might be. In fact, of the seven hundred slaves listed at the plantation, my information from his overseer is that only four hundred are fit to work. Yet the remainder, nearly half, have been maintained, clothed and fed, at your husband's expense, or perhaps I should now say, at *your* expense, for several years.'

'What will happen to those poor people?' Penelope asked.

'I would not really like to say. I'm afraid they may find their new owners less indulgent. And then, I hate to speak uncharitably of the dead, but Titus was a compulsive gambler, as you must have been aware, Mrs Meigs.'

'I knew he liked cards, and horses,' Priscilla

Meigs said. 'But he always told me he won at least as much as he ever lost.'

'Yes,' Renseller agreed in his driest tone. 'I'm afraid we must say that he was rather over optimistic about his winnings. And then there was the lifestyle he pursued, that lavish trip to Europe three years ago, and that sort of thing. These things add up, Mrs Meigs, and unfortunately cotton has been going through a slump recently. But Mr Meigs would never let that bother him. He always said, my credit is good, and things will certainly get better, and went off and borrowed another hundred thousand. Well, of course he was right, up to a point. However, as I said at the beginning, things are not entirely black. The plantation debt will be taken care of by placing it on the market, together with the crop. Those debts were secured by the plantation and the crop, thankfully, and specifically by nothing else. That means you have only the mortgage on this house to concern yourself with. It is, alas, also being called. However, I understand that negotiations are in progress...' he looked at Jonathan.

Who sighed. 'The Driscoll Line, which apparently holds the Greenacres mortgage, is prepared not only to tear up the deed, but also to purchase the *Penelope* from us for sixty thousand dollars.'

'Which, in my opinion,' Renseller said, 'is an act of quite unprecedented generosity. Sixty thousand dollars is considerably more than I should have expected you to get for this ship, even had you been in a position to sell her. But as she belongs to Mr Driscoll anyway, for him now to offer to buy her...'

'That is not correct, Mr Renseller,' Edward said. 'Mr Driscoll has no title to the ship.'

'He has title to this house, Captain Anderson, which is vastly more important. Now, Mrs Meigs, as I was saying, thanks to Mr Driscoll's generosity, you will be cleared of all debt, you will retain Greenacres, and everything in it. I'm afraid you will no longer be able to consider yourself a wealthy woman, but you will by no means be destitute. Of course, in my opinion you will have to sell most of your slaves, and I also feel that you should consider placing most of your horses, and such valuable items as your husband's collection of porcelain, on the market as rapidly as possible, but these are details which we can thrash out once the main points are agreed.'

'May I ask what you intend Mrs Meigs and her family to live on?' Edward asked. 'Or is it to be the money received for the sale of the porcelain?'

Renseller flushed. 'That was intended merely to tide them over,' he said. 'Obviously what happens next must also be discussed, as soon as possible. But I considered it my duty to secure Mrs Meigs' home for her, so as to enable her to maintain her position in the community.

As for the future...'

'There is no future,' Edward said. 'There can be no future, for any of us, if we lose the ship. The ship is all we have that is capable of earning an income.'

'May I point out that her maiden voyage has certainly not earned any income, Captain Anderson. One passenger, and a few tons of freight, will not even meet the coal bill, much less the crew's wages, or the repairs I am informed are necessary.' He looked at Jonathan.

'I'm afraid that is true, Edward,' Jonathan said.

'She was a disaster,' Penelope muttered. 'From the very beginning, a disaster. Oh, I hate her. *Hate* her.' She started to turn her head, as if she would have looked at Edward, then turned away again.

For a moment Edward could think of nothing to say. She was reacting in her usual over-emotional manner, but even he had not expected it to be quite so vehement. Besides, he still had no idea how the ship *could* be made to pay, sufficiently to help the Meigs, much less finance a new design.

'Yet there is a good deal in what Edward has said,' remarked Priscilla Meigs. 'Are you expecing Jonathan to go out and take a position as a clerk, Mr Renseller? Or perhaps you think I should advertise for paying guests?'

Renseller sighed. 'I am aware that the prospect before you is a sad one, Mrs Meigs. But

I can offer no easy options. To keep the ship will involve selling Greenacres. That will leave you with no home at all. You suppose your wealth will soon be restored by operating the *Penelope*? I have gathered some figures here. We will forget about this first voyage, which was, I suppose, in the nature of an experiment, but presume the vessel will sail from now on fully laden, with passengers and freight. You are still not likely to gross more than twenty thousand dollars a voyage. Let us suppose you make even twelve voyages a year, that is, a straight turnaround without a day's holiday for the crew, you are still talking of no more than two hundred and forty thousand dollars a year. Now, ma'am, wages and fuel, not to mention upkeep, are going to come to roughly two hundred thousand. And that makes no allowance for damage and repairs, or ultimate replacement of the ship. That doesn't leave you too much to exist on here. And remember, you won't have Greenacres.'

Priscilla Meigs looked at Jonathan, and they both looked at Edward. Who for a moment had nothing to say. Renseller's figures could not be argued against, even supposing he dared contemplating using the *Penelope* on a regular Atlantic run.

'Sell it,' Penelope said. 'Oh, sell it. I never want to think of it again.'

There had to be a way. There had to be a way to overcome this hysteria, this creeping acceptance of disaster. There had to be a way to make up to Titus Meigs, and to Mandy, too, for the catastrophes which had overtaken them.

Jonathan said. 'I guess I'll ride into town after the funeral, and see Driscoll. Believe me, Edward, I'll have a word with him about restoring your place as master. He's given to these outbursts of temper, but he must understand that you were feeling pretty damn desperate.'

'No,' Edward said. He felt almost sick with sudden excitement as the answer to their situation came to him as if a bomb had gone off inside his brain. 'Selling the ship will involve us all in ruination.'

'My dear Captain Anderson,' Renseller protested.

'Because she *will* make our fortunes,' Edward insisted. 'You say that grossing two hundred and forty thousand dollars a year will barely keep our heads above water? What about grossing one and a half *million*?'

They stared at him.

Then Renseller smiled, pityingly. 'It would be very nice indeed, Captain Anderson. But may I point out that there has never been a ship launched which ever grossed anything remotely like half that figure?'

'The *Penelope* will do it,' Edward asserted.

'Would it be impertinent for us to inquire how?'

'There is a clipper ship in Charleston now,'

Edward said. 'Undergoing repairs. She has seventy people on board as passengers, and each of them is paying one thousand dollars to be carried around Cape Horn to San Francisco and the California goldfield. Simply because it takes twice as long to go across country.'

'I am aware of the gold fever, Captain Anderson,' Renseller said, severely. 'Two of my own clerks have recently left for California. Crazy fools. I told them so. But with respect, sir, the voyage takes four months. And four months back with by no means so valuable a cargo. I cannot see where this million and a half can be realised.'

'Anyway, Edward,' Jonathan objected. 'You couldn't possibly carry sufficient coal for such a purpose. And there are no coaling stations in the South Atlantic. Or the South Pacific for that matter.'

And the *Penelope* would never weather Cape Horn, anyway, Edward thought. But that was irrelevant beside the huge idea which had suddenly sparked in his mind. 'I have no intention of keeping my passengers at sea for four months, Jonathan,' he said. 'But it may interest you to know that it is only one thousand seven hundred miles from Charleston to the port of El Bluff in Nicaragua. That journey I can do in five days, *and* carry sufficient coal to get back again. It is in fact a run for which the *Penelope* could have been especially designed.'

Because, of course, it was through much

smaller seas and better weather conditions in general than were to be found in the North Atlantic, except when a hurricane was actually blowing—and hurricanes were not all that common in the Gulf of Mexico. But he did not elaborate on his remark.

'So I will return empty of cargo,' he went on. 'I can still make the voyage every fortnight, and with a hundred people on board. Those prospectors don't mind sleeping rough. That's twenty-six voyages in a year, at a hundred thousand dollars a time...my God, that's *two* and a half million. And in fact, as we shall be getting them to California in about a third of the time it will take them by clipper ship, we'd be entitled to charge more than the going rate.'

'They will walk to California, from this place...El Bluff?' Renseller inquired, with another pitying smile.

Which Edward returned. 'At this very moment an Englishman named Dutton is also in Charleston. He is trying desperately to get to El Bluff himself, to manage the railroad there. The cross-isthmus railroad, Mr Renseller. It ends on the Pacific Coast.' He looked around the Meigs family. 'The journey takes about ten days.'

'By God,' Jonathan said. 'By God. But... what happens when they reach the Pacific? They're still a thousand miles and more from San Francisco.'

'They'll be met by another ship', Edward

202

said. 'Which will take them on the last leg of their journey. As we will have to buy what we can on the spot, and I don't suppose it will be very fast, we had better allow for two ships, so one is always available.'

'Railroad? Two ships? Where does the money for all of this come from in the first place?' Renseller demanded.

Edward drew a long breath. 'If Mrs Meigs were to sell Greenacres, lock stock and barrel, she would, you say, realise more than two hundred thousand dollars. Of which she owes one hundred thousand. That leaves a hundred plus. I am also sure that between us we can borrow a few thousand more. Besides, if we collect in advance from our passengers that'll meet the cost of the rail fares. So, if we leave you, Mrs Meigs, and Penelope, say, twenty thousand dollars to settle down in Charleston, and Jonathan and I take the remainder, we should have ample cash in hand to buy ourselves a couple of schooners or whatever on the west coast of Nicaragua. One will do to start with. We can buy the other one in 'Frisco.'

'I have never heard such a hare-brained scheme in my life,' Renseller said. 'How do you propose to find these thousand-dollar-a-head passengers?'

'We advertise, Mr Renseller. There are certainly an enormous number of people waiting to get to California. The *Penelope* has to be refitted, anyway. That will take a fortnight or so. Ample time to accumulate passengers. If we act right away.'

'But...a hundred people are a lot to be transported by rail,' Jonathan said. 'Won't we need a trip down there first, to organise things?'

'Not if we have Dutton in tow,' Edward explained. 'He's been told it will take him several weeks to get down to Central America, even supposing he can find a ship going that way. We'll say to him we'll get him there in five days, if he'll wait here a fortnight and if he'll guarantee us places on his railroad. He'll be happy about that. And about handling a hundred fare paying passengers every fortnight after that. His job is to make that railroad pay, and we are offering to fill his carriages for him.'

'But...the ship needs a lot of work, I'm told,' Priscilla said. 'How do we pay for that?'

'Bartell will give us credit until this place is sold, Mrs Meigs. I have no doubt about that. Just as the crew will wait for their wages, if we explain to them what we are doing, and what the prospects are. We can scrape together enough cash to coal her, certainly.'

Priscilla Meigs looked at Jonathan.

'Well,' he said.

'I am bound to say,' Renseller said. 'That this entire scheme sounds the maddest of mad gambles. With respect, Mrs Meigs, I should have supposed you would have had your fill of mad gambles. You're gambling on obtaining credit until you can sell this house, on selling this house at all, for its full value, on Captain Anderson here being able to take his ship where no self respecting American master has ever ventured before, on a railroad none of us has ever even heard of, much less seen, operated by some itinerant Britisher, on being able to buy a seaworthy vessel on the other side, and most of all, on this absurd gold rush lasting more than a week.'

'May I point out, sir,' Edward said, 'that it has already lasted some two years. It only has to last one more and our fortunes are entirely restored.'

'I must still advise against anything of this nature in the strongest possible terms. In fact, Mrs Meigs, if you were even to consider it, I should have to *re*consider my own position as your counsel.'

Priscilla Meigs was again looking at her son. 'Well?' she asked.

'I think it might just work,' Jonathan said. 'It might just work. And if it didn't, would we be any worse off than we are now?'

'We'd still have the house,' Penelope shouted, jumping to her feet. 'And we wouldn't have that deathtrap of a ship. My God, you people make me despair. You sit here, and talk about selling Greenacres, and moving into some rented apartment? You, Edward Anderson, can sit there and tell my mother that is what is best for her to do? Of course you can. You've never owned a damned thing in your entire life. Well,

205

we have. Greenacres is our home. I was *born* here. And now you want to sell it, just like that.' She snapped her fingers.

'Death ship?' Jonathan inquired, frowning. 'It killed Father, didn't it?'

'It could just as easily have saved him,' Priscilla Meigs said. 'If he'd had just a little more faith in Edward here. And in the ship. I think we *will* go along with Captain Anderson, Mr Renseller. I am sorry to act against your advice. But I certainly cannot envisage us locking ourselves up in Greenacres, with nothing to live on, no slaves, no horses, no nothing. We may as well be completely bankrupt as half bankrupt. So there it is. Greenacres goes on the market.' She looked around her, gave a little shiver. 'You may have been born here, Penny, but it has always given me the absolute creeps. And that was your father's real mistake, trying to buy his way into the Carolina gentry. It would have been a mistake anyway, but especially when he hadn't properly consolidated his plantation.' She stood up, held out her hand. 'Edward, you have yourself a deal.'

Penelope stared at her mother for a moment, then at Edward, then ran from the room.

Edward waited for her as they walked away from the graveside. 'Your father befriended me,' he said. 'When I had no friend in the world. He was almost a father to me as well as to you and Jonathan. I am sure he would wish us to do what we are doing.'

She glanced at him, her face cold, then resumed walking.

He sighed. He was terribly tempted to remind her that their affair had been entirely her idea and her doing. That it had been she who wished to pray for the storm to delay their return. But undoubtedly it was that knowledge which was so oppressing her.

'I can only ask you to be patient,' he said. 'And I will prove it to you. Penny...believe me, I know exactly how you feel. I think I feel a little that way myself. What we did was terribly wrong, and it is impossible not to feel we have incurred...well, the wrath of God. But we did it because we loved each other. Would it not compound crime upon crime for us now not to be at least friends? I am trying to do my best for you, and for your family. I give you my word that our first profits shall be devoted to buying Greenacres back for you.'

She stopped, and turned to face him. 'What we did was an act of madness,' she said. 'I do not see...' she hesitated. 'How I could have been so...so demented. And now you pretend you are doing your best for me, for my family? You are doing your best for yourself, Edward Anderson. That is what you are doing. I hate you. I wish you had never been born. Or at least, that I had never set eyes on you. I never wish to set eyes on you again. For God's sake leave me alone.'

James Driscoll slowly climbed the gangplank to board the barquentine *Regina*. Henry Driscoll frowned at him. It occurred to him that his uncle had aged considerably in the last two months.

But he could be as acerbic as ever. 'You're two weeks late,' he snapped.

'Well...' Henry smiled depracatingly. 'We ran into some weather on the homeward voyage, and I thought it best to heave to.'

'For two weeks?'

'Good Lord, no. For four days. But, well, we were a little late in leaving Bordeaux.' He looked around the harbour. 'We're still home before that coffin ship of Anderson's, eh? Oh, she made a fast passage to France. In fact, she left Bordeaux to come home the day before we arrived. My God, what's happened to her? She *should* have been back by now. Don't tell me she foundered? With Penny Meigs on board?'

'The *Penelope* returned to Charleston on schedule, on the seventh of May,' James Driscoll said, speaking evenly. 'That was five weeks ago, Henry.'

'My word,' Henry said. 'Then where is she?'

'She sailed again two weeks ago.'

'For France?'

'For Nicaragua.'

'Nicaragua?' Henry scratched his head.

208

'She's been sold, you mean? I'm not even sure I know where this Nicaragua is.'

'You'd best come below,' James Driscoll said. 'There's been quite a lot happening since you went away.'

Henry poured them each a glass of brandy, listened to what his uncle had to say.

'My God,' he remarked, when James Driscoll had finished. 'By God. Titus Meigs, a suicide. And a bankrupt? Well, well. And now you own Greenacres?'

James Driscoll shrugged.

'I don't see why you had to help them at all,' Henry said. 'Mind you, us owning Greenacres could come in handy...yes. But Anderson. There's the scoundrel who must be stopped.'

James Driscoll raised his head. 'Stopped?'

'Well, for crossing you. For...for everything. He *is* a scoundrel. An utter scoundrel. You can see it in everything he does.'

'I'd say he has more gumption than almost any man I know,' James Driscoll said, pointedly. 'Oh, sure, he drives me crazy every time I talk with him. But hell, he's a man with brains as well as ambition, guts as well as perseverance. Stop him? I wish him all the success in the world.'

Henry stared at his uncle in disbelief.

James Driscoll smiled. 'Mind you,' he said. 'I wouldn't mind getting my hands on a set of the plans for the *Penelope*. No, sir. I've approached Bartell, and I've offered the Meigs widow a fortune for them, and do you know, they both refused? That's another mark of a man, Henry lad. The ability to inspire loyalty in other people. Oh, yes, I wish him joy.'

'Mr Driscoll is here to see you, Miss Penny,' said Maybelle, the maid. She was the only one of the Greenacre slaves that Priscilla Meigs had retained; Priscilla could not contemplate existence without at least a maid.

For a moment the name did not even register on Penelope's consciousness. Few things registered on her consciousness nowadays. Five weeks ago her world had come to such an abrupt end she sometimes thought she might well have died herself. How she wished, indeed, that the *Penelope* could really have capsized in that storm, that she could have died there and then, standing next to Edward and laughing as the sea broke over them, still in all the glory of their love, still unknowing of the tragedy that lay in wait for them.

That forty-odd other people, including her own mother, would necessarily have died with them, could hardly have compounded the burden of guilt she carried in any event.

But she had not died, and she had had to face up to the guilt. At first, she had wanted only to escape, from Edward, and from the ship which had been so grotesquely named after her. In her desperate self-anger, and anger too at the whim of Fate, even of Heaven, which had so visited her with catastrophe, she had turned her self-hate on those two objects, the things she had loved most dearly in all the world. And still loved, most dearly. Loved them even while she hated them, prayed for their safe return even as she prayed for them to be lost—except that with Edward on this occasion there was also Jonathan. And she had wreaked enough catastrophe in her short life; she would not even be twenty for another few weeks.

And now, Henry Driscoll. Come to sympathise, and, knowing Henry, also come secretly to consider how he could turn the situation to his own best advantage. And he would be seeking an answer to his proposal of marriage. Henry Driscoll! But undoubtedly in marriage to Henry Driscoll she would be able to lose herself in misery for the rest of her days.

Because the most confusing, hateful thing of all was that now, if she wished, she could marry Edward. Mother would certainly be delighted, and so would Jonathan. Even had they not had their affair it would seem the entirely logical thing to do, as he was now so firmly their business partner.

And they would lie in bed together, or stare at each other across a dining table, for the rest of their lives, in mutual horror at the swathe they had cut to achieve their ambitions.

Besides, she knew now that Edward was just as much of a gambler as ever Father had been. He was gambling now, as Renseller had said, with their money and indeed their lives, and with his charm and his forceful personality he had managed to carry Mother and Jonathan along with him. But even if their love was sufficient to rise above their mutual misery, it would have to be great indeed for her to contemplate spending a lifetime as Mother had done, waiting for calamity.

Henry Driscoll was no gambler. And Henry Driscoll would soon be in a position to throw his protective net over them, no matter what happened to Edward's wild gamble.'

Besides, Henry Driscoll was all she deserved.

CHAPTER 6

'Penny. My dear, dear Penny.' For a dreadful moment Penelope thought he would kneel before her, but he merely bowed very low as he took her hand to kiss it. 'I came as soon as I heard the news. Oh, my dear girl, I don't know what to say.'

Penny sat down again on the settee and Henry sat beside her, giving a quick glance around the little parlour; the apartment contained only four rooms—Maybelle had to sleep on the floor in the kitchen.

'And now you are reduced to this,' he said. 'My God, it makes my heart bleed. I'm afraid

I have quarrelled with my uncle.'

She turned her head to look at him inquiringly.

'Well, I think he behaved abominably,' Henry said. 'Throwing you out of Greenacres.'

'Somebody had to buy it, Henry,' she pointed out. 'And as your uncle held the mortgage, it seemed appropriate.'

'Then he should have given it right back to you and your mother to live in. That's what...' he paused as he heard the baby cry. 'What in the name of God is that?'

'That is Robert Anderson,' she explained.

'Robert...?'

'Amanda Anderson's child. You knew she died in childbirth?'

'I had heard. And you mean the babe has been foisted on you?'

'It lives here with us certainly,' Penelope said. 'Mother looks after it. There is a wet nurse, of course,' she added hastily.

'But...my God, that fellow Anderson *is* a scoundrel. I always knew he was a scoundrel. And now I learn that he has abandoned you, and gone off on some hare-brained scheme to Central America.'

'Why, yes,' Penelope said. 'So he has.'

'With your ship.'

'It's partly his ship, you see,' she said.

'And you still are fond of the fellow,' he grumbled.

Penelope looked him in the eye. 'I hate and

abhor Edward Anderson,' she said. 'I think he is the lowest rat that ever crawled on the earth. But he has managed to hoodwink Mother and Jonathan into going along with him. There is nothing I can do about it.'

'By God,' Henry said. 'Oh, yes there is. Penny...' he seized her hand again. 'Penny, how would you like to live in Greenacres again? With all the horses and all the slaves you ever had, with all...'

The door burst open to admit Priscilla Meigs, hastily cramming a hat on to her head. She looked at Henry in a scandalised fashion for a moment, then at her daughter. 'Penny,' she shouted. 'They're back. The *Penelope* is in the harbour. I've just heard. Flying all her flags. They've made it. And they must have made a huge success, too. Oh, Penny, they're back.'

Penelope pulled her hand free and ran behind her mother, down the stairs and out on to the street, hurrying towards the dock.

Henry Driscoll stood at the window to watch.

'Paid in full.' Bartell carefully wrote the words across the account, ruffled the pile of bank notes Jonathan Meigs had placed in front of him. 'I can't tell you what a pleasure it is, Jonathan, Edward, to be able to write those words. Mind you,' he hastily added. 'If you want to leave the account for another voyage...'

'We aim to keep ourselves up to date,' Jonathan said. 'While we can.'

'I just can't believe it,' Priscilla Meigs said. 'I can't believe it. Oh, if only Titus had *waited*, to see this...' she glanced at them, and flushed, and then laughed. 'Come along, tell us again. El Bluff...'

'Is just a mud hut village,' Jonathan said. 'Really and truly. It lies at the mouth of this river, the Escondida they call it, and is bang in the middle of a swamp. I mean, you can't even see it from the sea. Edward was navigating completely blind.'

'Poor old Dutton,' Edward said. 'I really thought he was going to have a seizure. And when we finally managed to anchor and go ashore, and he said he'd come to see the railroad, they just stared at him: "What railroad, senor?" '

'That must have given you a bit of a turn as well,' Bartell suggested.

'Well, it did,' Jonathan agreed. 'And we weren't too happy when we discovered that there was a railhead, three days journey away. To be reached only by canoe and mule train.'

'What did your passengers think of that?' Priscilla asked.

'They weren't too happy. But of course the mutiny had nothing to do with that, in my opinion.'

'A mutiny,' Priscilla said. 'Oh, it terrifies me just to think of it. And you mean you didn't know this man Walker?'

'Never saw him before in my life,' Edward

said. 'He was just another prospector to us. A young fellow, but real tough-looking. No, I suspect he only came along with the intention of making trouble.'

'So what did you do?' Bartell asked.

'Clapped him in irons, and sent him clear across the country like that. He'd paid his fare to California, so I sent him there.'

'So everything worked out?'

'Well,' Jonathan said, 'after some argument. Of course no one there spoke English, and between us we only mustered a few words of Spanish, but we got there in the end. And found just what we were looking for on the west coast, a three-masted schooner whose owner had just died. The family were quite pleased to get rid of it, especially as we offered them well over the odds.'

'And that's where Mr Malewski has gone?' Priscilla asked.

'He should be in San Francisco by now,' Edward said. 'I gave him forty thousand to buy another schooner up there. I doubt we'll get as good a bargain; the *Pacific Belle* is one of the sweetest craft I've ever seen. But he'll get something.'

'You say Reynolds went with him?' Bartell asked.

'Why, yes. He'll command the new ship. We have to have reliable people in command, because frankly, obtaining sound crews on the Pacific Coast is a bit of a problem. Everyone thinks of only one thing, gold. So I'm using Mark as my mate as well as my engineer. I think he's having the time of his life.'

'And you're sure Malewski and Reynolds won't be tempted to scurry off to the goldfields themselves?'

'Not them,' Edward said. 'They know too well that we're sitting on a gold mine of our own.'

'Supposing that Dutton can keep the railroad going,' Bartell remarked.

'He will,' Jonathan said, confidently. 'And if he can't, why, we'll hire a mule train. We'll still get our customers to San Francisco before anyone else. The Nicaraguans are all for the idea.'

'You mean the government?' his mother asked.

'If you can call it that. It's very primitive, in every way. A few great landowners lording it over the rest of the country...' he grinned. 'Rather like South Carolina. But they get things done. Just as we do. It'll work. It is working already, Mother. Think of it. We've liquidated all our immediate debts, bought two new ships, well, virtually, and we've still got cash in hand. And customers queueing up to get a berth. How many at this moment, Edward?'

'We've a hundred and seventeen applications for a hundred berths,' Edward said. 'And they've all paid for their places. One hundred and seventeen thousand dollars in the bank.'

He smiled at Priscilla Meigs. 'You'll have Greenacres back before you know it.'

'I don't want Greenacres back,' Priscilla said. 'We're going to do this right, this time. Penny and I are quite happy here. We're not moving out until we can really afford to.'

Edward glanced at Penelope, who sat on the other side of the room, looking out of the window. She alone had taken no part in the celebrations at their return. Yet she had hurried down to the dock with her mother. And then had turned and walked back up to the house again.

'Although Penny may soon be moving out in any event,' Priscilla said. 'You can't imagine who came to call, yesterday? Henry Driscoll.'

'Henry?' Edward demanded.

'Well...' Priscilla gave a coy smile. 'He's in love with Penny. Anyone can see that.'

'Or he's after the plans for the *Penelope*,' Jonathan said with a grin. 'Mind you don't go *too* soft on him, Penny.'

Penelope got up and left the room.

'You really shouldn't tease her so,' Priscilla Meigs said. 'She is in a most strange mood, all the time. She seems pleased to see Henry, and then she won't give him a firm answer. She was desperately excited when she heard you all were coming home, then she went into this brown study again. Ah, well, she'll get over it, I suppose. I think marriage is the best possible thing that could happen to her. Edward...'

218

Edward's head jerked. He also had been in a brown study.

'Won't you come in to see baby?' Priscilla Meigs asked. 'He's such a lovely child.'

Edward hesitated.

'Amanda would have been proud of the way you stood up for what you knew was right, Edward,' Jonathan said. 'You really cannot blame Robert for her death. She would not be proud of you for that.'

Edward hesitated a last time, then accompanied Priscilla into the little bedchamber. He allowed the babe to be placed in his arms. Robert cooed happily and dribbled on to his father's collar.

Priscilla Meigs sighed. 'I wish...so many things. I am so terribly sorry about Mandy, Edward. As sorry about her as I am about Titus. But *she* had no choice. And as Jonny says, she would have been so proud of you. We are all so proud of you.'

'Except for Penny,' he said, and replaced the baby in the cot.

'Yes,' Priscilla said. 'I sometimes wonder... you and she used to be such friends, Edward. Why, on the voyage to Europe, I sometimes felt...well,' she blushed. 'Mothers think these things, sometimes, about their daughters, and of course it was very wrong of me to do so, then. While now...I know it is far too soon after Mandy's death to speak of these things, but I would throw my hat into the air for joy if you and she…' she hesitated, watching him.

'I thought you wanted her to marry Henry Driscoll,' Edward said.

'I said, I wanted her to *marry*. But of course, he wants to marry *her*. As I said, she doesn't seem able to bring herself to say yes. Which must mean she doesn't really love him.'

'I don't think Penny is in the mood to love anyone, at this moment, Mrs Meigs,' Edward said. 'We shall have to give her a little more time. Now I must get back to the ship.'

'Mr Driscoll not in?' Henry hung his hat on the peg by the boardroom door.

'No, Mr Henry.' The male secretary hovered, nervously. 'He sent down to say that he wouldn't be coming in, today. He's not feeling very well.'

'Ah,' Henry went into the office, there hesitated, and then continued through to his uncle's private domain. The old man very seldom came in, nowadays. It really was absurd that he did not retire altogether, instead of clinging so feebly to the reins of power, while all the time…Henry sat behind the huge oak desk, riffled through the reports and manifests and sailing schedules that lay there. The fact was, of course, that the Driscoll Line was so well organised it just about ran itself. And yet, returns were definitely down. Almost entirely due to the current American preoccupation with what was happening in California. He had never known a nation so utterly obsessed with the lure of gold. No matter that for every man who made a fortune, a hundred found themselves destitute after selling up all their belongings to prospect, and not a few of that hundred found themselves dead. Everyone supposed that *he* was going to be the lucky winner.

Mundane, ordinary matters, like shipping cargoes to and from Europe, no longer seemed to be relevant.

But James Driscoll refused to consider the gold rush, for all that it had now been going on for well over two years, as anything more than a passing aberration. Henry had tried to persuade him to send some of their own ships on the long, dangerous, but lucrative passage round Cape Horn to California, and he had refused. 'We don't have any clipper ships,' he had declared. 'Anyway, not even the clippers can compete with young Anderson. How the devil could we? You wait, the rush will be over in another month or so, and they'll all be back here begging for freight cargoes. Which we will already have.'

That had been six months ago.

And always it came back to Edward Anderson. Edward Anderson. In every possible way that scoundrel lay across Henry's life like a deep shadow. At a time when his life should not have had any shadows at all. Clearly he was about to step into his uncle's shoes, which was

221

all the professional ambition he had ever had. He was young, and healthy, knew exactly what he wished to do with his life, but he was being restrained from reaching his goals by an upstart ex-ferryman. It was not merely the ability Anderson seemed to possess to be able to turn disaster into triumph time and time again. There had, over the past year, been a much more personal element creeping into their rivalry. Incredible though it appeared to him, he could no longer doubt the evidence of his own eyes and ears, that Penny Meigs was actually in love with the fellow. He should have known from the beginning, of course, from the way she kept saying so vehemently that she loathed him. There was a typically feminine attitude. But she betrayed herself over and over again in the way she could not stop her eyes from dancing whenever the wretch's name was mentioned, the way she could not stop herself hurrying down to the docks whenever the *Penelope* was signalled, because that she loved the ship as well was equally certain. He had made no progress whatsoever in his tentative attempts to persuade her to allow him a sight of the plans.

And thus he dangled on a string. She wouldn't definitely tell him no, went riding with him, and with him attended balls and supper parties, but she couldn't bring herself to accept his offer of marriage, while there was a chance that Anderson might get over his wife's death and decide to marry again. Which also meant, quite apart from her almost motherlike protection of his design secrets, that she permitted *him* no greater intimacy than a squeeze of her hand or a peck on the cheek, while all the time she was growing into quite the most lovely young woman in Charleston.

He might have been tempted to throw the idea of a romance between them in her face—after all, as he kept reminding himself, he was now Commodore of the Driscoll Line, and the way things were going with the old man, obviously soon to be President as well; there was hardly a girl in Charleston would not be happy to find herself his wife—but for the fact that, much as he hated to admit it even to himself, he wanted *this* girl, and this girl alone. It was not merely a matter of rivalry with Anderson, although the thought of that scoundrel possibly being married to Penny, sharing all that she could give as a woman...because there was the real crux of the matter. Watching her, spending so much time with her, wanting her...why, *he* had fallen in love with her himself, where in the beginning he had merely selected her as a suitable wife because she was Titus Meigs' daughter and because she was a somewhat unusual girl. But now, with her father a suicide bankrupt, it was totally absurd. And yet, it was *her* he wanted to marry. And her he would marry.

Which made Edward Anderson doubly much

of an enemy. Because it was all very well for Uncle James to prate about the freight trade to which the prospector-carrying ships must eventually return. What would happen when Edward Anderson brought that sleek, fast devil-ship back to the Atlantic run? And with perhaps sufficient capital accumulated to build one or two more?

And that was a problem *he* would have to face. Not Uncle James. He realised that his entire life might be caught up in the prosperity, or the destruction, of Edward Anderson.

So what was he going to do about it? What *could* he do about it? What could anyone, while Uncle James indulged this curious admiration for the fellow? But Uncle James was not going to be around very much longer. Then all the decisions would be his.

He leaned back in his uncle's chair, stared at the ceiling. Presumably, he thought, it was a question of how badly he wanted Anderson destroyed.

He rang the silver bell on his uncle's desk. 'Is that fellow Walker still in Charleston?' he asked the secretary.

'I have heard so, Mr Henry, but your uncle forbade him to come here again. He said he was a scoundrel.'

'I know that, Marley. I've no doubt at all that he *is* a scoundrel. But there are some questions I wish to ask him. Find him for me, will you.'

'I tell you, Mr Driscoll, your uncle is passing up a great chance. Central America is the key to the future of this entire continent. And Nicaragua is the key to Central America. I've been there. I know the country. I know the people. They're all at sixes and sevens. They want to be led. They want to be shown the way. With forty men, and the right financial backing, of course...it's money that counts. But with the right backing, I could take over that country in a weekend.'

William Walker was certainly no older than himself, Henry thought. A true soldier of fortune, tall and lean and stoop-shouldered, as if perpetually avoiding a flying bullet or a sweeping sabre, with curiously flat, blue eyes and a mouth which appeared too slack for decision at first glance, but which could harden like a steel trap. His black hair was as lank as his physique, and his clothes, of good material and cut, were carelessly worn, and had not been pressed or laundered in months. Clearly he looked as if he could be a dangerous man, but Henry wondered whether it would be the instinctive, responsive deadliness of the moccasin snake, or the slow but sure and determined enmity of the swamp alligator.

'I seem to remember,' he observed, 'hearing that you thought the same thing of California, and even Sonorra in Mexico.'

Walker smiled; his lips drew back from his teeth, and then closed again. 'I didn't have the backing, Mr Driscoll. But there's an empire out there, waiting for the man with the guts, and the backing, to seize it. Remember Aaron Burr? He felt the same way about Texas.'

'And damn near got himself shot for treason,' Henry observed.

'But he was proved right, in the end, Mr Driscoll. Anyway, Nicaragua; there ain't anybody in the States going to get excited about Nicaragua. Not right now.'

'I'm quite sure you're right. And my uncle is the least likely of all men to become excited about Nicaragua. I cannot imagine what made you bring your crazy scheme to him.'

'Well, sir, there's a Charleston shipping company dealing through Nicaragua right this minute.'

'Then why not *go* to Anderson?'

Walker pulled his nose. 'He don't have the money. And I doubt he'd see my point.'

'Because he once locked you up?'

'He had me in irons, right across that country,' Walker said. 'And all the way to 'Frisco. Him and that Malewski. By Christ...'

Henry nodded. 'You don't want a country, an empire, Walker. You want to get your own back on Anderson. And you've heard there's bad blood between him and my uncle.'

'I'll get my own back on Anderson, soon enough,' Walker said.

'I think you should do that first,' Henry said, quietly.

226

Walker's head came up.

'And maybe, maybe, we can talk about empires after. I can't back you with Driscoll money. I don't control it. Yet. But I've a little of my own I might be prepared to invest in a venture. A venture which, if it were to be successful, might lead me to back you on a bigger scale. When I can. Which may not be too long in the future. What do you say to that, Walker?'

Walker's long tongue came out and circled his lips. 'I'd say that sounds pretty fair to me, Mr Driscoll,' he said. 'You tell me what you want done.'

Edward Anderson stood on the quarterdeck of the *Penelope* and watched the deep blue water surging away from the sides of his ship. It was, as so often in the Gulf of Mexico, a hot and almost airless day; the engines throbbed, and the ship marked her passage as usual by the huge plume of black smoke she left behind.

The sea was so calm that although they were not running at anything like full speed they were still making fifteen knots. It was for conditions like these, in fact, that he might especially have designed the *Penelope*. Just as she might especially have been created to ferry gold prospectors to California by the quickest possible route. He could take no credit for either of those. He could only marvel at the way things had turned out, the immense stroke of

227

luck with which he had been visited. The only credit he could take was for recognising that luck, and acting on it.

All of which had led him to a realisation that there was no such thing as guilt and retribution, in concrete matters. His guilt was inside him, and would remain there. It could not be expiated by physical disasters. The retribution lay in the knowledge that all he now had to do was take the woman he desired above all others into his arms, and love her, for her to love him back. And he could not bring himself to do that. His feelings towards her were still too confused. Towards any woman, he supposed. Certainly he could not contemplate taking *anyone* into his arms, and least of all Penelope Meigs, without having Amanda's soft smile, Amanda's intense vitality, immediately come between them. Marriage to Penelope Meigs would indeed be to bring retribution on to his head, and hers. They shared a guilt as deep as if between them they had murdered Amanda. Together, they would surely drown in each other's misery.

What made the situation even more unbearable, and confusing, was that he *was* sure that Penny would be more than willing to forget the past. Her initial reaction had been too clearly a self-anger, the bewilderment of a girl who had never been refused anything in her life, at having that life so savaged by Fate. But she was growing up, learning to accept what had happened. The fault now lay entirely with him. In direct contrast to her experience, where his initial reaction had been that they were too closely yoked together ever to separate, it was time that was now doing the damage. He had lost his wife, and the circumstances of that tragedy had made it impossible for him ever to love the one woman who could have replaced her.

Even *knowing* that, he could not make himself warm towards her. As she could see, and thus relit her own hatred at every disappointment. But he could not even warm towards his own son, and there lay an even more sombre prospect for the future.

Thus Fate exacted her own penalties, compounding his misery because, after having been forced, with Amanda, to scrimp and save and suffer, always in the *hopes* of prosperity, he had now, in the space of only two years, become a wealthy man. If the trade had not been quite as lucrative as he had anticipated, in that time the firm of Meigs-Anderson had grossed well over two million dollars. Their expenses were heavy. They were meeting the operating costs of three ships—but was that not itself a singular stroke of fortune that he should so suddenly find himself Commodore of an entire fleet—but they could still look on a good quarter of that sum as sheer profit. Obviously they would not be able to maintain such a tremendous rate of gain. There were already indications that the great impetus dragging people west was beginning to die down. There were stories that the gold was being worked out, and certainly it seemed true that all the best claims were already taken up.

But even two years had been sufficient. They were in profit, they owed not a cent to a soul, and the ship was proving herself. And he had solid reasons for supposing they would continue to operate at a profit. He had not wasted his time on his visits to Nicaragua, had made more than one journey by Dutton's creaking, gasping little train, at least as far as the capital, Managua, had there talked with most of the leading men. The country was still in a very unsettled state, even thirty years after it had achieved its independence from Spain. Indeed, the whole of Central America was unsettled; the people of the small states of Nicaragua and Costa Rica, Salvador and Honduras, equally afraid of the swelling power of Mexico to their north, kept making uncertain moves towards a political unity of their own. Moves in which he had more than once been invited to join, and perhaps even lead; the presence of a relatively shallow draft steamship which could be armed, and which could transport armed men in haste, was an attractive prospect to ambitious politicians.

He had not been tempted. He had not even bothered to discuss them with his partner. He was a shipmaster, not a Cochrane. Besides, even had he been tempted, there were too many changes of power in the various capitals, and changes of policies. Too many men to whom he had been introduced as staunch allies had suddenly become bitter enemies. But he had met no one, friend or enemy, who did not seem to be aware that financial stability was essential to their future prosperity, and that such stability depended upon trade. And therefore ships. If the *Penelope* would not carry their soldiers from point to point, they were at least determined that she would carry their produce. On this voyage her holds were as usual full of Nicaraguan sugar cane, for sale in Charleston. Here was the beginning of a freight line of which he would have a monopoly. Obviously the returns at the moment were virtually non-existent, although the people of South Carolina, having as they did an abrasive relationship with tariff conscious governments in Washington, were just as likely to buy sugar from Nicaragua as they were to buy sugar from Louisiana. But he had another, and more important prospect in view. The United States Government was moving towards the annexation of California. The causes would be the same as those which had erupted into the war with Mexico a few years before, for the Mexicans were quite incapable of keeping order in a territory they claimed as their own, and already Malewski and Reynolds had brought back tales of attempted *coups d'état*, with the design of declaring

California an independent country. That was exactly how the Texan business had begun. And indeed, the latest of these abortive revolutions, led remarkably enough by the itinerant scoundrel William Walker, bent as usual on stirring up as much trouble as possible wherever he happened to be, would have succeeded but for prompt action by United States troops. Once California became a U.S. territory, she would inevitably become a State, and speedy and reliable communications between her and the east coast would be even more important.

The physical future, in fact, had never looked so bright, and so foreseeable. And even if it seemed destined to be a lonely future, emotionally, it was time to start making plans all over again. Firstly, to restore Priscilla Meigs to her home. The money was there. It had in fact been there for several months, but Priscilla, still determined never to make her husband's mistake and overreach herself, had steadfastly refused to spend it. But now she would have to be persuaded. It was more than an act of contrition, of repayment, on his part, for the way she had supported him in that catastrophic hour two years ago, or the way in which she had acted the mother to Robert since that time. There was also the fact that he could not spend any of their accumulated profits on a new design until that debt was settled.

Because there at least he was sure Amanda

would be happy for him. He spent his time on these sunlit voyages, thinking and watching the performance of his ship, and dreaming, just as he spent all his scanty leisure hours in Charleston devouring all the literature he could discover on the progress of steam engineering and of steamship design, learning all he could about men like Samuel Cunard, the Canadian-born Britisher who had taken the Atlantic by storm with his conventional steamships, or his American rival, Collins. Both Cunard and Collins were subsidised, Cunard by having been given the contract to carry Her Majesty's Mails, and Collins, by direct grant from the United States Government. Neither actually ran at a profit, so far as Edward could discover. And neither had shown any inclination to advance the theory of steamship design, but seemed content to chug along at a maximum of twelve knots, with their engines set low in the hulls of ordinary sailing ships, their funnels poking out amongst the masts, their sails available not only to make up for any shortage of coal, but to increase their seaworthiness should there be bad weather. And certainly while both of them had shown an interest in the *Penelope*, they had recognised at once that she was entirely unsuitable for the North Atlantic. They regarded the problems he was attempting to overcome as insoluble.

Down to this last voyage he had been forced to agree with them, and had all but despaired.

There seemed no way that a true ocean-going ship could be constructed without accepting the limitations of having to sail her for some half of the journey—or at least be prepared to do so; there was simply no way a steamship could carry sufficient coal to guarantee her passage under steam alone, except under the most perfect conditions of wind and weather. Thus all the old objections he had sought, unsuccessfully, to obviate in the design of the *Penelope*, the deep draft and the high freeboard, necessary to sail a ship safely in strong winds, remained, with the inevitable result of bringing down her maximum speed. Granted, the clipper ships which were now being developed by men like Donald McKay were very fast, but they were sailing ships pure and simple, and thus they were still helpless when the wind was not blowing. While building bigger and bigger steamships in order to carry more coal was self-defeating, as of course the bigger ships required bigger engines and thus burned the same amount of coal, space for space, as, for instance, the *Penelope*. Certainly, size had been the solution adopted by Isambard Brunel, the Englishman who had built both the *Great Western* and the *Great Britain*, ten years before, in his new design, which was apparently to be called the *Great Eastern*. She was to be a mammoth vessel, nearly seven hundred feet long and only eighty feet in the beam, a ratio of more than eight to one, and she would be powered by paddlewheels as well as a propeller, intended to develop a considerable speed. She was being designed with sufficient bunkerage to carry all the coal she would need for a voyage from England to Australia without refuelling—but Brunel was giving her masts and sails as well, just in case.

There were not wanting critics who supposed that such a hybrid monster would never sail at all. Well, that remained to be proved, in time. But Edward remained convinced that sheer size could not be the ultimate answer. And when he had been home this last time he had read an article by a man named John Elder, who claimed to have developed an engine capable of producing steam at a much higher pressure than had ever been achieved before. His argument was that such steam could be used *twice*. Thus each ton of coal would actually be performing twice, and thus at a stroke double the range of any steamship. If that were the case, all the problems were solved. Because then it might be possible to design a ship which would not need sails at all, and *that* raised all manner of possibilities.

He had thought of very little else throughout this voyage, could hardly wait to regain Charleston and begin a communication with Elder, seeking more information. Trethowan, remarkably, with whom he had discussed it, was sceptical. Not about the possibilities of using steam twice—he called it double expansion—

for in fact he could see no reason, providing the pressure could be raised sufficiently, why steam could not be used *three* times, but rather as to the practical possibility of relying upon engines alone, because of the risk of breakdowns. But these were surely minor problems which would be overcome in the course of time. The important thing was to get the new ship designed. The *Amanda*. The name at least was settled in his mind.

'Smoke on the starboard bow, Captain Anderson.' Carruthers, the mate, pointed.

Edward frowned, and took the telescope. The last thing he wanted was some other steam vessel muscling in on his preserves. Presumably it had to happen one day, but now was too soon. He frowned into the eyepiece. 'She's a sailing vessel,' he said. 'I can't see a funnel. A...By God, she's on fire.' He gave the glass to the mate, rang down to the engine room. 'Give us everything you've got, Mark,' he shouted. 'There's a schooner on fire over there.'

The engine revolutions increased, the *Penelope* commenced to surge through the calm water. Edward summoned the boatswain, gave his orders. 'We may not be able to get alongside,' he said. 'Although that is certainly what we shall attempt. Have the hoses rigged and damp canvas hung over the bulwarks. But if the fire is too severe, we must take the crew off in boats. Have both pinnaces swung out.

236

We shall also need blankets and some drink, I should think. Soup laced with brandy. You'll pass the word to the cook.'

'Aye aye, sir,' the boatswain cried, and hurried forward.

Carruthers had continued to study the schooner through his glass, although she was now coming close enough to be observed by the naked eye. 'It seems to be a deck fire,' he said. 'And they've managed to take all sail off her. It looks very strange to me.'

Edward took the glass back, realised that the smoke did indeed appear to be rising from the deck rather than issuing from any hatch cover. And he could see no flames. Which could of course mean that her entire cargo was ablaze, and that the deck had opened up. And yet... like Carruthers, he would have thought that with a fire that immense, giving off so much smoke, he would have been able to see flames. It also occurred to him that if the fire was so intense that it had caused the deck to burn, then it would certainly also have opened up the hull; she should have sunk long ago.

He switched his attention to the crew, gathered right aft. And the passengers, apparently; there were at least forty people there, far too many to be required to handle a schooner. All were men, and there seemed an equal mixture of light and dark complexions. But at least there was no panic, and indeed they had not even launched a boat, despite their desperate situation on board a ship which had to be at the point of sinking.

It was quite the most unusual situation he had ever come across. He lowered the glass, and looked at Carruthers, who was looking at him. Then they spoke together. 'Pirates, by God!'

Edward ran to the helm. 'Hard a port,' he said.

The *Penelope* slewed round, already within a cable's length—two hundred yards—of the schooner. The men watched them in surprise, and one or two shouted. Edward returned to the rail, biting his lip. If they were genuinely on fire, and now went down...

There was an explosion, and then another, and he saw the flashes of light as the rifles were fired. Now every man on the schooner was armed with a rifle and was firing; a bullet crumped into the wooden gunwale beside him.

'Take cover,' he shouted, and returned to the helm. 'Get down, cox. I'll take her.'

The rifles continued to crack, but such was the *Penelope*'s speed that she was already drawing out of range. Nobody had been hit.

Trethowan came on deck. 'Pirates, by God,' he said. 'I thought they were extinct. Odd we haven't seen them before.'

'I don't think it's odd at all,' Edward said, looking back at the ship, where the burning bales of straw were now being heaved over the side as they had obviously failed in their purpose, while other men were hastily setting sail, as if they had any hope of catching the steamship. 'She was waiting there, Mark. For us.'

'That is utterly incredible,' Jonathan Meigs said. 'And you reckon they were sitting there, waiting for you to appear?'

'I reckon,' Edward said. 'The whole thing was just too coincidental to be an accident. Hell, they would know within a few miles of where our track had to be, as we always sail straight from Banco Gorda to the Yucatan Channel, before turning up for Key West. And that's a pretty empty stretch of sea. Another thing, they were well on fire before we sighted them. That meant they had lit their straw the moment they saw our smoke over the horizon. We're the only steamship operating in those waters.'

'But who would possibly wish to do such a thing?' Priscilla Meigs inquired.

'Some people in Nicaragua who don't care for our operation?' Jonathan suggested.

'I doubt that,' Edward said. 'They need us as much as we need them. That goes for all political parties. No, I think it would have to be someone with considerable knowledge of the sea, and considerable contacts in the shipping world, too.'

Jonathan frowned at him. 'Driscoll? I can't believe that. Anyway, he's very seriously ill,

I've heard. He's not really expected to last the month.'

'Yeah,' Edward said. 'I wasn't thinking of Jim Driscoll. He and I may have had our differences, but he's always dealt straight up, even with his opponents.' He went outside, on to the small verandah of the apartment, looked down King Street towards the dock. He had not really given the Driscolls a lot of thought in recent years, as either past employers or potential rivals. Because they were not potential rivals, in any way. They had stayed with their Atlantic trade, and he had left it. His only concern had been the possible marriage of Henry Driscoll to Penelope, with all that might mean for the future of the Meigs-Anderson Line. But as that did not seem to be ever likely in view of Penny's refusal to give Henry a definite answer...he pulled his nose. Henry must also be aware that it was not ever likely. And might well consider him as the cause. But piracy...?

He turned his head as Penelope stepped outside, closed the door behind her.

'I...is it true, about the pirate craft?' she asked.

'We survived.'

'I...I had no idea there was any danger, in that run.'

'Neither did I. Actually, there isn't, as long as we keep our wits about us. But I'd still like to find out who was behind it.'

'Have you no idea?'

'None at all,' he lied.

She gazed at him. 'Do you hate me, so very much?'

The question took him by surprise. He felt himself flush, even as he attempted to frown his bewilderment. 'I had supposed it was the other way around,' he lied again.

'You know that is not so. You said to me once, the day Papa was buried, that for us to be enemies was foolish and wasteful. That was over two years ago.' She bit her lip. 'I opposed you then. I know now that I was wrong. I thought you were clutching at straws. Now I know that I was wrong there too. You have made Mama very happy, and Jonathan, too. You would have made Papa both happy and prosperous, had he trusted in you, sufficiently. And you would have made Amanda very proud. Is it true that you have made a bid for Greenacres?'

His flush deepened. He had not intended her to discover that. 'Jonathan handles our finances,' he said.

'He would not have done it without consulting you.'

Edward shrugged. 'I do not think we have been very successful. Old Driscoll is too ill to conduct any business, and young Henry refuses to consider it until his uncle is well again.'

'It was the thought. I am sure there are many

more important things you could think of, to do with the money.'

'We are but repaying the investment made by your mother and yourself,' Edward said, gently. 'Once that is done, why, yes, there are things I would like to do with our profits.'

'A new ship,' she said.

'What makes you say that?'

'Is it not your dream? You told me there were modifications you would like to make to the *Penelope*. Or to her successor.' She half smiled. 'I was going to have Papa make them for you, remember?'

'I remember, Penny.'

'Then I should be grateful if you were to discuss your plans with me, whenever you can spare the time,' she said. 'I should so like to help you, if I can.'

He gazed at her. 'When I can, Penny,' he said. 'I give you my word, when I can.'

The clods of earth sounded dull as they fell on the coffin, and the onlookers shifted their feet uneasily. There was no one present who had not been aware for some time that James Driscoll had been dying, and his actual passing was but one more apsect of the burial of the prosperity and certainty that the people of South Carolina had enjoyed in the past. Driscoll had helped to build that prosperity with his shipping line and had played his part in leading the citizens of his state in what he, and they, considered the right direction for all of the United States. Although never taking his place on the wider stage, he had maintained his interest in politics, and the Driscoll Company had always backed suitable candidates for office, those men who could be relied upon to support the principle of States' rights. As a young man he had spoken in favour of the Missouri Compromise; a quarter of a century ago he had been one of the leaders in the opposition to the Tariff of Abominations, and in 1832 he had been prepared to consider the secession of South Carolina from the Union rather than accept President Jackson's Tariff Act.

Since then he had been less active on the national front and had concentrated more on his business, turned inward by the death of his childless wife, which had caused him to look to his dead brother's son as the heir to his commercial empire. He had played no part in the recently agreed Compromise of 1850. But as no one could doubt that the storm clouds were again gathering over the slavery question in all the arguments about what was to happen to the new territories of Kansas and Nebraska, equally no one could doubt that the President of the Driscoll Line, Charleston's main shipping concern, would have to interest himself in that. Nor could anyone doubt what point of view they might have expected from James Driscoll.

Now they had to consider an unknown quantity. Still in his middle thirties, Henry Driscoll was regarded by many as too young to have control of such a large financial institution. It went against the grain for white-haired would-be senators and congressmen, judges and even state governors to have to apply to a somewhat callow youth for financial support. And Henry was undoubtedly callow, in the eyes of his seniors. His reputation was mainly that of being Charleston's leading man about town. Even this might have been accceptable, had he spread his favours, suggested that a daughter of one of Charleston's best families might soon be the Driscoll bride. Instead of which he devoted most of his time in the clearly unsuccessful pursuit of the Meigs girl, daughter of a suicide bankrupt, who had not even been a Carolingian by birth, and whose brother was in partnership with a somewhat disreputable shipmaster.

No one could say for sure *why* Edward Anderson was disreputable. It had to do with his having been born a Yankee, with his having quarrelled with old Jim Driscoll, with his having operated a chain ferry for some years, and most of all with his newfangled ideas—a collection of crimes against society compounded by his actually having made a success of himself, although here again, the idea of trading with some place called Nicaragua, populated entirely by mestizoes or mulattoes, was as disreputable as anything else—few of the good people of Charleston were at all sure where

Nicaragua was.

But Henry Driscoll seemed determined to carry over none of his late uncle's grudges, walked with the Meigs family even as they left the cemetery, oblivious of the disapproving looks he received from James Driscoll's friends. 'In many ways, of course, it is a relief,' he remarked to Priscilla Meigs. 'Poor Uncle James had been ill for so long, I am sure it was a relief for him as well. Not that I relish the prospect of owning the Driscoll Line. Dear me, no. As I am sure you know only too well, Ned, even on your small scale...what is it, three ships?... the problems of a shipping company never diminish.'

He met Edward's gaze with a pleasant smile. Although what the fellow was doing here at all, looking as insufferably confident as ever, when his beastly steamship should be at the bottom of the sea and himself a bankrupt, was incomprehensible. He hadn't actually intended any harm to befall either Edward or any of his people, had insisted on that to Walker—his aim had been to cripple the scoundrel's business, not have a murder on his conscience—but suddenly he wondered if he had not been a trifle soft-hearted. When he laid his hands on that useless layabout William Walker...but there were more important and immediate considerations.

'May I drive you home, Penny?' he inquired. She hesitated, glanced at her mother—or was

245

it actually at Anderson—and then inclined her head. 'If you wish, Henry.'

She sat beside him in his phaeton, while he flicked the whip and they drove past the equipages of the other mourners, bowing and even smiling at them.

'I am sure you should at least *pretend* you mourn your uncle,' she suggested.

'I'm no hypocrite. The old fool should have died long ago. He had no thoughts for the future. No plans. While I...there is so much to be done. I suddenly feel there is so little time.' He glanced at her. 'So little time for anything. Penny! Would you not say I have been the most patient of men?'

'You have been the most patient, the most generous, of men, Henry,' she agreed.

'Then do you not suppose I am at last entitled to ask for a definite answer? One would suppose you had no desire ever to live at Greenacres again.'

She looked ahead of them down the road. 'I had supposed you did not wish me to live there, Henry, as you have refused Jonathan's offer for it.'

'I do not wish *you* to live there, Penny. I wish *us* to live there. Will you marry me? You simply must answer me, one way or the other.'

At last she turned her head. 'Then I must answer no.'

He drew rein instinctively, he was so surprised. 'No? You mean you will not?'

'I have said no, Henry.'

'But...Penny, I love you.'

'But I do not love you, Henry.'

He stared at her. 'Anderson,' he said. 'You *are* in love with the scoundrel. And you suppose he may one day marry you.'

She did not even blush. 'I certainly mean to wait and find out, Henry.'

'Mr Walker is here, Mr Driscoll,' said the secretary.

'Show him in.' Henry bit off the end of his cigar, struck a match, leaned back in his chair, the chair his uncle had sat in for so long, and gazed at the door. He could not let the freebooter suspect that his mere presence made him nervous. So he arranged his features into an aggressive expression and pointed with the cigar butt as the door closed behind the tall, thin figure. 'I am surprised you have the effrontery to come back to Charleston at all, Walker. Suppose Anderson had still been here?'

Walker sat down. 'So I waited until he'd left again, didn't I? Anyway, he don't know I had anything to do with that business. I kept out of sight.'

'So successfully,' Henry sneered, 'that the entire project turned into a fiasco.'

Walker shrugged. 'What the hell? Your friend Anderson ain't quite the fool he looks. Now, if you'd let me mount a cannon, then we'd have brought him down.'

'The plan was yours,' Henry said, coldly, and sat up. 'No doubt you are here with some fresh hare-brained scheme.'

Walker grinned, helped himself to a cigar. 'I've been hearing that you're the boss, now.'

'So?'

'Well, you want Anderson ruined? I'm partial to that myself. But it's the main chance you want to be thinking about, *Mister* Driscoll. There's an empire there, waiting to be took. Think of this: even if we was just to destroy that railroad, Anderson's Line would come tumbling down. And the whole country behind him.'

Henry stroked his chin. It was, of course, something of which from time to time he had alllowed himself to dream. But it really was, only for the realms of dreams. Private citizens did not interfere in the affairs of foreign countries, inspire revolutions and *coups d'état*. At least, certainly not in pursuit of a business rivalry—even when that business rivalry had developed into a personal hatred he would not have supposed himself capable of feeling.

But was he now allowing words to overcome him, rather than realities? Nicaragua was not a foreign country, in the sense of France or Britain or even Holland. It was a tiny speck on the map, occupied by warring half-breeds, which happened to span a vital part of the American continent. And the goals were enor-

248

mous, for the Driscoll Line as well as for himself personally. If that vital span could be controlled, quite apart from his private satisfaction...it all came down to the *will*. He had never considered such a positive attitude to life before. He had been born a Driscoll, had no sooner been old enough to look around him than he had realised that one day the Line would be his. He had sought nothing more for the major part of his life. When he had gone off to war for the United States against the Mexicans it had been purely because it had seemed the thing to do, a necessary part of occupying his life until the vital moment arrived.

Now it was here, and it was for the first time necessary for him to make a decision, whether he continued in the same old conservative mould fashioned by his uncle, or whether he struck out into new fields. His uncle had actually considered competing in the North Atlantic run, with Collins and Cunard, and had decided that the risks were too great. There at least the old man had been right. But Central America...and with Anderson gone, the Anderson Line itself might fall into his lap. *Would* fall into his lap. Penny would have no one to turn to then, but him.

Did he want her so badly, that he would kill for her? That was not a question he really wished-ed to consider. Well, then did he hate Anderson sufficiently to wish him dead? That also was dangerous ground. But if he considered the matter from sheer ambition, then the question was whether he had the necessary drive and ruthlessness to reach out and grasp new markets, even if it meant tearing them from another's grasp, that was entirely different. That was the stance upon which nearly all the great men of history had founded their success.

That such a project might involve civil war and loss of life, that included in the casualty list might be a man whom he cordially loathed more than any other living creature, well, a ruthless man could ignore such consideration.

And where was the risk, for him, personally? Merely financial, and perhaps not too much of that either.

He stubbed out his cigar, leaned across the desk. 'How much would you need?' he asked.

CHAPTER 7

Edward rang the engine room telegraph for reduced speed. He studied the approaching coastline, absently hearing the hubbub of conversation arising from his passengers, grouped beneath him in the waist of the ship. There were only twenty-seven of them on this voyage, twenty-five men and two women—California was steadily losing its magic lure. But he no longer needed them, however interesting he invariably found them, and their reaction to their landfall.

It was, he supposed, an approach to make the stoutest heart wish he was securely back in New York, or Boston, or Charleston, or wherever he might have originated. The coast was very shallow for some distance offshore, and was littered with islands and sandbanks, through which the *Penelope* now threaded her way, while ahead of them was nothing but an endless vista of mangrove swamps and fast-running streams, from which rose, even above the noise of the engines, the calls of the birds, a huge variety of tone and sound, while in the noonday heat the jungle seemed to steam.

It was an approach he knew now as well as he knew Charleston Harbour, having been in and out more than a hundred times. Yet it alway required caution, just as it never failed to terrify strangers, especially as they had no concept where they were headed; Nicaragua changed but slowly, and the town of El Bluff, if it could yet be called a town, remained hidden behind a finger of land equally overgrown with trees and mangroves, and was therefore not visible until the ship had actually entered the estuary of the River Escondida. By then, they would be able to see the new town of Bluefields, on the other side of the river, their actual departure point. Then they would be faced with a mule train journey of three days to the actual railhead. Like his first-ever passengers they would curse and swear and wonder why they had paid a small fortune for so much discomfort, but they would still reckon it would be worth it when they reached the goldfields.

He supposed, idly, that California was a place he must one day visit; Malewski and Reynolds both told glowing tales of the strange mixture of frontier town, sea-port, and elegant city that composed San Francisco. Perhaps it might be an idea for his honeymoon. Because suddenly that required consideration. A marriage between himself and Penelope Meigs had not even been discussed as yet, but no one doubted now that it was going to happen.

As it had always been going to happen? He sometimes wondered what might have happened had Amanda been standing on that dock, Robert in her arms, to welcome him home that day four years ago. Would it have been possible for him to spend four years meeting Penelope almost every day, watching her grow into a quite startlingly lovely young woman, knowing that she loved him, and yet be able to resist the temptation to take her in his arms? Instead of which he had held no woman at all in his arms for four years. Yet even four years ago, in the guilt and shame which had all but overwhelmed him he realised now that he had known they would one day marry. They had needed time. More time than he had suspected, or had felt they possessed. But now the time was past, they could both recognise that they shared a never-diminishing love, and increasing mutual desire that transcended their original sin, that was the great driving power in their lives, that could not be gainsaid.

A strange mood in which to approach a wedding. And yet an honest one. And a true one. On the day of her father's funeral he had suggested they were yoked together. And he had been right. But his mind could again soar at the thought of possessing her, and of being possessed by her. The night they slept together for the first time as man and wife would set the seal upon the happiness that kept threatening to obliterate all his memories, however much he mistrusted it.

He realised that the decision, slowly hardening in his mind over the past few months, had suddenly been taken, almost unconsciously. He had indeed thought of little else, had not even pursued the question of Henry Driscoll's possible involvement in the abortive piratical attempt on his ship. And no doubt his life as well. Henry had failed there, just as he had failed with Penny, just as he had failed in so many ways—and just as he would undoubtedly fail as President of the Driscoll Line. There were more important things in life for Edward Anderson to consider than Henry Driscoll. He had done what he had set out to do; the *Penelope* had had her day and served her purpose; she was now becoming an old lady. If her speed was undiminished, her engines needed more and more attention. He did not doubt that Mark would be able to keep them going for some time yet, but it was time for him to close this episode of his life, and start a new one. With Penelope, and Robert, and the new design. Letters from John Elder lay on his desk back in Charleston, offering him a demonstration of the double compression engine. Neither Elder nor anyone else could guarantee him that such an engine would be sufficiently reliable to enable him to do away with sails altogether, but if it could double his range that might not be important. And anyway, it was a problem, like all the other problems, which would certainly be solved in the course of time.

Suddenly he was desperately impatient to be home again, to say everything that needed to be said to Penny, to start drawing and designing, to arrange the details with Bartell...he joined the passengers in a shout of excited relief as the *Penelope* crept round the tree shrouded headland into the broad, shallow, suddenly brown waters of the estuary, and they saw houses, and docks, and people, waiting for them. The engine room telegraph clanged, and the screw was put astern, as the ship glided quietly alongside the only deep water wharf, and Carruthers saw to the running out of the gangplank.

'Wait there, wait,' Edward shouted, as the passengers surged forward. 'There are formalities.' He looked for Colonel de Soto, all pale blue uniform and gold braid, who usually came on board to inspect his papers—not that the colonel ever did anything more than drink a glass of brandy, no matter what the time of day—frowned as he did not see him, was instead confronted by a man dressed in a brown uniform and a peaked cap, and armed with a drawn revolver. He looked past this intruder, realised that the people on the dock, although few of them were actually wearing uniforms, were not interested spectators after all; every man was armed with a rifle and a revolver, which was now being levelled at the crew of the *Penelope*, while as the warps had already been secured there was no chance of pulling away to sea again, in a hurry.

'May I ask what is the meaning of this?' he asked in his best Spanish.

'The meaning, senor,' the brown clad officer said, coming on board followed by a dozen of his men. 'Is that this ship is under arrest, and all who sail in her.'

'Are you out of your mind?' Edward demanded, and pointed at the stern. 'That is the American flag. Where is Colonel de Soto?'

'Colonel de Soto is dead,' the officer said, and smiled, briefly. 'I hanged him. And I was warned that you might prove difficult. Seize him,' he told his men. 'Seize them all.'

Edward bunched his fists and was checked by the revolver thrust into his chest. A moment later his arms were seized and his wrists bound behind his back. Carruthers had also been pinioned, and Mark was held as he came up the ladder from the engine room.

'You can't do that,' Jehu shouted, emerging from the main companionway. 'You can't treat Mr Edward so.'

The officer swung his pistol; the barrel caught the Negro across the face and sent him tumbling to the deck, whence he was immediately pulled up and bound like his master, blood streaming from his split cheek.

'By God, you filthy greaser,' shouted one of the passengers, a New Yorker, who now drew a revolver himself. There was an explosion, and the man gave a gasp and buckled forward, landing on his knees before falling on to his face, blood trailing away from his chest. The captain replaced his revolver in its holster. 'I will kill anyone who resists arrest,' he said. 'Throw down your weapons. Quickly now.'

They stared at him, then threw a variety of handguns on to the deck. One of the women screamed.

The captain turned to his sergeant. 'You may take the women,' he said. 'But do not kill them.'

'Move!' The sergeant dug his rifle muzzle into one of the girl's thighs.

'Ow!' she cried. 'Ow! My God, Captain Anderson, you going to allow this? They're gonna rape us. We paid good money...'

Another poke from the rifle muzzle made her gasp, and a push sent her staggering down the gangplank. Her companion ran behind her. Edward had never doubted for an instant that they were both prostitutes, on their way hopefully to reap some of the rich pickings that were to be had by willing females in the goldfields, which might even include marriage to a wealthy and sex-starved prospector, but they were certainly his responsibility until they reached San Francisco.

As was Jehu his responsibility at all times.

'By God,' he said. 'If you touch those ladies, I will have you hanged. As I will have you hanged for piracy, if you do not leave my ship and my crew this instant.'

The captain gave another of his brief smiles. 'When you are freed, senor,' he said. 'If that ever happens. Take them ashore.'

Rifle muzzles were thrust into their backs, and they staggered down the gangplank. The two girls had disappeared into one of the waterfront houses, but they heard a scream.

'My God,' Trethowan said. 'It's like some nightmare. What in the name of God can have happened?'

'There's been some sort of revolution,' Edward said, looking left and right as they gained the dusty street. There were people standing around, looking at them, raggedly-dressed mestizo women and children, and a handful of men, the same people who had always gathered to stare at the American steamship whenever it arrived here. Some of them Edward even thought he recognised. But they gave no sign of recognising *him*. Whatever happened had been accepted by these apathetic, undernourished people as they accepted storms and disease, debt and poverty—their situation could hardly change for the worse. While all the port officials, such as the mayor and his fat smiling Indian wife, had disappeared, like de Soto. Had they also been shot?

It was too much to take in at this moment. Only an hour ago he had been a prosperous shipmaster, navigating his ship with easy confidence through the narrow, twisting channels, dreaming of his future plans and his future wife...now he and his officers, as well as his crew and his passengers, were being marched out of the town along a dusty, uneven road, towards the distant jungle. Were they to be shot, as well? It seemed unbelievable. He had to suppose that he would suddenly roll over and wake up and realise that he had eaten too much cheese with his dinner.

He looked over his shoulder at the ship. The captain and his soldiers were still on board, roaming the decks, staring up at the masts, coming and going from the cabins. All of that luxury, all of that delicate machinery, all of his navigational instruments, his charts and his books, at the mercy of men who had never been on a ship before...

'Halt,' called the sergeant, and his feet immediately stopped moving. Thus quickly, he reflected, does the human mind accept a total change in its situation.

He looked along the road at the group of horsemen approaching, also wearing the brown uniforms of the revolutionary army, and very heavily armed with swords as well as rifles and revolvers. And at their head...Edward's eyes narrowed in disbelief.

'Walker!' he said. 'William Walker.'

'General Walker,' snapped the sergeant, and once again thrust his rifle into Edward's midriff, causing him to gasp. 'On your knees, before the general.'

Another paralysing blow had him kneeling before he really meant to, looking up through a red haze of anger at the smiling face above the horse, now reined to look down at him.

'Captain Anderson,' Walker said. 'We have been waiting for you.'

'By God, Walker,' Edward said. 'By God, when I get home...'

'When,' Walker commented.

'Do you wish this man hanged, general?' the sergeant asked.

Walker appeared to consider. 'No,' he said at last. 'Not yet. I wish him to discover what it is like, to be a convict, in Nicaragua. But he is an insolent dog, sergeant. Flog him. Flog him all the way to the gaol.'

Henry Driscoll stood before Priscilla Meigs twisting his hat in his hands, his face contorted with distress at what he had to say. 'It really appears very serious, Mrs Meigs,' he said. 'As you know, I sent one of my own ships down there to investigate as soon as Edward became overdue...I mean, Anderson and I may have had our differences, but I could not conceive of anything happening to another Charleston shipowner and not doing something about it. And my people were fired upon, from the shore.'

'But the scoundrels could see the American flag, surely?'

Jonathan was scandalised.

'The *Penelope* would also have been flying the American flag,' Henry pointed out. 'Mind you, that is our best hope. They did fire at the flag. I have of course made out a full report and despatched it to Washington. If we can get the Navy to take action...'

'But what has *happened* to them?' Priscilla shouted. 'A ship with twenty men and a whole lot of passengers on board cannot just disappear.'

'Ah, well...' Henry sighed. 'My captain did manage to make contact with some of the Indians who live on the coast. And they told him that there has been a great revolution, and that the whole country is in a state of civil war. And apparently the revolutionary forces seized El Bluff and Bluefields, that is, the entire mouth

260

of the Escondida River, just before the arrival of the *Penelope*. They arrested the ship in order to use her for their own purposes. Of course Edward tried to resist them, and there was some shooting. The Indians could not be sure, but some of the gringoes, that's what they call us white people, you know, were killed.'

'Oh, my God,' Priscilla said. 'Oh, my God.' She hugged little Robert, just four years old and staring at the agitated grown-ups with enormous eyes.

Penelope said nothing. She just sat on the settee beside her mother, put her arm round her shoulder.

'I know,' Henry said, looking about to burst into tears. 'It is quite the most shocking thing I have ever heard. American citizens, being shot at and killed by halfbred revolutionaries...'

'But *Edward*,' Jonathan shouted. 'What news of Edward? Was *he* shot?'

'I'm afraid that seems to be the case,' Henry said. 'Those of the crew, and passengers, who survived the battle were apparently marched off into the interior. The Indians did not know what eventually happened to them. But... Edward was not with them. They were sure of that.'

Jonathan also sat down, his shoulders bowed.

'Believe me,' Henry said. 'I am utterly shattered by the news. Quite apart from the insult to the flag, the personal element, and you...to have lost Edward, and your ship, all at one

261

blow, really, I don't know what to say. If there is anything I can do, anything at *all*...' he gazed at Penelope and watched the tears rolling silently down her cheeks.

No nightmare can last forever. Therefore, Edward realised as he carried the wooden sleeper to drop it into place, extending the railroad by another three feet, this was no nightmare. Therefore everything which had happened *before* his arrest had to have been a dream, a happy dream, from which he had so suddenly and brutally been awakened.

It was simple to think in terms of dreams and fantasies, because he was lightheaded all the time, from exhaustion, malaria, fever, lack of food, dysentery, general debility. He supposed he was lucky to be alive, if alive was a fortunate thing to be. Walker had shown considerable acumen in sending him to the slow death of the railroad gang rather than the gallows. Here he could be visited, from time to time, and flogged, and laughed at. Dutton had not been so lucky; he had been shot and killed attempting to preserve his precious railroad.

The absurd thing was that Dutton no doubt would have appreciated seeing his line extended, no matter at whose behest. Or was the amazing thing that a scoundrel like William Walker should have been able to carry out so successful a revolution that he had installed his own puppet as President of Nicaragua, and, as himself Commander-in-Chief of the Army, ruled the country as absolute dictator? Or was it even more amazing that no outside force had interfered? But why should anyone interfere? Nicaragua was an independent country. All independent countries in this part of the world suffered revolutions from time to time. The Government in Washington was probably quite pleased that it was an American citizen controlling this vital transcontinental link, would no doubt supply the Nicaraguans with additional rolling stock once the new railway was complete. That the citizen might be widely known as a scoundrel, and that his revolution might have involved a few other American citizens was neither here nor there. And after two years, he doubted they were even remembered.

Because there was the *truly* amazing aspect of the situation, that he should have lived and worked in these conditions for two years, reduced to wearing a pair of home-made drawers and nothing else, his feet bare to the stings of ants and the burrowing of chiggers, his back exposed to the sun and to all the other insects which feasted off his perpetually raw, whip torn flesh, his hair grown long and lank, his beard a matted mess of fleas and filth— and not gone mad. As Mark Trethowan had gone mad, and worked in solitary silence, locking his brain up in the imponderable mysteries of ship design, speaking only occasionally, and cryptically, as to say, 'a double bottom, Edward, a double bottom. And sheathed in iron.'

Or as Carruthers and so many other of Edward's erstwhile crew and passengers had succumbed and died of fever, as Reynolds shivered and shuddered his way through each day, because the Pacific ships of the Meigs-Anderson Line had also been seized and impounded by the new regime. Only Cas Malewski, big and strong and tough-minded, and Jehu, no less tough and more emotionally equipped to withstand the rigours of the prison camp, faced the daily agony with grim determination.

And their captain. But there the determination was beginning to weaken. The will to survive, to accept whatever was hurled at him, to resist the temptation to hurl himself at the throat of one of his tormentors and enjoy the merciful relief of a bullet in the belly, had been based upon a simple fact: back in Charleston were his friends and business partners, and the woman who loved him. They would certainly come, or send, looking for him. Two years ago that had seemed as sure as anything in this crazy world. But they had not come. No one had come. Not even Penelope had sent after him. She had forgotten him too. And therefore there was going to be no escape from this living hell, and like Carruthers, he would eventually die. Even Jehu and Malewski would eventually die. It was incredible, unbelievable, but it was true. The vital force that was Edward Anderson, all the plans and dreams, which had been on the point of coming true, for great steamships roaming the world, all the newly-awakened desire, the sheer bliss of looking forward to holding Penny in his arms, as he could just remember doing on that oddly happy but guilty voyage, all would just disappear into oblivion, along with his aching body.

Clearly they thought him dead, and the ship lost. Well, they were right. So what had they done about it? What was Robert thinking, about his lost father? What was Penny thinking, and doing? But those were impossible considerations, as he trudged to and fro with a wooden sleeper draped across his shoulders.

The whistle blew for the ten minute rest they were allowed every second hour, and he fell to his hands and knees, and then on to his face, to lap the filthy water from the nearest muddy puddle left beside the track by the last rainstorm.

'You staggered just now, master,' Jehu said, kneeling beside him. 'Are you all right?'

Edward drank some more. 'Sure,' he said 'Sure. I'm all right.'

Jehu worried about him all the time. Apart from actual illness, he felt it shameful that his master should have to work until he dropped from exhaustion. In the beginning he would even have carried Edward's loads for him, had not a guard with a whip convinced them both that there would be no shirking in this camp.

'Edward...' Malewski knelt on his other side. Another worried friend. Because he fears for *my* sanity, Edward thought. But am I not already insane? If I were sane, would I not long ago have had the sense, or the manhood, to commit suicide? Is that not true madness, to continue living when there is no rhyme or reason to do so?

But he smiled, and shook his head. 'I'm all right, Cas. Really and truly.'

They listened to hoofbeats, turned their heads. Walker, Edward wondered? That would surely mean another flogging. He did not think he could stand that. But then, he had never supposed he could stand a flogging the first time, when he had shouted and cursed, less at the pain of it than from sheer humiliation, sheer inability to believe that such a disaster could be happening to *him*, Edward Anderson. Now he merely wept, from pain. And perhaps still from humiliation as well. He, Edward Anderson, a man of courage and determination, once, a man who had laughed with sheer joy as he had faced a hurricane, reduced to tears, by the agonising sear of a leather thong across his back and shoulders.

He became aware of a restless stir amongst the work gang. They moved in these *stirs*, worked together when the whistle blew, collapsed together inside their wire pen in the dusk, scrabbling for the scraps of food which were thrown to them. They seldom fought over much else now. In the beginning there had been considerable anger. Then a man had needed a friend, and with Trethowan already a broken reed, Edward had thanked God for the presence of Jehu, just as the day Malewski and Reynolds had been thrown in beside them, he had almost wept with joy, even as he had known sorrow for his friends' plight. Up to then he and Jehu had had to battle alone, and not only against the Nicaraguans and Indians who shared their confinement and were interested in whatever of value they might possess; those of the passengers in this pen had felt a bitter resentment against the sea captain who, as they saw it, had inveigled them into such a desperate situation, after having relieved them of a thousand dollars each. And had they not been right? Even as he had swung his fists and kicked at their bodies and clawed at their eyes, even as he had exerted the essential willpower to force himself to destroy them, that he might not be destroyed himself, he had felt the guilt of his inadvertent crime weighing heavily on his shoulders.

But those days were far in the past. Nowadays it was unusual for the work gang to stir for anything save work or food. He sat up, beside Malewski and Jehu, watched the group of horsemen draw rein at the foot of the embankment on which they were laying the sleepers. There were four horsemen, and one... horsewoman?

Instinctively Edward rose to his knees, and then his feet, like all the other men. They had seen no women, except for the odd Indian squaw gaping at them from the roadside as they were marched from site to site, for over a year. And this was a young and even pretty woman, Spanish by descent, obviously, with her fine dark hair and eyes, her bold, handsome face, her full figure well-dressed in a deep green riding habit and a broad brimmed black hat... but with her wrists tied together and then to her reins.

She was staring at them with equal interest, but her features were contorted with disgust at what she saw, and with fear as well.

'Get down, senorita,' the officer in charge said. He leaned across, and released the rope holding her wrists. 'Get down.'

'You cannot do this,' the woman said, her voice high with protest. 'You cannot *do* this.'

The captain swung his riding crop, and caught her across the shoulder. The force of the blow knocked her from the saddle and she sprawled on the muddy ground, her hat flying off and dirty water splashing over her face and hair.

The captain looked up at the watching prisoners. 'This woman has been sentenced,' he shouted, 'to work on the railroad. With you.' He smiled. 'Use her well,' he said, and turned his horse to ride away.

The work gang exchanged glances, unable to
268

comprehend what had happened, unable to consider the crime she must have committed to have received so dreadful a sentence.

The sergeant in charge of the guard stood above her, swung his foot. His booted toe crashed into her thigh, and she rolled and rose to her knees. Now her entire habit was coated with mud, as was her face. 'Up there,' the sergeant said. 'Or I'll take the skin from your arse.'

Slowly she pushed herself to her feet, biting her lip now to stop from screaming, looking at the tree fringe a few hundred yards away.

The sergeant smiled at her. 'Try it, senorita,' he said. 'Just try it.' He jerked his head. 'Up there.'

She hesitated a last time, inhaled—the men watched the bodice of her habit rise and then fall again, and there was another enormous *stir*—and then she climbed the slope. The sergeant blew his whistle and the men picked up their tools. The woman stood in their midst, gazing from one bearded face to the next, from dribbling lips to hands openly holding erect penises, tears now streaming down her cheeks, fists tight curled as she tried to stop herself from having hysterics.

'Get to work,' the sergeant said, and strode into their midst to push her towards one of the wooden sleepers. 'Get to work.'

She stumbled forward, stooped, but could not lift the sleeper from the earth. Without a word Malewski lifted it for her, only to be sent sprawling by a blow from the sergeant's stick. 'She'll do her own work,' he said. 'If she has to crawl with it, she'll do her own work. Crawl, slut, crawl.'

The woman crawled, dragging the block of wood behind herself.

The whistle blew, the men dropped their tools; the sun was beginning to sink into the trees behind them, and the mosquitoes were rising from the soaked ground in their myriads.

But the men did not care. They watched the woman. All afternoon she had crawled to and fro, with painful determination, pushing and pulling her sleepers into position, refusing to look at the man who waited with hammer and steel pin, desperate not to be kicked or beaten any more. She never raised her head, however often one of the men contrived to have his shoulder brush against hers. But no man had risked more than an inadvertent touch. They were prepared to wait, for the whistle. And the pen. Edward supposed this would be the first time any member of the work gang would actually have looked forward to being returned to the pen for the night.

The woman got up, slowly and cautiously, as if she did not trust her muscles. Her riding habit was stained with mud, as were her boots; as she had crawled to and fro the watchers had seen the frilly white hems of her petticoats and even obtained occasional glimpses of white leg, and had again *stirred*. Her hair was matted to her neck and across her forehead, by a combination of mud and sweat. Her once-manicured nails were already cracked and broken. But her torment had clearly not yet begun. And this she knew.

'Fall in there, fall in,' bawled the sergeant, and the men formed their usual column of fours. The woman was taken into their midst, several rows in front of Edward and Jehu and Malewski and Trethowan and Reynolds. But still no man made a move against her. They feared the sergeant's whip.

The whistle blew, and they set off, stumbling over the uneven ground. 'What will we do?' Malewski asked.

Edward felt an enormous sensation of warmth, that his friend had not thought it necessary to ask *if* they would do anything. As if they could do anything. Three men and two cripples against forty-odd? And why should they risk their lives? He had never laid eyes on this girl before. And he wanted a woman very badly. So instead of considering dying in some absurdly gallant gesture, why did he not merely take his place in line, and have her, even after forty others?

Because his name was Edward Anderson and once he had known pride? And the sight of the woman had awakened his pride? That was not true. The sight of her had merely awakened his manhood, so now he would fight for her, to possess her. But there were forty other men whose manhoods had also been awakened.

The gates of the pen swung open, and they marched inside. There was nothing inside the wire fence, as the woman was now realising; Edward saw her head jerk as this fresh horror was revealed to her. No huts, no tents, no shelter from the rain or the sun...and therefore, no privacy. Just beaten earth, as sweet smelling as the gigantic cesspool it had become, littered with puddles left by the day's rain, and an enormous cauldron filled with a greasy looking liquid which contained the odd lump of putrid meat floating in it, and beside it, a pile of handleless bowls. Their supper.

She turned to face the gate, as if she would make one last appeal to the humanity, or at least the sexuality, of the guards. But the gate was already swinging shut. 'Sleep well, senorita,' they shouted. 'When you can.'

She looked left and right, her face the strangest mixture of concentration and threatened collapse. That would be easiest, for her. But even that required an initial act of will.

One of the prisoners went to the cauldron, picked up a bowl, dipped it, and walked towards her, holding the bowl in front of him. She gazed at him, incredulously, then slowly stretched out her right hand, as with her left she pushed mud streaked hair from her forehead. He had made her feel like a woman again, for a moment.

But such had not truly been his intention; as her fingers were about to close on the bowl he dropped it. It fell to the ground at her feet, and as she stared at it in dismay, he uttered a shrill laugh, and drove his hands forward, to seize her breasts through the cloth. She jerked away from him and the linen ripped, exposing the straps and frills and flesh that lay below. The rest of the men had watched, as now they watched their leader reaching for her again. Then they surged forward in a mass, sweeping her legs from the ground, throwing her heavily on to the earth so that she lost her breath and could not even scream; the only sound above the gasps for breath, hers as well as the men's, was ripping material.

Edward glanced at Malewski, and then ran forward, clasping his hands together and swinging them left and right, catching one man on the side of the head and sending him spinning away from his prey, kicking another in the face, knowing that Malewski and Jehu were beside him, the Pole using his giant strength to even more purpose. And not only Malewski and Jehu. Trethowan had shrugged off his mental blackness to fight with them, and even Reynolds, barely able to stand after a day's labour had sapped his already meagre strength, was in the middle of the fray. And if they were weak, the others were even weaker. They turned with feeble protest to face the Americans, stumbled backwards, leaving the girl, gasping for breath, her skirts and bodice already ripped to shreds.

The guards stood grouped at the gate, laughing and making bets on the possible outcome of the fight as they watched.

The man who had led the assault drew his lips back from his teeth in a wolfish smile. 'There is no need to fight for her, senors. She will satisfy us all,' he said. 'Do you take her first, if you are in such a hurry. We will wait until you are finished.'

'I'll kill the man who touches her,' Edward said, sucking his lacerated knuckles.

They stared at him, while Trethowan helped the girl to her feet.

'Fetch some food, Cas,' Edward said, and took her other arm to help her into a corner of the compound. She shrank away from him, and he realised that, as he looked no different to any of the other prisoners, she would necessarily assume his intentions towards her must be the same. 'I will not harm you,' he said. 'Neither will my friends. We are Americans.'

'Americans?' she asked, her eyes enormous. 'You are the Captain Anderson?'

Edward frowned at her. 'You know of me?'

'Walker told me, he would put me in with the Captain Anderson,' she said. 'And let me suffer with him.'

'Walker? You have met Walker?'

Cas and Jehu had returned with six bowls of

stew. The girl took hers, hesitated, nose wrinkling—but she was too hungry not to eat. 'I know him,' she said, her mouth full. 'I was his mistress. My name is Dolores de Soto. He had my father hanged, and took me as his mistress.'

'I knew your father,' Edward said.

'And he spoke to us of you,' she said. 'I hated Walker, but there was nothing I could do against him. And I think he hated me as well. When he tired of me, he told me he would condemn me to a living death. In here.' She shuddered, gazed at the other prisoners, also eating now, gathered in a group on the far side of the compound, and staring at them, while several of them still nursed cuts and bruises from the brief fight. 'Will they not attack us again, tonight?'

'I doubt it,' Edward said. 'I doubt they have the strength, of either body or mind.' He turned, at the sound of boots hitting the earth behind them, to look into the muzzle of a rifle.

'As you *men* do not want her,' said the sergeant of the guard. 'We will take her, for tonight.'

Remarkably, she did not scream, but got to her feet and went with him without a word. Even more remarkably, when she returned an hour later, an hour punctuated by loud laughter from the guards' tent, she lay down next to Edward.

'I am sorry,' he said, inadequately.

'Bah,' she said. 'They are only men, not animals like those. But you fought for me, Senor Captain Anderson. If you wish me...'

It would certainly have been a pleasure to accept her offer, had he possessed the strength. In the circumstances they shared, that she had just been raped several times could interest him no more than it apparently did her. But as she had said, those had been men, not animals, and even *had* he possessed the strength, his commonsense told him that the ascendancy, as much moral as physical, which he and his friends had just established over the other prisoners would be lost if they now proved themselves no better.

And in fact it *was* a pleasure, just to have her company, her blooming femininity. There was no means by which, in the pen and on the railroad, she could hope to preserve any part of herself from the most complete intimacy with the men around her, and thus they rapidly got to know her almost as well as they knew themselves, could even ask her how she was when she returned from the sergeant's bed, for he sent for her several times a week. Her remarkable composure in the face of all she was forced to endure was a source of strength even to them. Her well-being became something to be worked for, and they had not possessed any goals for too long. Thus the five of them even practised a friendly rivalry as to who could procure her the most palatable-looking food.

But she was important for more than herself alone. She had news of the outside world. Granted little of it was at all to their advantage. Walker had apparently established his authority beyond the slightest question, had driven all his would-be opponents either into exile or into the forests; his regime had been recognised by the neighbouring states, however much Dolores felt they did not approve of it.

She was also able to tell them that there *had* been inquiries made after them, by Henry Driscoll, of all people, on behalf of the Meigs family. But if this was reassuring the fact that Driscoll had been told they had died in attempting to defend the *Penelope* was crushing. Even if it was as they had feared and expected. Of the *Penelope* itself she had no information.

'So that is it, my friends,' Malewski said, one evening as they sat and ate their monkey stew. 'We are lost souls, doomed to spend the rest of our lives here on this railroad track, supposing we do not die even sooner than that.' He looked at Reynolds, and Jehu, and Trethowan, and then at the girl. It had taken no more than a fortnight to reduce her physically to their level. Out of her destroyed garments she had managed to rescue but a single shift, and even this was split to the thigh. She was as filthy as they, and suffered even more from the mosquito bites which brought her flesh up in festering red sores. And yet she remained the most attractive thing in their lives. Just to watch her move, to watch her breasts swell as she breathed, the muscles in her legs ripple as she walked, was to remind them that they were not *yet* dead.

And her brain had not yet been killed by despair, either. 'If you remain here, then you are right,' she said.

They gazed at her.

'Is there somewhere you could go, should you get out of here?' she asked.

'We are not three days away from El Bluff,' Edward said. 'Perhaps even closer. If we could get there, and the *Penelope* is still there...'

'But it is not possible to leave the pen,' Malewski said.

Dolores smiled at him, and then glanced at the gate, where the guards clustered; they found as much pleasure in looking at her as did the inmates. 'It would be possible if you had a weapon,' she said.

Edward also looked at the guard, then back at her.

She shrugged. 'If they catch me out they will flog me. I have been flogged before. Do you *wish* to die, in this swamp?'

He really had no reply to make to that. Her presence had indeed reawakened his manhood in every sense. For all his physical weakness and his mental uncertainty, he did not really wish to dwindle here. No matter what had happened, there were still dreams to be dreamed, and plans to be made...and perhaps even realised, if he could once again find himself standing at the helm of the *Penelope*.

Her smile widened. 'I will get you a weapon, Senor Captain Anderson.'

Edward heard the gate clang shut, the bars drop into place. It was about eleven at night, the usual time for Dolores to return. It was a moonless night, and as usual the mosquitoes hummed through the darkness, seeking even this thin blood which was all that was available. And again as usual, he slept in a corner of the wire enclosure, together with his four companions. Since Dolores had joined them the other prisoners had definitely regarded them as their enemies. No doubt they felt some satisfaction at the way she was summoned almost nightly to the sergeant's bed, thus doing the gringoes out of their prize.

But tonight, for the first time in a long while, he was conscious of a real excitement. Tonight...undoubtedly the chances against their succeeding were slim. Perhaps they could blast their way out of the camp, but to hope to escape...and yet, why should they not? If they could but regain the *Penelope*...

But whether or not they escaped, whether or not they were soon to go down in a hail of bullets, they would have *lived*, for a few glorious moments. Entirely because of the woman. For that, at the least, they must be grateful.

She knelt beside him, put out her hand to touch his shoulder. 'Are you awake, Senor Captain Anderson?'

'Yes,' he said, and felt the revolver being pressed into his hand.

'There are six bullets,' she said. 'And the guards on the gate have many more. But it must be done now, Senor Captain. The sergeant has become careless with me. When he wakes up and finds his weapon gone, he will beat me to death. And he will not be careless again.'

'I understand,' Edward said, and sat up.

She could not see his face, but something in his voice must have warned her. 'You have killed men before, Senor Captain?'

There was no temptation to lie. 'No,' he said. 'I have never killed anyone.'

'But you must kill now. Do you understand this? There can be no hesitation, no offers of mercy.'

'I understand that,' he said.

He heard her breath whistle as she smiled. 'Just remember what they have done to you, and your friends. And to me.'

'Yes,' he said, and shook the others awake.

'You must leave me here, Captain,' Reynolds said. 'I will be nothing more than a hindrance.'

'We go together, or we don't go at all,' Edward told him. 'Besides, who's going to steer us home? Now stay here, and you, boatswain, lie still. They will come to us.'

'Give me the gun,' Trethowan said. 'Give me the gun, Ned. I want to kill one of them.'

'You'll get a gun,' Edward said. 'Lie still.'

He carried the revolver under his left arm, invisible in the darkness as it was pinned against his ribs. He went to the gate. 'Senors,' he said through the wire. 'My boatswain, Reynolds, he is dead.'

'Bah,' said one of the guards.

'He is dead,' Edward insisted. 'And will have decomposed by morning.'

'We'd best get him out,' said another man. 'Stand back there.'

The bolts were drawn, the gate swung in. There were four guards on duty; two of them stood with their rifles pointing into the compound, while the other two accompanied Edward, their rifles slung, one of them carrying a lantern. This he gave to Edward as they approached the Americans. 'Hold it high,' he said, and stooped over Reynolds.

Edward swung the lantern with all of this strength. It caught the man across the side of the head in the same instant as the glass shattered and the paraffin ignited, exploding his hair into a spume of flame. He screamed as he fell to the ground, throwing his rifle away. Edward had already levelled his revolver and squeezed the trigger, shooting the second guard in the chest.

'Get the others,' Edward shouted, throwing himself to the ground behind the fallen body,

281

and emptying the revolver at the gate. The two remaining soldiers returned fire, but had little to aim at in the sudden darkness, while their position was clearly delineated by the gleam of the steel gate uprights. And now Malewski and Trethowan had seized the discarded rifles and were pumping bullets in that direction as fast as they could load.

The guards ceased firing, but the entire encampment was a huge buzz of sound, as the prisoners were awakened as well as the rest of the soldiers.

'Now,' Edward shouted. 'Now's our time.'

He leapt to his feet, ran at the gates, expecting at any moment to be cut down by a bullet. But both the guards were dead. He paused long enough to pick up their rifles and drag off their bandoliers, and was then running towards the embankment, aware that Dolores was at his shoulder, and that Malewski and Trethowan and Reynolds were immediately behind him. And also that the rest of the prisoners were following them out of the camp, shouting and cheering. Which was as he had intended. The soldiers hurrying from their tents began to fire into the main mass of fugitives rather than the five who were out in front. They scrambled up the embankment and down the other side with only stray shots coming behind them.

'Free,' Dolores screamed. 'Free!'

Ahead of them lay only the trees, and the jungle.

They panted, gasped, and staggered, fell to their knees, tore their flesh on thorns and swinging branches, slapped at mosquitoes and stinging ants, stumbled into water, unknowing whether or not it contained snake or alligator. They followed Edward, as if he knew where they were going. But occasionally, through the trees, he could see the stars, and at least he knew he was leading them in a generally easterly direction, towards the sea. And the *Penelope*.

That was all the hope they had. And it was a slim one. By dawn they were too exhausted to go any further. But at least by dawn he reckoned they had thrown off their pursuers, if there had ever been any.

He stopped walking and sank to his knees, and his companions did the same. But not the girl. She went on a few more steps, and then came back to them. 'There is water,' she said. 'We must drink.'

He crawled forward, followed by the others and lay on the edge of the little stream, and drank. It was the cleanest water he had tasted in two years. He drank until he could drink no more, then lay down, his eyes flopping shut. He could not even think, he was so exhausted.

When he awoke the sun was high, and penetrating even the foliage, to warm his body. And there was something resting against him. He sat up in alarm, reaching for the nearest rifle, saw that it was a pile of fruit, most of which

283

he had never seen before. He picked up one large yellow apple-like ball, cautiously bit into the skin, spat it out as it was bitter, but discovered underneath the most delicious pulpy yellow flesh.

Dolores smiled at him. 'It is called a golden apple,' she explained. 'And here are mangoes, and sapodillas, and bananas. All good to eat.'

He shook his companions awake, to share his feast with him, to feel the strength flooding back into their muscles. And to watch the girl.

She had moved a few yards downstream from them, and knelt in the water to bathe, and rinse her hair. She did this over and over again, with luxurious patience, slowly extracting all the filth which had accumulated during the previous fortnight, moving from hair to body to groin to feet, totally immersing herself before once again kneeling and resuming her delicious chore. Watching her made him aware of his own filth, just as watching her naked body made him aware of other things he had not known for too long. As he knelt beside her he experienced his first erection in more than a year.

'You will soon be strong again,' she said.

'Thanks to you,' he said. 'You have saved our lives.'

'And also my own,' she reminded him. 'When you reach your ship, will you take me with you, Senor Captain Anderson? To America?'

284

'I will take you wherever you wish to go,' he said.

'Then take me now,' she said. 'Please. Make me feel a woman again, and not a toy. That way you will save *my* life.'

They went a little way into the forest. None of the other four made any comment. He presumed that only Malewski might possibly be in any condition to emulate him. But that was a question for afterwards. Because here was a sensation he had forgotten existed, the burning heat of a woman's loins, of his own, the touch of her lips, the stroking of her tongue, the eternal splendour of feeling a woman's naked breasts against his own, of sifting his fingers through her hair.

'I took a knife from one of the guards,' she said later. 'I will cut your hair and beard.'

She cut all of their hair and beards, as best she could, and then shaved their chins. They stared at each other in amazement; they had almost forgotten what they looked like. She infected them with her own confident composure; they could no longer doubt that she would see them fed until they reached the coast.

That was Edward's responsibility. But suddenly he shared her confidence. Refreshed, rested, fed and washed, they resumed their march in the afternoon, away from the setting sun, towards the *Penelope*.

The mood of euphoria did not last. The sudden intake of fresh fruit gave them all diarrhoea, left them weaker than before. They were further away from the coast than they had supposed, and the country grew increasingly swampy; they spent most of their time wading thigh- and waist-deep in muddy water, their bodies infested with bloodsucking leeches. There were no more clear running streams, no more delicious baths, and as the realisation of the immense task they faced grew upon them, no more delicious moments in the forest, either. And by the second evening after their escape, it became plain that Reynolds could go no further.

He lay and panted, his skin drawn so tight over his bones that it seemed no more than a covering of thin paper. 'You must leave me, Captain,' he gasped. 'You'll never make it, with me along.'

They had found a momentarily dry piece of ground, a hummock in the surrounding swamp. 'We'll rest here for the night,' Edward decided. 'And tomorrow we'll make up a litter. We'll not leave you, old friend.'

'He is dying,' Dolores said, lying with her head nestled into his shoulder as she liked to do.

'No doubt you're right,' Edward said. 'But he will die in the Lord's good time. Not ours.'

He slept, and awoke to the sound of a rifle shot, realising what had happened even before

286

he reached his feet.

'He was a brave man,' Malewski said.

'And a faithful one,' Edward agreed.

Trethowan and Jehu said nothing at all. They could not even bury him, could only walk away from his body. Now they no longer smiled. Edward found himself filled with a deadly, implacable anger, a resolve that when he had sailed the *Penelope* back to Charleston he would raise a private fleet and a private army, if he had to, and return here to settle with William Walker, just as he would discover who had financed him and deal with them as well. He would see them all hang, in revenge for all the misery they had inflicted. The hatred, the obsession, became a driving force even greater than the will to escape, urged him onwards, enabled him to lead his companions onwards, although even Dolores was now beginning to flag.

But on the fourth day they found themselves on the banks of the Escondida and that afternoon they came in sight of El Bluff, with Bluefields waiting on the further bank. And the *Penelope*. Or part of her. What they saw was a burned out hulk sunk beside the quay.

CHAPTER 8

'What can have happened to her?' Malewski asked in bewildered horror.

'They have burned her,' Edward said. His heart seemed to have slowed. He lacked the strength even to think. Trethowan sank to his knees and burst into tears, while Jehu stood with bowed shoulders.

Dolores stared at the ship, and then the town, frowning. 'We will find friends here,' she said.

'Friends? In Nicaragua?'

She pointed. 'That is not Walker's flag. That is the old flag.'

Edward squinted in the glare, at the red and blue bunting floating in the breeze. 'By God,' he said. 'You're right. El Bluff must have been taken by counter revolutionaries.'

Once again he found life, the power to move, to plod through the trees, carrying Trethowan now, between himself and Malewski, until they were stopped by the click of a rifle bolt. 'Who comes?'

'Dolores de Soto,' Dolores called. 'And Captain Edward Anderson. And others. Escaped from the prison at Ramo.'

The picquet showed themselves, half a dozen

men. 'You have escaped from the prison at Ramo?' they asked. 'No one has ever escaped from that prison.'

'We have done so,' Dolores said. 'Who is your leader?'

'General Chamorro.'

'Frutos Chamorro? I know him well.'

'I know him also,' Edward said, having met the liberal leader when he had last been in Managua. 'He will help us.'

The picquet conferred amongst themselves, then gave the five fugitives an escort. It was a walk of about half a mile, through very well-prepared defences, before they arrived at a ferry across the river to Bluefields, which wore the appearance of a military encampment; the rebel force—or the loyalists, Edward supposed, depending on one's point of view—could hardly number less than two thousand men, and were well armed with rifles, and even a battery of four cannon.

'Anderson? You are Edward Anderson?' Frutos Chamorro was a heavily built man, with a walrus moustache. 'We had heard you were dead.'

'Not quite,' Edward said. 'Although most of my men are.'

'And you have walked fifty miles through the jungle? My God!' He gazed at their scratched and torn bodies, their blistered feet, their scanty clothing. 'You must have food, and drink, and medical attention...'

'And a hot bath,' Dolores said. 'How I would like a hot bath. Will you share my bath with me, Senor Captain Anderson?'

But already the sense of isolation from human affairs which had threatened to overwhelm him during the past two years was beginning to fade. Life was beginning, all over again. 'What happened to my ship?' he asked.

'I do not know for sure,' Chamorro said. 'I think they tried to sail her, the rebels that is, but when they could not get the engine to work, they burned her. We found her like that when we captured these towns, two months ago.'

'Do you hold much territory?'

'Only a few square miles. But we are consolidating. These arms were brought in from Honduras. They wish to support us against Walker.'

'Do you ever have ships calling here from the United States?'

'No, senor,' Chamorro said. 'If we had help from the United States, we would have finished with Walker before now. There *were* American ships here, but they were trading with Walker. When we took over the town they stopped coming.'

'These ships,' Edward said. 'Do you know which port they came from, in America?'

'Why, senor, they came from Charleston, like yourself. The Meigs-Driscoll Line they sailed for.'

'The *what?*' Malewski shouted.

The Meigs-Driscoll Line,' Chamorro repeated. 'I understood it is the major shipping company in the southern United States. But as I said, they stopped coming four months ago, when we gained possession of the port. But I think maybe we can ship you to Honduras, and thence to Mexico, and thence to your country. It will be a long journey, but you will be going home.'

A long journey, Edward thought. And what did he have to go home for, now? The Meigs-Driscoll Line. So Jonathan, and Penny and Mrs Meigs had sent to inquire after him, and been told he was dead, and no doubt, that their ships had all been commandeered or destroyed. They had gone into partnership with Henry Driscoll. It was unbelievable, but it was true. And why should Henry wish to be partner to Jonathan Meigs, a man without ships, with very little money, in shipping terms, and with nothing else at all. Save a sister.

There could be no doubt what had sealed *that* partnership.

A partnership which had even embraced his son, as he was to all intents and purposes a Meigs? But did he have a son? Could he have a son, after the boy had spent two years as a Driscoll?

And under Henry's influence they had even been prepared to trade with Walker. The man Henry had supported from the beginning? He

291

did not know that for sure. But he meant to find out. Some day.

But there were so many people to be dealt with, and Henry must wait. With Penny. Because he did not know *how* to deal with her. He knew only hatred, and anger, and lust for revenge. And here in Nicaragua was one object upon which he could fasten that hatred and anger.

'You mean to fight Walker?' he asked.

'Of course. He is a tyrant. We will bring him down.'

Edward looked at the burned out hulk of the *Penelope*, and listened to the sound of Dolores splashing in her hot bath in the next room, waiting for him.

'Then we will help you, General Chamorro,' he said. 'To bring him down.'

Frutos Chamorro sat his horse and studied the distant bridge through his binoculars, for several minutes, before handing the glasses to Edward. 'It is a strong position,' he remarked.

Edward looked at the bridge. It had been left intact, enticingly enough. A bait to lure them to the assault. But beyond, he could see the earthworks and the cannon, emplaced amongst the trees. Walker had chosen the strongest possible position for a decisive encounter; his right wing was protected by the river, broad and deep; his front was protected by the tributary stream, neither wide nor deep, but

292

sufficiently both to slow and disorganise any charging force, and his left wing rested on the swamp.

And once, in their optimistic ignorance, the patriotic commanders had supposed the American adventurer lacked the will to fight. In the early days, a year ago, they had supposed an assault on Bluefields was imminent. Then they had trained, and prepared their defences, and recruited their army...and argued amongst themselves. They might have been doing it yet had not Edward bullied them into marching on Managua.

When he had determined to settle with Walker before anyone else, he had not considered spending the rest of his life in Nicaragua. And certainly the time was right. From all over the country there were coming reports of discontent and misery under the harsh rule of the dictator, of people being shot and imprisoned without trial...but they had remained the only organised force capable of resistance, and they were cooped up in Bluefields. Surely, he had said over and over again, at every council meeting, and with greater vehemence as his health and strength had returned, if we were to march on him, rallying the country to our cause...he will fight, if we march on Managua, their fainter hearts had complained. Can you hope to crush him, without fighting? Edward had demanded.

So, at last, they had marched, made their way

through the forest to the road, taken the road for Managua...and encountered no opposition at all. The men had laughed and cheered as they had marched, and certainly they had attracted a large number of willing volunteers, young men anxious to leave their farms for the glory of a campaign. But these were a rabble who would have done more harm than good to the cause of freedom, Edward had insisted, and be useless when it came to fighting; the volunteers had been sent home again. For victory they must rely on their fifteen hundred well-trained and equipped men, and their four cannon. And now these men had come face to face with their foe.

'How many people does he have, do you think?' Chamorro asked.

'To hold that position, that frontage, in any strength,' Edward said, 'not less than two thousand.'

'He will certainly also have a reserve,' said Colonel Esteban. 'Perhaps another five hundred men. They outnumber us by nearly two to one, and we must do the attacking? That is madness.' Esteban had always been one of the doubters.

'We must outmanoeuvre him,' Chamorro said. 'A holding attack here in front, and a main attack through the swamp.'

'The swamp?' Esteban said. 'That also is madness. We will never keep control of our men, even if we can get through at all.'

For only the first time in the year he had known the man, Edward found himself in agreement. 'If we flank him,' he said. 'It must be by the river.'

'The river?' They stared at him in bemusement.

'We have boats,' Edward said. 'Sufficient to carry a couple of hundred men.'

'And will they not see you, and shoot you to pieces?' Esteban demanded. 'Men in boats are the easiest of targets.'

'Not if we go upstream by night,' Edward said.

'At night? On the river? That way implies even more certain catastrophe than through the swamp. How will you see where you are going? And there are too many sandbanks for navigation in the dark. While if you show a light you will be seen.'

'I will lead the boats,' Edward said. 'We will be in position, half a mile behind Walker's lines, by dawn tomorrow. You must commence firing as soon as the darkness begins to fade. And begin your assault at first light.' He looked around the frowning, anxious faces. 'We came here to fight, senors. And win. And thus free Nicaragua. All we now need is courage.' And enough hatred, he thought, not to care whether we live or die.

'I will come with you,' Dolores announced. She very seldom left his side, had assumed almost a position of his wife. And in fact, she had become a necessary part of his life.

He kissed her on the forehead. 'You'll stay here,' he told her. 'I will see you tomorrow, after we have won.'

'But Edward,' she protested. 'If you are killed, what will I do?'

'Find yourself another man,' he suggested and went to the boats, where two hundred men waited, hand-picked from amongst the motley force of patriot insurgents. And here too were Malewski and Trethowan, and Jehu, prepared to follow him yet again. From sailors they had become desperate fighting men, who already had blood on their hands, and were soon to have more. Like him, they each wore a sabre, and carried a revolver hanging from their belts.

Jehu was also armed, and ready. After all they had experienced together, it no longer seemed the least incongruous to arm a slave, and have him as a comrade rather than a servant.

They possessed ten boats, a local form of large canoe called a *pirogue*, each capable of holding twenty men. And the night was dark as pitch. Edward had the boats roped together, stern to bow, in a long line, took his place in the bows of the lead craft, Jehu at his side. Malewski commanded the last boat, Trethowan was in the centre. 'No speaking now,' Edward said. 'Just follow my lead. And no firing, no matter who fires at us.'

Chamorro and Esteban and their officers stood on the bank to watch them leave, instantly disappeared into the gloom. The paddles rose and fell rhythmically, seeming from close at hand to make a great deal of noise, but in reality a gentle slither of sound, far quieter than rowing boats could ever be, mingling with the rustle of the wind in the trees, and the whisper of the river itself. Edward Anderson, he thought, going forth to do battle, with men, where before he had only ever engaged the wind and the sea. Yet he felt the same sense of exhilaration as when he had grasped the spokes of the wheel on his ship and had seen the breaking water to either side, the gale whistling.

Slowly the flotilla made its way upstream. Edward had led them across the river to the far side, guided them by staring into the darkness until he could make out the deeper gloom of the trees. Twice they ran aground, and the boats cannoned into each other with loud thumps. There was some swearing, but all in low tones, and no panic; they trusted their American commander. Edward himself jumped over the side of the lead boat and was waist-deep in the swirling current, careless of piranha fish or lurking alligator, because this night he was careless of life itself—he had waited too long to launch himself at Walker's throat—and led them back to the channel.

There came a challenge from across the river.

It was repeated a moment later, and someone fired into the darkness. 'No reply,' Edward said.

They went on paddling, listened to a good deal of noise and shouting and some more shots, and then to the sound of hooves. Walker was sending back a patrol of mounted men to check the banks. But Edward reckoned they had gone far enough. Carefully he lowered the grapple he had prepared over the bow and into the water, while his men stopped paddling and let the stream carry the boats backwards. Soon the anchor gripped on the mud of the river bottom, and they lay silently, immediately upstream of the enemy position, he estimated.

Now was the most difficult part of the operation, as his men had to sit tight for more than an hour, while the mosquitoes tore at them and their own apprehensions mounted. But Malewski and Trethowan kept them well in hand, and it seemed no time at all before the first flicker of light appeared in the sky and the guns began to roar.

'Give way,' Edward said. 'Pass the word. Give way.'

He heaved up the anchor, and the *pirogues*, cast adrift from each other, surged in a line across the river and into the slowly growing light, their shouts drowned by the cacophony arising from the bridge. The boats slid into the shallows by the far bank and Edward leapt ashore, crashing through the bushes. He was instantly met by a belated challenge; the patrols on the river side had been distracted by the assault coming from behind them. 'Nicaragua,' he shouted, giving the agreed password, and at the same time bringing up his revolver to shoot the man at point-blank range.

A quick glance behind him assured him that all his men were ashore, and he holstered the revolver and drew his sword instead, waving it above his head. 'Follow me,' he shouted, realising with a start that he had never wielded a sword in his life before.

The fire was slackening from in front of them, as the initial assault withdrew before the volley fire of Walker's well-entrenched soldiers. But now they were being challenged by other sentries, and a bugle call rang out to alert the enemy commanders that there was a sizeable force in their rear. Edward could hear orders being given, as he parted the bushes, stared into the gloom, and found himself on open ground, facing a town of tents and picketed horses, moving restlessly to the sound of the rifles. And here a force was being hastily assembled, riflemen being supported by a cannon, now being wheeled into position.

Beyond the camp he could make out the bridge through the tree fringe, and also the rifle pits dug in along the banks of the stream. Here was the decisive moment.

'Form line,' he shouted. 'Take aim. Hold

your fire for the command.'

His men lined up, marshalled by Malewski and Trethowan, their rifles presented, staring at their countrymen, now two hundred yards distant, also forming line. Edward gave them another couple of precious seconds to regain their breaths, then shouted, 'Fire!'

The explosions rippled down the line, smoke from their powder rising into the still dawn air. Much of the shooting was wild in the extreme, but several of the government troops went down, and their line dissolved into clumps of men.

'Now,' Edward shouted. 'Fix bayonets. Charge.'

He ran across the open ground, leaping the latrine trenches which had been dug behind the tents, watching men levelling their rifles and realised that for the first time in his life he was wondering what it would feel like to be hit—it had not seemed the least important during the brief exchange of fire in the prison camp—or even if he had already been hit and was unaware of it. But he was now up to them, swinging his sword left and right, scattering the two men nearest to him, gasping for breath and watching another man run at him also waving a sword, only to encounter his own point as he thrust, taking it in the chest. Blood spurted and coated Edward's hand and forearm. Some even splashed on to his face, while the force of the impact drove the sabre so deeply into the chest of the already-dead man that he lost his balance and himself fell to his knees. Yet the stumble no doubt saved his life, as he heard an explosion from very close, and almost felt the wind of the bullet passing over his head.

He dragged the sabre out of the corpse at his feet, swung it sideways, felt it jar as it cut through flesh and muscle and bone to bring another man heavily to the ground, and caught a blow himself on the back of the head which sent him tumbling forward, mind spinning into oblivion.

He was unconscious for only seconds, then was aware of being pulled to his feet by Malewski and of a sickening pain in his head, and blood running down his neck.

'Are you all right?' Malewski shouted.

'I don't know,' he admitted. 'What hit me?'

'A rifle butt. The fellow's dead.'

Jehu was swabbing his neck with a wet cloth. 'You going be all right, Mr Edward,' he said. 'It just a bash.'

Edward blinked, and drew a long breath, hearing his men cheering for the government troops were retreating on their comrades by the river. Yet would they soon rally again, if given the chance. For a moment he thought of retraining the abandoned cannon, then decided it would take too long, even had he possessed any gunners. He stooped to regain his sword and pointed it in front of him. 'Come along,' he called. 'We must charge them again.'

Yet were they on a suicide mission if Chamorro did not grasp the situation and order an all out assault across the stream. He ran forward and was met by a shattering volley from a concealed rifle trench. Instinctively he dropped to his knees; heard the shrieks of several of his people falling; looked left and right; watched Trethowan writhing on the ground, his entire shirt front a mass of blood. He crawled across to his friend and lifted his head. Trethowan's eyes were closed but he opened them at Edward's touch.

'I've got the answer, Ned,' he said. 'Two propellers, two engines. There's the answer. Two propellers.'

Then he died.

Edward wondered why *he* was still alive, why indeed all of his men were not being cut down, listened to the shouts coming from the bridge, the increasing snarl of musketry, and the deeper roar of the insurgents' cannon. A ball came tearing through the trees and he realised that they were in danger of being blown to pieces, but by their own people.

'Bugler,' he shouted. 'Sound the call.'

The notes rang out in the morning, while Edward gathered his men together. Not many more than a hundred, now, but sufficient to win the day. For the government forces were breaking as they had to face the stream again, conscious that a rebel company still remained behind them. Men were looking over their shoulders and hurrying for the doubtful safety of the swamp.

'Nicaragua,' Edward yelled. 'Nicaragua!' and ran forward, listening to the answering shouts coming from in front of him. But he sought Walker, charged towards a small group of horsemen which had hitherto been directing the battle but was now itself turning away from the fight in search of safety. 'Cas,' he shouted. 'To me. We want Walker. To me.'

He urged his weary legs onwards, dropped his sword to draw his revolver, now identifying his enemy. Walker's lean face contorted with anger as he gazed on the ruination of his brief empire, turned his horse and drove his spurs into the animal's flanks.

Edward fired, and the horse came down, crashing on to its knees and throwing Walker forward over its head. He struck the ground heavily, lay still for a moment, and then pushed himself to his feet, still staggering from the blow on his head.

Edward levelled the revolver. 'You'll surrender, Walker,' he said.

Walker gazed at him, lips drawn back in a savage grin. 'You, Anderson,' he said. 'Always you. I should've hanged you, three years ago.'

Edward's finger went white on the trigger at the memory, and Malewski touched him on the shoulder. 'He is not worth murder, Ned,' he said.

Edward lowered the gun, and Walker's smile

widened. His own hands hovered close to the pistol at his belt, but he made no move. 'Twenty thousand dollars for my life,' he said. 'You'll find gold in my saddle bag.'

'I'll give you your life, but not your freedom,' Edward said. 'If you'll tell me who financed you. Who made all of this possible.'

Walker appeared to consider the offer, and then looked past him. 'It is no longer your decision,' he said.

Chamorro's hat had been shot away and there was a sabre cut on his arm, which had been hastily bound up. Esteban was at his shoulder. Both were elated. 'The day is ours, utterly and completely,' he cried. 'They are routed.' He clasped Edward's hand. 'Thanks to you. Nicaragua is forever in your debt.' He looked at Walker. 'And now we have the tyrant himself.'

'He would bargain,' Edward said, the white heat suddenly faded from his mind as he looked at his beaten foe. He was aware only of exhaustion.

'I am sure he would,' Chamorro said. 'So we will not give him the chance. You stand before us, William Walker, a tyrant and a usurper, condemned by the god of battle. Have you anything to say in your defence?'

Walker looked at him, then at Edward, his face for a moment contorted with fear and the desire to live. Then he shrugged, and gave his twisted grin. 'I guess not,' he said.

'Take him away and shoot him,' Chamarro said.

The bands played, and the people of Managua cheered. No doubt, three years before, they had cheered William Walker just as vociferously, when he and his victorious army had entered the city. But he had proved just as much of a tyrant as all the previous Nicaraguan leaders, and now the people were again ready for a change. Frutos Chamorro was the man of the moment. Frutos Chamorro and his American sea captain friend, who had led the flanking movement in the great battle. They rode together, down the main street into the square to be blessed by the bishop on the steps of the cathedral, while young girls ran out from the crowd to throw rose petals before their horses' hooves.

Then it was time to listen to the plaudits of the city leaders, with difficulty restrained from smothering them in their joy. Chamorro made a speech, in which he promised good government and justice for all men—having a week before executed every one of Walker's officers that he could discover, without trial. But civil war, Edward reminded himself, is by its nature the most savage of conflicts. It was entirely possible that Chamorro would turn out to be an excellent president.

'What will you do?' the victorious general asked him. 'I would be more than pleased,

305

Nicaragua would be more than pleased, if you would remain here, Edward. Stay and become First Admiral of the Republic. We face the sea on both sides of our country. It is certainly necessary for us to have a navy. And you will command it, for the rest of your life. You have my word on that.'

Edward looked around the interested faces, dark-moustached and passionate, men who had supported Chamorro through thick and thin, but who were already whispering behind their hands, making plans for when he failed to succeed in everything he would attempt, as, being human, he must. Then he looked at Malewski, who was watching him. One of the only two survivors of all the men who had followed him so willingly. He picked out Jehu's familiar black face in the crowd.

'What will you do?' Dolores asked, lying in his arms as the night ebbed away and the cocks began to crow. 'I have heard it said you will stay here, and be admiral of our navy. I should like that. I should like that more than anything.'

'I am a sea captain,' he reminded her. 'Not an admiral. I fought because I had to. Now I wish to return to my profession. There are things to be done.'

Supposing they had not already been done, by someone else, during the years he had languished at Ramo.

She raised herself on her elbow. 'There is a woman you must go to,' she said.

He hesitated before replying. But was that not equally true? Even if he knew, almost certainly, that she had turned to Driscoll in his absence. But at least he must go and see, and see her, too, one more time. And then there was Robert. He had refused to consider the boy ever in the past out of anger at what his birth had cost and then out of despair at his own sense of failure. The boy would not even remember what his father looked like.

But Robert was at least a reasonable cause for what he knew he must do, before he could think of again picking up the threads of his life.

'I have a son,' he said.

'Then you have a wife?'

'My wife is dead.'

'But there is a woman,' she repeated intuitively.

Edward sighed, 'Yes,' he said. 'There is a woman. But I promised to take you with me, when I left Nicaragua. I will not break my word.'

'That was when Walker ruled,' she said. 'Nicaragua is my home. I would share it with you, Edward. I would not share you with another woman.' Her turn to sigh. 'Go home to her, Edward. If she has waited for you, for four years, then she is worthy of your love. If she has not, then come back to me. I shall wait for you. For a year.'

307

Penelope Driscoll sat in the rose garden of Greenacres Great House and watched her children playing. Robert Anderson, busy with his lead soldiers, was eight years old. James Driscoll was two, and Yvonne was one; they could watch their elder companion, unable as yet to join in his manoeuvres. But she counted them all her children.

She spent a good deal of her time sitting here in the shade, watching the babies. She sometimes supposed they were her sole reason for living, and certainly she had entirely replaced her former active, enthusiastic lifestyle with her interest in them and her anxiety for their wellbeing. Because they were vastly more than she deserved.

She seldom dreamed, nowadays. It was not a luxury she dared permit herself. When she did she was forced to consider herself some latter day witch, not in any active sense, of curses and incantations, but in the utter disaster in which she had time and again involved all of those with whom she had come into contact, and attempted to love. But that was the easy way. The alternative, to which she was always led, was to recognise that all of those disasters had been brought about *by* her endless daydreams, which had led her into wilful selfishness, and this was unacceptable, to be combated wherever possible. But it could not be combated during her darkest midnight hours, when she lay beside a snoring Henry, and remembered that it had been her own determination to set her cap at Edward Anderson, and her determination to encourage Father to invest his last penny in the ship, and her determination to have it named after her, and her determination to accompany Edward on her maiden voyage—no matter what might have happened to Amanda, she could not escape the certainty that had she and her mother remained in Charleston, even the supposition that the *Penelope* had been lost at sea, with the financial disaster that entailed, would not have been sufficient to drive Father to suicide.

Then she had abandoned will and drifted, in a sea of futile anger, to be sure, but also supposing that by so doing she could end the dreadful cycle of catastrophe. As if she ever could, now. So, the *Penelope* was a burned-out wreck at the bottom of the Escondida River, according to the reports of Henry's sea captains, and Edward, by the same account, had died in attempting to defend her. Then indeed she had considered suicide herself. Only the presence of Robert, the assumption of full responsibility for him, had even preserved her sanity. That, and remarkably, the renewed badgering of Henry for her hand, and her body. She had remembered that she had once thought she deserved no one better than Henry Driscoll. And marriage to Henry had appeared to solve so many problems, not least the problem of money, and the future, for Jonathan and Mother. She had been able to bargain, and without pretence. She did not love Henry, and probably would never love him, and she had yielded up her virginity to the man he loathed above all others. Amazingly, he had not been concerned; Anderson was dead. He had offered her security and peace in exchange for the possession of her, and he had promised to bring Robert up as his own, just as he had offered Jonathan a seat on the board of the Driscoll Company. He had done better than that; the company had been retitled the Meigs-Driscoll line, an act of quite remarkable generosity, on the surface; only she and Mother and Jonathan knew that he had done his own share of bargaining, had insisted that, in return for the directorship, Jonathan should hand over all the remaining Meigs—Anderson assets, and not only their bank balance, effectively to make them utterly dependent on him, but also the plans for the *Penelope*. Henry had been pleased. He had scooped the pool, for the knowledge that she had once loved Edward. He had not realised that in marrying a succubus he was assuming her mantle of disaster. Thus he had built a sister ship to the *Penelope*, named her the *Priscilla Meigs*, and sent her to sea—and she had disappeared in a gale in the Gulf Stream with the loss of all on board. No one knew for sure what had happened, but there were mutterings that she had had too shallow a draft, and been carrying too much sail, and been generally unsafe. Everything, in fact, that had been said about Edward's ship before he had sailed her so triumphantly. But *she* could remember that it had been Edward's seamanship that had made the *Penelope* such a success, and that he had also had his doubts.

But Henry, undismayed, had then built the *Angela Driscoll*, named after his dead mother. The *Angela Driscoll* had actually made two Atlantic crossings, before her timbers opened up and she had foundered within sight of Fort Sumter, fortunately with little loss of life.

That second catastrophe had been sufficient even for Henry, although Penelope suspected that he had been appalled more by the loss of money than of life. The third ship in the class, to be called the *Yvonne Driscoll*, remained uncompleted in the yard. Yet had his misfortunes multiplied. With Jonathan's agreement—after considerable heartsearching—he had attempted to take over the Nicaragua trade route, using fast sailing ships, and dealing with the revolutionary leader down there, the American William Walker. If Walker could be held responsible, at least indirectly, for the loss of the *Penelope* and thus Edward's death, Henry pointed out time and again that business should never be confused by sentiment or personal feeling, and that Edward himself had made the Nicaragua trade route viable—it would be utterly senseless to sit back and let some other

311

shipping line scoop the pool. After all, he had insisted, revolutions in Central America were as much an occupational hazard as hurricanes, and one never took a personal dislike to the wind.

But was not the Nicaraguan revolution itself just an emanation of the contamination which spread over everything with which she had even the remotest contact? In any event, as a counter revolutionary movement had grown, the Meigs-Driscoll Line had been forced to abandon the project, and in fact as the whole shipping world was undergoing a trade recession, there were several ships lying idle in Charleston Harbour, while Henry had been forced to put a veto on *all* new building.

But he put no vetoes on any of *her* activities, should she ever reveal the wish for anything—which was seldom. Incredibly, after everything that had happened, he loved her. He adored her. He adored her to such an extent that she had been forced to respond, could even pretend to an eagerness to accept his embrace, and sometimes, even to orgasm. He was the most perfect and loving and attentive husband. It was merely his misfortune not to be Edward Anderson.

And he had given her James and Yvonne. In them she was finding more happiness than she had expected or deserved. But that was only another aspect of her evil influence, that she personally should be at least content, while so

312

much misery spread around her. She was almost able to see, in the increasing rancour between North and South, between slave state and free state, in the growing bloodshed along the Kansas-Missouri border, fresh aspects of her baneful power. It was not a question she truly understood. Her slaves had always been happy people. No doubt there had been occasional floggings and other punishments on the cotton plantation, and there were a great many cotton plantations—but there were floggings and other punishments, just for example, in the army. No one argued that there should not be an army, or that there was any way to have an army without severe discipline. The same thing surely applied to slavery. And economically, of course, the preachings of men like the Illinois lawyer, and now candidate for the Presidency, Abraham Lincoln, were absolute nonsense. She could not help but accept Henry's interpretation of the situation, that it was largely inspired by jealousy. The Southern States of the Union were a prosperous and contented rural society, in tremendously pleasant contrast to the industrial grime of the North, the hustle and bustle and anxiety of the Yankees.

But the trend, the possibility, that a man like Lincoln *could* be elected, if all the Northern States decided to support him, the certainty that should that happen he would seek to impose his concept of the United States upon all the South, was alarming. Men and women recalled the dictatorial tendencies of Andrew Jackson and recalled, too, that their fathers had been prepared to resist the encroachments of the Federal Government by force if necessary. Certainly both Henry and Jonathan were deeply concerned about the immediate future. They knew only too well that a clash between the government of the United States and that of South Carolina could only result in financial disaster for the Meigs-Driscoll Line.

Which would of course be but one more aspect of her ability to spread misery around herself.

She listened, to the sound of hooves, the shouts of excited grooms, turned her head and then got up, solemnly watched by her children. She faced the french windows which opened on to the lawn, saw her husband hurrying towards her. His face was white and his hair was dishevelled from hard and hatless riding.

'Henry?' she asked. 'What on earth has happened? Not another wreck?'

He panted, stopping in front of her. 'Anderson,' he said.

'Anderson?' Her heart seemed to slow. 'Edward Anderson? What about Edward Anderson?'

'He's here,' Henry gasped. 'He's here in Charleston. He's on his way here now, with Jonathan.'

'But...' she just could not take in what he had said. 'Edward is dead.'

'He's not dead,' Henry shouted. 'He's alive. He's...' he faced the house as they heard more hoofbeats.

Penelope forgot about the children, forgot even about her husband, gathered her skirts and ran for the house. In the hall she met her mother coming down the main staircase. 'Have you heard?' Priscilla Meigs shouted. 'Have you heard?'

'Yes,' Penelope said. 'Oh, yes.'

'Penny...' Priscilla said warningly, but Penelope had already run to the front door, to watch Jonathan and Edward coming up the stairs. Edward? Oh, it had to be Edward. The body was more spare and muscular than she remembered, and the fair hair had wisps of grey. And the face...it was Edward's face, but there were ridges of hardness at the corners of his mouth, and his blue eyes were like pieces of flint. 'Edward,' she whispered.

'Mrs Driscoll,' he acknowledged, his voice flat.

'The man himself,' Jonathan shouted. 'Back from the dead. The man himself.'

'Edward!' Priscilla Meigs threw herself into his arms. 'Oh, Edward.'

Edward kissed her on the forehead and gazed at Penelope over her head. She did not know what to say, or do, or even think. So she looked over her shoulder at Henry.

'Edward, my dear fellow.' Henry had got himself under control. But she found it difficult

315

to understand why he should have been so upset in the first place. She was *his* wife. For whatever might have happened in the past, it was Edward would have to bear the guilt. 'My God, but this is a happy day.' He had taken the additional precaution of arming himself with Robert. 'Rob, lad,' he said. 'This is your father.'

Edward at last looked away from Penelope, sank to his knees before the little boy. 'Robert,' he said.

Robert looked at Penelope.

'He is your father, Robert,' she said. 'Go to him. He *is* your father.'

Edward held the boy close, while they stood around them.

'Well,' Jonathan Meigs said. 'To have you back. There is so much...so much for you to tell us.'

'And so much for you to tell me,' Edward said, releasing Robert and standing again.

They looked at each other, and Priscilla Meigs assumed the duties of spokeswoman. 'It seemed to be the logical thing to do,' she said. 'To merge the two companies. Without your expertise, your drive, Edward...well, we needed all the help we could get.'

'We thought the Driscoll clippers and the Meigs steamships together...' Jonathan bit his lip. 'The Anderson steamships, I meant.'

'But they turned out badly,' Henry said. 'The whole steamship concept has turned out

316

to be a disaster. Collins has gone bankrupt...the government has withdrawn his subsidy, you know, because he lost two ships as well. Cunard is in financial straits, so I've heard...the *Great Eastern* has proved to be a complete white elephant...' he smiled. 'Well, we aren't exactly in clover ourselves. But we'll pull through. Of course there's a place for you on the Meigs-Driscoll Board, Ned. Oh, indeed. And a command, if you wish it.'

'I'm sure the last thing Edward wishes to discuss at this moment is business,' Priscilla said.

'On the contrary, Mrs Meigs,' Edward said. 'What else *is* there for me to discuss?'

Once again he was looking at Penelope.

'So now you're a famous general as well as a famous shipmaster.' Henry signalled his butler to refill Edward's brandy goblet, smiled down the length of the crystal laden dining table at his wife. 'My word. Did you actually see Walker?'

'I was present at his execution,' Edward said, gazing at him. 'But I had known him before. I carried him as a passenger, oh, nearly ten years ago, at the beginning of the gold rush.'

'Did you now,' Henry remarked, meeting his eyes. 'What a small world it is, to be sure. He must have been a remarkable fellow.'

'A remarkable scoundrel,' Jonathan Meigs said. 'I remember him too, from that first

317

voyage. We had to put him under restraint.'

'But he died well,' Edward said, still looking at Henry. 'He would not tell us the names of his backers. Because he certainly had them.'

'It all sounds so horrible,' Priscilla Meigs said. 'Civil war, murder, revolution, people being shot...did you really spend two years in a prison camp, Edward?'

'Two years, Mrs Meigs. And three months and four days.'

'But you survived, Edward,' Penelope said, softly. 'Oh, you survived.'

'While watching my men die, Mrs Driscoll, one after the other,' he said. 'And I would *not* have survived, but for the love of a woman.'

'Then shall we soon have another Mrs Anderson?' Henry cried. 'You must bring her to Charleston to be married, Ned. It will be a famous occasion. Now, tomorrow you must come down to the office, and we will get down to business. I have a clipper ship for you, Edward. What do you think of that? A clipper ship, presently trading between Charleston and San Francisco. It is a long voyage, but a profitable one. Although, you know, as you are such friends with the new president of Nicaragua, I look forward to having that route reopened. Oh, yes, indeed. I see a whole new chapter of prosperity opening in front of us.'

It was more than an hour before Penelope could find herself alone with him, by following him on to the porch as he smoked a

318

cigar, a *tête-à-tête* most surprisingly engineered by Henry, who engaged Jonathan in sudden conversation when he would have accompanied them.

'I think we are all still a little shocked,' she said. 'By the suddenness of your return. The joy of it.'

He turned his head, looked at her for several seconds. She had dressed with great care, wore a ball gown of white tarlatan with flounces and rosebud trimmings beneath an amber taffeta bodice and overskirt; her neck and shoulders were bare, and there were crimson roses in her hair. She might indeed have been dressed for a ball instead of a family dinner—Henry's eyebrows had arched when he had first seen her. And Edward had not seen her in more than three years.

Yet she would not have been able to say for sure *why* she had so dressed herself.

'Is it joy?' he asked at last.

She sighed. 'We thought you dead, Edward. We were told that, quite definitely. And all our ships were gone as well. Then Henry made us a very fair offer. What would you have had us do?'

'What sort of an offer did he make *you*? Apart from Greenacres?'

She did not reply, and in the darkness her expression was difficult to determine.

'I'm sorry,' he said. 'That was unfair.' He smiled, sadly. 'I have sometimes felt life to be
319

unfair, these last few years.'

'But...you said at dinner that you had found someone to love,' she said 'Will you not go back to her? Or bring her to Charleston?'

'I don't know,' he said. 'There are so many things I don't know. So many dreams I dream-ed...I am grateful to you, Penny, for caring for Robert.'

'I have adopted him,' she said. '*We* have adopted him,' she added. 'It seemed the best course. And he is welcome to stay here, until... until you have a home for him.'

'If you have adopted him,' he said. 'I have no rights to him.'

'It was done when we supposed you were dead, Edward,' she pointed out. 'He is your son. You have every right to him. Much as I have grown to love him, I would never stand in your way if you wished him back.'

'But as you say, I've no home to offer him.'

'You will have a home. Do you still dream of building great steamships?' she asked.

'Yes. That dream was all that kept me alive. That dream, and another. But the other has become a nightmare.'

They stood in silence for some moments, while a succession of the wildest thoughts raced through her brain. And, she hoped, through his as well. But he made no move towards her. It was she must surrender, and offer, and admit the guilt of having married. That was not something she could bring herself

320

to do. Certainly not so soon after his return. But would she ever dare act with such selfish abandon again? She was a wife and a mother.

She drew a long breath. 'We were not meant to love, Edward,' she said. 'When I made you love me, I committed a crime. I am only sorry, terribly sorry, that you should have been involved in my punishment.'

She went up to her room. Did she mean that? How could she possibly mean otherwise? He was alive, and safe. There was joy. But he was back to torment her mind, and her body. There was misery.

Henry stood behind her as she brushed her hair. 'Did he take you in his arms, tell you how much he loved you?'

She gazed at him in the mirror. But perhaps it was what he had actually anticipated would happen, hence his distraction at the news of Edward's return. Certainly there was no point in taking offence. 'No,' she said.

'Then what did you talk about? You spent a long time, out there.'

She shrugged. 'What he is going to do, in the main. Will you really offer him a ship?'

'Certainly. I think it is the least we can do for the poor fellow.'

'I think he would like to build again.'

'Now that is not possible, and you know it. Not in the present economic climate at any rate. And I suppose he is thinking of a steamship. I would not let him build one of those even if

321

we had the money. They were a flash in the pan. Believe me, even Edward will realise that when he sees all the facts and figures. Did he speak of Nicaragua at all? Of Walker?'

'Not of Walker.' She frowned into the mirror. 'Did you ever know him? Walker?'

'Of course not. What makes you think that?'

'You seem so interested in what he did, in what he might have said before he was executed.'

'Well...I corresponded with him, of course. When we were setting up the trade route. And I *am* interested. In what drives a man so hard. I think he was a fascinating character.' His hands rested on her shoulders. 'Do you still love him? Anderson?'

She turned her head to look into his face; it remained expressionless. 'I do not think it matters,' she said. 'Because he no longer loves me.'

'Our entire concept in the past has been wrong,' Edward declared, looking the length of the boardroom table at the three pessimistic faces. 'Steam is steam, and sail is sail. In trying to combine the two, we have been merely suffering the worst of both. Believe me, I know my design for the *Penelope* class was faulty. I realised it on her maiden voyage. The ship lacked both the stability to stand up to the North Atlantic, and the strength to stand up to being constantly driven at high speeds through rough seas, however successful she might have been

322

in the Gulf of Mexico.'

'Pity you didn't make that knowledge public,' said Peter Harman, the firm's attorney.

'I had not intended to build any more *Penelope*'s', Edward said, and looked at Henry, at the opposite end of the table. 'Nor could I have any idea that anyone would take over my design in my absence.'

Henry looked at Jonathan Meigs.

'That was my decision, Edward,' Jonathan said. 'And my mistake, I suppose. But the fact is, that Henry is quite right. Steamships have without exception proved financially disastrous to their builders and their owners, quite apart from the mere matter of lives being lost. Collins' ships cost over five hundred lives between them.'

'Cunard has never lost a life,' Edward said. 'And he is still operating.'

'Purely because of the mail subsidy being granted him by the British Government,' Henry said. 'As for these compound expansion engines you're speaking about, they've been tried. And sure, they cut coal consumption in half. But they're no more reliable than any other engine. If steam has a future anywhere, it's on inland water. Then when the engine breaks down you can just anchor and wait for help.' He smiled. 'That's not practical in the middle of an ocean. The man who goes to sea without sails is begging for trouble.'

'Sails would not be necessary,' Edward said. 'If you had twin screws.'

They stared at him.

'Two engines,' Edward said. 'Each driving a separate shaft and a separate propeller. So you'd always have one engine in reserve. You'd have to be damned unlucky to have both engines break down at the same time on the same voyage. And if you used them together, then you'd really have speed. While consider the manoeuverability you'd possess. It would be the same as twin paddlewheels, save that the propellers would be far safer and more efficient.'

'You'd tear your hull apart,' Harman objected.

'Not if you built in iron. And put in a double bottom,' Edward said.

The other three men gazed at each other.

'You're talking in terms of a hell of a lot of money,' Henry said.

'We'll also *earn* a hell of a lot of money.'

Henry shook his head. 'It's not a risk we can contemplate at this moment. Even if I believed it would work. And I don't.'

Edward looked from him, to Jonathan, who gave a helpless shrug. There was no use looking at Harman, who was Driscoll's creature.

So what was he doing here at all? He had not returned to Charleston to do business with Henry Driscoll. Even while the compliments had been flying last night, and the optimistic platitudes about the future, he had known in his heart he would not really get any support here, had been stupid to allow his dreams to take hold of him all over again. It would make far more sense, having seen the truth, having discovered that there could never be anything here for him again, for him to return to Managua, and Dolores' arms. However Trethowan had also dreamed, his plans had at least kept him from the uttermost dark pit of madness. It was unreasonable to ask anything more of dreams. Certainly he could never be brought back to life, any more than Penny could be regained. As she had truly said, they had not been meant by Fate to love, and no human beings can successfully confront Fate. As for Malewski and Jehu, they would follow him wherever he went, without question, whether it was into the uniform of a Nicaraguan admiral, or a Meigs-Driscoll shipmaster.

And all his life, all his mistakes, all his tragedies, from the cargo of wine onwards, and including Amanda, would have been meaningless, because he would have accepted defeat. From a man he in any event suspected of having been one of Walker's backers, and who had robbed him not only of his shipping firm, but of the only woman he could ever love. Because there it was. He owed Dolores his life, and she would make him a good wife, he had no doubt at all. But he would never love her, not after having seen once again the consuming beauty, and remembered the supressed passion, that was Penelope Meigs.

Penelope Driscoll!

He realised, perhaps for the first time with absolute honesty, how badly he wanted her, and as he could not have her, then how badly he wanted to oppose Henry, on common ground. And crush him. And that could only be done, effectively and completely, by means of one of those other beautiful, wooden or steel ladies which ruled their lives.

'Then I'll build her myself,' he said.

'What with?' Henry demanded.

'Where?' Jonathan asked. He had taken no part in the discussion, but that he was also entirely on Henry's side could not be doubted. But Jonathan had always possessed an easy facility for supporting what he supposed was the main chance.

'I'll go back to Bartell,' Edward said. 'As for money, half the capital I left when I was taken prisoner by Walker was mine, as I had a half share in the Meigs-Anderson Line.'

'All that capital, including the bank balances, was taken over when we absorbed the line,' Harman pointed out.

'I was not a party to that agreement,' Edward said, 'nor do I propose to be a party to it now. By my reckoning you owe me three hundred thousand dollars, Jonathan. I'll be obliged if you'd let me have your cheque.'

Jonathan looked at Henry, who gave a deprecating smile. 'Now, really, Ned, let us be sensible about this. Where do you suppose we can lay our hands on three hundred thousand dollars, just like that? And do you think we really want to see you going out and ruining yourself over some damn fool idea? You have a seat on this board, and the mastery of the finest ship we possess. You also have an urgent task awaiting you, in re-establishing the Nicaraguan route. And you have your Spanish senorita to marry. What more can you reasonably ask?'

'You can keep your directorship, and your clipper, Henry,' Edward said. 'And you can re-open the Nicaraguan route, if you can. There are dead men to whom I owe too much just to let their memories fade away.' He got up, pointed the length of the table. 'You find that money, Jonathan. I've a ship to build.'

'Two engines, two screws.' Bartell pulled his nose. 'And in iron. There's a tall order, Edward. Exciting, mind. But expensive.'

'We'll find the money, Bartell,' Edward said. 'We'll get it, if I have to take Jonathan Meigs to court.'

'Yes,' Bartell said, doubtfully. 'Oh, I'll go along with you, Edward. You built the finest steamship in the world once before. You'll do it again, I have no doubt. You say Mr Elder himself will come over to help with the engine installation?'

'You read his letter,' Edward said. 'He's as excited about the project as I am.'

'Then I'll get to work,' Bartell said. 'Ordering the iron. By God, it'll be like old times.'

'Aye,' Edward said. 'Like old times.'

He left the office, paused for a moment to look at the almost derelict shipyard—for like most other yards Bartell's had been feeling the pinch—and then went down the stairs to where Jehu waited with the horses, and where there also waited a gig, in which sat Penelope Driscoll and Robert Anderson.

'I was told I'd find you here,' she said. 'Robert had hoped we'd receive another visit from you, before now.'

Edward raised his hat. 'I'd not supposed I would be welcome at Greenacres,' he said.

'Because you are suing Jonathan for your share of the Anderson Line profits? I think you are entirely justified. Will you ride with us?'

He gazed into those amber eyes. What devilment was she up to now? She was a wife and a mother, the legal and sexual partner of a man he knew to be his rival, and suspected of far more than that. It was impossible for her not to share Driscoll's secrets, while she remained in his house, and at his side.

Besides, to ride with her, to sit beside her, to allow himself to touch her, would be once again to find himself on that slippery path down which he had slid so dizzily once before.

'No,' he said. 'I will not ride with you, Mrs

Driscoll. But I'd be grateful if you'd leave Robert for a while, and we will talk, about sea and ships. Jehu will return him to Greenacres in time for supper.'

Henry Driscoll stamped into the hallway of Greenacres Great House, threw his hat to a waiting slave, dropped his gloves and stick on a table and walked towards the gardens at the rear. Because *she* would be there. Waiting. For him? It could not be anyone else.

Except in her mind. He did not doubt that. He had never doubted that; he had no objection to her dreaming of dead men while she yielded her body to his living one. Walker, he thought. God damned Walker. Walker had sworn that Anderson was dead. But Walker had sworn so many things. And now he was shot, himself.

Had he told any tales? Anderson undoubtedly suspected much of the truth. Henry had a notion that Anderson had suspected ever since that attempt at piracy. But he could prove nothing, and with Walker dead he would never be able to prove anything. Yet *was* he proving himself to be an implacable and determined foe, prepared to fight on any ground, from the courts to the shipyard. And who could be sure he would not win, in both places? The ship he talked about was like something out of an overwrought imagination, but if anyone could make it work, Anderson would. Then why not...

He shook his head, as if that would clear his

mind. The temptation had to be resisted. He had taken that path twice before, and accomplished nothing, gained nothing save a perpetual headache. Besides, trusting other people, using other people, was to make himself too vulnerable. He had hardly slept a full night since first employing Walker. A hired assassin...

It was not a matter of conscience. At least it had not been, up to now. Business, love, life itself, was a matter of survival. Edward Anderson was a man who seemed destined to block his path wherever he had turned. He had never *meant* the fellow any physical harm, just intended him to be removed from competition with himself. But yet he had been greatly relieved to learn that he *was* dead. As he should have died. As he might still die. But those were unthinkable thoughts. It was far better to use the weapons *he* had to hand, and he was not bereft. Especially now. He wondered what Anderson, a Northerner, would be thinking at this moment?

He saw the children, and his wife, seated beneath a huge parasol and wearing a broad brimmed hat; it was being a bright and delightful November.

She looked up. 'Why, Henry. You're home early.'

'The results have just come through,' he announced. 'Lincoln has been elected.'

She frowned. 'But...I thought you said that

was not possible?'

'Of course it was possible.' Henry sat beside her on the bench. 'If all the Northern States voted for him. And they did. He didn't get a single vote in the South. But that doesn't alter the fact that next March he is going to be the President of the United States.'

'My God,' she said. 'But...what are we going to do?'

'Secede,' he said.

Her mouth sagged open. 'Secede? South Carolina is going to leave the Union?'

He waved his arm. 'Not just South Carolina. Virginia, North Carolina, Georgia, Alabama, Louisiana, Mississippi, Texas...all of us are going to leave the Union. There's been a meeting of delegates called to settle the matter.' He inhaled, importantly. 'I've been invited to attend, as one of the representatives from Charleston.'

'My God,' she said again. 'But...won't that be rebellion?'

'They can call it what they like. We shall be our own country. We've been chased by those northern bullies for too long. We'll show them.' He pointed. 'You'd best get rid of that Yankee bastard for a start.'

Her chin came up. 'You'll not touch Robert, Henry. We have adopted him, and he is our son no matter what happens. It was part of our bargain.'

'Our bargain,' he sneered. 'Because you're

331

still in love with Edward Anderson. And you reckon as long as that boy stays here you must see him, from time to time.'

She stared into his eyes, refusing to admit her guilt. 'If you wish to believe that, Henry,' she said. 'then you are welcome. But I am *your* wife, and that is *our* son, whether he came from my womb or not.'

'Yes,' he agreed. 'And you'd best not forget it.' He pointed again. 'Well you can tell the boy that he won't be seeing too much of his father, from now on.'

John Elder turned out to be an amazingly young Scotsman, only in his middle thirties, but the possessor of a remarkably controlled enthusiasm and a tremendous knowledge of engines.

'This is my first visit to America, ye'll understand,' he told Edward. 'A great country. Oh, indeed a great country.. But fighting over black people...' he glanced at Jehu. 'Ye'll take no offence, old fellow. But I'm no believer in civil war.'

'Neither are most Americans, Mr Elder,' Edward said. 'So we've a new president who says some hard things about the way of life down here. We've had presidents like that before. And there's been talk of secession before. But we've a way of compromising those issues, in the United States. You're here to tell me about engines.'

'Engines,' Elder agreed. 'Engines.' His eyes gleamed as he entered the building shed and gazed at the keel of the *Amanda*. 'That's a big ship, Mr Anderson.'

'She's going to be three hundred feet in length, and have a beam of forty,' Edward said. 'Is it sufficient for you?'

'Oh, indeed, sir. Indeed. Ye'll understand I've never built engines to that scale before. Ye'll be thinking of two thousand horsepower and more.'

'But you can do it?' Edward asked.

'Oh, aye, the formula is the same.'

'And your engines have been tested?' Malewski asked.

'Oh, aye. They were used on gunboats in the Crimea, during the war. Successfully too. And they're in general use for the Cross Channel packets, over in Europe. They've never crossed the Atlantic, yet. But they will, sir. They will. And I'd be happy were they to do so for the first time in this ship. Oh, aye. But... they're not cheap. Not at that size.'

'That's not a cheap ship, Mr Elder,' Edward said. 'She is going to be the last word in luxury. We're aiming for the top passenger trade as well as the best freight trade. And to do that we not only have to offer comfort, but we have to guarantee delivery, and quicker than anybody else. I'm looking for a cruising speed of fifteen knots.'

'Aye, well, as I was saying, that'll be costly.

Would it be too much to inquire the name of your backers?'

'I'm financing the ship myself,' Edward said.

The Scot raised his eyebrows. 'Entirely by yourself, sir?'

'That is correct.'

'There's a risk. I'll have to be uncommonly impertinent, and ask you for guarantees.'

'You shall have them. I have the capital, sir.' Edward said. 'Or I will have it. I have just won a law suit against my former partner in the amount of three hundred thousand dollars, the money to be paid over four years in quarterly instalments of eighteen thousand seven hundred and fifty dollars. My partner is now a partner of the Meigs-Driscoll Line, so there can be no question of his ability to meet these payments. I have already reached agreement with my bankers, and if you will accompany me to see them tomorrow morning, they will supply you with whatever financial guarantees you may require. I intend the *Amanda* to be the finest ship in the world. And the first ever to be designed for steam alone. She will make your fortune, Mr Elder.'

'Indeed she will,' Elder agreed. 'A bold concept, sir. A bold concept. Well, I'll get down to my plans. Indeed, I will. You'll have your fifteen knots, sir, I promise you that. Now...' he looked at the door as there came the sound of cannon fire from down river. The men, and the workmen, ran outside on to the river bank,

334

stood on the slipway to look at the distant houses of Charleston. Now they could see the smoke clouding into the air, and now too they could see the vessel flying the Stars and Stripes which had been about to enter the harbour, putting about and returning to sea.

'In the name of God, what has happened?' Bartell demanded.

They watched a horseman spurring towards them.

'We've done it,' the man bawled, as he approached the shipyard. 'We've done it. We've shown those damn Yankees.'

'Done what?' Edward demanded, running into the road to catch the man's bridle and bring him to a temporary halt.

'The battery down at the harbour,' the man panted. 'It fired on the *Star of the West* when she attempted to enter, with supplies for Fort Sumter.' He threw his hat in the air. 'She turned tail and ran. You can still see her, beating out to sea.'

'You fired on a Federal warship?' Malewski was aghast. 'But...that's rebellion.'

'Rebellion hell,' the man shouted, and pulled his bridle free, anxious to continue on his way, spreading the news up the river. 'We've declared war.'

CHAPTER 9

The cannon roared, and the crowds lining the waterfront of Charleston Harbour cheered their gunners. The shooting was remarkably accurate, thought Edward Anderson. The balls screamed through the air, dotted the sea around Fort Sumter, plunged into the island itself. Already flames and smoke were issuing from the roofs of the buildings; telescopes had become the most valuable article to possess in the city, were being passed from hand to hand.

'Great stuff, eh, Edward? Great stuff?' Old John Dart, retired from business now, pushed his way through the throng.

Edward shook his hand. 'I hope these people will think so, Father, in a year's time.'

John Dart grinned at him. 'In a year's time we shall be recognised and established,' he said. 'The Confederate States of America. Lincoln is all bluff and bluster. The people in the North won't fight for him.'

'You had best pray you are right, Father.' Edwards said, and walked away. There could be no going back now. To fire on a warship, to band together and declare secession from the United States, to shout and rave...these were all matters which could have been resolved by compromise and diplomacy. Even to fire upon a Federal fort on Sumter *might* have been capable of a peaceful resolution. But this bombardment was being pushed home, and the return fire from the fort was weakening. Soon Major Anderson would be forced to surrender, and the people of Charleston would have a great victory to celebrate. While the people of the North went to war.

'What will you do?' Malewski asked.

What will I do, Edward thought? I am forty years of age, a man who time and again has grasped at success, at triumph, but who has never properly secured his hold. And now the possibility of triumph had once again been torn from his grasp, for the foreseeable future. There could be no more payments from the Meigs-Driscoll Company in time of war, and in any event there could be no more men and materials available for building the *Amanda*, while South Carolina was fighting for its very life. She must remain in Bartell's yard, a keel and a dream...for how long? Elder had already taken himself home to Scotland.

'Father! Father! Isn't it grand?'

His head jerked, and he gazed at Robert, sitting in the gig beside his adoptive mother. Penelope's face was tight, but only at the sight of Edward. Her eyes sparkled, and there were pink flushes in her cheeks. She too was carried away by the excitement of it, the glory of it. The exhilaration of actually being present for the first shots of the war.

Because she had never experienced war. Neither she, nor any other of these cheering women had ever known the horror of being thrown into a prison camp with forty sex-starved men. So this was the United States, and not Nicaragua. Who could say what passions would be released by today's bombardment?

Malewski had tactfully wandered away. Edward leaned into the gig as he raised his hat. 'Yes, Robert,' he said, and ruffled the boy's hair. 'It is grand.' He looked at Penelope. 'So your husband and his warlike friends have had their way, Mrs Driscoll.'

'They are defending the way of life their forefathers created, Captain Anderson,' she said. 'There can be nothing dishonourable about that.'

'None indeed,' he agreed. 'But it is sometimes a painful process.' He realised that the carriage had been surrounded by a crowd of men, turned his head to send them away.

'There's the Yankee bastard,' someone drawled.

'Aye, that's the scoundrel,' bawled someone else.

'Lynch the rat,' came the cry.

'Oh, my God,' Penelope shouted. 'Climb up, Edward. We'll ride through them.'

But his arms had already been seized, before he even properly understood what was happening. He pulled himself free, landed a punch

338

which sent a man tumbling, knew that Malewski had returned to his aid and was also swinging his fists, and then was sent to the ground by a crashing blow on the head. Half senseless he was again dragged to his feet, found himself being marched towards the nearest lamp-post, heard Robert shouting and Penelope screaming, but from the tones of their voices knew that they were calling after him rather than in any danger themselves.

He tried to think, tried to fight, but it was impossible with the searing pain in his head, the press of bodies crowding against him. Once again he was obsessed by the feeling that he had somehow been caught up in a nightmare, as on that day in El Bluff, and only dimly heard the shouting of other voices, the cracking of whips, found himself suddenly released and sprawled on the ground, to be yet again jerked to his feet, this time by soldiers in blue uniforms, while the mob sullenly retreated. He blinked at his rescuers, only slowly being able to focus on the officer who was saluting him.

'Captain Anderson?'

Edward drew a long breath. 'I am Captain Anderson, yes.'

'I have come to escort you to Richmond, sir.'

Definitely a dream. But not necessarily any longer a nightmare. 'Richmond?' he asked stupidly.

'Yes, sir. We are to leave immediately. President Davis wishes to meet you, sir, and discuss certain matters of great importance.'

'He's going to offer you a command,' Malewski had said, half jokingly.

'You ain't going to forget me, Mr Edward, if you going to a warship?' Jehu had asked, very seriously.

And this war was ostensibly being fought to secure people like Jehu their freedom. But his only concern, like Malewski's, was to remain at Edward's side.

They *wanted* him to fight for the South. To accept a command. Against his own people, in the North? But were they his own people? It was better than twenty years since he had last lived amongst them. He had supposed the people here in Charleston were his folk, now. But last week had given the lie to that.

So why was he here at all, wearing his best blue jacket, sitting in an antechamber watching anxious secretaries and *aides de camp* hurrying to and fro, listening to the martial throb of the city outside? Richmond was only a hundred miles, as the crow flies, from Washington itself. He supposed that never in history had a war commenced between two capitals so close together. Or between people so close together as well. So close he did not even know to which side he belonged.

Certainly he could never take a command against the North. But equally certainly, could he ever fight against Penelope Driscoll, no matter how he might enjoy seeing Henry at the end of a rifle sight?

And his opponents might even include his own son.

The secretary stood before him. 'The President will see you now, Captain Anderson.'

Edward stood up, straightened his jacket and followed the man into the huge office, where the spring sunlight streamed through the windows. There were several men in the room, but he recognised only Davis himself, a rather slight man, but possessing strong, aquiline features and a short goatee beard. He had been a famous soldier in his time, Edward knew, who had led his Mississippi volunteer riflemen to glory in the war against Mexico, a dozen years before. Now he had been called to command on a much larger field. He did not look unduly worried at the prospect.

'Captain Anderson,' he said, and offered a firm, dry handshake. 'I did not know if you'd come, as I've been told you're a Yankee by birth.'

'And a Carolingian by adoption, sir,' Edward said. 'Which leaves me straddling a sharp pointed fence.'

Davis studied him for several seconds. 'They tried to lynch you, I've been told,' he said at last. 'Do you still regard yourself as a Carolingian?'

'It's difficult, sir.'

'But as a Southerner?'

341

'I cannot accept a command against the Federal Government, sir.'

'If you'd agreed to do that, Captain, I'd have had no use for you. I'd expect no man to *fight* against his own people. No worthwhile man, at any rate. I'd have you meet my Secretary of the Navy, Stephen Mallory.'

'Anderson.' Mallory shook hands. He was heavy set with bulldog-like features and exuded a tremendous suggestion of energy. 'I would say it would be both to your taste and your interest to see our civilisation here in the Confederate States survive, at the least.'

'I won't argue with that, sir.'

'Well, Captain, it can only survive if we show the North that they can't defeat us. We're not afraid of meeting any Yankee soldiers on the open field. Man for man our boys are each worth three of theirs. And we have no aggressive intentions against the Federal Government. All Abe Lincoln has to do is recognise the Confederacy and we're content. But he's not going to do that so long as he thinks he can crush us. Trouble is, Captain Anderson, he can. Not in battle, as I have said. But because we don't manufacture here in the South. We buy our guns, we buy our ammunition, in the North. And they're not going to be selling us any more for a while. So we have to get what we need from Europe. We're already in contact with the British. They're all for us. There's even a chance they might come in on our side, sometime. But that's in the future. It's the next twelve months we're worried about. We need guns, and to pay for those guns we need to export our cotton to Lancashire. So we have to ship it. And Abe Lincoln knows that. He knows that all he has to do is impose a close blockade on our coastline, and he can strangle us, maybe without hardly firing a shot. And, Captain Anderson, he has the ships to do it.'

He paused, and Edward waited. Because he knew what was coming next, in principle, if not in form.

'Now, Captain,' Davis took up the tale. 'I'm told you command the fastest thing ever launched.'

'I don't command anything, right this minute, Mr President.'

'But you did, once.'

'Sure I did. And now she's at the bottom of the Escondida River, in Nicaragua.'

'We want to replace her.'

Edward stared at him, his heart commencing to pound. 'Well, sir, I *am* now building a twin screw steamship which will outrun anything in the world. Work has been stopped on her since the commencement of hostilities, but if you'll give me the men and the materials, and the money, to finish her...'

'How long would it take?' Mallory asked.

'A year. Maybe eighteen months. It's obtaining the iron that's the difficulty.'

'You're building in iron?' Mallory sighed.

343

'My dear Captain Anderson, there's going to be no iron at all, until this war ends. Anyway, a year...'

'There'll be a Federal general sitting right here, in a year's time,' Davis said. 'Unless we get moving. What about the *Yvonne Driscoll*?'

Edward frowned at him.

And Davis smiled. 'I endeavour to know what's going on, Captain Anderson. I *have* to know what's going on. Is it not true that there is a half-completed ship on the stocks in Driscoll's shipyard, Charleston, called the *Yvonne Driscoll*, which is an exact sister ship of your *Penelope*? Is it not true that her engines are already installed, so there'll be no delay there? And that she's being built in wood? We have a lot of wood. And is it not true that she can be completed in three months?'

Edward's turn to sigh. 'That is correct, Mr President. All of it. But it is also true that I am no longer connected with the Meigs-Driscoll Line. They'd rather give that ship to the devil than sell it to me.'

Davis's smile was grim. 'They'll sell it to the Government of the Confederate States of America, Captain Anderson. You may leave that to me. Will you take her to sea? I'm not asking you to exchange a single shot with any Federal warship. I'm just asking you to outsail them and outrun them. I'm told you're the man who can do that. Perhaps the only man who can do that.'

A dream. Certainly a dream. Which made all of the nightmares in his past fade into the glow of a brilliant dawn. A ship, and a purpose. Even a cause, with which he basically sympathised. And a cause for which Amanda would certainly have had him sail.

Davis was watching him. 'There'll be a tenth share of all profits in it for you, Captain. And the guarantee of this Administration that the moment hostilities cease, and our independence has been secured, we'll finance the building of your iron steamship. How about it?'

Here was everything he had ever wanted, just falling into his lap. The parcel even, incredibly, included an element of revenge against Henry. And he knew he could do it. Or was he again being impelled by that carelessness of his own life, which had cost so many others?

He drew a long breath. 'I have to tell you, sir, that the reason the *Yvonne Driscoll* has never been completed is because the design is basically unsafe. I discovered that on my maiden voyage with the *Penelope*. I had not intended ever to build *any* sister ships to that design. Unfortunately, while I was a prisoner in Nicaragua, two similar ships *were* built, and both were lost.'

'I've been told they were incompetently handled,' Mallory said.

'I cannot judge that, sir. I can sail the *Yvonne Driscoll*, and I have no doubt at all she is faster than any Federal warship, by several knots. I'll deliver your cotton and I'll bring back your guns for you. But she has an inherent instability factor which makes her unsuitable for the North Atlantic, and I would feel obliged to make this fact plain to my crew, before sailing.'

'The North Atlantic?' Davis cried. 'Who said anything about the North Atlantic?'

'But...' Edward scratched his head. 'You spoke of trading with England.'

'And England has an empire,' the President said. 'She has some islands just a couple of hundred miles from Charleston, called the Bahamas. Once inside those islands and you're in British territorial waters. Beyond that is the Atlantic. No Federal cruiser can interfere with any British ship on the high seas without risking British intervention in the war. But they sure can stop them from coming into Charleston or Savannah or Wilmington. They're entitled to do that by international law, once they've declared a blockade. Now, the British will take their guns to Nassau in the Bahamas, and they'll pick up our cotton there. That they've already agreed to. They won't come any closer to the mainland than that. Your job, Captain Anderson, will be to ferry between Nassau and Charleston, cotton out, guns and ammunition in. Simple as that.' He leaned forward again. 'Will you do it?'

Henry Driscoll's face was stiff with outrage. 'I have to tell you, sir, that I regard your proposal as an act of outrageous tyranny. Of daylight robbery, sir. It is nothing less than piracy.'

General Beauregard bowed. 'You are entitled to voice your protest, Mr Driscoll. But I feel sure that a brief reflection will convince you that you are entirely wrong. The Government is not expropriating your ship; it is buying her from you. The Government will complete the vessel, and sail her for the duration of the war. When peace comes, she will be restored to you. I would say that you are getting a very good bargain. You will also *appear* as a most patriotic citizen. In any event, sir, I am not in a position to discuss the rights or wrongs of the matter. My orders are plain. That ship is regarded as of supreme importance in the fight of the Confederacy against the Federal Government, and as even being essential to our eventual victory. We do intend to gain that victory, Mr Driscoll.'

'Of supreme importance,' Henry sneered. 'She will be a floating coffin, like all her sisters. Has Anderson not warned you of that?'

Beauregard nodded. 'Captain Anderson has pointed out certain design faults in the vessel. These we are prepared to accept, as he is prepared to take her to sea.' He got up, placed his hat on his head, turned to the door, and then checked, and looked back at Henry. 'I may say, Mr Driscoll, that as of this moment, the *Yvonne Driscoll*, or the *Penelope Driscoll*, as Captain Anderson actually intends to call the completed vessel, is under the protection of the Government of the Confederacy. So is her captain, and all the members of her crew.' He nodded to Jonathan, who had remained silent throughout Henry's protests. 'Good day to you, gentlemen.' He left the room.

Henry glared at Jonathan. 'You did not support me.'

'I could see little point. Nor do I feel that your protests are justified. We may feel the ship is unsafe, but undoubtedly she could have been designed expressly as a blockade runner. As for her being captained by Edward, well, I think right now is the time to bury the hatchet, at least for the duration of the war. And if Edward is prepared to sail her, well...I reckon he's the only man who can.'

'Edward,' Henry sneered. 'The man is a millstone hung around our necks. Those ships are millstones hung around our necks. I should have burned that hull, years ago.'

'Well,' Jonathan said. 'I'm rather glad you didn't. I've a notion the entire Confederacy might be rather glad of that. And Edward is obviously not wishing to crow. Or he wouldn't be planning to rename her the *Penelope Driscoll*.'

Henry stared at him for a moment, then got up, crammed his hat on his head, ran downstairs, and spurred his horse out of town. His whole being seemed to be on fire, as if he had a furnace burning in his belly. The *Penelope*

Driscoll. Could there be a more blatant declaration of past conquests? Why, it was sufficient grounds for calling a fellow out. He drew rein, wiped sweat from his forehead. There was the solution to all of his problems at a single stroke.

But the scoundrel was under governmental protection. Jefferson Davies would certainly forbid a duel. And if they fought it clandestinely, the winner might well find himself charged with murder. Even supposing *he* was the winner. It was impossible to admit he was afraid of Anderson. Undoubtedly he was a far superior shot. And yet, the fellow had such a habit of coming out on top, no matter what the odds...

He kicked his horse forward again, galloped through the grounds of his estate, tossed his reins to a waiting Negro groom, but retained his riding crop. He stamped across the hall and into the schoolroom, where Robert Anderson sat with his governess, but looking up with an excited smile at his foster father. 'Uncle Henry?' he cried. 'There's been a battle?'

Henry pointed at the door. 'Out,' he told the astonished young woman. 'Get out.'

She hesitated, glanced from her employer to her charge, and then gathered her skirts and ran from the room.

'We've lost it,' Robert said disconsolately, still misinterpreting Henry's mood. 'Don't say we've lost it.'

'Bend across that desk,' Henry commanded.

'Drop those breeches and bend across that desk. By God, I'm going to take the skin from your arse.'

'Uncle Henry?' Robert stared at him in total amazement.

'Across that desk,' Henry seized the boy's shoulders and thrust him over the wooden table, himself yanked down the breeches. 'God damned Yankee scum,' he shouted, raising the crop.

'Henry,' Penelope snapped, closing the door behind her.

He turned to face her. 'Get out,' he snapped.

'Have you lost your senses? Release Robert this instant.'

'I shall not. I'm going to whip him within an inch of his life.'

'You *have* lost your senses,' Penelope said, coming across the room to take the crop from his hand. 'Leave us, Robert.'

Robert glanced from one to the other, dragged up his pants, and ran from the room. Henry sat down, shoulders slumped.

Penelope stood above him. 'What on earth can have happened?'

'That Anderson,' he muttered. 'Your *lover*,' he shouted, raising his head.

'That was twelve years ago, Henry,' she said. 'And it is futilely ill-mannered of you to keep dragging it up.'

'Twelve years ago,' he sneered. 'You expect me to believe that? Do you know what he is renaming the *Yvonne Driscoll?* He means to call her the *Penelope Driscoll*. Twelve years ago, eh?'

Penelope frowned at him, unable to understand a word he was saying, even as her heart was commencing to beat most wildly. 'The *Yvonne Driscoll?* How on earth does Edward Anderson have anything to do with the *Yvonne Driscoll?*'

'Because he's taken her, that's what,' Henry shouted.

'*Taken* her?'

'He's sweet-talked Jeff Davis into requisitioning her as a blockade runner, with him in command. By God, I should have set that mob on him just a few minutes earlier. Then he'd have been over and done with. By God...'

Penelope stared at her husband. '*You* set that mob on Edward?'

Henry flushed, bit his lip, and then got up, strode to the window, looked out at the lawn. 'I told them where to find a damned Yankee sympathiser. It was my duty to do so.'

He turned his head as he heard the door close. Penelope had left the room.

'Where are we going, Aunt Penny?' Robert sat beside her in the gig, looking back at Greenacres, and then at the carryall she had hastily packed for him, waiting in the back of the vehicle.

Where indeed, she wondered. *I* am going nowhere. And once I release you, dear little

351

boy, I have no more means of even the slightest communication with *him*. As she had so accurately realised, on the day Edward had returned from the dead, he had brought her a greater misery than she had endured even when she had supposed him lying drowned at the bottom of the Escondida River.

But he had renamed the ship, the *Penelope Driscoll*. And meant to take her to sea. He did not realise the curse that hung over everything to do with those ships.

'We're going to see your father,' she said, and drew rein at the gate to the Driscoll Yard, above which there now flew the red and black design of the Confederate States of America, and before entering which she had to state her name and business. 'Why, to see Captain Anderson,' she explained. 'This is the captain's son.'

In hardly a week an enormous amount of work had been done on the long unfinished vessel. Her hull was complete, and she would be ready for launching in a few days. The entire yard was filled with the sound of hammers, the rasp of saws, there were workmen everywhere, scurrying to and fro. And there was Edward, on the deck of the ship, surrounded by experts with their pads and pencils, by blue-coated naval officers, all drawing and discussing...the *Penelope Driscoll*.

'Is Father really going to take her to sea?' Robert asked.

'Yes,' Penelope said. 'Yes, he is.' She watched him climb down the ladder, with all the energy and power of a young boy. She watched the pleasure in his face at the sight of them being rigidly controlled into a cold, watchful expression.

'I'd prefer no recriminations,' he said. 'This was Jefferson Davis's idea.'

'I have no recriminations to offer,' she said. 'Was the name his idea, as well?'

Just the trace of a flush. 'No,' he said. 'The idea of the name was mine. The first *Penelope* proved a lucky ship for me, until the very end. I'm hoping the name will again bring us fortune.'

'I shall still take your choice as a compliment. May I have a word with you?'

He hesitated, then looked around, and summoned Jehu. 'Show Master Robert over the ship, Jehu.'

'I going do that thing, Mr Edward. Come along, Master Robert.'

'He is very fond of you,' Penelope observed. 'Jehu, I mean. But all the men who sail with you seem fond of you.'

He waited.

'That is why...Edward, please don't take her to sea.'

His eyes narrowed, then he snorted. 'Really, Mrs Driscoll, I had expected a *little* more subtlety.'

'Henry did not send me, if that is what you

353

are supposing, Edward,' she said. 'I came of my own accord. Edward, please believe me. These ships are unlucky. Because I am unlucky. They have brought nothing but death and disaster to all who are associated with them. You say the first *Penelope* brought you luck? Isn't she now a burned-out hulk? Are not all who sailed on her, saving only yourself and Cas and Jehu, dead? How can you describe her as a lucky ship?'

'The *Penelope* was burned by men, Mrs Driscoll. And my people were killed by men. Not by anything supernatural. Just as the *Angela Driscoll* broke up because her timbers could not take the speed with which she was being driven across the Atlantic, and the *Priscilla Meigs*...well, no one will ever know what happened there. But it was almost certainly human error.'

'And do you suppose you can never make an error?' she cried.

'Everyone does, eventually,' he agreed. 'And when I do, I will no doubt lose my ship. And most likely my life with it. But that applies to every master who ever put to sea. It was a shabby design, Penny, coming here to try to put me off where Henry has failed.'

'Do you really believe that is why I came?' she asked.

Once again he hesitated, but now they were distracted by the return of Robert and Jehu. 'What do you think of her, boy?' Edward asked.

'I think she's great, Father. I'd love to sail in her.'

'Aye, well, she's going to war. In a sense.' He glanced at Penelope.

'Yet must you make arrangements for him, Edward,' she said.

He frowned at her.

'He can no longer live at Greenacres,' she said. 'That was the real purpose of my visit.'

'Ah. I should have thought of that. I had not realised your antagonism would bite so deep.'

She flushed. 'It is not *my* antagonism, Edward. It...' she bit her lip.

'Uncle Henry wanted to flog me, Father,' Robert explained. 'Why did he want to do that?'

'*Did* he flog you, boy?'

'No, sir. Aunt Penelope stopped him.'

'I hope you thanked her.' He hugged the boy against him. 'Do you wish to come and live with your Dad?'

'Oh, yes, sir, Father. But...wouldn't it be possible to live with you both?' He looked from face to face.

As they also looked at each other. If you were to say just one word, Edward Anderson, Penelope thought, that would be possible as well. I would come to you, as an adulteress, a traitor to my family, a fallen woman in every sense of the word. I would even abandon my children, for that grasp at happiness. Just one word, is all I ask.

'No,' Edward said.

'No,' Penelope said, her shoulders sagging. 'No, it is not possible, Robert. What would I do with Jimmy and Yvonne?' She held out her hand. 'As she will go to sea, Edward, whether I like it or not, then I am delighted she will be under your command. If any man can drive her to success, it is you. God speed to you, Edward, and to all who sail with you.'

She went back to the gate and the waiting gig. She wondered if he had noticed the tears in her eyes.

'Do you suppose,' Henry Driscoll demanded, 'that you can just take my son, and give him away?'

He stood in the centre of the hall, his hands on his hips. For all she knew he might have been standing there since she had left Greenacres, several hours before.

'*Your* son?' Penelope handed her gloves and whip to the waiting maid, went up the stairs, taking off her hat as she did so.

Henry had almost to run to keep up with her long strides. 'You made him so. You insisted on it.'

'And you promised to play the father,' she said. 'Not the tyrant.' She went into the bedroom, where her maids hovered anxiously.

Henry followed her. 'Out,' he said to the black girls. 'Get out.'

They hesitated, looking at their mistress,

who nodded. 'You had best leave. I will ring for you when I am ready to change.'

They sidled round their master, and through the doorway. The last one closed the door behind herself.

Penelope sat herself on the settee by the window, arranged her skirts and placed her silk hat beside her on the cushion.

'And what of *your* promises?' Henry demanded.

She looked at him. 'I have kept them all, Henry.'

'Ha,' he said. 'You have spent the last hour closeted with your lover.' He pointed. 'That gives me the right to call him out. Do you realise that? To have him in the sights of my pistol. By God, I shall enjoy that.'

'You would be arrested for murder, and possibly even treason,' she said, with a composure she did not really feel. 'Edward is now an officer in the Confederate Navy. As you, I understand, have obtained a commission in the Army.'

'Well, of course I have. I'm a veteran of the Mexican War. Jefferson Davis knows I can fight. By God, it'll be good to wear uniform again.'

'I'm sure it will,' she said, still gazing at him. 'Does President Davis's knowledge of your abilities explain why all the Mexican War veterans amongst his officers have been given at least colonelcies, and you are remaining a captain?'

'Well...' he flushed. 'You know there was that talk, because Uncle James bought me out. He needed me.' He squared his shoulders. 'As the Confederate Government, Jeff Davis himself, will soon know how much they need me.' But his anger was already fading as he gazed at her, wanted her...even after nearly four years of marriage, he still wanted her.

He sat beside her. 'You've no right to treat me so, Penny. I'm going off to war. It is me that you should be spending your time with, not Anderson.'

'I do not spend any time with Edward Anderson, Henry,' she said. And got up in turn. 'But I do not feel like spending any time with you, either, at this moment. Will you leave me, please? I wish to change my clothes.'

He hesitated, and then went to the door. 'I hope she sinks,' he said. 'By God, I hope the *Penelope Driscoll* goes down, with all aboard her.'

He left the room.

Cas Malewski saluted the bridge. 'All loaded and all hatches in place, Captain Anderson.'

Edward returned the salute. 'Then raise steam, Mr Malewski.' He turned to Jefferson Davis, who with almost his entire cabinet, waited on the quarterdeck. 'Time, Mr President.'

Davis clasped his hand. 'You know they're waiting for you, Edward? There's been too

358

much publicity.'

Edward nodded.

'And you're sure you won't mount even one gun?' Mallory asked. 'You're entitled to defend yourself.'

Edward shook his head. 'My business is to land cotton in Nassau, Mr Mallory, not fight a battle.'

'Then Godspeed to you, Edward,' Davis said, and turned for the gangway.

Edward scooped Robert from the deck, hugged him tight. 'You do what Grandpa says, now.'

'When can I sail with you, Father? When?'

'Soon as you're old enough,' Edward promised. 'Next year, maybe. Maybe the war will be over by then. You belt him if he's bad, Father.'

John Dart winked. 'I reckon we've a lot of fishing to do. You hurry back, Edward.'

'By the end of the week,' Edward said. 'If my cargo is ready in Nassau.' He watched them go ashore, waited for the steam tugs to pull the ship away from the dock. Standing beside Drayton, the pilot, he cast a last look shorewards, and saw the gig standing by itself. Of all her family, with whom he had experienced so much, she alone had come to see her namesake leave. Perhaps that was understandable. It was the only aspect of their relationship he dared allow himself to understand. Their strange, sinful honeymoon still lay at the back of his mind as the happiest occasion of his entire life. But it could not be recaptured without spreading too much more misery and disaster all around them both. If, indeed, after everything that had happened over so long a period of time, it could ever be recaptured under any circumstances. He had loved, and lost, too many times. His business was the sea, until the day, as he knew must eventually happen, when the sea claimed him for its own.

Then what fatalistic compulsion had made him name his ship the *Penelope Driscoll? He* was no believer in luck.

The guns on Sumter fired a salute. 'Damned fools,' Drayton growled. 'They're letting the whole coast know you're putting out.'

'Don't you reckon the whole coast already knows that?' Edward asked. He levelled his telescope, surveyed the empty ocean.

'She'll be waiting round a headland,' Malewski suggested.

'Oh, they want us at sea, all right,' Edward agreed. 'Question is, is it a she or a them?' He rang down to stop engines, shook hands with Drayton. 'Monday, Mr Drayton.'

'Monday,' Drayton said, doubtfully, and waved from the deck of the pilot cutter as she made sail back for the safety of the harbour.

Edward studied the sky, checked the wind. It was out of the north-west, and quite brisk. 'We'll have her working canvas up, Mr Malewski,' he said, and opened the speaking tube to the engine room. 'Are you ready down there, Mr Ritchie?' he asked Trethowan's successor.

'Pressure's up, Captain,' came the reply.

'Well, you keep it up until we dock in Nassau,' Edward said. 'That'll be tomorrow night. If I need you, it's going to be in a hurry.' Or rather, he supposed, when. He stood by the helm. 'Course is one three five, boatswain. The sooner we get under the lee of Grand Bahama the happier I'll be.'

The *Penelope Driscoll* was out in the swell by now, breasting the Gulf Stream, choppy today as the wind was blowing across the direction of the current; the low ship was already tossing spray over her shoulders, making the decks slippery. Edward and Malewski both had their glasses ready, sweeping the fast disappearing shoreline, the creeks where a Federal cruiser might be lurking, and then the heaving whitecaps which lay ahead of them...'There,' Malewski said.

The Federal gunboat had not only known her quarry was about to put to sea. She had known where must be her destination. And thus had waited just below the horizon on the direct course between Charleston and the North West Bahama Passage. The *Penelope Driscoll* was left with several choices. She could turn back for Charleston. She could turn north up the Amcrican coast. She could turn south for Florida. Or she could run for the open ocean, confident that she could not be caught. But if she did any of those things the warship would have accomplished its purpose; the blockade runner's cargo of guns waited for her in Nassau, and nowhere else—as did the British ships waiting to load her cotton.

The boatswain turned his head, anticipating a command, while Edward continued to study the warship through his glass. She was not very large, and was of a conventional design, three-masted, and with a funnel, to be sure, but more intended for sail than steam. While her broadside was interrupted by the huge paddlewheels. She was undoubtedly fast, by conventional standards, and would carry a powerful pair of chasers in her bows. But she would not be fast enough, and he had known what he had to face, before he had cast off. 'We'll stand on, cox,' he said. 'Steady as she goes.'

The *Penelope Driscoll* surged over the gentle waves, making, Edward estimated, a good ten knots under sail—which could well be misinterpreted at a distance as her maximum speed. Certainly the distance between the two ships was closing fast, and through his glass Edward could make out the activity on the gunboat's deck, as her cannon were prepared. On the *Penelope Driscoll*, by contrast, although both watches were on deck, no man moved. They waited at their posts, knowing what they would have to do when the time came, as Edward had

362

spent the past fortnight in training them. But there was many a white face and a bitten lip, as they glanced aft, towards their captain, and then forward, at the guns.

A puff of white smoke rose from the gunboat's foredeck, but there was no corresponding splash; she was adhering rigidly to the rules of war and calling for surrender.

'Heave her to, Mr Malewski,' Edward said. 'Hand her sails.'

The orders were given, the sails came clouding down. To heave to the *Penelope Driscoll* had to turn up to the north, facing the wind. But the coxswain had also been carefully trained, and now let her fall away again, so that she slowly turned, to point in her original direction, rolling heavily in the swell. No doubt, Edward hoped, the officers of the warship would be discussing the incompetence of the helmsman, and also of the master, who had taken all canvas off to leave his ship quite out of control. But he was also determined to obey all the rules of war, and did not actually strike his flag; with fortune that too would be considered an oversight by the navy men.

He opened the speaking tube as the *Penelope Driscoll* slowly lost way. 'Stand by, Mr Ritchie.'

'Aye aye,' came the reply.

The warship was slowly turned, to present her broadside. No doubt her captain could not really believe his fortune, that the much-touted blockade runner should be prepared to surrender so tamely. But he was taking no chances; those broadside guns would all be loaded and trained. And thus *he*, Edward thought grimly, was gambling as heavily as he had ever done in his life.

A boat swung out from the gunboat's davits, slowly lowered towards the sea. Edward waited until it was within a few feet of the water, then thrust the telegraph forward. 'Now, Mr Ritchie,' he bawled down the speaking tube. 'Now's your time.'

He doubted Ritchie actually heard him, in the tremendous rumble of sound which welled out of the interior of the *Penelope Driscoll*, accompanied by the huge gush of black smoke from her funnel, the sudden whirr of power from her propeller. The ship surged forward, leaping instantly to five knots and steadily gaining speed. Edward continued to watch the warship. The boat was let run into the sea, and almost immediately her broadside exploded. The water astern of the *Penelope Driscoll* became a maelstrom of miniature waterspouts. But the shots all fell astern. The blockade runner was already past the gunboat, and streaking for the south-east. She'd be hull down long before there was any hope of the warship regaining her pinnace and turning in pursuit.

The crew gave a resounding cheer. Even the reserve stokers, faces black with coal dust, came on deck to wave their shovels in triumph.

And Malewski slapped his captain on the shoulder. 'You've done it,' he shouted. 'You've done it.'

'*We've* done it, Cas,' Edward said. 'But that was only trick Number One. We'll have to go through the entire pack, before we're finished.'

CHAPTER 10

Penelope Driscoll listened to the sound of gunfire, rolled over, pressed her pillow across her ears. There was gunfire every morning, as there had been gunfire every morning since the Federal fleet had seized Fort Wagner at the entrance to Charleston Harbour, just a year ago. Now they had dropped a few shells into the city every dawn, and the city batteries replied, whenever they had sufficient powder, which was increasingly seldom, nowadays.

Through the noise of the guns she heard her daughter wailing. With a sigh she got out of bed and went along the hall to the nursery. She picked Yvonne up and held her close. 'There's nothing to worry about, my darling,' she said. 'Those guns cannot reach Greenacres. Not *those* guns.' But the other guns, those which were coming closer and closer as Sherman led his ever victorious army through Georgia...*they* might one day be able to drop a shell on even these quiet woods.

'I'm not afraid of the guns, Mama,' Yvonne protested; she was a very grown up five year old. 'But I was wondering if Father Christmas will be able to come down from the North Pole, with all of that shooting.'

'Father Christmas can travel through *any*thing,' Jimmy said, from the next bed.

'Of course he can,' Penelope agreed, and laid Yvonne down again. 'Now you go back to sleep. It's not time to get up yet.'

And when it is time, she thought as she returned to her bedroom and wrapped herself in her dressing gown—for in only a few minutes she had become thoroughly chilled—there will be nothing to get up for. Just a cold, empty, miserable house, in the midst of a cold, largely empty, miserable park. Father Christmas? Oh, he would come this year, as he had always come in the past. But he would bring precious little in his knapsack.

When she remembered the Christmas of 1861, the excitement and the exhilaration of the end of the first year of independence, with nothing but victories to show for it, the uniforms and the bands, the laughing women, the huge ball at the Assembly Rooms…it was incredible to suppose that had only been three years ago.

Henry had obtained leave for the Christmas holiday, and even Henry, in his biscuit and yellow, had seemed handsome that night, someone to be proud of. Until Edward Anderson had appeared. He had docked that afternoon, after, apparently, another of his famous and hair-raising brushes with the Federal cruisers. But he had, as usual, brought the *Penelope Driscoll* safe to port, with her precious cargo of guns and ammunition, and was prepared to commence loading cotton the very next morning, even if it was Christmas Day. On that occasion the band had played *See the Conquering Hero Comes* for him, as it had once done for Henry, when he had returned from Mexico. But unlike Henry, Edward was a genuine hero, especially to the people of Charleston, anxious to forget, and have him forget, that they had once tried to lynch him. He was no longer the only blockade runner. The war had spawned an entire fleet of fast, shallow-draft ships, which raced to and fro between Nassau and Wilmington, or Charleston, or Savannah, risking the lives of their crews to keep the South supplied; indeed most of the remaining Meigs-Driscoll fleet, unable to obtain any legitimate business *because* of the blockade, had taken part. But the *Penelope Driscoll* had been the first, as she was the fastest, and thus still the most successful of them all, and as she had survived, where none of her rivals and accomplices had lasted more than a year; there simply *was* no Meigs-Driscoll fleet any more. The ship alone could not be given all the credit for that. It was her captain, who by consummate seamanship and the use of every trick in the trade, had made the perilous journey so many times with such success.

And who viewed life, it seemed, with a grim cynicism, seldom smiled, and never laughed. At least in Charleston. But she doubted he even smiled in Nassau. He was a man who seemed able to turn everything into gold merely by touching it, and yet who could never achieve the things he really wanted. Thus he sailed a ship he had in effect designed, but did not trust and no longer even liked...and was making a fortune at it. And thus his experiences with women had left him unable to love, or perhaps even desire. Or was it that, despite all, he still desired *her*? They had gazed at each other across the crowded ballroom, before he had been swept away on the arm of one of Charleston's bright young things. And she had danced with Henry.

That Christmas Eve, three years ago, had been the last time she had seen him. There had been no ball in 1862. By then the euphoria had gone out of the war, as the casualty lists had mounted, together with a sombre understanding that President Lincoln meant to prosecute this conflict until it was won, regardless of defeats in the field, of the cost in either men or money. And by 1863 the Federal net had begun to draw more tightly around the sea coasts, even as the name of Grant had begun to loom ever larger out of the west. The capture of Fort Wagner had effectively sealed the port of Charleston, except for those small craft which would sneak into the bayous and bring their cargoes across the Neck. For ships like the *Penelope Driscoll* that was impossible. Edward had started using Wilmington, further up the coast, instead. There the Federals were still excluded.

He had persuaded old John Dart to move up the coast as well, with Robert. At least in her weekly visits to the boy, if she had never managed to time one for when Edward was actually home, she had been kept up to date with information about him. For the past year she had lacked even that.

But even Edward, she supposed, as she gazed out of the window at the still beautifully-tended grass lawns of Greenacres, must now know that he was backing a losing side. As if it would matter to him. He must have made a great deal of money out of his blockade running, and he was a Northerner by birth. He had no roots to be torn out of Southern soil.

She listened to shouting, and her mother scream. Some fresh disaster? She hurried on to the gallery, looked down the great staircase, watched her husband coming up. His uniform was torn and mudstained, his face was grey with fatigue. 'Henry?' she asked. She had not seen *him* in three months. 'Henry? Whatever has happened?'

He gasped up to her, kissed her on the cheek. 'Savannah has fallen,' he panted. 'Sherman has reached the sea.'

'It's the end,' Priscilla Meigs wailed. 'Oh, it must be the end.'

'We shall hold them,' Henry declared. He was a colonel by now, and had undoubtedly grown in stature. Nor could any one any longer doubt his courage; he had been commended by General Lee himself for bravery in action. 'But the next line of defence must be here in Charleston. I only obtained this forty-eight-hour furlough to put my affairs in order.'

'Charleston?' Priscilla shrieked. 'Oh, my God, Charleston. What are we to *do*?'

'Leave,' Henry said, and looked at Penelope.

'Leave?' she queried. 'You mean...leave Greenacres?'

'Lock the place up, pack whatever you feel you need, and go north. Wilmington, or some such place. Believe me, Penny, it's the only safe course. And it must be done *now*, before this news spreads and everyone else has the same idea.'

'Now?' she asked, stupidly; her brain seemed to have gone quite dull. 'But...tomorrow is Christmas Eve.'

'So you'll spend Christmas on the road. You can celebrate it when you get to Wilmington. You must pack up now, and be on the road by tonight.'

'Wilmington,' Priscilla Meigs said. 'Yes. That is much closer to Richmond.'

Quite apart from being the capital of the Confederacy, Jonathan was stationed in Richmond.

'We shall need five wagons, I think,' Priscilla decided, now quite prepared to take charge of the entire operation. 'That will mean ten men. I should prefer them to be white men, Henry. So they may be armed. And...'

'Mother,' Henry said. 'There are no men. And there is only one wagon. And you must leave as secretly as possible, or you will cause a riot.'

'*One* wagon?' Priscilla exclaimed. 'But that is quite impossible.'

Penelope got up, walked to the window, looked out at the park. She had been forced to leave Greenacres once before, and had hated it then. And then she had not doubted for a moment that she would one day come back. But this time...

She watched the yardboys still weeding away. 'What of the Negroes?' she asked.

'I wouldn't take any of them,' Henry said. 'You'll be safer on your own, if you leave before anybody else. If we win, we can round up the slaves. If we lose...well, they'll be rounding *us* up, I guess.' He stood beside her, put his arm round her waist; insensibly she rested her head on his shoulder—suddenly she felt quite exhausted. 'Penny, you must go. I was one of the rear guard left to hold Atlanta. We

371

left the city after the Feds were already in it. Things I saw...Penny, you cannot stay here to be overrun by Federal troops. Their mission is to destroy, everything. And then there are deserters, rogues of every description who hang about the fringes of the armies. You cannot stay here.'

She turned to look at him. 'And where will we flee, after Wilmington? To Richmond?'

He sighed. 'If we can hold them outside Charleston, there is still a chance. They aren't making any progress in the wilderness. There is always the chance of a negotiated peace. If Charleston falls...' he hesitated.

'Yes?'

Another sigh. 'Then you must make for Richmond.'

'I think we should leave the country,' Priscilla Meigs said. 'There are still blockade runners operating out of Wilmington. We could reach Nassau, anyway, and stay there until things settle down.'

'That is madness,' Henry snapped. 'Those fellows are sunk on every voyage. You'd be committing suicide. I absolutely forbid it.'

'The *Penelope Driscoll* hasn't sunk yet,' Priscilla pointed out.

Henry stared at her for a moment. 'I forbid it,' he said, and turned back to Penelope. 'Listen. I have ten thousand dollars in gold, in my safe. I've kept it there since the beginning of the war, just in case of something like this. You'll take that, Penny. That will get you and the children, and Mother, to Richmond, and keep you there until I can come for you.'

And what then, she wondered? 'Henry...'

'I love you, Penny,' he said. 'I have always loved you. I want you safe, when this war ends.' He kissed her on the cheek. 'Whatever has happened between us in the past, I want you safe. Now pack, and run. While there is yet time.'

He was begging her, as desperately as he dared, without putting his fears into words.

She hesitated, then kissed him in turn, held him in her arms for a long moment. 'Then you keep safe as well, Henry,' she said. 'And come to us, when you can.'

So then, she wondered, as she wrapped her weary fingers yet again around the reins, and jerked them to urge the equally tired horses onwards; am I at last falling in love with my husband?

She would not have supposed that could ever be possible. She knew him too well, and at that, she was aware that she did not know enough about him. He lived a convoluted, twisted life, a life of secret deals and manipulations, manipulations which in the past she could not doubt had included Edward Anderson's destruction as their objective. Certainly she could never forgive him for setting a mob on Edward that April day in 1861. Just as she had no doubt that having lost his fleet he was involved in vast plans for the future, whenever the war should end, plans which did not necessarily include the survival of the Confederacy.

But yet a man who redeemed himself by his love, for her. Not to respond to that would be inhuman. Although in any event his fears were groundless. She and Edward had seen each other but a handful of times in five years. They had not spoken since the day she had returned Robert to him, and had attempted to dissuade him from taking the *Penelope Driscoll* to sea. She, as usual, had been wrong, and he had been triumphantly right. But that day he had hated her. He hated her no less than her husband. She had never allowed herself to understand that before, but now she knew that had been the root of the matter since his return from Nicaragua. He had come back to marry her, and she had been married to Henry. That she had only done so because he had been officially reported as dead was no consolation. So, for all his desire, he had included her in his hatred of Henry.

And now, no doubt, he did not even any longer desire her. Why should he desire a woman of thirty-five, whom he had not seen in three years?

'Jonathan will look after us,' Priscilla Meigs said, with a gallant attempt at brightness. She sat beside her daughter on the driving seat of the wagon, huddled beneath a coat and a blanket, bonnet pulled close over her ears and tied tightly beneath her chin, for it was very cold, and during the night there had even been a flurry of snow. But Penelope, equally well wrapped up, had kept driving. The night hid what might lie around them. Now the cold grey of the dawn revealed it only too well, the tangled morass which bordered either side of the lonely coast road. To the right, to be sure, they could hear the rumble of the surf through the mangroves—that was the Ocean. But to the left there was the silent swamp, its eerie noiselessness broken only by the rumbles of their wheels, the splashes as they struggled in and out of vast puddles, and occasionally the *crack* of a splitting branch, which had them sitting up, heads twisting to and fro in alarm.

'How far do you think we've travelled?' Priscilla wanted to know, yawning.

Penelope considered. They had left Greenacres immediately after dusk, and had been on the road for twelve hours. They must have covered at least eighteen miles, she supposed, even at the crawl which was the best she had been able to persuade out of the horses. And surely in daylight they would be able to increase speed. But they were still more than a hundred miles from Wilmington.

'I have no idea, ' she decided was the least depressing reply.

'Well, I think we should stop and have some breakfast.'

Penelope looked over her shoulder at the still sleeping children. They had been aghast at the idea of leaving their warm, secure home, their horses and their dogs, their toys...and the Negro servants who had been their friends. The slaves had not understood either, had stood around and gaped at them.

'But where you going, Mistress?' they had asked.

'Why you ain't taking any of we, Mistress?'

'You coming back, Mistress?'

'What we going do, Mistress?'

To all of which Henry had told silly lies, about an entire wagon train on its way to collect them and carry them behind their mistress —as, amazingly, most of them seemed to desire. No doubt they would not be *too* disappointed when they realised the truth. Certainly there had seemed little point in telling them to board the house up. If the Federal troops intended to burn it, or to loot it, then they would knock down any boards as easily as they would knock down closed doors. The whole evening had taken on the appearance of some ghastly nightmare. She had known enough of them in the past, but they had always been self induced, and therefore capable of being self ended when they became unendurable. Besides, in settling for Henry and Greenacres, and thus position and security, she had thought to put nightmares behind her forever. But this...it had seemed incredible that she should be packing, just one box each for herself and the children, and that she should be looking at her bed for the last time...yesterday afternoon she had lain in that bed, with Henry, because he had wanted it, perhaps for a last time. And for all their lengthy separation they had both been so preoccupied and disturbed by what was happening they had been able to do no more than hold each other tightly.

And now, that she should have sat on this box for twelve hours, driving down an empty road, her muscles aching and her bottom raw from sitting on the boards, coming from nowhere, and going nowhere...'I think we should let them sleep a little while longer, Mother,' she said. 'They'll only complain when they wake.'

'Well, I just have to stretch my legs,' Priscilla Meigs said. 'Stop a second, and I'll walk.' She glanced at Penelope. 'You look an absolute sight.'

Penelope regarded her mother's straggling grey hair, escaping from beneath her bonnet in every direction. 'So do you,' she said. 'But we're not likely to meet anyone on this road.' Which was why Henry had chosen it for them.

But as she applied the brake and brought the wagon to a lumbering halt, she heard the sound of splashes, from close at hand.

'What's that?' Priscilla Meigs asked, head turning as she changed her mind about getting down.

Penelope said nothing, but reached behind her into the carryall to find the weapon Henry had given her. It was one of the new Colt pistols, with six bullets carried in a central chamber which revolved as the trigger was squeezed...Henry was not even sure how well it worked. But it was an impressive-looking firearm. She placed it on the seat beside her, beneath the blanket. 'I don't think we'd better stop right here, Mother,' she decided.

She flicked the reins, the horses stepped forward, and then she braked again as the bushes parted some fifty feet in front of the wagon and two men stepped through. Her heart gave a little leap of relief as she saw the biscuit-coloured pants, and also the kepis they wore. But a glance at their tattered jackets and at their bearded faces as well as the mud which coated their bodies, convinced her that they were no longer fighting soldiers, although one of them carried a pistol at his belt, and the other a rifle.

'Well, what do you know,' said the first man.

'Howdy folks,' said the second, coming closer, rifle resting in the crook of his arm. 'You got soldiers in that wagon?'

'Of course not,' Priscilla said, prematurely in Penelope's opinion. 'We are on our way to Wilmington. If you boys want a ride...'

'Now that's real good of you, lady. Say, Mike,' he called. 'Lady's offering us a ride.'

378

A third man pushed through the bushes, out of the swamp. He wore a slouch hat and carried a rusting sword; there were three stripes on the arm of his uniform jacket. He raised his hat. 'That's mighty kind of you, ma'am,' he remarked. 'Me and my boys are all beat up, having been in that swamp damn near a week. A Merry Christmas to you.'

'And to you,' Priscilla said.

Penelope sighed; suddenly she felt twice as exhausted as even five minutes ago. But there was no way to avoid a confrontation now. She watched the sergeant's eyes drifting over the wagon, calculating what they might have inside, or who, and how many. And over her as well. In her case he did not have to do so much calculating. He could tell she was a woman, and he could see she was as good looking as any woman he had ever met in his life. And he could tell, from the quality of the material of her gown, the value of the rings on her fingers, that she was a lady. Thus he would reckon there'd be money to be had, as well as satisfaction—even if he might not actually expect to stumble upon ten thousand dollars in gold.

Yet she was not actually aware of any fear, only an overwhelming breathlessness. Until she saw one of the men begin to sidle past the wagon, and heard too the sound of Yvonne stretching in the back.

'Are you men wounded?' she asked, surprised at the evenness of her voice.

'Now, why should we be wounded, ma'am?' The sergeant moved closer.

'Because if you're not, shouldn't you be down south, fighting the Yankees?'

'We've done that,' said the man with the pistol. 'We've had that, but good, lady. Say, you got food in that wagon?'

'A little,' Priscilla said. 'We were just considering stopping for some breakfast. You boys are welcome to share it with us.'

'Ma'am, you are *generous*,' said the sergeant.

'Well, lookee here,' called the man with the rifle, from behind them. 'Kids.'

'Ma,' Yvonne shouted. 'There's a man looking at me. Ma!'

'You get out of here,' Jimmy cried, his voice high with outrage. 'You get out of here.'

'What on earth...' Priscilla Meigs turned to look into the wagon, was seized from behind by the skirt of her gown and pulled backwards, with such force that she fell out of the seat and struck the ground with a thud, arms and legs scattering, quite unable even to cry out in her breathlessness. With a tremendous surge of her heart, Penelope drew her hand from beneath the blanket, holding the revolver, telling herself that she had to fire it, and more, that she had to kill someone, if she was going to save their own lives.

Yet she could not stop herself hoping such an irrevocable step could be avoided, brought

380

the weapon up to level it at the sergeant. 'Call your men off,' she said. 'Call your men...'

She was hit a tremendous blow on the body, an embracing *thud* which paralysed every muscle, even her brain. Nothing like that had ever happened to her before, and her first reaction was only surprise. Surprise that she could not breathe, surprise that she should be lying in the mud beside the wagon, without any knowledge of how she had got there, surprise that she felt nothing, absolutely nothing. And for the moment could not hear anything, either, save for a tremendous ringing in her ears.

Then she saw faces, looking down at her. She had not realised her eyes were open. And now she *could* hear, Mother screaming, a long way away. And the sergeant speaking, also from a long way away, although his face was quite close to her as he stooped. 'For Jesus' sake,' he was saying. 'You've been and gone and killed the bitch. And I was looking forward to a piece of her. That I was.'

'She'd have shot you, sarge. She'd have shot you,' said the man who had fired the pistol.

'Ten to one she'd have missed,' the sergeant said. 'And she was a damned good-looking woman.'

'There's still the old one,' the man said, eagerly. 'And the kid. I ain't never had a little kid, before. Say, that'll be sport, eh, sarge?'

The sergeant grunted, knelt beside Penelope, raised her left hand and pulled off her wedding and engagement rings, dropped them in his pocket. She kept staring at him, but he didn't seem to notice. And now she could feel, great waves of the most sickening pain surging upwards through her chest, and a ghastly sticky wet sensation soaking her gown. And a huge lump, beneath her right breast, the side on which she was lying, the side where she had been hit by the bullet.

'Ah, well,' the sergeant said, and turned away. 'Let's have a look at this little one.'

'No,' she said. 'Not Yvonne. Take me instead. I'm worth taking, even if I'm dying. Take me.' But apparently she hadn't actually said anything, as they did not turn their heads.

'Please don't hurt the children, please,' Priscilla said, her voice quavering. 'You've killed my daughter. Please leave the children. Take the wagon, but please leave the children.'

Yvonne screamed as she was dragged from the wagon, and Jimmy shouted his anger, a shout which ended in a gasp and the sound of a fist hitting soft flesh. We are all going to die, Penelope thought. All four of us. We'll just disappear, like the crew of the *Angela Driscoll*. And there was nothing she could do, because she was already dead.

Save perhaps make herself more comfortable. With a tremendous effort she rolled, and at last got rid of the lump in her breast. Because it had been caused by her right hand, pressed into her flesh, and still holding the revolver.

Yvonne screamed again as her clothes were torn. Priscilla moaned as the two enlisted men knelt to do the same to her. Penelope found herself on her belly, her chin bumping on the earth, squelching in the strange mixture of mud and blood which was welling about her. But both her arms were out in front of her, and she held the revolver between her hands. It would fire six times, Henry had said. Oh, pray to God it would fire six times.

'You're hurting me,' Yvonne cried. 'You're hurting me.'

'So lie still,' the sergeant recommended, and stood up to take off his pants. Penelope squeezed the trigger, once and then twice. The sergeant's back exploded into flying red, and as he sagged the second bullet took away the back of his head—he had only been five feet away from her. He disappeared, and she looked at the man with the rifle, just turning towards her in alarm. She fired again, once, twice. The first bullet struck him in the groin and he gave a high pitched squeal and doubled forward. The second hit him exactly in the centre of his scalp, seemed to split his head as if she had used an axe.

He also disappeared, and the third man scrambled off Priscilla Meigs' body, hastily dragging up his pants. 'For God's sake, lady,' he shouted. 'Give me a break. For God's sake...'

Penelope fired again, once and then twice.

Penelope was aware only of pain, sometimes sharp, sometimes dull, but ever present. She rather thought, with bursts of surprising clarity of mind, that when the pain was dull she was sleeping, or at least in a coma, because then everything else was dull as well. But when the pain was sharp she was clearly awake, and able to think, and understand the creaking, jolting motion of the wagon, the chattering of the children, the constriction of the bandage which Mother had bound around her chest. She was able to be aware of her dreadful thirst, and to suck greedily at the cup of water which was held to her lips by Jimmy. Jimmy cried all the while as he held the cup to her lips. But at least the sight of his crying face reassured her that she was still living, if only just.

That, and Mother's quiet control of the situation. Mother fed them and kept their spirits up and drove the wagon. Without her they would surely have died.

But then there were houses, and people. She had never been to Wilmington before, but presumably this was it, a bustling place, as befitted the last remaining seaport of the Confederacy. There were people, peering at her, whispering and muttering, and then lifting her from the coach. There was Mother, fussing and commanding. There was a good deal of pain.

Then there was a room, small and bare and airless, and a man, stripping away her bloodstained clothes, making clucking noises with his tongue against his teeth.

'Good work,' he said. 'Oh, good work, Mrs Meigs. Yes, indeed. You are to be congratulated. I could not have done it better myself. Mind you, Mrs Driscoll has been very lucky. The bullet struck the rib and exited cleanly. And your bandaging prevented the rib from splintering and penetrating a lung. Yes, indeed. Her main problem is loss of blood; the rib will knit very well, I should think. But you look pretty done up yourself, if I may say so, ma'am.'

Pretty done up. And I have been lucky, Penelope thought. She held her mother's hand, tightly. 'Yvonne...'

'Is as right as rain,' Priscilla promised. 'That sergeant didn't have the time to harm her. She's not even too disturbed. I think she and Jimmy are too delighted to discover their mother is at once a crack shot and a heroine, to be shocked.'

More liquid, and blessed rest. Actual sleep, because she no longer felt any pain, just sank beneath the influence of the sedative the doctor had given her into a deep coma, was reluctant to return to the land of the living and feeling, the land of pain. She opened her eyes, hesitantly, and gazed at Edward Anderson.

'I've brought Robert to see you,' he explained.

She stared at him, his face as grave as ever,

but his mouth unusually soft. And then at Robert, a husky teenager now, wearing seaman's clothing, peering at her in almost comical distress.

She licked her lips, because speaking was still an immensely difficult business, and she was again very thirsty. But Jimmy was there with a cup of water.

'We've been so lucky,' Priscilla said. 'The *Penelope Driscoll* was alongside, loading. Penny...Edward will give us berths. We'll be in Nassau the day after tomorrow. Think of it, Penny. Nassau! Away from all this blood and war and hate. Nassau!'

Penelope turned her head in alarm to gaze at him again. Nassau, she thought. But it could have been Timbuktoo, so long as it was anywhere outside of the tortured Confederacy. And so long as she was taken there by Edward Anderson.

But she couldn't sail with Edward, in the *Penelope Driscoll*. Whatever would Henry say? Whatever would Henry do?

Edward observed the expression on her face, but misinterpreted it. He held her hand. 'I've explained to your mother,' he said. 'That it is a dangerous journey. The Federal ships know all of our tricks by now, and they're getting pretty cute themselves. But they haven't stopped us yet.'

'It can't be any more dangerous than living here,' Priscilla said. 'If anyone thinks I am going to travel across country to Richmond, and risk more deserters...anyway, the voyage only takes just over twenty-four hours. And then we'll be away from it all. It'll be worth it, Penny. Believe me, it'll be worth it.'

Penelope made a great effort, attempted to speak, and sank back with a sigh.

'But I cannot promise to take any special precautions, because you and your children will be on board, Penny,' Edward said. 'You must understand that. There are still guns and munitions waiting to be brought in, and without them your people cannot continue fighting. You must think of that, and you must make the decision. *You* must make it, Penny. I imagine you could stay here until the war is over. That cannot be too long delayed now. I agree with your mother about risking the journey to Richmond. Or would you rather go to Nassau?'

She stared at him, and then at Robert, and past him at her mother, and her own children, anxiously waiting for her decision. Because, as he had said, it must be her decision. As if there could be the slightest doubt in her mind as to what she *wanted* to do. But Henry...yet Henry could come for her in Nassau as easily as in Richmond. Perhaps more easily.

Then what was she afraid of? Because Edward had asked for *her* decision, might have meant more than just a determination to risk the voyage? Because she knew, or hoped, that if she went with him they would renew their love? Edward had not seen her in three years, and before then had not touched her for more than fifteen years. What had happened between them was far in the past, and she was an old married woman of thirty-five, with a great gash beneath her right breast. Whatever remained, remained strictly in *her* mind, not his.

She filled her exhausted lungs with air. 'Please take me to Nassau, Edward,' she whispered. 'Please.'

She rode in another wagon down to the dockside, was placed in a stretcher to be carried on board. Stevedores stopped work to stare at her, women clustered on the quay; the fact that she had killed three men in defence of her own had spread. So then, she wondered, do they consider me a heroine? Or a coward, for fleeing them to the safety of the Bahamas?

More likely, she thought, they think I am mad, to risk myself and my children beneath the guns of the Federal cruisers.

She was carried up the gangway and on to the deck. The *Penelope Driscoll*. Her very own ship. And there were Cas Malewski and old John Dart to greet her, and Jehu. They had not changed, save perhaps to have grown in confidence from three years of successfully outstripping the best Federal warships. Although she gathered that John Dart did not actually make the Bahamas Passage, but remained in Wilmington to act as Edward's agent.

But the ship herself had certainly changed. There was little to be seen of the polished brightwork, and the decks had not been holystoned in some time; she never spent long enough in port. While in several places her bulwarks had been patched, and Penelope could even tell that it had at some time been necessary to replace her mizzen mast; the wood was of quite a different colour from the others.

Edward stood beside her. 'They do manage to hit us, occasionally,' he said. 'But as I said, they've not stopped us, yet. And they're not going to. You'll be safe, below.'

She was carried down the companion ladder into the great saloon. But here too there was no resemblance to the elegance she remembered from the old *Penelope*. The mirrors and pictures had all been taken down, and the huge dining table had been removed, as the carpets had been rolled up to leave bare decking. And almost every square inch of the large room was filled with bales of cotton. So were most of the twelve staterooms, but two had been cleared, and into one of these she was carried, and placed on the lower bunk.

'Can't I stay on deck?' she whispered. 'I so want to see.'

'When we're clear of the Federal fleet,' he promised.

But he joined them for supper, with Malewski and Robert, after the ship had been remoored, clear of the dock. They would not attempt to run the blockade until after dark. 'No problem tonight, you see, Aunt Penny,' Robert explained. 'There's no moon. And some cloud.'

He had become a sailor, wore a blue pea jacket and a peaked cap and had much of the confidence of his father. His father! She was afraid to look at him, for fear she might not be able to look away. He was as lean and hard and grim faced as she remembered him from the Christmas Eve Ball of 1861. But on board his own ship he was also confident and easily good-humoured. And he had come to her rescue. Could there possibly, after all of these years, remain a spark of love?

But thoughts such as those were far more dangerous than merely looking at him.

'I worry so, for Jonathan,' Priscilla was confiding. 'Up there in Richmond, with that dreadful man Grant coming ever closer...' No one would suppose that she had recently survived a far greater ordeal than almost anything Jonathan was likely to be subjected to. 'Edward, what *is* going to happen?'

He sighed, gazed at Penelope. 'I'm very much afraid the Confederacy is going to have to surrender, some time. Or be wiped off the face of the map.'

'But...''

'We'll never surrender,' Jimmy declared. 'Jeff Davis can lick Abe Lincoln any time.'

'Maybe he can, man to man. But there are

390

just too many Abe Lincolns in the North, Jimmy,' Edward said.

'Then why...why are you still risking your life, twice a week, for our cause?' Priscilla asked.

'Because I gave Jeff Davis my word that I would do so, Mrs Meigs,' he said. 'I took an oath, just as much as any fighting man.' Again he looked at Penelope. 'Just as much as Henry. I hear he's been decorated.'

'Yes,' Penelope said. And on impulse asked, 'Have you forgiven him?'

'Him?' Edward seemed surprised by the question, as if he had not really considered the matter recently. 'Why, I suppose I have. There hardly seems any point in bearing grudges at this moment, does there?'

They gazed at each other. But have you also forgiven me, she tried to ask, with her eyes.

'All ready, Captain,' Malewski said. He spoke quietly, even while the ship remained on her mooring. It was a habit which had become common to the entire ship's company. And he rubbed his hands together and held his jacket tightly against his chest as the temperature was only just above freezing.

'Very good, Cas.' Edward opened the speaking tube. 'Stand by, Mr Ritchie.' He closed the tube. 'Cast off, Mr Malewski.'

The *Penelope Driscoll* had been towed away from the dock and placed on a mooring buoy out in the river, during the afternoon. Everyone, including the Federal spies who were undoubtedly in the town, knew she was about to put to sea. But it helped for them not to know the exact time of departure. And when she did cast off, as now, there would be no tugs fussing around her to give her away.

Edward took the helm himself. It was eleven o'clock, and utterly dark. The *Penelope Driscoll* had set no sail, and her engines were just ticking over. A long, low, dark wraith, she slipped quietly through the darkness, towards the river mouth, still three miles away, and Fort Fisher. It was a journey few men would dare, in the darkness, and without lights. Yet, Edward, with his usual careful approach to any problem, on his first voyage here after the closure of Charleston, had spent three days in his pinnace, going up and down between the town and fort, charting every inch in his mind, until, as now, he could quite confidently make the journey blindfold.

A possible encounter with a sandbank was the very least of his problems. Beyond the fort he had been informed there were at least six Federal gunboats, steaming slowly up and down; he could make out the flashes of their signal lanterns even from in here. But they could not approach the river mouth too closely without coming under the guns of the fort. As long as Fisher was held for the Confederacy, Wilmington would be kept open. When it fell, as it must undoubtedly fall, then would the end of the war be in sight.

The Confederacy would lie in shattered ruin, and with it, every dream of Edward Anderson? Not this time. His endless voyages, to and from Nassau, every one with a laden ship, had made him into a wealthy man, and the money was on deposit in Nassau itself, where it could not be touched by either a greedy or a vengeful Federal government. He would complete the *Amanda*, the very moment he could regain possession of her. For that reason, perhaps, he even anticipated the end of the war. Yet he would not abandon his twice-weekly run, his twice-weekly joust with death or captivity. He had given his word to Jefferson Davis, and the preservation of that word was essential to the preservation of his honour. It was sufficiently tarnished.

He had never thought like that before to-night. He had concentrated on the essentials, for three years, as was necessary, in war time. He sailed his ship to the limits of her endurance, as he worked his men, and himself, to the limits of their endurance, as he relaxed and enjoyed himself, to the limits of his constitution, during his brief stays in Nassau. That was the only way to live, in wartime. Wars had a habit of blotting out the past, and drawing a huge, black curtain down across the future. That much he had learned in Nicaragua. And this was war on a much vaster scale than any he had previously experienced.

Yet it seemed that even war could not *entirely* blot out the past. Not when it could rise up out of the swamps to slap him in the face. He had wondered once, how she would react to being thrown into a pen with forty men, how her carefully protected personality, nurtured on dreams, would cope with so primeval a situation, his conception tinged with contempt at her probable collapse. So now she had killed three men, to save her family. Spoiled, wilful, selfish, she was still everything a woman should be, everything any man could ever desire. And now she lay, only twelve feet beneath him, her rib broken and her body a mass of bandages, but sailing in his ship for the first time in fifteen years.

To await her husband, in safety.

The fort drew abeam, and a single light winked at them. It was time to concentrate, on the looming bulk of Smith Island and Cape Fear to starboard, on the open sea and the warships to port. Still the *Penelope Driscoll* slipped almost silently forward, bows rising now to the Atlantic swell, while Malewski and Jehu both studied the horizon with their glasses, identifying the waiting ships.

'I have three to port,' Malewski said.

'I got one down here, Mr Edward,' Jehu said. His was the starboard side.

'We were told six,' Edward said thoughtfully, and rang down for a slight increase in speed.

The warships would not yet know he was out; the *Penelope Driscoll* showed no lights, and the swell was sufficient to keep her topsides below the horizon for two minutes out of every three. He swung the helm to port, to gain an offing from the dangers extending east of Cape Fear, and thus closed on the three ships. But he only held that course for three miles, and then swung back, to the south east, and the Bahamas. Now he was already outside the more southerly of the patrolling ships, but he was under no illusion that this was going to be an easy passage; there was no such thing, nowadays.

Sure enough, a lantern was signalling from one of the northerly gunboats and being answered by the southern; some keen-eyed lookout had spotted them. Edward promptly threw the telegraph lever over, and the engines thumped into full speed. The *Penelope Driscoll* seemed to shake herself free of a restraining leash as she leapt forward, in the same instant as all four warships fired star shells in her general direction. For a minute the entire sky was illuminated, and while Edward could hardly make out the enemy, so dazzling were the exploding lights above him, he knew that *they* were as clearly delineated as if the sun had been noon high.

Then the lights were gone, and the night seemed darker than ever. But now the warships had a memory to aim at. Guns exploded and the night became filled with rumbling thunder. Edward swung the helm hard to port and the *Penelope Driscoll* slewed round to leave the initial broadsides behind her. But at this speed her bubbling, white wake was clearly discernible even at several miles distance, and the firing continued. Edward brought the helm back, and the ship zigzagged, while shot exploded all about her, sending huge spumes of water high into the air, that spray scattering as if they were in a gale. And one of the shells struck home, high on the mizzen mast, bringing the wood thumping down, to trail half over the side, reducing the ship's speed by more than a knot. But instantly Malewski was leading a party of men with axes to cut the timber and the halliards away, and soon the *Penelope Driscoll* was leaping ahead again, with the water spouts and the flaring lights beginning to trail astern.

'She's yours, cox,' Edward said, relinquishing the helm. His shirt and jacket were drenched with sweat, despite the cold, but he could grin at Malewski. Nothing more expressive than that, now; they had merely completed a job of work. Edward rang down to the engine room to reduce speed somewhat, as the ship plunged onwards into the darkness, reached for the glass of rum Jehu had waiting for him. 'I'll turn in for an hour, Cas,' he said. 'We'll set some canvas at dawn, when we see if they're chasing us.'

Winter sunlight sparked from the waves of the Gulf Stream as the *Penelope Driscoll* skimmed over them, under sail alone now, for behind her was a brisk northerly. The wind was cold, but in the sun it was quite warm; they were past the thirtieth parallel of North Latitude, and approaching the sunlit waters of the Bahamas.

'We should sight Grand Bahama by dusk,' Edward told Priscilla Meigs. 'It's just a huge, empty sandbank and mangrove swamp, really. Nobody lives there. But it's British territory.'

'Do the Federal warships never follow you into the Bahamas?' Priscilla asked.

'Oh, yes, indeed. Or they used to. They've practically given it up now. They have to stick to the well defined deepwater channels, you see, like the North East or the North West Bahama Passage, not only because of their draft but because they cannot approach within three miles of any of the islands.'

'Whereas you can keep inshore and go across the banks?'

He winked. 'Some of them, Mrs Meigs.'

But she knew what he really wanted to do with his afternoon, and took her grandchildren on yet another inspection of the ship, leaving him alone with Penelope, who had been brought on deck, cocooned in blankets, and lay on a mattress in the stern, enjoying the breeze and the sunlight. Edward wondered what

Priscilla really thought about the situation, what she really hoped might happen. But no doubt she was as confused as any of them, while as aware of the emotions which were swirling about their heads.

Yet it had been her idea to approach him. Had she not done so, he would never have known they were in Wilmington at all, much less offered them berths on his ship; he did not spend sufficient time ashore to listen to all the local gossip.

He knelt beside her. 'Did you manage to sleep?'

'Eventually,' she said. 'I was terrified, when all that shooting was going on. Do you have that every voyage?'

'Except when there's mist, or a gale of wind. Were you really terrified?'

She smiled. 'Not really. I...' faint colour crept into the still bloodless cheeks. 'I still can't quite believe I'm here at all.'

'As I told you once,' Edward said. 'This is a lucky ship. And now she bears a lucky name. Do you still doubt that?'

'I don't doubt the skill of her master, Edward. I have never doubted that.'

He sighed, and looked forward, where Robert was instructing Priscilla as well as Jimmy and Yvonne in the art of tying a bowline knot. 'Those are two fine children,' he said.

She did not reply. She did not know what he wanted her to say.

He stood up. 'We'll be in Nassau by dawn tomorrow. Ever been there?'

She shook her head.

'Well, it's a bit of a boom town. But there's a good hotel, the Royal Victoria. They always keep a suite for me, so they'll put you in there. I'm afraid it'll be a bit noisy, but at least it's clean and comfortable, and you'll be well looked after.'

'But where will you sleep?' she asked.

'Oh, they'll find me a room somewhere. Or I can stay with the ship. We make a fairly fast turnaround.'

'Back to challenge the gunboats?'

'That's my job,' he explained, simply.

'I...' she was obviously racking her brains for something to say, so that he should not leave her. 'You will have to tell me what we owe for this voyage. The passage, I mean.'

He frowned at her.

'I have money,' she explained. 'I...' she bit her lip. 'Henry gave me a considerable amount in gold.'

He knelt again. 'What will Henry say when he learns that you have gone to Nassau, with me?'

She gazed at him, and then smiled. 'It is also with Mother, and Jimmy, and Yvonne. I don't even know if *he* hates *you* any more. As you said yesterday, hatred, except of the enemy, seems rather pointless, in war time.'

'Even of the enemy,' Edward said. 'There's

no passage money involved, Penny. Just having you on board is a pleasure.' His turn to flush, and recollect himself with a guilty smile. 'After all,' he added, 'the ship's named after you. You just had to sail in her, at least once.'

'Perhaps I shall be able to sail in her again,' she said. 'When the war is over.'

He stood again. 'I should think you will be able to do that,' he agreed. 'Because then she will belong to Henry again.'

Once more she bit her lip, conscious of having said the wrong thing, and he turned away, checked, as there came a hail from the masthead.

'Smoke, bearing one six five.'

Edward's head jerked; their course was one six zero, so the ship approaching them was virtually dead ahead.

Malewski hurried up with the telescopes.

'That's two ships,' Edward muttered, peering through the glass. And now he could make out their masts and sails as well. And a moment later the shapes of their hulls. 'By Christ,' he said. 'Federal cruisers. Two of them. The ships which should have been outside Wilmington. Just waiting for us.'

'What will you do?' Malewski asked.

It was a long time since he had asked that. There had never been any question during the past three years; the *Penelope Driscoll* always stood on, accepted every challenge. But never before had she carried passengers, and children, much less a wounded woman—much less Penelope Driscoll herself.

Edward chewed his lip. But only for a moment. They had known the risks they were running. 'You'll take Mrs Driscoll below,' he said. 'Mrs Meigs,' he called. 'Those are two Federal warships, out looking for us. Will you go below, please, and take the children? Hand those sails, Mr Malewski.'

'Won't we make even better time with sail *and* steam?' Malewski asked. 'The sooner we're past them the better.'

Edward shook his head, pointed at the black clouds which drifted lazily across from time to time, each passing accompanied by a freshening of the wind. 'I aim to zigzag, Cas, and with sails up, if there was a sudden squall, we'd risk a knock down. This is a business for engines alone.' He opened the speaking tube. 'I'm going to need everything you have down there, Mr Ritchie.'

'You shall have it, Captain,' came the reply.

Priscilla stood beside him. 'Are you going to fight them, Edward?'

'I don't have a gun on board, Mrs Meigs,' he said. 'I'm going to try to wriggle past them.' He pointed. 'See that low, green hump on the horizon? That's Grand Bahama. If I can get into the shoals over there, we have a pretty good chance.'

'But...they're *between* you and the island,'

she protested. 'Wouldn't it be safer to turn away, and outrun them, and come back after dark? Or even go right round the islands, and come in from the other side.'

'They'll still be there, after dark,' Edward told her. 'And to go round to the Atlantic would add at least another twenty-four hours to our journey.'

'What's twenty-four hours, compared with the safety of the ship?'

'Mrs Meigs,' he said, as patiently as he could. 'I have a cargo of rifles and ammunition waiting for me in Nassau. Bullets and weapons which General Lee has to have by the end of this week if he is to have any chance at all of stopping Grant. I don't aim to go on any Atlantic cruise while he's in that situation. So you go below. Jehu will give you life jackets, and mind you put them on.'

'I just wanted to know *why*,' she said, and blew him a kiss. 'I'm on your side, Edward.'

He went aft to Penelope. 'I think we should strap you into your bunk,' he said.

'So when you sink I'll be first to drown?'

'So you won't fall out when I start throwing her about the place,' he said. 'We won't sink, Penny. At least, not if I can help it. Off you go, now.'

'I'd much rather stay here,' she grumbled. But she allowed the sailors to carry her below.

'They're separating, Father,' Robert was studying the warships through his telescope.

402

'They're wanting to catch us whichever way we turn,' Edward said. 'Well, that's our best chance.'

The sails were down by now, and Malewski had come aft to join him. 'Straight through the middle?' he asked.

'Straight through the middle,' Edward said.

As usual, when approaching action, he took the helm himself, but he kept the speed at a moderate cruising rate of about eight knots, while the gap between the *Penelope Driscoll* and the Federal cruisers slowly narrowed. There was no room for any subterfuge here. But he doubted that subterfuge would work, any longer, anyway. The gunboats' skippers must have exchanged a hundred tales of his tricks and ruses during the past three years. They were not likely to be taken in now. But they had still not been able to discover an answer to his greatest trick of all, sheer speed. Because, very simply, there *was* no answer—save yet more speed. And that they lacked.

Now the ships were clearly visible to the naked eye; he could even make out the men on their decks. And soon came the first explosion, a puff of white smoke in the bows of the starboard ship, to be instantly followed by another from the port vessel. Columns of water leapt forty feet into the air only fifty feet from the *Penelope Driscoll*'s bows. That was accurate shooting. Too accurate by far.

Edward thrust the telegraph lever away from

403

him, and the engines roared. The *Penelope Driscoll* cut through the calm seas beneath a long plume of black smoke, her wake streaming astern. Now the gunboats commenced shooting in earnest. Clouds of powder smoke soared upwards from their decks, from time to time quite obliterating them. Vast columns of water exploded into the sky and scattered as spray across the steamship's decks. It was too hot to last very long. Edward twisted the helm, first to starboard, for five minutes, then to port, for a similar period of time, to set up a shallow zigzag, while his heart seemed to leap and his brain became filled with the wild exultation he always knew when handling a ship at speed and in moments of dangers. Yet he knew he was only waiting for the inevitable, and a moment later there came a crash and a cloud of flying wooden splinters from forward. The entire ship seemed to shake, and for a moment she even lost speed, but immediately she regained it, thrusting her now crumpled bow into the waves.

'Damage report,' Edward snapped, and Malewski hurried forward. Edward's hands were wet on the spokes of the wheel, partly from sweat and partly from salt water. He looked at Robert, who was still calmly studying the warships through his telescope.

'We're nearly out of range, Father,' he said.

'Five minutes more will do it, I reckon,'

Malewski hurried aft. 'We'll need a new

bowsprit,' he said. 'And some of the forestays have been shot away. But we're carrying out extra guys now. The mast will hold, even if we'd better not put any sail on it.'

'People?'

'Edwards, von Heller, and Johnson have been wounded by splinters.' Malewski drew a long breath. 'And Mason has been killed.'

Edward chewed his lip. He had had the same crew from the beginning, all volunteers found by Stephen Mallory, and he had licked them into a perfect team, just as he felt they regarded him as the perfect skipper. In the three years he and they had played at this hazardous game he had lost only two men, and one of those had gone overboard on a stormy night.

'I've had him taken below,' Malewski said. 'He was hit in the throat by a splinter. Must have died immediately.' He grasped Edward's shoulder. 'It was not your fault, Ned.'

Except that he was the master. But there were still the living to be cared for. Desperately he twisted the helm to and fro, snaked in and out of the flying columns of water, listened to Robert shouting, 'They're falling astern. We're through, Father. Through.'

Edward seemed to be picked up by a giant wave, which lifted him right over the bridge rail, still, it seemed, carrying the wheel with him. He looked down and saw the main deck rushing up towards him, smothered in an enormous blackness.

CHAPTER 11

The impact of the explosion drove the *Penelope Driscoll* over on to her side, and Penelope, all but falling out of her bunk, felt a stab of pain as the rope holding her cut into her bandages. The list only lasted a moment, before the ship came upright again, and continued at undiminished speed, but now she could hear a good deal of shouting, and suddenly she smelt the acrid tang of burning wood.

Priscilla appeared in the cabin doorway. 'The ship's on fire,' she announced, with massive calm. 'We must get on deck.'

'Are the children all right?' Penelope hastily released the rope, cautiously got out of the bunk, holding on to the upright, for the entire vessel was vibrating violently as she hurtled onwards.

'They're okay,' Priscilla said. 'Come along, children. No running now.' Jimmy and Yvonne wore their lifejackets, and carried one for Penelope. They were more excited than scared. Priscilla vigorously inserted her daughter's head and shoulders into the kapok garment and pushed her towards the door. Penelope leaned on her mother's arm as they made their way into the main cabin, coughing at the smoke coming down from a gaping hole in the decking above, although they could hear the reassuring clack-clack of the pumps dousing the flames by now and the staircase seemed undamaged. But they could also hear the shouts from above, and the word 'Captain' repeated several times, with great urgency.

'Edward,' Penelope gasped, and released her mother to hurry to the stairs, only to be overwhelmed by a tremendous weakness and fall to her knees at their foot. From there she saw two sailors descending, led by Malewski, carrying Edward between them. He looked terribly inert.

'Is he...?' she could not frame the words.

Malewski shook his head. 'He's broken his left leg, and his left arm, so far as I can see. I must get back on deck. Can you help Moffat bind him up? It should be done before he regains consciousness.'

'Yes,' Penelope said. 'Yes, we can.' She wanted to scream her joy that he had not been killed, or even too desperately hurt. 'But...the ship...'

'The shot struck just aft of the mizzen mast,' Malewski explained, 'and brought down what was left of that as well as making a hole, and exploding upwards, which blew Edward and most of the wheel on to the lower deck. But Robert is handling the emergency tiller, and doing a great job.'

'What's burning?' Jimmy wanted to know.

'The bas...I beg your pardon, ladies. The Federals were trying red hot shot, believe it or not, against an unarmed merchantman. But the blaze is under control, and we're just about clear. Put the Captain on the floor,' he told the sailors. 'That way he can't fall any further.'

Edward was laid on the cabin sole, and the two women knelt beside him, while Moffat the ship's carpenter brought in hastily cut down lengths of wood. Priscilla tore away Edward's blood stained trousers, to reveal the leg, and a very serious looking fracture—the splintered bone had penetrated the flesh.

'Ugh,' Yvonne commented. But there was nowhere she could be sent. Besides, Penelope reflected, she had watched the three deserters die.

'Easy, now, easy,' Moffat commanded, helping Priscilla slowly to straighten the limb, gently easing the bone back into place. Penelope dragged herself to the steward's galley to get some water, to wash away the blood; the flesh was blue next to the puncture, but the wound itself looked clean enough. But now Edward was starting to moan and twist his body as consciousness threatened to return him to a world of pain.

Moffat had the splints in place and Priscilla was passing cord round and round them, pulling them tight against the leg. 'I've seen worse breaks than that mend in a fortnight,' the carpenter said, cheerfully. 'And the skipper's a tough man. Now let's look at his arm.'

This was twisted and dislocated, but there were no bones broken, and Moffat easily jerked it back into place. Penelope was more concerned about the huge, swelling, purple lump on Edward's forehead, but when she applied cold water to it, his eyes opened. For a moment he clearly did not recognise her, and his face twisted with pain.

'Laudanum,' Priscilla decided. 'He must have laudanum. The doctor gave me some for you, Penny. It's in the cabin.'

'No laudanum,' Edward said. 'I've a ship to command.'

He attempted to raise himself on his good elbow, sank back with a groan. 'The ship...'

'Is just off Grand Bahama,' Penelope told him. 'We've escaped the warships. And we'll be tied up in Nassau by dawn.' She didn't know how much, if anything, of that was true, but it seemed the right thing to say. He definitely relaxed.

'And I've been hit,' he said. 'First time ever.'

'They're only fractures,' Priscilla said reassuringly, 'you'll soon be up and about.'

'It would never have happened,' Penelope said. 'If I hadn't been on board.'

He smiled at her, through the pain. 'That's nonsense, Penny. I've been riding my luck for three years. Besides...I wanted to come down here and spend the rest of the voyage with you.'

The sun soared above the horizon, played over the calm waters of the North West Bahama Passage. Edward pointed with his good arm. 'New Providence. Well, Hog Island. New Providence lies beyond.'

There were so many islands. Through which they had glided with consummate confidence during the darkness. From time to time they had seen a light, but no more. Now the entire southern horizon was dotted with low, green humps, each with its inner fringe of white sand and then its outer fringe of surf and green water. Most of them were clearly just uninhabited atolls. It was difficult to suppose there was a town or a harbour anywhere within a hundred miles. But every one of them was a fascinating paradise, Penelope thought, because she was approaching them on board the *Penelope Driscoll*, and because she was in the company of Edward Anderson.

She had remained on deck all night. She probably would have done so anyway, as Mother and the children had also slept on deck, wrapped in their blankets. The fire might have been extinguished easily enough, but the entire cabin stank of scorched wood and smouldering cotton, for some of the cargo had also caught fire and had had to be thoroughly soaked in salt water. But she had also remained awake, because after his gallantly reassuring remarks, Edward had insisted upon being carried up to con his ship through the shallows. And she had sat at his side to watch him do it. Clearly he was in great pain, and from time to time Jehu had brought them both a cup of coffee laced with brandy, but despite that, and despite her own discomfort, all of the years seemed to have rolled away, and they were out in mid-Atlantic on board the old *Penelope*, tilting at the entire world.

As they would do again? She did not know, and for the moment she did not care. Her wound, no less than the brandy, no less than her recent experiences, had drawn a veil over reality, left the future entirely irrelevant. She could not believe that one week ago she had sat on the lawn at Greenacres, to watch the children play and listen to the yardboys singing as they worked. It was difficult to believe that that life had ever really been. But what then was she to make of the woman who had shot and killed three men, or of the ship which had twisted its way through a barrage of shells? If those things were real, then Penelope Driscoll had never existed. Certainly Henry could never had existed. A meeting with Henry, at some time in the future, seemed so remote as to be impossible. As for sharing his bed again, *knowing* him...

But right this minute she did not wish to know any man. Not even Edward Anderson. It was sufficient to be sitting here, feeling the first warmth of a tropical day caress her flesh, and knowing that she was alive, and for the moment, anyway, utterly safe.

But then, she had never felt anything less than utterly safe, when in Edward's company.

He caught her looking at him, and she flushed. He pointed. 'The harbour.'

She had been so wrapped up in her reverie that she had not been watching the approaching land. Now she realised that they had rounded the western tip of the over-grown sandbank he had described as Hog Island, and that the much larger bulk of New Providence had opened before them. Here was a reasonably substantial island, more than twenty miles long, she estimated, and with a low hill forming a raised backbone. And climbing up the hill was the town of Nassau, a cluster of white and pink walled houses, square towered churches, towering shade trees, all dominated, half way up the hill, by a great dome, glistening in the morning sunlight.

'The ballroom of the Royal Victoria Hotel,' Edward explained.

But her interest had already been taken by the harbour itself, formed by the breakwater of Hog Island, which ran parallel to New Providence, with only narrow entrances at each end, guarded by shoals, a totally enclosed roadstead in which it would probably be possible to moor the entire United States fleet, she thought. And in which there were presently anchored not less than a hundred vessels, ranging in size from great four-masted clipper ships through a variety of paddle steamers—both stern-wheelers and sidewheelers—and down to little brigs and coasting schooners. And all was a bustle, with boats coming and going from the shore, with ships being warped alongside the docks for loading, with others leaving the harbour and dipping their ensigns to the *Penelope Driscoll* as they came abeam, and others in fact just having entered the anchorage ahead of them and still in the act of mooring up.

She glanced at Edward in wonderment. 'I had no idea...and this is only two hundred miles from the mainland?'

'A shade less, if you measure due west from Florida,' he said. 'I'll not pretend it was the least like this when I first came here, three years ago. But it's grown. Every get-rich-quick artist in the world has turned up in Nassau. It's just made for blockade running. Or piracy. This harbour was the home of the pirate fleet, a hundred and fifty years ago, you know. In these shallows they were virtually uncatchable. Now they're all running guns. It's quite a town.'

The *Penelope Driscoll* was feeling her way into the very heart of the harbour, engines slow ahead, Robert Anderson at the wheel, handling her with all the skill and confidence of his father. And the men on the other ships were noticing the shot damage, the shattered bowsprit, the stump of the mizzen mast, the scorchmarks on the after hull, and were calling out their questions even as they inspected her through their telescopes.

Inspecting *her*, as well, Penelope realised. And she had spent the night on deck. Her face was unwashed and her hair unbrushed. Because this was not the desert island she had anticipated, but one of the most busy places in the world. She hurried below to dress herself.

The *Penelope Driscoll* was the queen of this motley fleet, Penelope realised, as space was hastily made alongside the dock for them to be warped into position. Men crowded forward to hear first hand accounts of the battle and to inquire after the wounded and the dead. It occurred to her that Nassau had indeed become the shipping capital of the world as she listened to the clipped tones of the Britishers, the guttural growls of the Germans, the soft cadence of the French, the liquid drawl of the Spanish and Portuguese, the excited gabble of the Italians...even to the jabber of pidgin English as spoken by several Chinamen waiting on the dock.

There was also an enormous crowd of black people, passing their inimitable comments to and fro.

Now there were other men, sea captains by their dress, coming on board to shake Edward's good hand, to stand with Malewski and peer at the shot damage, to slap Robert on the shoulders and congratulate him on having survived. She and Priscilla and the two children stood in a corner of the quarterdeck and listened and stared in amazement. Never had she felt so totally irrelevant.

But there were also dock officials, and then a very resplendent black gentleman who wore a red frock coat and white knee breeches, white stockings and black shoes, as well as a white wig, and was apparently the representative of the Royal Victoria Hotel, and a close friend of Jehu, who had been appointed to look after them. They were taken ashore, Penelope with difficulty declining the use of the stretcher which had hastily been prepared for her, and placed in a carriage for the ride up the hill, a ride which took them through crowded Bay Street, the main thoroughfare, a quite amazing experience, for while the shops and offices lining the street had obviously been built many years before, and in wood, they had all recently been repainted and re-signed—and in many cases the lettering was in gold leaf. While the street itself was as smooth as the deck of a ship, having been covered in tarmacadam, as well as being lit, every few yards, by gas lamps, an innovation which had not yet been brought in to Charleston.

The carriage took them up the hill, through an avenue of red flowered poincianas and then into the gardens of the hotel itself, where they seemed to have entered some sub-tropical Eden. Here were not only the poincianas, the orange-flowered oleanders, the huge red and yellow blooms of the hibiscus, and the bristling spiky green leaves of the cactus, the whole dominated by the stately Royal palms which waved gently in the breeze, but the entire ground was covered in brightly coloured periwinkles, regarded as weeds by the Bahamians, apparently, and carelessly trampled underfoot.

The drive itself was composed of crushed conch shells, which cracked agreeably under the carriage wheels, before they arrived at the huge, high-pillared portico of the hotel itself, to be greeted by a small army of red-coated Negro busboys and red-gowned waitresses—Penelope had to remind herself that none of these people were any longer slaves, Emancipation in the British Empire having taken place in 1834. Yet they were as friendly and eager to help her as ever Jehu.

At the top of the steps there waited a smiling red-and-white striped vested English manager, who welcomed Jehu like an old friend and assured the ladies that Captain Anderson's suite was ready and waiting, as ever, and also that he had already sent for a doctor to check Penelope's wound and bandages. Then they were escorted through the huge ballroom, dominated by the great glass dome she had observed from the sea, through which the morning sunlight streamed to glint from half a dozen enormous crystal chandeliers and the

416

wealth of polished wooden floor. At the far end of the room an immense portrait of Queen Victoria and her German consort gazed benignly down.

By now Penelope was feeling quite exhausted, and she was grateful to be assisted up the stairs and into a palatial suite of rooms, in which the door knobs and the faucets on the bathtubs and washbasins were plated in gold, the carpet beneath their feet was so soft she thought she would very likely sink entirely out of sight, should she fall down, and the beds themselves were the largest she had ever seen. She was immediately encouraged to lie down in one, while a maid produced a glass of ice-cold lemonade for her to drink, and she listened to the shouts of laughter and clink of glasses rising from the central garden courtyard to the opened windows. Jimmy, who had been exploring, sat beside her on the bed, in a state of total wonderment, to whisper, 'Mama, I saw a man light a cigar out there...and he did it with a dollar bill.'

'Not too tight, I hope, Mrs Driscoll?' asked Dr MacNee, dragging on the bandages.

Penelope had to brace herself against the bed to stop herself from being pulled over. She looked at herself in the mirror. MacNee was very correct, had insisted that she encase herself from the thighs downwards in a sheet, and wear a bed jacket tucked up under her breasts, so that only her midriff, where he was actually working, was exposed to view. And that he was a most efficient doctor could not be doubted, even though her most close fitting corset had never held her in quite such a vice. 'It's not tight at all, doctor,' she lied with a gasp, and endeavoured to smile at the male nurse.

'Good. Good. Because it's a good clean wound. Healing well. Oh, yes, indeed, Mrs Driscoll. Healing well.'

He tied the last knot. 'Now you sit yourself down. Because that's what you must avoid more than anything. Fatigue. Fatigue, Mrs Driscoll. That's what you must avoid.'

Penelope sat down, cautiously; she had a distinct feeling that she had just been sawn in half.

To her surprise, the doctor sat beside her. 'You're not leaving Nassau soon, I hope?'

'Not for a while, doctor.'

'Good. Good. You'll be able to rest.' The doctor's rather chubby face screwed itself into an anguished ball. He looked at his nurse, who merely raised his eyebrows, then at Penelope, then at the floor, while a beetroot flush spread from his neck over his entire features. 'Now, my dear lady, my dear Mrs Driscoll, I...ah, have a favour to ask of you.'

'Of course, doctor.' She had no idea what he might have in mind.

'Well,' he said. 'I...we...my colleague and I, have formed an opinion that you might possess some influence with Captain Anderson. After all,' he said defensively, 'you did arrive in his ship. He does not usually carry passengers.'

'That is quite true,' Penelope agreed. 'And I will confess that the captain and I are old friends. But as to possessing any influence over him...I do not think anyone has that.'

'Yet must we try, Mrs Driscoll,' MacNee said, becoming suddenly professional again as she had not taken offence at the suggestion that she might be Edward's mistress. 'He is a very badly injured man. That leg, admirably set, mark you, admirably set, needs absolute rest if it is going to knit properly. The slightest accident, even a jar, could leave him with a permanently bent leg, or even worse. Yet despite my advice, he insisted upon attending the funeral of his dead seaman, and standing throughout the service, when the Reverend would have been perfectly willing to allow him to sit, and now, he is talking about taking his ship back to Wilmington, tomorrow night.'

'Edward?' she cried. 'But that is impossible.'

'Quite, my dear lady. Unfortunately, Captain Anderson regards it as entirely possible. And indeed, essential.'

Penelope got up. 'Where is he?'

MacNee raised his eyebrows. Presumably he had expected her to know that. 'He has been given a room just down the corridor. We thought, Nurse Randall and I, that perhaps if

419

you were to have a word with him...'

Penelope went to the door. 'I shall certainly do so,' she promised, and hurried down the corridor to the door of Edward's room, where she found him sitting up in bed surrounded by bills of lading and manifests, and work sheets, supplied to him by Malewski and his local agent, who stood one to each side. Robert sat in a chair by the window, but hastily got up as she entered.

Edward's left leg was entirely encased in bandages, and his left arm in a sling, while there was a bruise on his head the size of a fowl egg. But he looked quite delighted to see her. 'Why, Penny,' he said. 'You are looking quite well. No ill effects from the voyage?'

'None,' she said. 'But I cannot say the same thing about you, Edward. You're not seriously proposing to go to sea tomorrow night?'

'I see no reason why not. Malewski assures me that the repairs will be completed by then. They are rigging a jury mizzen now, and the new bowsprit is already in place. She'll be ready by tomorrow. And the cargo is already being loaded.'

'But *you* will not be ready by tomorrow, Edward,' she said. 'You have a very badly broken leg. The slightest jolt, even the movement of the ship, could cause the bones to separate again, and you'd wind up with a permanent limp.'

'Oh, come now,' he said. But he gave

Malewski an embarrassed glance; obviously the mate had made a similar point. 'What you do not seem able to understand,' he said. 'Any of you, is that there is a war on, and that we have a job of work to do. General Lee must have those munitions. According to that quack MacNee, I am going to be virtually a cripple for something like three weeks. That represents six voyages. The war could be lost by then.'

'Edward,' Penelope said. 'Don't you think that Mr Malewski is capable of commanding the *Penelope Driscoll*?'

'Cas?'

It was Malewski's turn to look embarrassed.

'For heaven's sake,' Penelope declared. 'He's sailed with you for twenty years, Edward. And he commanded his own ship in the Pacific before the Nicaraguan revolution. Why shouldn't he be able to command this one?'

Edward looked at Cas.

Who shrugged. 'I would be happy to act for you, Edward,' he said.

'They'll be waiting for you, Cas. All the way to Wilmington. You know that.'

'They are always waiting for us, Edward,' Cas said. 'Somewhere.'

Edward looked at Robert.

'I'll go as mate, Father,' Robert said.

Penelope bit her lip; she hadn't intended that Robert should sail without his father.

'Yes,' Edward said, drily. 'Yes.' He attempted to move his leg, could not without a

421

grimace of pain. 'Yes,' he said again.

But he was like a cat on hot bricks, insisting upon being carried up to the highest of the Royal Victoria's balconies to oversee the *Penelope Driscoll* leave harbour and watching her through his glass until she was out of sight. And then fretted for the next four days.

Jehu did his best to entertain his master. He arranged carriage drives down to the east end of the island, which sheltered under an ancient sugar mill which had been given the picturesque name of Blackbeard's Tower—the pirate Edward Teach, nicknamed Blackbeard, having sailed out of Nassau for several years, before, oddly enough, Penelope thought, removing himself to the South Carolina creeks, where he was eventually brought to book. The east end of the island was a mass of reefs and shallows, seeming to stretch forty-odd miles through a succession of little cays all the way to the original British settlement of Eleuthera. But westward, where also Jehu drove them, were to be found delighful sandy beaches, protected from the ocean by reefs several hundred yards off shore, where it was a delight to laze while drinking cold lemonade laced with rum, and where the children could take off their shoes and stockings and romp in the shallows.

Because Priscilla and Penelope, as well as Yvonne and Jimmy, more often than not accompanied the men on these jaunts. They were insidiously enjoyable, as Penelope could not help but reflect that it was very much like a family outing, Papa and Mama, Grandma and children. Just as she could not help but reflect that Henry had never shown the slightest interest in sitting around a beach and watching his children paddle.

But then, would Edward, but for his broken leg? In many ways the two men, for all of their long antagonism and the very real differences in their characters, were surprisingly alike, both driven by a burning energy which prohibitied the slightest true relaxation.

Penelope spent a good deal of her time in considering her situation. For *her* wound was healing very fast; the jagged tear in her flesh, belatedly stitched together by the doctor in Wilmington, had completely closed and was now hardly more than a purple stain on the smooth flesh. Two days after the *Penelope Driscoll* sailed she was able to discard her bandages altogether, as Dr MacNee, delicately probing her with his finger, came to the conclusion that her broken rib was mending neatly.

'But no violent exercise, Mrs Driscoll. No violent exercise.'

'No violent exercise, doctor,' she had agreed, with a rueful smile. Because here she was, shipwrecked on the desert island of her dreams— and with all the civilised appointments that in a dream desert island she would certainly have found—with the man of her dreams, and effectively entirely in his power, as she had always dreamed...and there was absolutely nothing either of them could do about it.

Would he have wanted to, had his leg not been shattered? It was impossible to say. Over the lonely years he had become too self-contained and revealed little of what he was thinking...save his agitation at the thought of what might be happening to his ship and his son. But his leg would not always be shattered, and his ship would surely return safely, as she had always done in the past. She had no doubt that eventually the decision would have to be made, the urges would have to be faced. Besides, it was what she wanted.

She had written Henry a letter, to be delivered by Malewski, at least to Army Headquarters in Wilmington. It was something she had to do, anyway, to inform him what they had done, where they had gone. The letter had been very matter-of-fact; she had mentioned the incident of the three deserters only in passing, and her own wound only incidentally. She had advanced solid reasons for leaving the Confederacy, in all the circumstances, and had conveyed the impression that the decision had been hers rather than her mother's. But she had also mentioned, just as casually, that they had sailed in the *Penelope Driscoll*. Henry would have to draw his own conclusions from that, and from her disobedience of his direct command. Supposing he ever received the letter. Supposing he *lived* to receive it..but these were unthinkable thoughts.

And as, at the moment, there were no conclusions for him to draw, *she* had to make up her mind, now, while she had the opportunity. She loved. She had always loved. And in the implementation of that love she had committed a great crime—for which she had been punished, time and again. Surely sufficiently. Surely now that the pair of them jointly approached middle age they could be allowed to find each other once again, to achieve at least a modicum of happiness before it was too late?

But that would be to commit another great crime. A whole series of them, in fact. Henry loved her. He had always loved her, it seemed, just as she had always loved Edward. Whatever his faults, whatever dubious paths down which his ambitions and his hatred of Edward had led him, he loved her. And to desert him would not merely be a moral crime; it would also be a crime in the eyes of the law, and would carry with it, undoubtedly, the sacrifice of her children. Unless she kidnapped them and sailed the seas forever with Edward. But Edward did not wish merely to sail the seas. He wished to build, and experiment, and create—and to interfere with *that* vision, *that* ambition, *that* determination, would be the greatest crime of all.

Yet would she do all of that, she knew, and more—if he but held out his hand. And that could not happen until the *Penelope Driscoll* had returned. As she did, four days later, quite unscathed.

'We were lucky,' Malewski said. 'Fog going up...'

'And a north-easterly gale coming down,' Robert said. 'Oh, it was magnificent, Father. We saw a Federal sloop, but it was all she could do to keep from being overwhelmed. We ran down under sail *and* engine.'

Edward's head turned, sharply, to look at Malewski.

The big Pole flushed. 'Well...she handled very well, really, Edward. There was no danger.'

Edward made no comment, but Penelope remembered him wrestling with the *Penelope* during that mad, exciting race across the Atlantic, sixteen years before. Yet however disturbed he might have been, he insensibly, and even reluctantly, she thought, began to relax. Obviously he had only contemplated leaving the ship to his friend for a single voyage. But his leg was still a long way from being sound again, and Lee was still fighting for his life in Virginia, waiting anxiously for each shipload of munitions. And now it was easier to wave them goodbye on their next voyage. Certainly it was the safest time of the year for blockade running, with either fog or high winds constantly sweeping the Gulf Stream and the vicinity of Cape Fear.

426

The measure of his mood was that, the second night after their departure, he escorted her to the dance. There was a dance every other night in the great ballroom of the hotel; she had several times been kept awake by the booming music and the shrill laughter, much of it emanating from the gardens beneath her window, as the revellers overflowed from the overheated dance floor. It was more than three years since she had been to a ball, and indeed, she had brought no proper gown with her. But at Edward's command Negro seamstresses descended on her, measuring and taping, and within twenty-four hours she was radiant in a pale pink gauze gown decorated with white stripes and white flounces and with lace ruffles at her hem. They had even found a crinoline for her to wear, the weight of which she was prepared to risk as she did not suppose she would be doing any actual dancing. There was no hairdresser capable of coping with her long brown hair, so they tucked it up and smothered it in flowers and for jewellery she wore the one piece she had brought with her from Greenacres, her pearl necklace. She thought she at least measured up to Edward, in his black tail coat with its silk revers, his black trousers with the braided seams, his black satin waistcoat, his white shirt, and collar and tie. And this night he had shrugged away Jehu and his wheelchair, and merely used a stick to lean upon, while she was able to support him on the other side.

Their entry was greeted with a burst of applause, then by a more general round of cheering, while the band struck up *For He's a Jolly Good Fellow*. Because for all of her observation of the respect in which he was held by these hardbitten sailors who weekly risked their lives, whether for money or for patriotism, she had not before tonight truly understood how much he was *loved* by them. He was the original. As the hotel manager, Mr Danvers, never tired of telling her, when the *Penelope Driscoll* had first sailed into Nassau Harbour she had found an empty roadstead, save for the ship from England which had been waiting for her. The Bahamas, it seemed, hardly more than several hundred tiny sandbanks dotted on top of one immense sandbank, had nothing to offer the world. Even their shelter from the wind was hardly appreciated by seamen because of the innumerable coral reefs which littered their pale green waters. That they were British at all was an accident. They had been left deserted by the Spaniards, who had deported the entire Indian population to Hispaniola to work the mines there, and had remained deserted for a hundred years, until a band of Englishmen, called the Eleutheran Adventurers, fleeing religious persecution in the British colony of Bermuda, several hundred miles to the north, had sailed due south and eventually bumped into the island called by the Indians Cigatoo, but which they had renamed after their dream, Eleuthera, the Greek word for freedom.

There they had stayed, ekeing out a precarious existence by fishing, while to the south, in the huge natural harbour of New Providence, the scum of the seven seas had insensibly accumulated, ex-privateers thrown out of employment by the Peace of Utrecht in 1714, criminals and law-breakers of every description, seeking a community which had no law at all, issuing from amongst their sandbanks to prey on the merchant ships seeking a passage from the still wealthy West Indies to Europe. Their bloodstained paradise had eventually become such a nuisance to those who sought only to sail in peace that the English Government had been forced to take action, and they had been brought to order by the famous Woodes Rogers, after which the islands had again sunk into a sleepy, impoverished somnolence. An influx of Tories from the United States, following the British defeat in the War of the Revolution, had briefly revived a modicum of prosperity, as they had attempted to grow cotton and cane. But these attempts to make something out of the soil-less sand had also come to naught, and only three years before the islands had been as decrepit and derelict as ever.

Edward Anderson, and the men who had clustered behind him to take their share of profits from running the Federal blockade, had ended all of that. And now Nassau, as Penelope had observed, was one of the most prosperous communities in the world. Yet, like all boom towns, it remained a place of strange absurdities. She had not supposed she would be required to dance. But those white women of New Providence who regarded themselves as respectable, shunned the Royal Victoria, with its drinking and its gambling and its oaths, and its *men*, as a haunt of the devil. It had immediately been obvious to her that she and her mother had been the only white women actually living in the hotel—or rather, the only two *women* at all, except the maids. She had not, however, expected to find herself the only white woman at the dance. There were, in fact, only a dozen women all told; the others were mulattoes of various shades, pretty and vivacious, yet marked down by their heritage as fair game, and entirely aware that the evening would end with their services being obtained by the highest bidder. Had Edward ever secured one of these brown-skinned beauties for himself, she wondered?

They were in continuous demand as dancing partners, for there were some sixty men present. But every man had eyes only for the already famous Mrs Driscoll, and took a lesser substitute only when forced to. She spent the entire evening on the floor, thankful that neither Mother nor Doctor MacNee were here to oversee her, waltzing from man to man, while sweat soaked her temples and dribbled down her back, and she was assailed over and over with questions about the battle and the deserters, as that fracas had now come to be considered, and about what it was like to sail on the *Penelope Driscoll*, intermingled with the most curious confessions about themselves and those they had left behind in Liverpool or Hamburg or Bordeaux or Cadiz or Naples, the wives and the children they had not seen in some time, but to whom they looked forward to returning, soon, their pockets filled with gold. Because few supposed the war could possibly last much longer, however much they were all resolved to milk it for the last penny.

And certainly there was not a man present who was not by any ordinary standards absurdly wealthy. Every sea captain was at least as well-dressed as Edward, and most, unlike him, sported huge diamond or ruby rings on their fingers, and diamond-studded pins in their shirts. Their pockets were invariably stuffed with bank notes, and they were indeed as likely as not to thrust one into a passing candle flame to light their cigars—not quite as extravagant a gesture as might be supposed, as in this money mad city even a box of matches was likely to cost several dollars. What their suite was costing she had no idea, but they were never presented with an account, so she had to suppose that Edward was taking care of it. An outrageous assumption of responsibility for them, but not one she was prepared to dispute.

Because throughout the evening he sat on his chair, with a stool placed for his leg, surveying the scene with benevolent pleasure, exactly like the potentate he had become.

And when, with the waiters' aid, he heaved himself to his feet, the music stopped, and the man with whom she was dancing immediately released her and bowed from the waist.

Suddenly she was aroused, and it had been so long since she had been sexually excited. But now she was back on board the *Penelope* again, surging through the Atlantic swell, and knowing that soon she would hold him in her arms. She had been drinking champagne, although he, she thought, was absolutely sober. But she wanted him to be sober, because tonight she wanted him to send her through all those magic gateways at which she had so often in the past merely lingered.

She held his arm as they went up the stairs. The suite she was occupying with her mother and the children came before his bedroom, and at the door she hesitated. They had not spoken since leaving the dance floor.

Now he said, 'I love you. Oh, how I love you, Penny.'

Yet could there be no mistakes, this time. When last he had loved her, she had been a girl.

'I have changed,' she said. 'You must know that. I have fought, and killed, and learned how to hate.'

'And how to die, if necessary,' he said. 'Had

you not changed, Penny, I would not love you. Once, I only *wanted* you.'

'I have dreamed of you, every night, for twenty years,' she said.

'And Henry? The children?' Because he too would not risk a mistake, this night. She must know, and accept, exactly what she was doing.

'And the world,' she said. 'And heaven and hell. And the deep blue sea.'

He gazed at her for some seconds, but he was already moving forward, along the corridor, carrying her with him. 'They all have a habit of seeking their revenge.'

'This time I shall let them,' she said. 'The only mistake I ever made was in not loving you, always.'

The bedroom door was opened by an astonished Jehu.

'Go to bed, Jehu,' Edward said.

The Negro gave Penelope a delighted glance. 'Yes, *sir*, Mr Edward,' he said, and hurried down the corridor.

Edward sat on the bed, while she closed and locked the door. 'I'm afraid I cannot undress myself,' he said.

'I shall do it.' Gently she laid him on his back, unlaced his shoe.

'Nor, I'm afraid, can I behave in any very orthodox fashion,' he said.

She lay on her elbow beside him. 'I do not want orthodoxy from you, Edward Anderson. I want love. We have hands, and lips, and

433

thoughts, and feelings. We need nothing more.' She kissed him on the lips.

Here then, at last, was what she had always wanted, what she had spent her entire life dreaming of. As, for most of her life, he had been there—and for most of her life she had not had the sense to go to him.

But that was in the past, and suddenly, as she lay in his arms and listened to a cock crowing as the dawn light slowly spread over the island, she could see the future falling into place. Henry would grant her a divorce. As he loved her, he would surely do that, where so much of her own happiness was involved. Nor would he seek to retain the children. To him they had never been more than the necessary adjuncts of marriage. Undoubtedly there would be recriminations, and some tears...but it would be done. Because she willed it so. Because she had come to the understanding that she could not live without Edward Anderson...she could only exist. As she had but existed for sixteen years.

'Do you mind if I stay a while longer?' she asked.

'What of your mother?'

'She will have to be told, today,' Penelope said. 'If you wish me to tell her at all.' Because, of course, *her* will was not sufficient. Or even important.

'I wish you to stay with me, always, if it can

434

be done,' he said.

'It can be done,' she promised.

Priscilla Meigs was already up, and breakfasting with the children, when Penelope returned, to bathe and dress for the day. She gazed at her daughter, eyebrows arched.

'I have been with Edward,' Penelope said.

'Oh, my dear,' Priscilla said. 'Oh, my dear, dear girl. But are you *sure*? There will be a lot of trouble.'

'I am sure,' Penelope said. 'And so is he.'

'Then am I the happiest woman in the world,' Priscilla said. 'I never doubted that he was the man for you, Penny. Oh, I am the happiest woman in the world.'

In the most amazing fashion, it seemed that the entire hotel knew of it, and also, was realising for the first time that before last night she had *not* been Captain Anderson's mistress. This was not a society of genteel hypocrisy. Every man here knew his purpose in life, and did not disguise it. Their attitude to human relationships was on a similar lusty, vulgar scale; however Penelope was a little shocked to receive a vast bouquet of flowers from the hotel management, with a card, 'To your future happiness,' almost as if she and Edward had been most publicly married.

Yet there could be no embarrassment, as she went downstairs for lunch on Edward's arm, to be greeted by the staff and residents, almost expecting to be asked exactly how it had been.

435

They drank champagne with the meal, compliments of the management, and made plans for an afternoon drive out to Love Beach, on the north western coast, and also for the celebration they would have when the *Penelope Driscoll* returned, the next day, and listened to a swelling hubbub from the harbour which had men running on to the verandah.

'It is a Federal warship,' Mr Danvers came to tell Edward. 'Entering Nassau Harbour. Now there is a strange event. Like a fox entering a hencoop, eh? But she can touch nothing here. Not without risking war with Great Britain.'

Edward was frowning, and suddenly an immense icy hand seemed to close on Penelope's heart, as the men crowding the porch parted, and she watched the blue-uniformed captain of the Federal ship coming up the stairs and entering the room.

'Captain Anderson,' he said.

Edward held on to the table to stand up. His face was expressionless, but Penelope could see the little muscles at the base of his jaw curling into tight balls.

The captain held out his hand. 'Commander Evans, sir. I apologise for the news I must bring. You have fought us long and well, and it is a pity it had to end this way.'

'You have taken my ship,' Edward said.

'No, sir. The *Penelope Driscoll* was not intended by God to be taken, in my opinion. But

I watched her go down, yesterday morning.'

'Go down?' Penelope whispered. 'You mean you sank her?'

'No, ma'am,' Evans said. 'She capsized in a squall, off Grand Bahama, and sank in seconds. There was only one survivor. But he at least is your son, sir. Robert Anderson.'

Robert had been long enough in the cold January sea to have suffered from exposure, as he was also clearly suffering from shock. He had been kept wrapped in blankets on board the warship, and was transferred to the hotel to be put immediately to bed with hot water bottles. But by now he could tell them what had happened.

'It was a squally day,' he said, his teeth chattering. 'And we were running down before a north easterly, maybe twenty-five knots, no more. Then we saw the warship, and Cas told Mr Ritchie to give us all the steam he had, as well. It was like nothing I've ever known before, Father.'

'You used full steam power, while already sailing before a twenty-five knot wind?' Edward asked.

'I was on the helm,' Robert said. 'But I couldn't hold her. I swear we were making twenty knots. So Cas came as well, and the boatswain. It was almost like flying, and we went past the cruiser before she could even take aim, I reckon. She was almost out of sight, and

Cas was just ringing down to reduce speed, when there was a sudden line squall. It happened with a windshift. The force must have increased to above forty knots, for a few seconds and went more easterly at the same time. It really all happened so fast I can't remember much about it. We were just thrown off the wheel. I got hold of a shroud and I looked down, and saw the rail dipping under the water at the starboard side. You know, Father, we've dipped a rail before, but we've never doubted she was coming back up. This time I knew she wouldn't. It was the most curious thing I've ever seen. It seemed to take so long, but I guess it couldn't have been more than a few seconds. She just went over and over and over. I remembered thinking, I must let go of this shroud, or she'll take me down with her. But I didn't want to. I wanted to hold on, forever.' He sighed. 'But I let go.'

There was silence in the bedroom. There were so many questions they all wanted to ask, but they could only wait, for him to speak again.

'I found myself swimming,' he said. 'There was nothing else at all. The ship must have filled and gone straight down. There was only me, and Cas, swimming.'

'Cas?' Edward cried. 'You mean he survived, too?'

Robert sighed. 'He didn't go down with the ship itself. I guess he must have been washed

438

off, like me. But then he said, "I've lost the ship," and he just went under. He was only about twelve feet from me. But when I got to him he had disappeared. I thought I would drown too, but then I saw the warship steaming after us.' He looked at Captain Evans. 'It was a miracle they saw me.'

'It was really the most horrifying thing I have ever seen, Anderson,' Evans said. 'The *Penelope Driscoll* just went right over, without the slightest hesitation. It couldn't have taken more than a few seconds, and then she was upside down. And a moment later she was gone.'

'Yes,' Edward said. 'I thank you, for saving the life of my son.' He got up, using his stick, and limped on to the balcony outside the room. After a moment, Penelope followed him. 'All of those men,' he said. 'All of those men.'

For a moment all of the old fears welled up inside her. As he had said, only last night, the sea and the sky, heaven and hell, have their ways of exacting penalties from mortals who seek to defy them.

But that was superstition. It had to be superstition. And she had turned her back on superstition.

'She was being oversailed, Edward,' she said. 'You know that. And Cas knew that, too.'

'Oh, aye,' he said. 'She was being oversailed, all right. But it was the design which was wrong.'

'Cas knew that too,' she insisted. 'He knew

439

the risks he was taking. The risk he *had* taken, in carrying too much sail.'

He nodded, and sighed, and she waited. Once again their love had coincided with tragedy. So now they must either part forever, driven to desperation *by* that superstition, because it is an inescapable part of human nature, or they must square their shoulders and boldly face the future, together. But the decision had to be his.

He was staring out of the window at the harbour, where every ship wore its colours at half mast, including the Federal cruiser, and then at the sea beyond. The wind remained fresh from the north-east, and there were white-caps beyond Hog Island.

'Do you know,' he said, half to himself. 'I have now sailed for nearly thirty years, and I have never been wrecked? Every one of the four *Penelope* class steamers has now gone down. Even the *Regina* was sunk last year. And I have never been in a shipwreck. Not even a stranding. There is a strange record.'

'A proud one,' she said. 'If you had been on board, the *Penelope Driscoll* would still have lived.' She bit her lip, knowing what she had just said.

'Yes,' he mused. 'I should have been there instead of here.' He turned to look at her, and her heart constricted.

'I must not make that mistake again,' he said. 'I must be there. And the ship must have

440

no weaknesses. The *Amanda* must be the safest ship that ever put to sea. I must make sure of that.'

She waited, scarce daring to draw her breath.

He took her hand. '*We* must make sure of that,' he said.

CHAPTER 12

The shipyard had been burned. Much of Charleston had been burned; there had been a fire the entire length of Market Street, Edward saw. The city no longer truly existed, as the Charleston he remembered from five years ago. Now there were few white faces to be seen, unless they happened to be wearing the uniform of a Federal soldier, and those houses which had survived the holocaust were shuttered and locked. Truly, he thought, was he looking at the face of defeat.

But at least the shipyard was in the process of being rebuilt, even if the labour here, surprisingly, was almost entirely white. An angry, suspicious labour force. He was halted at the gate with a surly demand for his business.

'I seek Bartell,' he said.

'Bartell?' The man gave a brief laugh. 'He's gone. This yard belongs to Sanders, now.'

'Sanders?' Edward frowned at him. 'Well,

then, I seek Mr Sanders.'

'What about? He don't own no Bartell debts.'

'I had business with Bartell,' Edward said. 'Before the war. Presumably Mr Sanders will be able to continue that business?'

'Business, eh?' The man looked Edward up and down. He had carefully refrained from wearing the uniform of a shipmaster, but his broadcloth suit was well cut and there could be no missing the gold of his watchchain. 'You'd best come in. What did you say your name was?'

'I didn't,' Edward said.

The man hesitated, and then walked in front of him, over that so well remembered roadway, past the slip, now covered in green slime, and up to the main building shed. Here the roof had fallen in, and was now in the process of being cleared away. But as he had hoped and expected, the iron keel and hull of the *Amanda* still lay where he had left them, rusting now, but capable of being restored. His heart swelled with relief, and also pride.

'Pretty, ain't she? Belonged to Anderson, the blockade runner. You'll have heard of him. I'm Don Sanders.' The man was short and solidly built, shock headed and strong fingered. He spoke with a quick Illinois accent.

'And now you own the yard,' Edward said.

'It was going cheap,' Sanders said. 'Everything around here's going cheap. But we're

442

busy. Maybe you'd tell me your name and business.'

Edward drew a long breath; there was no way he had been able to estimate properly the risk he was running in returning here at all—which was why he had come alone, save for Jehu. But he *was* here. 'My name is Edward Anderson,' he said. 'And my business is that ship.'

Sanders stared at him for several seconds, his eyes narrowing. But he did not lack either nerve or confidence. 'Well, well,' he said. 'You know, Anderson, we figured you'd come back. Eventually. You'd best come in to the office. My partner will want a word with you.' He opened the door, showed Edward inside. 'Here's the man you've been waiting for, Mr Driscoll.'

Alone of everything he had seen this day, Edward thought Henry had changed least. Except perhaps for his expression. Too often in the past he had been prepared to dissemble, at least towards his rival. Today he no longer considered it necessary. 'Anderson,' he said, and leaned back in his chair. His eyes seemed to gleam with pleasure—but it was a malevolent pleasure. 'I never thought you would have the nerve to come back here.'

'As we wondered why you didn't seem to have the nerve to come to Nassau,' Edward said, speaking with a confidence he did not really feel. He couldn't doubt there was trouble ahead. 'Or even to reply to Penny's letters.'

'I did not consider it a subject that could be adequately settled, by letter,' Henry said, and sat up straight. 'Where is my wife? Where are my children?'

'They are in Nassau,' Edward said. 'As Penny told you in her letter. I'll take you to them, if you wish.'

'Oh, I will come for them, when I am ready. And I will come accompanied by a Federal marshal. There is also a matter of ten thousand dollars.'

'That's in Nassau as well.' Edward said. 'Waiting for you. I'm not so sure about Penny. But that's a matter for you and her. I've come for my ship.'

'Your ship? Don't make me laugh, Anderson. That ship is part of the assets of Bartell's Shipyard, which now belongs to Mr Sanders here. He and I, in partnership, are combining Bartell's with Driscoll's, and merging the old Meigs-Driscoll Line into a new Sanders-Driscoll Line. There is no room for more than one shipping line out of Charleston. That ship belongs to us.'

'Bartell had no money in the *Amanda*, Henry,' Edward said, speaking very evenly. 'Every cent that was spent on that boat came out of my pocket.'

'*Your* pocket?' Henry demanded. 'You mean it came out of *my* pocket, by means of that

444

absurd court judgement you obtained against Jonathan Meigs. Well, that's over and done with. The Court which gave that judgement no longer exists. Jonathan Meigs no longer exists...'

'Jonathan?' Edward asked. Part of his mission had been to discover what had happened to Jonathan.

Henry waved his hand. 'He was killed in the battles outside Richmond.' He frowned. 'Doesn't Priscilla know that? Doesn't Penny know?'

'We've been rather cut off, these past few months.' Edward said. 'Since the *Penelope Driscoll* went down, and the Federal fleet closed Wilmington.'

'Ha,' Henry said. 'And that's another thing. You took my ship. Well, you lost her, as I knew you would. So I'm taking the hull of the *Amanda* in part payment. And you can take that to any court in this land, Anderson. As an ex-blockade runner you'll get short shrift from the Federal Government, I can promise you that.' He waited for some reply, and not receiving any became bolder. 'And as a seducer of a man's wife, a kidnapper of his children, you'll get even less. I'm in the process of obtaining a court order now, demanding their return to me. A suit against you for damages will follow.'

He paused again, staring at Edward, his cheeks flushed. But his eyes were expectant. Because he was working to a plan, Edward realised, gradually increasing the hostility and

445

rudeness of his words, laying a trap, which Edward could see even as he stepped into it. But he *was* going to step into it. He was too angry to wish to avoid it.

'You are a lying, cheating scoundrel,' he said, quietly. 'I have always known you for that. I have always known you as the man who backed Walker. Now I can see for myself how rapidly you've gone into business with this carpetbagger.' He gave Sanders a contemptuous glance. 'Well, by God, you do your damnedest, Driscoll. You may be able to sequestrate the hull of my ship, but I'll build another one which will make her obsolete before she ever sees water. And I'll make you pay for the deaths of my men in Nicaragua, if it's the last I ever do. As for Penny and the children, they stay with me until they choose to leave. Your Federal marshal won't have any jurisdiction in Nassau.'

Henry looked at Sanders.

'Them's insulting words, Driscoll,' Sanders said. 'And uttered by a man who's run off with your wife. You've rights, you have. Rights as a man and as a husband.'

Henry stared at Edward, slowly licked his lips. He made Edward think of a tiger watching a lump of raw meat being pushed into his cage.

But he wanted to end it, here and now. 'Any time you choose,' he said. 'And any place.'

'Well, then,' Sanders said. 'I reckon we could make it at dawn tomorrow morning, Captain Anderson. Right here in this yard. That way we'll be sure of privacy.' He pointed. 'You be here, now, or I'll paint you a coward as well as a wife stealer, from here to San Francisco.'

Already the white heat was fading. Hate was not a sufficient part of his personality.

Had he also meant to provoke a duel? To kill Henry Driscoll would certainly be the simplest method of ending their lifelong enmity. Henry certainly saw it that way.

Nor could he really discover any prick of conscience; the man deserved no better.

But he had not come to Charleston to fight or kill anyone. He had thought to leave all that behind him; up to now, he *had* managed to leave it all behind him, from the day of Walker's execution. And Henry was Penny's lawful husband, just as he was also the father of Jimmy and Yvonne. There would be something horribly primeval about shooting down your mistress's husband, whatever his crimes. What a dismal tale he would have to carry back to Nassau, Jonathan dead, as well as old John Dart—as he had ascertained during his stop at Wilmington—and now Henry...

And if he did kill Henry, he knew in his heart that it would not be because of Penny. It would not even be because of Walker, and Trethowan, and Reynolds, and all the others. It would be out of anger at having lost the hull of the *Amanda*. Because that she was lost was certain.

447

Henry was undoubtedly right in his estimation of the support he would receive from the Federal courts, especially as he had had the foresight to team up with a Northerner himself. While he...

He called at Bartell's home, which had suffered only partly from fire or looting, gazed at the frightened faces of the shipbuilder and his prematurely old wife. 'They've done a big job on you, Ned,' Bartell said. 'Driscoll has made everybody aware that you're a New Yorker born, but that you sailed for the South. There was even talk of a warrant, at one time. But they reckoned you'd committed no treason, as you'd declared for the South from the beginning, and as you'd lived here twenty years before the war began. Your old friend Stephen Mallory argued that one for you, and won.'

'So I'm grateful,' Edward said. But he could not keep the bitterness out of his voice.

Bartell sighed. 'Driscoll was unhappy about that. That's when he went after the *Amanda*, I reckon. He figured that would fetch you back. He'd showed no interest in my yard before, because it was just a burned out wreck.'

'And you sold it to him, at first asking,' Edward said.

'What was I to do?' Bartell shouted. 'We were starving. You were safely tucked away in Nassau, with no word if you were ever coming back. And I hadn't made any fortune out of running guns.'

'You weren't risking your life every day of the week, either,' Edward reminded him. And sighed in turn. 'I'm not blaming you, Bartell. I'm just weary. It seems my entire life has been a business of starting all over again. Don't get me wrong. I'm going to build that steamship, if it takes me the *rest* of my life. And I still want you to build it for me.'

Bartell hesitated, glanced at his wife, then shook his head, his shoulders hunched. 'I've no yard.'

'I'll find you a yard.'

'There's none to be had. Not for me, and not for you.'

Edward smiled. 'We'll see about that, when they see the colour of my money. I'll get you a yard, Bartell. And when I do, you'll build the new *Amanda* for me. You remember that.'

But he was just talking. *His* memory retained two frightened faces. Bartell was just as much a casualty of the war as if he had lost a leg at Gettysburg.

'Mr Bartell going second you, Master?' Jehu asked.

'Nope,' Edward said. 'You're going to second me, Jehu. And you simply have to stop calling me Master. You're not a slave any more, you know. You're just as free as any of your friends in Nassau.'

'Well, I am knowing that, Mr Edward,' Jehu said. 'But what else *can* I call you. I been calling you Master for near twenty-five years. How

449

you expecting me to change now? And me, second you against Mr Driscoll? Man, he ain't going to like that.'

'He's not supposed to like it,' Edward said.

Yet he spent a restless night. Bartell's words and warnings clustered around him. He had not supposed that the hatreds and the antagonisms would continue so long and so deep after the conclusion of the struggle. But undoubtedly Edward Anderson had caused the North as much trouble as even General Lee himself. On the other hand, there had been no warrant out for Lee's arrest.

On the *other* hand, Lee had not been born in New York.

So why take the risk, of remaining in Charleston a moment longer, of stirring up some more of that terrifying antagonism he had experienced in the past. He had more responsibilities now, in Penny and Robert, and even in Priscilla and the children, than he had ever had before. So why not leave now, and return to them, and the sun-bathed Bahamas, and consider his next step from that safety?

Because he had allowed himself to be inveigled into a senseless exchange of fire with Henry Driscoll. And however senseless it might be, to run away from it would do neither his reputation nor his prospects any good at all. So the next morning he and Jehu presented themselves at the gate of Sanders' Shipyard, and were admitted.

'Man,' Jehu muttered. 'I ain't liking this, Mr Edward.'

There were at least a dozen of Sanders' workmen present, far more than was necessary to witness a duel.

'Well,' Edward said. 'You remember where you've got that six-gun tucked away, just in case we need it.'

'Man, Mr Edward, how I going shoot down any white man? They would hang me too quick.'

'I'll do any shooting that has to be done,' Edward told him. 'You just see that I get the gun when I need it.' He nodded to Sanders and Henry, who waited in front of the spectators.

'Couldn't you find a second?' Henry sneered.

'I have my second,' Edward said, and indicated Jehu.

'A Negro?' Henry was scandalised.

'That's fair enough,' Sanders said. 'He can have a Negro if he wants. Hey, you, Sambo, you know what a pistol looks like?'

'I've seen one, I guess,' Jehu said.

Sanders flipped open the pistol case. 'Well, you have a look in here, and decide which one you want. They're both loaded.'

Jehu glanced at Edward, who shrugged. So he took out the first pistol. 'This one.'

'There's a good choice. You ever fought a duel before, Anderson?'

'No,' Edward said.

Sanders raised his eyes to heaven. 'Well, I've
451

marked out the distances. You go stand over there, and you don't raise your arm, you don't even twitch, until I drop my handkerchief.' He looked at Jehu. 'Nobody twitches. Now, this here is Dr Timpson. He'll take care of any wounds, or sign any death certificates, or what have you. As I understand it, this duel is to be fought until one of you is dead, or so badly hurt he can't continue. Right?'

The thought had not crossed Edward's mind. He had assumed it was to be a simple exchange of fire. 'That's up to Driscoll,' he said.

Henry stared at him. 'We'll fight to the death,' he said.

'Okay,' Sanders said. 'Now, it's my duty, before the law, to ask you two fellows to forget this quarrel and shake hands. If you do, you'll both be called right yellow-bellied southern cowards by every right-thinking American man, but you'll both still be alive. If you don't, one of you's going to be dead in less than five minutes. It's up to you.'

Why are we doing this, Edward wondered? To satisfy the amusement of this lousy little rat? Or because, one way or the other, Henry finally intended to settle with him? In which case, he was indeed being a fool, standing here to be shot at until he was dead.

But there was no alternative, after everything that had been said. Besides, suddenly they *were* fighting over Penelope. Only his sense of loss, perhaps even his love for her, could justify

452

Henry's determination to carry their quarrel to the extreme.

He felt curiously calm.

'Right,' Sanders said. 'You'll take your places. Over there, Anderson, where I've put the paint.' He grinned. 'Don't forget your weapon.'

Edward closed his fingers on the butt of the pistol, slowly walked to the splodge of white paint on the grass. The watching men spread themselves along the wall of the shed which contained the skeleton of the *Amanda*, at right angles to the shooting. Edward ignored them, gazed at Henry, who had also taken his position, turned correctly sideways to his opponent, arm hanging at his side with the pistol protruding from his fingers. Sanders had not asked *him* if he had ever fought a duel before. Presumably he had considered such a question unnecessary.

So, he thought, it all came down to how badly he hated this man. At this moment. There had certainly been moments in the past when he would cheerfully have looked at Henry Driscoll down the barrel of a pistol, and with murder in his heart. And perhaps he had always one day anticipated doing so. But now...

He became aware that Sanders' handkerchief was fluttering to the ground. His head jerked in surprise, as he watched Henry's arm already high, the pistol already levelled. As he watched, too, the puff of smoke rising into the air.

It had all happened so quickly his own arm had not yet even moved. But then he heard the bang of the explosion, and knew that he was unhurt.

Henry realised it too. An expression of utter incredulity spread across his face, and he looked down at the pistol, as if he considered the catastrophe was entirely the fault of the weapon. While Edward's hand was instinctively beginning to rise.

Henry started to move, away from the line of fire, and then checked himself, remembering that the duel was only just beginning. He stared at Edward, and Edward could see the blank horror in his eyes. That was surely victory enough. In these few seconds was he making Henry pay for all the death and misery had had himself caused. Surely he could allow himself a magnanimous gesture, and fire in the air?

Except that then the whole business would start over again, and he might not be so lucky the next time. Henry would certainly not consider any generosity as regards him. This had to be ended here and now, or it would end in his death.

He sighted along the pistol, could see the sweat standing out on Henry's face. He knew he was a good, if slow shot. If the sights were true, he could probably hit a stationary target wherever he chose. There was the important factor. He drew a long breath, held it, looked down the barrel, and squeezed the trigger. Henry's body half turned under the impact, and he staggered backwards, but did not fall. The ball, as intended, had struck him in the right shoulder, and blood now streamed down his jacket sleeve.

'Don't move, gentlemen.' Sanders signalled Jehu, and came forward. 'We will recharge the pistols for you.' He grinned at Edward. 'You should have killed him when you had the chance, Anderson.'

Edward threw the pistol on the ground. 'He'll not shoot again.'

'He must,' Sanders said. 'He has another arm.'

Edward realised that the carpetbagger did not much care which of them was killed; Henry had only been necessary to get hold of the Charleston shipyards, legally—now he was redundant.

He brought up his hands as Sanders reached him, tucking his enormously strong, helm-hardened fingers into the lapels of the little man's jacket, and half raised him from the ground. 'The duel's done, Sanders,' he said.

'For Christ's sake,' Sanders shouted. 'Help me. You...'

The men against the wall started to move forward.

'Jehu!' Edward snapped.

Jehu drew a quick breath, and at the same time the revolver from his jacket pocket. The advancing men checked.

'A God damned nigger with a gun,' Sanders shouted. 'He'll murder us all.'

Edward let him go, and he sank to his knees. 'You'd best bind up Mr Driscoll's wound,' he told the doctor. 'And maybe you'll choose your associates with more care in the future, Henry.' He touched Jehu on the arm, as they both backed towards the gate. 'Let's get the hell out of here, Jehu.'

The chartered sloop slid through the narrows at the western entrance to Nassau Harbour, her Negro crew shortening sail as they approached the docks. There was no need to wait for a space to be cleared now; in all the vast expanse of water, along all the endless miles of wooden docking, there were only one or two fishing vessels to be seen. The armada which had thronged these seas for four years had disappeared as if Neptune himself had waved his wand; the translucent green waters contained only fish.

Nor were there any eager shipmasters waiting on land to welcome him and exchange the latest gossip. There was in fact no one at all, not even a customs official, and he could not find a rig for hire, had to walk up the hill to the Royal Victoria Hotel, Jehu trailing behind him with his box. At the hotel at least some pretence of continuing fame, continuing prosperity, was preserved. The gardens were still carefully tended, there was still a resplendent major-domo on the front door. But the great bars, the huge ballroom, were closed and shuttered, slowly accumulating dust, just as the gas lamps down on Bay Street were no longer lit because there was no longer any gas and no money to obtain any.

In all the hotel, only half a dozen rooms were still occupied; Priscilla Meigs had moved into a suite of her own, and the children had separate rooms—Penelope and he slept together without subterfuge now. In many ways they were already married, and might always have been married. Which was just as well, he supposed, in view of the news he brought them.

'I knew Jonathan was dead,' Priscilla said. 'He would have written, had he been wounded, or a prisoner. I knew he was dead.' She looked at her daughter. 'Now it's just you and me, Penny.'

'But Henry...' Penelope sighed.

'You should have killed him, Father,' Robert said fiercely. 'You should have shot him down.'

Edward looked at Penelope, and then at the children, staring at him with wide eyes.'

'Can he take them, Edward?' Penelope asked. 'Can he?'

'There is no doubt that he is legally entitled to them,' Edward said. 'But it's going to take him a long time to enforce that, here in the Bahamas. He'll have to bring a suit under Bahamian law, and then we would have the

457

right of appeal to the Privy Council in England...Frankly, I'm not sure he's that interested. It's me he really hates. He's managed to do what his uncle once did, and have me blacked the length of the Eastern seaboard. I put in at Wilmington, before coming on here, and there's not a shipyard will touch my money. Even when I offered over the odds.'

'Well,' Priscilla declared. 'As you say, Edward, it was only what his uncle *tried* to do. And he failed. I'm sure there's another Titus just waiting to team up with you. Somewhere.'

Edward sighed. 'You may well be right, Mrs Meigs. But I can't go find him, without leaving you here. You see, if Penelope sets foot in the United States, Henry most certainly *can* take the children.'

'Yet you must build your ship, Edward,' Penelope said. 'I did not come back into your life to ruin it, yet again. What, will you spend the rest of your days sitting on this beach, just to be near me? Suppose you were to meet another man like Father tomorrow? And between you you built your ship? Would you not then seek to sail her?'

He frowned at her. 'Would you not expect me to?'

'Exactly. And then you would be away from me for weeks on end, unless I could persuade you to take me with you.' She smiled. 'I intend to do that, to be sure. But for a month or so I am prepared to pretend that I have failed. Do you go to the States, and find your shipyard and your backing. And build your ship.' She held him close. 'Because that is what I want for you more than anything else in the world.'

As the *Amanda* was lost to him, and he was being forced to start all over again in any event, he completely redrew his designs, to create a larger, and he hoped faster ship. Now he aimed at twenty knots. No vessel had ever cruised at such a speed, and it would bring the crossing from England to North America down to six days. It would, he had no doubt, revolutionise travel between the two continents.

If it could ever be built.

'This nation,' said Mr Brewster of Philadelphia, 'ain't interested in Europe, and it ain't interested in the Atlantic Ocean, Captain Anderson. We have enough to do, for the next hundred years and more, right here in America. Those Britishers and those Frenchies and those Spaniards have caused nothing but trouble over here, and so far as I'm concerned they can all go hang.'

Brewster at least dressed up his reluctance to involve his company in the venture under the guise of national policy. Others were more blunt. 'You sailed for the Confederacy, Anderson,' Mr Morgan of New Jersey told him. 'You want to build a ship, use a Southern yard.'

'There aren't any Southern yards, still in

Southern hands,' Edward said, with great patience. 'Save for Driscoll's. And he isn't going to build any ship for me.'

'Yeah? Well, maybe you should have thought of that, back in 1861.'

Mr Wright of Baltimore was more prepared to be friendly, if the ultimate answer was still no. 'The fact is, Anderson,' he explained. 'You've gone and got yourself a reputation as an unlucky shipmaster. Every ship you've ever skippered has gone down. Sure I know you've never even got your feet wet; they always sink the moment you step off them. But that don't make the rest of us any the happier. Now, I don't believe in luck, myself. So I'll tell you what's wrong. You're just in too much of a hurry. Crossing the Atlantic without sails, indeed. Sure, it'll happen one day. But not in your lifetime or in mine. Now look at this ship Driscoll is just completing. I'm told it's to your design.'

'It is my ship, Mr Wright,' Edward pointed out.

Wright nodded. 'It's tough, being on the losing side.'

'And she does not have sails,' Edward pointed out.

Wright shook his head. 'She has now, Anderson. Driscoll has a brain in that head of his. That ship has everything, iron hull, two engines, twin screws, and three tall masts with a good spread of canvas. I wouldn't be sur-

460

rised if she breaks every record there is, when she gets going. I'm told you once crossed from Bordeaux to Charleston at an average speed of fifteen knots. Well, Driscoll claims this new ship of his will equal that, maybe even do better. That's going some. If he puts that on the New York to Bristol route he'll bring the time down to eight days, I shouldn't wonder. *And* she'll keep the sea in any weather.'

The knowledge that Henry was actually bent on completing the *Amanda* and sending her to sea under her original name was a final insult, and drove Edward to the ultimate, the office of the Secretary of the Navy, Gideon Welles. 'A great nation has to have a great merchant marine,' he said.

'It's a point of view, Captain Anderson,' Welles said. 'But this nation is great, and is going to get greater, by private enterprise. Not by government subsidies.'

'I'm not asking for subsidies,' Edward insisted. 'I'm asking for the use of a shipyard, that's all.'

Welles studied him. 'You are a New Yorker, who fought for the South,' he said.

How that episode seemed determined to haunt him for the rest of his days. 'That is not so, sir,' Edward said. 'I *sailed* for my adopted state. I had lived in South Carolina from the age of twenty. But I never fired a shot at any Northern vessel.'

'And now you live in a British colony.'

461

'It is not convenient for me to return to the United States, right now.'

'Because you've gone and got yourself involved in some scandal. Taking a woman away from her husband, indeed. We don't hold with that sort of thing in this country, Anderson. If I were to give you the use of a Navy yard, there'd be an outcry you'd likely hear in Nassau. And why should I? We've *got* a merchant marine.' He leaned across the desk. 'And we're getting a new Atlantic clipper, built by Driscoll himself. You're sure this idea you have to build the fastest ship in the world isn't just rivalry with Driscoll? For God's sake, man, you've got his wife, and his children. Ain't that enough for you?'

Edward bit his lip. Welles' suggestions were uncommonly close to the truth. 'I meant to build the fastest, and the best, steamship in the world long before I fell out with Henry Driscoll,' he said. Which he supposed was not altogether true. He could not remember when he had *not* been falling out with Henry Driscoll. 'And sure I resent the way he has appropriated my ship.'

'You don't suppose he resents the way you have appropriated his wife?'

'Okay,' Edward said. 'So I'm a scoundrel. That doesn't alter the fact that he isn't going to break any records with the *Amanda*. It's just not in his nature to push a ship to her limit.'

'And it is in yours,' Welles agreed. 'With the

462

result that your ships have a habit of sinking with all hands. We can do without that. I'll tell you straight, Anderson, I don't hold with all this quest for faster and bigger and more powerful. Certainly not in merchant ships. Look at what happened to Collins. The four finest ships on the Atlantic run. So one gets stranded and the other sinks after a collision, both with several hundred lives lost. *Because* they were so big and beautiful and powerful. Those facts didn't stop them sinking. But it sure meant they were crowded with passengers. And they were subsidised by the United States Government. That's when I set my face against continuing any governmental backing for shipping. You want to model your ideas on Sam Cunard. Now there's a man who has the sense to know human limitations, to understand what's possible and what isn't. His ships don't break any records. They don't try to steam the whole way. I'm told they ain't even very comfortable. But they sure as hell get across the Atlantic and back, time after time after time. No accidents, no fatalities. And even they don't make a profit. Without the British mail subsidies Cunard would have gone under years ago. To cross the Atlantic in six or seven days is a waste of time, and money. Who the devil wants to? You're a brilliant shipmaster, Anderson. So I've been told. I ain't ever heard anyone say you were a brilliant ship designer. A man should stick to what he does best. And he should leave other men's wives alone. Good day to you, sir.'

'So there it is,' Edward confessed to Penelope. 'There is no one on the whole continent will touch me or my idea with a ten foot pole. Welles says I should take a berth as master. There isn't even anyone will offer me a ship.'

'Because of me,' she said. 'My God, but I'm an albatross. I've known it all my life, I suppose. And I thought, I hoped, that you and I could beat it, by just being together...' she sighed. 'Send me back to Henry. Then *his* ill luck will start all over again, and yours will change for the better. Send me back, Ned.'

'We don't believe in luck, remember?' he said. 'Everything that has ever happened has been by men's wills and men's mistakes, not by luck or any supernatural agency. It was Cas who lost the *Penelope Driscoll*, nobody else. And the fault was mine. I knew he never really understood how to handle that ship. And I still let him go. And drowned twenty-three men. But that was no act of God. Just as it's no supernatural force which is keeping man from successfully building faster and bigger, and safer ships. It's just the pessimism, the fear, of other men. There has got to be the ultimate ship, which can go anywhere, at speed, and in perfect safety. Someone is going to build one, one day. Why the devil shouldn't it be me? Because if I don't, Penny, don't you

464

see, everyone who has ever died, starting with Amanda and your father, will have died for nothing. Nothing at all. I *have* to build that ship, to make their deaths even remotely acceptable.'

She said nothing, because there was nothing to say. She knew as well as he that he could not build any ocean-going ship here in Nassau.

'So if my own people won't have me,' he declared, 'I'll look elsewhere.' He grinned, and kissed her on the cheek. 'If necessary, I'll sail for Sam Cunard.'

But he did not really have any intention of sailing *for* anyone, ever again. Instead he began writing letters, to the great shipbuilding firms in France and Germany, and most of all in Britain. Britain was the sea-going capital of the world. Her merchant fleets, supported and protected by the greatest navy the world had ever known, ranged the globe to exploit the greatest empire the world had ever known. And the British had pioneered the development of steamships, however much the originals might have been French or American. Surely in England there was a shipyard and a shipping company which would be anxious to look to the future.

The replies were bleak. 'It is our opinion,' wrote Horace Jerningham of the firm of Hartley Pownall, 'that steamship design has attained its final shape and form in the latest Cunarders. The newly launched *Java* is de-

465

signed to sail at fourteen knots, which is as fast as any ship can reasonably be expected to travel. May I respectfully point out that your record breaking crossing of the Atlantic in the *Penelope*, Captain Anderson, was accomplished very nearly twenty years ago, and in somewhat more pleasant latitudes than the North Atlantic. Your speed has never since been approached, until these new Cunarders went into service. Thus we are forced to conclude that you must have been served by freak conditions of weather, and in any event that you were at least twenty years ahead of your time. The concept of obtaining twenty knots from any large vessel designed to be driven through the sea is surely for the next century. In our opinion you should rest content with the laurels you have already gained.'

Always back, he thought ruefully, to the high point of his life. Twenty years ago. There was a confession of failure, that he should have hit the peak before the age of thirty, and never been able to regain it. But it was a far more sobering reflection that he would soon be fifty, and was wasting week after week sitting on a beach in the Bahamas.

But the French and the Germans, busy with their plans for dominating Europe, and on the verge of war between themselves, were even less helpful. While his family waited, and watched. He had secured a governess for Jimmy and Yvonne, and they were happy enough, with the sun and the sea. But Robert was equally wasting his life, as he passed his eighteenth birthday with nothing more to do than skipper a fishing boat which explored the reefs and sounds of the Bahamas in search of crayfish and turtle, conch and grouper. While Penny, however personally happy she might be, with his arms to find every night, with her children around her, and with at last an absence of the strains under which she had existed for so long, showed the pain of her love for him in her eyes every time she brought him letters.

But the Bahamas themselves had become painful to consider, painful to watch, as the islands and their inhabitants sank back into a sun-scorched somnolence, as potholes began to appear in the splendidly paved roads, as paint peeled from walls of the houses, as the miles of dock rotted into the translucent green waters.

The news which eventually arrived that the *Amanda*, flying the colours of the Sanders-Driscoll Line, had completed her maiden voyage, New York to Bristol, at an average speed of fifteen knots, to equal the existing record and claim the blue riband of the ocean, after eighteen years, completed Edward's descent into misery. Now he did not even have any laurels on which to rest. He accepted defeat, and sat down to write Samuel Cunard, applying for a berth as master. To stay in Nassau any longer, looking at the sea and a part of it and yet unable to take his place upon it, would be to drive him mad.

But it was a difficult letter to write. He had not asked a favour such as that for a long time. And why should Cunard employ an itinerant American sea captain who was now fifty years of age, however famous some of his past exploits? The fact was that none of those exploits were likely to appeal to the canny, cautious Nova Scotian who alone had made a success out of steamships in the Atlantic, by the very rule of always being canny and cautious. He had not finished the letter before the next ship arrived, with mail from England. And a letter from Sir Charles Austin, managing director of the shipbuilding firm of Austin and Graham. 'I find your project most interesting and exciting,' Austin had written. 'And if I have not replied before now it is because I sought the unanimous support of my colleagues, before doing so. This I have now managed to attain, at least in principle, and my board and myself would be most happy to meet with you and discuss your design, at your earliest possible convenience.'

'Man, Mr Edward, but this is a cold country,' Jehu remarked. 'You think it going warm up, when this rain stop?'

'I believe it always rains, in Liverpool,' Edward said. But he could hardly believe that they had actually reached their destination, as he

468

gazed at the docks and houses and church spires emerging from the wet mist. Since the arrival of Austin's letter he had existed in an ethereal world, had only really come down to earth on the crossing from New York, which they had made in the very *Java* which had been thrown at his head as the ultimate in big steamships. Certainly he had found her fascinating, three hundred and thirty-seven feet long, forty-two feet in the beam—a ratio of one-to-eight, which was the figure he had arrived at as the perfect proportion—and just short of twenty-eight feet in the draft. Her engine was capable, he had been told, of developing two thousand six hundred and fifty horsepower, which would drive her two thousand six hundred and ninety-seven tons at fourteen knots, by means of her single screw, with suitable assistance from her three masts and her thousand plus square feet of canvas. And certainly they had crossed the Atlantic very comfortably at thirteen knots, and had actually been at sea but ten days out of New York.

Edward had been allowed to see everything, because of his interest, and the pride Captain McIntyre had in his ship—and because he was travelling under an assumed name. This was less to protect himself than because of Penelope and the children. He would not leave them behind in Nassau, but the moment they set foot on American soil they were liable to be arrested and returned to their rightful father, even if

Henry, as Edward had expected, had not pressed in any British court for possession of his children. He merely intended to keep Penelope, and thus Edward himself, out of the States. So they had sneaked through as Mr and Mrs Smith, travelling with Grandmother Smith and the three Smith children, and the Smith Negro servant. The children, even Robert, found it delighfully exciting. Edward considered it but one more humiliation to add to all the other humiliations he had been forced to endure these past few years. But all other emotions were overridden by the consideration that this was the very last opportunity he was ever going to get to realise his ambitions and his dreams, to make his life anything better than a total disaster from start to finish. It was a challenge which alternatively filled him with the wildest exhilaration and plunged him into the depths of depression, which was not alleviated by their being passed by the Sanders-Driscoll flagship *Amanda*, pennants flying and decks lined with cheering passengers, as the American flag streamed in the breeze on their fifth day at sea. He should have been standing on that bridge.

Penelope had squeezed his arm. 'We'll pass *her*, one day, Edward,' she said. 'We'll leave *her* as if she was standing still. One day soon.' It seemed incredible that all of that so often misdirected determination, all of that tremendous self-confidence, should finally have been harnessed in his support. The fact was that far from being unlucky, she was his personal mascot. With her at his side he had first broken the Atlantic record, and ridden out the fiercest of storms. It was only when they had drifted apart that the disasters had begun. He discounted the events of the war. Luck did not come into that.

But luck surely did not come into anything. If only he could make himself believe that. He knew he possessed the design; had Henry not added masts and sails, and changed the entire concept, the *Amanda* would be travelling at least three knots faster than even the great speed she was already displaying. He knew that even if poor John Elder was dying up in Scotland, his engines were still the best in the world and were available. And he knew that he could sail her, whatever she was eventually called, better than any man afloat. Those were facts, not dreams. If only he could make sufficient people believe in them. But at last the moment was here, because they were reducing speed and yielding to the tugs, to be placed alongside the Liverpool dock. And there was Sir Charles Austin, waiting for them.

'Gentlemen, allow me to introduce to you, Captain Edward Anderson.'

Sir Charles Austin smiled at his crowded boardroom, and Edward, standing beside him, attempted to do the same.

He thought he had encountered some tough inquisitors in the past, but never had he come face to face with eleven gentlemen of quite such dignity, such arrogant aplomb, and such coldly composed features as these. Yet the mere presence of Charles Austin gave him confidence. They had spent almost every moment of the train journey from Liverpool, which had taken an entire day, in conversation—while Pansy Austin and her startlingly pretty daughter Charlotte had entertained Penny, Priscilla and Robert and Jehu and the children in another first class compartment—and Edward had been overwhelmed by the Englishman's grasp of the subject of ships and the sea, his knowledge of the history of hull design, and of engine design too, his acquaintance with the facts of Edward's career, and, above all, his enthusiasm, all hidden behind long, aquiline features, and his total confidence that because he was British he had merely to decide that something should be done and it would happen. Failure did not enter into his imagination at all.

And with all that he also possessed a sense of humour, and had in fact warned Edward that his colleagues on the board of Austin and Graham were, as he put it, 'a kettle of cold fish. Just like me, Anderson. Just like me. You'll have to spin us a good yarn. But if there's a fine ship at the end of it, then you'll have them on your side. I can promise you that.'

And now the moment had arrived. At Sir Charles' suggestion he had dressed as the shipmaster he was, in blue broadcloth, and wore his best cap. Now he was shaking hands with each man in turn, aware that several were knights, and three were lords, and one was even an earl. And he was an ex-ferry-minder from South Carolina. But if he could not convince these men then he might well find himself ending his days minding another ferry.

Sir Charles took his seat at the head of the table. 'The floor is yours, Captain Anderson,' he said courteously.

Edward laid his briefcase on the table in front of him, hoped that his nervousness was not apparent. He cleared his throat, looked at each face in turn. 'I'm here to talk about speed and about safety in ships,' he said. 'Because I believe the pair are inseparable. The faster any ship can get from A to B, the less likely she is to encounter bad weather. The faster she can travel from port to port, the higher her turnover of cargo, and therefore the more profit she will make for her owners. And therefore the better she will be maintained. Half the ships that are lost, founder, or strand, because their hulls or their equipment are in poor shape, or their crews aren't up to scratch, because their owners are penny pinching. I'm after the ultimate in ships, the safest, fastest thing that will float.'

'You wouldn't agree, Captain Anderson, that a clipper ship, I am thinking of the *Thermopylae* or the *Cutty Sark*, is the ultimate in ship design?' asked Lord Balmain.

'I believe my lord, that they may well be the ultimate in *sailing* ship design. But they are still sailing ships; without a wind they are helpless. And because they need the wind, and must take advantage of it when it is there, no matter how strong, they are driven harder than the average ship. Clippers founder, sir. Regularly. And they lose men, overboard or by accidents, regularly.'

'And the ship you will design will suffer none of these mishaps?' Balmain asked. 'It is surely impossible to guarantee that, of any ship.'

'Impossible to guarantee, sir. But it is possible to reduce risks to a minimum. There is an absolute limit to the size a sailing ship can be built, because of the beam and the draft she requires to carry sail at all, and thus there is also a limit to the speed she can attain. I do not believe there is any such limit for a steam-driven vessel, providing she relies upon steam alone. Yet we have handicapped ourselves from the beginning by building sailing ship hulls, and then putting engines in them, and calling them steamships, and expecting them to steam as fast as the best clippers can sail. Now, gentlemen, while I realised this long ago, and attempted to surmount it, I was handicapped by the impossibility, under conditions as they then existed, of carrying sufficient coal to guarantee an Atlantic crossing, regardless of the weather. I was thus forced to compromise yet again, and as you will be aware, my compromise was unsuccessful.'

'And how many lives were lost, Captain Anderson?' asked the Earl of Dover.

'Not one, my lord, on the *Penelope*, while she was at sea. I understood her tenderness, and I abandoned any idea of ever building her sisters. I knew the whole concept had to be changed. But it was necessary for me to earn a living while I worked on the design, and so I continued to sail her. Then Fate took a hand, and I was out of action for several years. In those years, unbeknown to me, my company was taken over by a rival, and that rival company built two more ships to my original design. Both of these were lost, but only one with lives involved. The fourth ship went down in time of war, while attempting to escape a warship. I may say that she was the very last of the blockade runners to be lost before the surrender of the Confederacy, and she had been the very first at sea, in 1861, which can be no bad record. But I am not attempting to deny that the design was too tender for anything but small seas and light airs. My new design will have no such drawbacks. She will be designed for steam power, and steam power only. She will be four hundred feet long, fifty wide, and she will have a draft of twenty-two feet.'

There was a gasp. 'Would she not break in two the moment she either hogged or humped?'

someone demanded. 'Four hundred feet is greater than the average Atlantic wave length.'

'She will not, sir,' Edward said. 'A ship is hogged when her bow and stern are supported by waves and her midship section is hung in the air, and she is humped when her midship section is supported by a wave and her bow and stern are both suspended. Now, gentlemen, I am not saying that if you take a four hundred foot hull and suspend it half in the air for any length of time it is not going to burst in two. But here's where speed comes in. Travelling at twenty knots she will never be suspended for more than half-a-second at a time, and thus the crucial stress point will never occur.'

'Travelling at twenty knots, she will, as you put it, Captain Anderson, surely burst herself in two anyway, merely from hitting the seas that hard over a period of time. No matter how much iron sheathing you put around her.'

'I agree, sir, that wood will hardly stand up to such a pounding. But iron will. The hull of our ship, gentlemen, will contain no wood at all except as fittings, but will be of iron in two skins, to make her virtually unsinkable.'

'The *Great Eastern* was built in iron,' someone objected.

'And she is still afloat, sir,' Edward pointed out. 'This despite hitting a rock outside of New York harbour and tearing open a gash eighty feet long in her bottom. You name me any other ship ever built which could have taken such a blow. As I understand it, the crew of the *Great Eastern* did not even know she had damaged herself until divers went down. And incidentally, she is two hundred feet longer than my design, and she never either humped or hogged.'

'I was thinking, Captain Anderson,' Balmain said, 'that the *Great Eastern* has proved an economic disaster to her owners, because of her weight, and the amount of power that was needed to move her. Now, sir, how much do you anticipate this ship of yours will weigh?'

Edward drew a long breath. 'Four thousand tons.'

They stared at him. 'The *Java* displaces two and a half thousand tons, Captain Anderson.'

'And the *Great Eastern* displaced eighteen thousand, sir. Four thousand tons is not an exceptional weight to shift.'

'It is at twenty knots. What horsepower are you looking for?'

'Three thousand on each engine, giving a full indicated horsepower of six thousand.'

'Has anyone ever built an engine of that size which works?'

'I have the designs of John Elder,' Edward said. 'Mr Elder is unfortunately too ill to take part in this project himself, but he is willing to offer his advice, and he is confident his engines can be built to any size.'

'But will it work? Will any accumulation of moving parts, that massive, work, day in and day out, under the pressure you seem to wish to apply to it? What happens to your ship when you suffer a breakdown?'

'That is the reason for having two separate engines, sir, each driving a separate propeller,' Edward said, patiently. 'To lose both engines would be the equivalent of being dismasted in a sailing ship. There would have to be an awful freak of nature, or more likely, a disastrous human error, for such a mishap to occur. I do not accept freaks of nature or human error on any scale in my ships.'

There was arrogance, he thought, as he stared at them. But he had realised that, being utterly arrogant, confident, successful men themselves, they would respond only to someone willing to meet them on their own ground.

'And you would of course be prepared to command this vessel yourself?' Austin asked, quietly.

'That is my intention, Sir Charles.'

'Is that practical?' someone asked. 'If she is to be British-built and registered, she will have to have a British crew. And captain.'

Edward gazed at him. 'She will be American-registered, sir. And she will fly the Stars and Stripes.'

'Here, I say...'

'But the profits, obviously, or most of them, will be British,' Edward said, with a smile. 'They will accumulate to the company which builds and owns the ship.'

'Supposing there are any profits,' someone grumbled.

'It seems like a devilishly ticklish international set-up to me,' said another.

'These are details, gentlemen,' Sir Charles said. 'Which can be thrashed out after we have come to an agreement on building the vessel.'

'I entirely agree with Sir Charles,' said George Graham, the firm's co-managing director. 'And before such a decision can be made it is necessary for us to ascertain the economics of this project. Captain Anderson's plans may be viable, and he may well produce the finest ship in the world. She may even be unsinkable. But she is going to cost an enormous amount of money. Double-skinned iron, three thousand horsepower engines...'

'She will also have to be fitted out to the very highest quality for her cabin passengers,' Edward said. 'There is no point in building the Queen of the Atlantic without making our passengers feel that they are travelling *on* the Queen of the Atlantic.'

'Oh, quite,' Graham agreed, drily. 'I take it you are not also an accountant, Captain Anderson?'

'You may take it, sir, that if I were not aware that this ship was going to cost a fortune to build I would not be coming to you for help.'

'Well, sir, you will then understand that we represent our shareholders, who expect a certain return on their investments. I have here a detailed analysis of all recent Atlantic crossings, in the past ten years, to be precise. Granted that these have been bad years, because your people in America have spent most of them killing each other rather than visiting Europe, but even if we suppose a hundred per cent increase in cross-Atlantic passengers now that the war is over, we are still talking of no more than a few thousand berths a year. That means that the Cunard ships are already travelling at a quarter capacity. And I believe the Sanders-Driscoll flagship which so recently equalled your record, Captain Anderson, and is, at present, *undisputed* Queen of the Atlantic, as you put it, carried only seventeen cabin passengers on her last crossing. That means she is sailing at a thumping loss. There is no hotel could operate never more than a quarter full and hotels do not have to steam about at twenty knots with all the fuel consumption that entails. I repeat, I have no doubt at all that you can build such a ship. And sail her. The point is, can you convince us she will ever earn back her cost?'

Edward could only gaze at him. Here was attack from a direction he had not anticipated. 'We will also carry freight,' he said, somewhat lamely.

'Not sufficient, sir. Again, there is just not sufficient freight crossing the Atlantic to make the project viable.'

Edward looked at Austin. Who did not seem

the least perturbed by the way the discussion was heading. He even smiled. 'Captain Anderson is concerned with ship design,' he remarked. 'Not with the economics of running a shipping company. Although I understand that you ran a very successful shipping company for several years, at the end of the 'forties, Captain. Am I not right?'

Edward also smiled, ruefully. 'My passengers were my freight, Sir Charles, and I could never find room for all who wanted to travel. They were people in a hurry.'

'People in a hurry,' Sir Charles mused. 'Are you aware, gentlemen, that on her last crossing to America the *Java* had approximately five hundred passengers? Granted only twenty-seven of them were cabin class. But there were still five hundred passengers. And I can tell you that the *Amanda* is sailing from Liverpool the day after tomorrow with six hundred souls on board apart from her crew, and as she was designed principally for the luxury trade, she has had to decline applications for passages from another thousand people who wanted to travel but could not afford the first class fare. People in a hurry, gentlemen. In a hurry to reach the promised land of the United States.'

'Steerage passengers,' someone sneered.

'Immigrants,' said someone else.

'Russians, most likely. Or Irish,' said someone else.

'My dear fellow,' Sir Charles said. 'They still

pay a fare. It may be a modest fare, but when you multiply it by several hundred, or several thousand, or several hundred thousand, in the course of a year, you arrive at a very large sum of money. A sum of money which will mainly go to the shipping company which first designs and builds a ship which will get these people where they wish to go in the shortest possible time, and then returns here in the shortest possible time to pick up the next load, but which has also been designed with specially large, and, within the bounds of economy, comfortable steerage quarters. In building Captain Anderson's ship we shall be the first in the field, and this field, I am positive, will continue to be the most lucrative in the shipping business for the foreseeable future. What is even more important, gentlemen, in Captain Anderson we have a man who knows this field, and has already made a success of it. It is the most important field in the world, gentlemen, the shifting of humanity, en masse, from where it is to where it wants to be. Combined, of course, with a restricted cabin class which will be offered accommodation to equal that of any hotel in the world. That is the future for shipping, and that is the future we are going to grasp.' He smiled at Edward. 'I think I may say, Captain Anderson, without fear of contradiction...' he looked up and down the table, slowly, 'that it is the unanimous decision of the board of Austin and Graham Limited, that we should enter into an agreement with you for the building of *two* steamships to your design, and that work should commence immediately.'

CHAPTER 13

'Aren't they marvellous?' Charlotte Austin stood on the gantry and looked down on the two hulls, lying side by side in the huge shed. One was all but completed, and would be launched in a matter of weeks; she gleamed in the Austin and Graham colours of black and red. The other was still nothing more than a hull, her unpainted iron sides giving off flashes of blue light as the welders riveted up her seams. But in her promise, especially as foreshadowed by her sister beside her, she was every bit as beautiful. 'I can hardly believe,' Charlotte went on, 'that they are actually going to sea.'

She glanced at Robert Anderson and flushed, her cheeks turning as red as her brilliantly auburn hair; her complexion, milky white with just a dusting of freckles, inclined towards quick flushes. But she flushed more often in Robert's company than any other. Although he was just a year her elder, his background was so different from hers, so incredibly romantic, she might be forgiven for sometimes wondering if he were any more real than the great ships.

Born as his mother had died; brought up in one of those great Southern mansions of which she had only ever read, and which were now gone forever it seemed, at least as great Southern mansions; taken to sea by his father at the age of thirteen to run the blockades; and already having had the experience of feeling a ship sinking under him. The only other person who could possibly eclipse him in the romantic stakes was his father himself, with his remarkable list of triumphs at sea, and in the Nicaraguan revolution, to set against his distinguished, if weatherbeaten countenance, his still strong and powerful body, and the devotion of the beautiful woman who clung, so illicitly, to his arm.

There had been some question, amongst Mother's friends, as to whether the Andersons, and Mrs Driscoll, of course, were socially acceptable. Mother's reply had been typical of the Irish heiress that she had been born. 'Of course they are not socially acceptable, my dear Countess,' Pansy Austin had said. 'They are Americans. But as they *are* Americans, they must be forgiven their sins and accepted. Besides, my dear, are they not such a lovely couple?'

Obviously such a description would equally apply to their children.

And Robert clearly found her, with her background of governesses—like him—and Swiss finishing schools—so completely unlike him—equally interesting. Now he smiled at her embarrassment. 'Believe me, Miss Austin,' he said, 'I don't think even my father really believes it is happening at last. And *two* ships... this is all he has ever dreamed of. I hope your father knows how grateful we all are to him.'

'The boot will be on the other foot,' she said seriously. 'When the ship captures the blue riband from Driscoll. That's what Father is after too, you know. To dominate the North Atlantic. Are you going to sail with her?'

'Of course,' Robert said. 'Where Father sails, I sail.'

'I'm going to ask Father if I can sail on her maiden voyage too. Do you think I could?'

'Well...' Suddenly it was his turn to flush. 'By yourself?'

'Oh, of course not. I'd talk Mother into coming with me. She's always saying she should visit New York, and has never actually got around to doing it. One of her uncles, or something, emigrated to America, oh, twenty years ago. During the great famine in Ireland, you know. So we've a whole lot of cousins we've never seen, in America.'

Robert scratched his head. He could not really envisage this delightful, laced and ribboned creature, who smelt of the sweetest soap and the latest toothpaste, embracing a New York Irish immigrant as uncle—but it was reassuring to know that she had similarly plebian origins.

'I'll fix it,' she said, confidently. 'Oh, I'd love to do that. Do you know, I've never been on a ship at sea? Not even one of Father's?' she giggled. 'I've never wanted to, before. Oh, there he is now.'

Sir Charles Austin had just entered the shed, and was signalling for Edward, who was in the first ship's engine room with Hargreaves, who would be Chief Engineer at sea. 'Some news,' he said, as he joined them on the gantry.

'And not good,' Edward commented. 'From your expression.'

'Well...it's more irritating than bad. Your Congress have refused us permission to register the ship in the United States or to fly the Stars and Stripes.'

'Well, hell,' Edward said. 'That's carrying resentment a little far.'

'They claim it has nothing to do with you, personally, Anderson. They say it is the law of the United States that only vessels built in a U.S. yard can ever be registered there. I'm afraid we'll just have to accept it. Needless to say, my Board members are delighted.'

'Yes,' Edward growled. 'Well, let's hope Congress is delighted when we take the blue riband away from Driscoll, under the Union Jack.'

'That's the other piece of news. Driscoll has been so pleased with the success of the *Amanda* that he is building a new ship, which I believe he intends to call the *Spartan*. In fact, she is very nearly complete, as he began her in the most utter secrecy. He's got the message, Anderson. One of the reasons she is being called the *Spartan* is not a play on strength or fortitude, but on the very large and somewhat Spartan accommodation he is building, for emigrants. How soon can we launch?'

'Well, we can quicken everything up...I reckon we could have her in the water in a month.'

'Then quicken everything up,' Austin commanded. 'He won't be launching before next year. By then I want the American route sewn up. I gather he's aiming at sixteen knots from this new ship. But as usual he's not being very imaginative. She's to be conventional in design, with masts and sails as well as steam, and only a few feet longer than the *Amanda*. I want her made obsolete before she even smells water.'

'Will do,' Edward agreed. 'Maybe we'd better start thinking of a name for ours.'

'I thought you'd chosen that.'

'Yeah,' Edward said. 'The *United States*. But she can't be called the *United States* and fly the British flag.'

'There's a point. Yes, well, we shall have to consider that one.'

'The *Charlotte Austin*,' Robert said.

'Eh?' The men looked at him together.

'Why not? You've always called your ships by girls' names before, Father. I think that's entirely appropriate. And it has a ring to it.'

487

Edward looked from his son to the blushing girl, realised that the couple had been standing together on the gantry, talking, for the past hour. He looked at Sir Charles. 'Well,' he said. 'That's fine by me.'

'The *Charlotte Austin*,' Sir Charles said. 'That's a splendid name. And I'm delighted that you've chosen it, Mr Anderson.' He winked at his daughter. 'You'll have to perform the launching ceremony, you know.'

'I'm going to do more than that,' Charlotte declared, seizing her opportunity. 'I'm going to sail her on her maiden voyage.'

'Well?' Penelope asked. 'Is she everything you have ever dreamed of?'

They had escaped the music and the dancing, the toasts and the congratulations, to climb to the bridge, whence they looked down on the foredeck, and beyond, the lights of Southampton. Beneath them the ship hummed, from the laughter and the thumping of the band, the clink of glasses and the thudding of feet. Only a handful of the people on board this evening were actually bound for New York; the main body of passengers boarded tomorrow. These were the lords and their ladies, the guests invited to the official farewell party, people intended to explore and remember the Adam fireplaces in the first class saloon, the huge vaulted saloon itself—unashamedly copied from the Royal Victoria Hotel ballroom in Nassau, complete with glass dome which broke the symmetry of the boat deck; the luxury of the staterooms, which in first class contained beds rather than bunks, and had silver-plated taps and door knobs; the discreet lighting of the bars; the potted palms in the vestibules and corridors; the deep pile carpeting on the stairs; the dining saloon with its reproduction of Maxim's in Paris...these things the guests would hopefully think of when next they sought to cross the Atlantic, and thus automatically book a stateroom on the *Charlotte Austin*, or her as yet unnamed sister.

But they had also been encouraged to delve below, into the steerage, euphemistically described as third class accommodation, but very comfortable, each four-berth cabin having its own washbasin, while if the dining room contained three long tables rather than a host of four-settings and there were no flowers or potted palms, a glance into the enormous kitchen behind at least guaranteed that those eating here would not go short of food, even if, unlike the first class passengers, they would hardly expect either caviare or smoked salmon with every meal. There was of course no promenade deck for the steerage passengers. If they were determined on fresh air, they could, in limited numbers and in fine weather, use the welldeck forward, supposing they could find a friendly steward to let them out. But this hardly seemed relevant, as the *Charlotte Austin* was going to make the journey from the Bishop Rock Light House off the Isles of Scilly at the south-western tip of England to the Ambrose Light, off New York in just on six days, at an average speed of nineteen knots. That was what her engines had been designed for, and that was what John Elder, just before his death, had promised she would do. Because the climax of the invited guests' tour of the ship had been the descent into the engine room, to gasp at the huge, gleaming mounds of machinery, each piston taller than a man, the propeller shafts, streaming away from their gearboxes before disappearing through their gland packings in the hull, each four feet in diameter, the purest gleaming steel rods. Daintily they had picked their way into the coal bunkers, to gaze at the enormous black tonnage stacked there, and then at the still cool furnaces which fed the huge boilers, the stokers and trimmers standing to attention, vests and faces white tonight, and for the last time before New York, and Mr Hargreaves, the Chief Engineer, in dinner jacket and black tie like the rest of the officers, but still eager to explain gauges and levers and control points to anyone who would listen.

'Yes,' Edward said. 'She is everything I have ever dreamed of. And you?'

'I can hardly wait to get out to sea on her,' Penelope said.

'Even if it means three weeks separation from the children and your mother?'

Penelope smiled, a trifle guiltily. 'That's rather a relief, if you must know. I was wondering if you felt, well, odd at not being in command.'

He shrugged. 'She's an English vessel, sailing under the Union Jack. So she must have an English skipper and crew. I think Captain Ransome understands the situation.' He had no intention of interfering, with either navigation or discipline. Yet Ransome, even as the senior captain of the Austin and Graham Line, had not the experience of someone who had run the blockade and had once in theory, held the blue riband of the Atlantic, even in the days before such things were thought of. Nor had he ever handled a steamship pure and simple. He had been delighted to know that Captain Anderson was also sailing, had made it clear that he welcomed the added knowledge—as if he, Edward thought, had ever commanded a ship like this, either.

But how he would love to command this one.

'The Congress will change their minds when you steam into New York.' Penelope said. 'You know, in many ways this reminds me of the *Penelope*'s maiden voyage. Of course that was west to east, but having Lady Austin and Charlotte on board...'

'While Sir Charles holds the fort at home. I know exactly what you mean,' Edward said. 'I've thought the same thing myself.' He glanced down at her with a sly smile. 'You don't suppose Robert and Charlotte are planning what we were planning, do you?'

'I think you should invite me to dance, Captain Anderson,' she replied.

'Did they really blow you right off your bridge, Captain Anderson?' asked Lady Cantrell.

'I'm afraid so, ma'am,' Edward said. 'Mind you, I don't remember much about it.'

'It must have been dashed exciting,' remarked Lord Prebble, seated opposite, and as usual having trouble with his adam's apple. 'I dashed near gave it a go myself, d'ye know, Anderson? Even chartered a ship and was on the point of crossing the Atlantic, what? And then the Confederacy went and surrendered. Poor show, what?'

'I'm sure they were equally disappointed at letting you down, my lord,' Edward said, and found some solace in glancing at Penelope and watching her trying to stifle a laugh. He reflected that it was just as well this voyage was only going to last six days; having to entertain these people to dinner every night was the most trying experience he had ever undergone. And tonight they were more than usually excited —earlier that afternoon they had overtaken Cunard's new flagship, the *China*, and passed her as if she had been under sail alone.

The voyage was, in fact, going to last only five days, for the *Charlotte Austin* was actually averaging twenty and a half knots, a quite fantastic speed. Of course they had been helped by the superb weather; in the three days since they had left Southampton the wind had never risen above ten knots, and the sea had never managed a wave larger than three feet. The *Charlotte Austin* might have been sailing across a gigantic bathtub. Edward had known the Atlantic this smooth, occasionally, but when it had been this smooth there had always before been the concomitant of fog, which necessitated a reduction in speed. But throughout this voyage visibility had never dropped below twenty miles. It had to be the most perfect autumn ever, designed especially for the maiden voyage of the finest ship ever launched. He wondered if his passengers were really aware of how lucky they were. In that sense, *he* had been the unlucky one, as he might have been entitled to suppose that for the first two days, anyway, about half of the mob—even first class was filled almost to capacity, so thorough had been Sir Charles' publicity, which had harped on the point that anyone who did *not* make this record-breaking voyage would regret it for the rest of his or her life—would be lying seasick in their beds. In fact the dining saloon had been as filled the first night as it was now, the white jacketed waiters as busy, the orchestra as appreciated, and himself required to make absurd conversation with equally absurd aristocrats. He understood there had been a few cases of seasickness down in steerage, but this was because there had been a slight leak in one of the funnel flues and some fumes had escaped. The leak had been immediately mended; if that was the greatest of their teething troubles the *Charlotte Austin* would indeed be the luckiest ship ever launched.

And now they were more than half way. He smiled at Penelope, and looked over the brilliant room, at the back of Robert's dinner-jacketed shoulders as he whispered in Charlotte Austin's ear, while her mother looked benevolently on, listened to the steady, relentless humming of the great engines so far beneath his feet, raised his glass in reply to one of the endless toasts which went round and round the Commodore's—as he was officially described— table, put the glass down again, and frowned as he watched the liquid continue to surge restlessly even after his fingers had released it. All the other wine glasses also had restless contents, and as he looked up, he saw that the huge chandeliers were shivering. The vibration was so slight he supposed he was the only person in the room to have noticed it. And in fact he had never been to sea in a steamship where there had been no vibration. Yet up to this moment the *Charlotte Austin*'s engines had been smooth as silk.

Whatever could have caused them to start shaking now?

Edward climbed the ladder to the bridge deck,

where Captain Ransome was making his final checks before retiring. 'We've logged fifteen hundred nautical miles since leaving Bishop Rock at twenty hundred on Tuesday,' he said. 'If we maintain this speed, we'll berth in New York by dusk on Friday afternoon. That's twenty-four hours early. I tell you what will happen, Anderson. Our passengers will complain because they're too early for their connections.'

'They're welcome,' Edward said, and checked the Log. 'Glass stays steady.'

'I've never seen anything like it, and this is my seventy-fourth Atlantic crossing. I don't see what can stop us now. Save mist as we approach the American coast. But with a day in hand...what did you think of the *China*, eh? She might have been standing still.'

'The passengers drank another few cases of champagne. They seem happy enough.'

'Well, they should be,' Ransome said. 'They'll never have an experience like this again. Ah, well, I suppose I shall have to go down and do my duty before turning in. There's some dowager duchess or something who always virtually asks me to dance. You'll excuse me, sir.'

'Have you noticed any vibration?' Edward asked.

'Began about half an hour ago. Thank God.'

Edward raised his eyebrows.

'Well,' Ransome said. 'I've never been on

495

a steamship which hasn't vibrated. She's had me quite worried these past three days. Too much glide. I like a ship to remember she's a ship. You coming down, Captain Anderson?'

'I've done *my* duty by the ladies,' Edward said, and waited for the captain to disappear. The bridge was shrouded, the only lights those at the binnacle and over the chart table. It was a quiet, composed, confident place. The helmsman stood at the wheel, hardly having to turn it at all, yet his deputy waited at his shoulder, ready to assist him should it become necessary. Second Officer Martin, whose watch it was, stared ahead of the ship into the night through his binoculars. There was nobody else on the bridge.

Edward also looked ahead. The night was clear; there was no moon but a host of stars, and visibility remained at least twenty miles. There was no danger out there, at the least.

And yet his uneasiness remained, and was growing.

He stepped out on to the wing, looking aft. It was so clear he thought he could still see the lights of the *China*, plugging along behind them. In another couple of hours those would be gone, and they would again be alone. The happiest of sensations, he had always thought, to stand on the bridge of a fine ship, racing through the night, feeling all of that power and grace and beauty beneath his feet. So why was he so reluctant to see the *China*'s lights disappearing beneath the horizon?

He went down the ladder, and then aft, and down more ladders, even deeper into the bowels of the ship, until he arrived on the upper platform of the engine room itself. Here the huge units pistoned back and forth with relentless intensity, the stokers shovelled their coal into the furnaces, the trimmers shovelled *their* coal from bunker to bunker as it was consumed by the stokers to prevent any risk of the ship becoming unbalanced and listing. The gauges flickered, the engineer officers walked to and fro, and the huge shafts whirred round and round, filling the vast space with a tremendous subdued *roar*.

Edward descended further, having spotted Mr Hargreaves. Here the heat was intense; the engine room had a quality of hell about it which had never failed to fascinate him, or to make him feel vastly relieved that he had always been a deck officer.

'Ah, they're sweet, Captain Anderson,' Hargreaves shouted. 'Sweet. I've never known engines quite so sweet.'

'Which one is causing the vibration?' Edward asked.

'Vibration, sir? These engines don't vibrate.' Hargreaves was clearly hurt. But he was also right. There was no trace of vibration here on the floor of the engine room, and immediately by the engines themselves, where surely it should have been greatest.

'That's odd,' Edward said, 'it's quite notice-able higher up.' He walked aft, away from the noise and the heat, through the opened water-tight bulkhead doors, to stand by the giant gearboxes which were coupled to the shafts and looked down at the gleaming steel shafts them-selves, spinning at their eight hundred revolu-tions per minute as they disappeared through their glands into the waters of the North Atlan-tic. And he realised that his teeth had suddenly started to chatter. 'That's it,' he said to Har-greaves, who had accompanied him. 'That star-board shaft is vibrating.'

Hargreaves peered at it. 'Could be,' he said.

'If you want to shut her down for a spell to check her out,' Edward said. 'I know Captain Ransome will agree. We've better than twenty-four hours in hand.'

'Bless you, Captain Anderson,' Hargreaves said. 'That won't be necessary. That propeller has picked something up, that's all. A mass of weed, or something like that. She'll cut her way through it in a matter of seconds. I've never shut down yet, for a bit of vibration.'

Edward gazed at him. He longed to give the man a direct command. But he did not have the right. Only Ransome could do that.

Hargreaves grinned. 'Really and truly, sir. You've only noticed it because there was no vibration at all, before. It happens all the time. But in most ships there's so much shaking and juddering no one ever notices it. This one is

498

just so quiet…' He saw that Edward was not entirely reassured. 'I tell you what, Captain Anderson, I'll keep an eye on it, and if it hasn't cleared itself in an hour or so, I'll shut down.'

Edward nodded, climbed the ladder, looked back down into the engine room. Hargreaves was muttering at the duty officer. Asking him, no doubt, how the hell that fellow Anderson had managed to obtain such a reputation when he got nervous at a little vibration. And perhaps the engineer was right. Perhaps I am growing old, Edward thought, and went on up, to the first class suites, and the best of them all, where Jehu was turning down the beds. 'Mrs Driscoll not down yet?'

'No, sir, Mr Edward. Say, Mr Edward, I hear those boys saying we're going to be in New York a day early. That is true?'

'Barring accidents,' Edward agreed.

'This is some ship, Mr Edward. Some ship.'

Some ship, Edward thought, and went on deck. But Jehu was absolutely right. She was some ship. His ship. There was nothing wrong with the design, this time. Never had he been aware of such stability, such responsiveness…it was, in fact, a disappointment for them not to have encountered bad weather. He would have enjoyed seeing what she could do.

'So there you are.' Penelope stood beside him. 'I was rather hoping you'd ask me to dance.'

'Do you mind if I don't, tonight?'

'Of course not, my darling.' But she glanced at him, curiously, as she wrapped herself in her fur stole. 'Is something wrong?'

He grinned, apologetically. 'Everything's going *too* well, I guess. I can't believe it's really happening.'

'If you won't dance,' she said. 'Come to bed.'

'Do you mind if I stay up a while longer? I'll be on the bridge.'

'I'll come with you,' she decided.

'You don't have to, Penny.'

'I want to,' she insisted, climbing the ladder to the boat deck in front of him, to stand at the top, looking at the two funnels towering above her, the black smoke and the occasional spark being whipped away by the breeze of their motion. She turned towards him as they heard recognisable voices, and an almost recognisable giggle, coming from the shelter of one of the davited lifeboats. Her mouth opened, and Edward shook his head, and held her arm to guide her into the bridge itself.

'Ships were made for romance,' he reminded her.

'But theirs began before they even got on board,' she said.

'Have you no objections?'

'Well...no, of course I haven't. She's a lovely girl. And Robert is everything even a knight's daughter could wish. Oh, I hope it does work out for them. I'd be delighted.'

'So would I,' Edward agreed. 'All well, Mr Martin?'

'Aye-aye, Captain Anderson. She's travelling like a dream. She's...' he hesitated as the entire ship shook, the vibration welling up from the engine room to send a pair of binoculars sliding across the chart table to crash to the floor, while from beneath them they could hear the tinkle of shattering glass; the chandeliers must have come down in the ballroom, Edward thought, listening to the shouts.

He leapt across the bridge, opened the speaking tube to the engine room. 'Hargreaves,' he snapped. 'Shut down the starboard engine.'

'The shaft,' Hargreaves shouted, his voice high with terror. 'The shaft...' there was a huge muffled roar, drowning his voice, and drowning even the grind of the engines. Penelope uttered a stifled scream, and Edward, turning away from the voice tube, stared through the skylight roof of the wheelhouse at the first funnel, immediately above his head, to see something he would have thought impossible before this moment—a jet of water mingling with the black coal smoke exploding into the air above the ship.

In that instant Edward knew that his ship was sinking. Yet the rapidity of it still took him by surprise. He turned back from the funnel, and felt the deck dropping away beneath his feet, saw water already bubbling over the welldeck

501

and surging at the ladder to the First Class Promenade. He listened to the terrified screams from the trapped steerage passengers, banging hopelessly on the locked gate which restricted them to their quarters, to the shrieks from the First Class Ballroom, where the gas lights still blazed but the music had abruptly died. Without thinking he unhooked a lifebelt from the rail and thrust it into Penelope's arms; she stood absolutely still, staring at him, her face frozen with shock. He heard Martin shouting something, watched him impotently jangling the engine room telegraph, then he was in the sea, and the sea had closed over him and was sucking him down into its eternal embrace.

The cold shocked him and all but made him inhale. His lungs seemed about to burst, and red lights flashed before his eyes. Something hit him in the face and he instinctively grabbed it, realised that it was a woman's leg. Then he was shot into the air and struck the surface of the sea with a gigantic splash. Now he *had* to gasp, and he inhaled salt water which made him choke and then vomit. He turned on his face, nostrils in the water, realised he was about to drown...and had his arm gripped.

'Edward,' Penelope shouted. 'Edward! For God's sake, Edward.'

She had retained her grip on the lifebelt, and this had saved her life, as holding on to her leg had saved his. Now she grasped him and brought him against the belt. He wrapped his fingers around the cord, and simply lay in the calm sea, unable to think for the moment.

'Captain Anderson?' Martin swam up to them. Amazingly, he still wore his cap. 'Are you all right? Mrs Driscoll?'

'Yes,' Penelope said. 'We're alive.'

'Help me,' came a shout. 'Help *me*.'

'Robert,' Edward muttered, and released the belt to swim through the darkness to the sound, aware that Martin was beside him. Robert Anderson was supporting an inert body.

'Take her,' he gasped, as the two men came up to him.

Edward dug his hands into the water, found Charlotte Austin's hair, swam backwards towards the lifebelt. Robert and Martin followed, and Martin located another belt, floating free, which the two younger men could share.

'I'll take her,' Penelope gasped, and held the girl's shoulders. Charlotte's head tilted back, her mouth sagging open, her eyes staring.

The lifebelt holding Robert and Martin bobbed against them, as they slowly became aware of the utter silence. A ship of four thousand tons, and carrying twelve hundred people, had just disappeared.

'Just us five,' Martin said. 'By Christ, just us five.' He began to weep.

'Just us four,' Penelope said, and released the dead girl.

Robert made a convulsive grab, held Charlotte's arm, staring into her face. Then he, too,

503

released her, raised his head and glared at his father. 'Murderer!' he shouted. 'Murderer!'

He gave a kick, and the lifebelt drifted away into the darkness.

Edward lay with his head on the kapok of the belt. He was very cold, and very tired. And very sad. One did not, after all, tilt against the gods. It was time to call a halt, surely, to ambition, and dreams of future conquests. Before he murdered another twelve hundred people.

He released the cord, drifted away from the belt, had his arm again seized by Penelope.

'Edward,' she shouted, lips against his ear, fingers biting into his flesh, wet hair flopping across his face. 'Edward, wake up. You can't die. This wasn't your fault, Edward. Edward, wake up, you've still ships to build. Great ships. Ships which *will* cross the Atlantic at twenty knots. Edward...' she dragged him back against the lifebelt, held him there, and looked above his head at the lights of the *China*, steaming confidently out of the calm sea.

The bedroom door opened. Edward, seated by the window, looking out at the winter lawn, turned his head, and then slowly stood up. He had been dreading this moment.

Austin closed the door behind him. 'How do you feel?' he asked.

'Feel?' Edward's smile was bitter. 'I suppose I have never *felt* so fit in my life.'

'I saw Penelope, downstairs,' Austin said.

'She has borne up remarkably well.'

'She was magnificent.' Edward sat down again. 'She saved my life. I don't know why.'

'Possibly,' Austin said, 'because she loves you. But also, possibly because she knows you have work to do.'

Edward raised his head again, for the first time really looked at the shipowner. Austin's face was sad; the grief lines were etched on those cold features, would probably never be eradicated. Yet his gaze was as clear as ever.

'I do not know what the Inquiry will find,' he said. 'But *I* am satisfied about what happened. We finished her in too much of a hurry. That was my decision, not yours, Edward. Perhaps one or two corners were cut. We shall never know. But I do know that the hull was just not strong enough. It is as simple as that. Iron is not sufficiently strong to be able to stand up to being driven at twenty knots and more, even in calm conditions. It might have happened sooner, had you hit rough weather.'

'Iron is stronger than wood,' Edward said.

'But not so strong as steel,' Austin said.

'Steel?' Edward frowned. 'There isn't that much steel in all Britain.'

'Then they'll have to make some more,' Austin said. 'I've ordered the hull of the...' he hesitated. 'The *Charlotte Austin*'s sister ship to be scrapped.'

Edward's shoulders hunched. He had not expected anything different.

'And I've ordered the same design recommenced, but in steel,' Austin went on.

Edward's head jerked. 'Have you any idea what that will cost?'

'Several times the cost of an iron ship, to be sure,' Austin agreed. 'But I've reached an agreement with the Government.'

'The Government?' Edward could not believe what he was hearing.

'The British Government. Because like her sister, Edward, she will fly the British flag. The Government will subsidise her cost up to two-thirds, if we agree to her being an auxiliary cruiser in time of war. That is, they reserve the right to mount a gun in her and use her as a commerce destroyer. I have agreed to this on behalf of us both.' He gave a grim smile. 'If there were to be a war with France they'd have her anyway. Of course, starting again from scratch means putting back our plans. I doubt she'll be ready for launching before the end of next year, no matter how hard we work, and the *Spartan* will be in the water in March. But we can still take the riband away from Driscoll, with the new ship. And I want you in command, Edward. Even if we have to make you a naturalised Englishman.'

'I have just drowned your wife and daughter,' Edward said, slowly.

'The sea did that, Edward. Pansy was my wife long before I was either a knight or a millionaire. We ran risks together when we

506

were young, and we knew there'd be more risks before the end. Charlotte...' he sighed. 'She was my only daughter, Edward. My only child. As Robert is yours.'

'Yes,' Edward said.

'He'll come back,' Austin said. 'He'll come back, when he realises that it wasn't your fault. It was all of our faults, mine as much as yours. But the ship you designed was viable, will be viable, built in steel. I know that, and I'm determined to build it. I've nothing left to do with my life now. Nothing at all. And don't you see, if I do not succeed, Pansy's death, and Charlotte's, will have been in vain.'

'I've felt that, often enough, about others who have died,' Edward said. 'Too many of them. But you can't escape the fact that I'm a jinx, Charles. I always have been.'

'I don't hold with that. I think your ideas have always been ahead of your time, and that other men, lesser men, have been unable to understand them, and therefore have come to grief trying to implement them. But if your report of what happened during the last hour that the *Charlotte Austin* was afloat is accurate, it seems to me that if you had been in command she would still be afloat. I want you on the bridge when her sister puts to sea.' He came across the room. 'Will you do it?'

'I don't know if I can,' Edward said. 'I don't know if I still have the nerve.'

Austin gazed at him for several seconds.

Then he said, 'They're going to give you a hard time, at the Inquiry. You know that?'

'Yes,' Edward said.

'They've appointed Milne to chair it. He's a Bible-thumping conservative who has no doubt whatsoever that the world was created between a quarter to four and four o'clock on the morning of Monday the first of June six thousand eight hundred and forty B.C. You must stand up to him. You must tell him, and the Court, what happened, without fear or favour. What truly happened, Edward. You must not let him break you. You must not. Or you will never take a ship to sea again.'

'Pray be seated, Captain Anderson,' invited Mr Humphries, the barrister representing the Crown.

Edward sat down.

'You will understand, Captain Anderson, that this is not a court of law,' Mr Humphries continued. 'Neither you, nor anyone else, is on trial here today. His Lordship...' he half bowed towards Lord Milne, 'may think fit, when the Inquiry is complete, to make certain observations, upon which he, and we, may hope that Her Majesty's Government might act, but our principle purpose is to discover exactly what happened to the Steam Ship *Charlotte Austin* on the night of the seventeenth of October 1869.'

'I understand that,' Edward said.

Humphries nodded, and consulted his papers, slowly, well aware that he was at the most important moment of the morning. Edward was enabled to look around at the Court, which was packed to the doors, the press section crowded, Penelope, having already given her evidence, sitting with Austin and Priscilla, with Second Officer Martin close by—Robert had left the room on completing his tale.

And over in the far corner, Henry Driscoll. Edward's head jerked, and he had to look again to make sure. But it was Driscoll, as yet unnoticed by Penelope, staring at him with the intensity of hatred. They had not laid eyes on each other since the day of the duel, four years before.

'Now, Captain Anderson.' Humphries reckoned he had allowed sufficient of a pregnant pause. 'We have heard from each of the other three survivors of the catastrophe. Mr Robert Anderson, your son...' he hesitated, so that no one in the room should be unaware of the fact, '...has told us that he can form no opinion of what happened. He was too shocked by the death of his fiancée. Mrs Penelope Driscoll, the lady who happened to be on the bridge at the time of the disaster, also has no opinion to offer. She says that the ship just seemed to fall apart. Mr Lawrence Martin, the Officer on Watch, has offered the opinion that there was some sort of internal explosion, well beneath the waterline, something which "opened her

509

up", as he put it. He even hinted at the possibility of an infernal device. This, you will appreciate, coincides to a certain extent with Mrs Driscoll's evidence. But it is incredible to us here that an iron hulled ship, built with a double hull and to the highest specifications, could possibly have been so damaged by any explosive device known to man as to sink within a matter of eleven seconds. That is the estimate given us by the master of the *China*.'

'There was no infernal device, and no internal explosion,' Edward said.

'Then can *you* account for her foundering in such a remarkably short space of time?'

'I can,' Edward said. 'It is my opinion that the starboard propeller shaft uncoupled itself from its bearings, and exited through the hull. It was revolving at approximately eight hundred revolutions per minute, and it was four feet in diameter. That is the diameter of the hole it would have left in each of the two hulls of the ship.'

There was absolute silence in the courtroom, while Humphries stared at him. 'But...' he said at last, 'I have never heard of a ship's propeller acting in such a fashion, Captain Anderson.'

'Neither have I,' Edward agreed. 'But on the other hand, several steamships have disappeared without trace. Such an accident could have been the cause. The ship went down so quickly it is a miracle there were any survivors at all. Seven people happened to be on the top

510

deck. Of these, the two sailors on the helm did not manage to get out of the wheelhouse, and one, Miss Charlotte Austin, drowned after entering the sea. But the remaining four of us would also have drowned had not the *China* happened to be immediately astern of us. In which case the *Charlotte Austin* would also have disappeared without trace, and no one would have been any the wiser.'

'I see,' Humphries said, although he obviously didn't. 'And have you any evidence to support this ejecting propeller of yours?'

'There was a slight vibration, noticeable at dinner, perhaps an hour before the actual disaster,' Edward said. 'When I checked this, I discovered it to emanate from the starboard shaft. It is now clear to me that this vibration began when the first of the bolts sheared. At that time, I think, only one bolt had sheared. But the strain on the remaining seven must have been enormous. And those other seven must all have snapped together. When that happened there was an enormous shudder which shook the ship from stem to stern. At that moment I spoke with Chief Engineer Hargreaves, and he mentioned the shaft. What else he might have said was ended by the inrush of water. An inrush so severe it even exploded through the funnels fifty feet above. Obviously, with a hole that size in her hull, the ship would sink very rapidly.'

Once again there was a brief silence.

511

Then Lord Milne leaned forward. 'You say you noticed a slight vibration an hour before the disaster, Captain Anderson. Did anyone else notice this vibration?'

'I should think most of the crew noticed it, my lord,' Edward said. 'Captain Ransome most certainly did.'

'But he did not take any steps to counter it?'

'He did not consider it necessary, my lord. As I have said, the initial vibration was very slight.'

'But it concerned you. You went down to the engine room, and there discovered that the starboard shaft was loose. But *you* did nothing about it, either?'

Edward gazed into the judge's eyes. 'The shaft was not *loose*, my lord. It was vibrating. At that time, very slightly. Mr Hargreaves was of the opinion that there was probably a large mass of seaweed wrapped around the propeller, which would soon be dispersed.'

'But you, Captain Anderson, with your years of experience at sea and in steamships, you felt that something more serious was wrong.'

'I was not entirely happy about it,' Edward said.

'Not entirely happy,' Lord Milne repeated, half to himself. 'But you did nothing about it.'

'Mr Hargreaves did not consider that anything needed doing about it,' Edward said again.

'Mr Hargreaves was the Engineer Officer. You were the designer of the vessel, and also

512

the senior representative of the shipping company on board. Could you not have *instructed* Mr Hargreaves to shut that engine down, or at least to reduce speed?'

'I possessed no executive authority, my lord,' Edward said, keeping his temper with difficulty. 'I could not instruct anyone to do anything on board that ship. I could only suggest. Mr Hargreaves was a competent and experienced officer. So was Captain Ransome. I had no right to interfere with their running of the ship.'

Lord Milne consulted his notes. 'You have just said that you have never before heard of a propeller shaft acting in such a terrible way, Captain Anderson. You feel it may have happened on other occasions, but you have no evidence to support your theory. Can you suggest a theory to explain why an iron bolt should suddenly perish?'

'I am forced to the conclusion that there was a flaw in the bolt.'

'You would not suppose it had anything to do with the colossal speed at which the ship was travelling? Mr Martin has told us she was logging twenty and a half knots. Is this not considerably in excess of any speed ever previously recorded?'

'That is correct,' Edward said. 'Obviously the speed had something to do with the accident. Had the shaft not been turning at all, the bolt would not have sheared. As to what speed would have caused it to shear, no one can be sure. The couplings, the gear boxes, the shafts themselves, were designed for the speed we achieved.'

'Yet you will admit that the *Charlotte Austin* was travelling faster than any ship has ever travelled before?'

'It is not a case of *admitting* anything, my lord. She was a fast ship. She was designed to be the fastest ship in the world.'

'Designed by you, Captain Anderson,' Lord Milne said. 'Would it not be correct to say that she was being driven at that, if I may venture an opinion, suicidal speed simply in order to *prove* that she was the fastest ship in the world?'

'She was being driven at her optimum speed, my lord,' Edward said. 'That is to say, her most economical speed, the fastest she would travel in relation to the amount of coal she would burn per hour. It is a mathematical formula based upon engine revolutions, not upon speed through the water. The *Charlotte Austin* was designed to cruise at nineteen knots. But conditions were so perfect she improved on that performance, while still maintaining her cruising revolutions.'

'She was doing all this because you were on board, and because you were determined to gain for yourself and your associates the so called blue riband of the Atlantic.'

Edward refused to lower his gaze. 'She was doing all this, as you put it, my lord, because that is what she was designed to do. That is

514

what her passengers boarded her to see her do.'

'The question to which I am seeking an answer, Captain Anderson, is whether the *Charlotte Austin* would have continued to steam at such an insensate speed had you not been on board. She was your design. She was your brainchild, if I may use the term. Your dream. For twenty years, we have been told, you had this dream. And now was your chance to realise it, regardless of the risks involved to anyone else.'

'She would have performed her optimum speed no matter who was on board, my lord,' Edward said. 'That was her sole reason for being built and launched.'

'Thus you disclaim all resposibility for what happened? You, who designed and controlled the building of the vessel?'

'As I designed and controlled the building of the vessel, my lord,' Edward said, 'I am most certainly responsible, ultimately, for her fate. I do not deny this. I cannot deny this. The lives of those twelve hundred people will always weigh heavily upon my soul. But if you are asking me to accept responsibility for the shearing of an iron bolt, which might have happened in any ship at any time, with similar results to those on board the *Charlotte Austin*, then I would say you are asking me to take on some of the prerogatives of the Deity Himself, and this, my lord, I will respectfully decline to do.'

515

Lord Milne stared at him. The courtroom was so quiet it was even possible to hear the sound of breathing. Then the judge leaned forward again. 'Is it not true, Captain Anderson, that after the ship had sunk, and you and the other three survivors were floating in the water, waiting to be rescued by the *R.M.S. China*, that Mr Robert Driscoll, your son, Captain Anderson, called you a murderer? He has testified to this.'

Edward felt the colour scorching his cheeks. There was no reply he could make to that. But he could now hear a rustle from behind and beside him. He did not suppose he had many friends in this courtroom, but even so the spectators were clearly feeling that his lordship had gone too far.

But was he not justified? Have I not, Edward wondered, just murdered twelve hundred people? Including Jehu, the man who had faithfully stood at his shoulder from the very beginning, who would have been singing happily to himself as he had turned down the bedspreads and poured their carafes of water, and who would have heard the muffled roar and just had time to go to the cabin door to see the wall of water that would kill him come storming up the corridor. How that image haunted him. He dreamed of it every night, just as he dreamed of the evening-gowned bodies that had floated on the sea when dawn had broken on that terrible morning, and the *China* had remained stopped in the centre of the catastrophe, still vainly searching for survivors.

Lord Milne had used his gavel to tap for silence. He was not accustomed to acknowledging the mood of his courtroom in his relentless search for justice. 'I have asked you a question, Captain Anderson.'

Edward raised his head, and the court gasped as they watched a tear roll down his cheek. 'Yes, my lord,' he said. 'That is the word my son used.'

Lord Milne leaned back. He had accomplished his purpose. He had destroyed this arrogant, over-ambitious mortal, and hopefully ended his fantastic and almost blasphemous dreams, forever. He could afford to be merciful, now. 'But as you have said, Captain Anderson, if the ultimate responsibility must be yours, you *cannot* be held responsible for the weakness in a small piece of iron, which caused the actual tragedy. That was surely the decision of the Almighty, in His wisdom, an example of His determination to prove to us mere mortals that there are paths down which we are not intended to tread. It may be some comfort to the relatives of the twelve hundred souls who perished with the *Charlotte Austin* to know that their deaths will not have been in vain if they have served to prove to men like yourself, Captain Anderson, that it is as unseemly as it is impossible to seek to challenge the dispositions of God, by seeking to drive a ship faster than

any vessel was ever intended to go...' he looked around the courtroom. 'Just as it is equally
blasphemous to attempt to fly, where no man
was intended to equal the birds. It would be
a fitting, and most satisfactory, conclusion to
this inquiry, Captain Anderson, if you would
acknowledge here and now that it is surely a
mistake for a mere mortal man to attempt to
compete with the forces of nature, and that
you, and hopefully all other shipbuilders, have
learned your lesson from the fate of the *Charlotte Austin.*'

The courtroom was again silent, as the judge
stopped speaking. Edward gazed at him for
some seconds, then turned his head, to look
at Penelope, leaning forward, lips slightly
parted as she attempted to will him to answer,
and at Austin, beside her, also staring at him,
face expressionless, but eyes glowing with an
almost demoniac intensity.

'Captain Anderson?' asked Lord Milne,
gently.

Edward drew a long breath. 'My lord,' he
said. 'With respect, I think you exceed your
authority or your knowledge, in attempting to
set a limit to the possibilities of human genius.
I myself cannot subscribe to such a doctrine,
nor will I.'

Lord Milne stared at him, brows slowly
drawing together. 'You mean you would actually contemplate building another such vessel, to
put another thousand lives at risk?'

'My lord,' Edward said. 'I desire to put no lives at risk. Anyone who sails in one of my ships does so of his or her own free will. They pay for the privilege. But as for the ship, my lord, why, her keel is already laid.'

CHAPTER 14

The courtroom exploded into pandemonium. There were some boos, but most of the noise came from cheers. Lord Milne could only bang with his gavel, and then, in despair, clear the court. Edward found himself in the vestibule, shaking hands with Austin even as he was hugged by Penelope, and then looking past them both at Henry Driscoll.

Penelope saw his change of expression, and turned her head, her mouth sagging open. She had not seen her husband since the moment she had left Greenacres, on Christmas Eve 1864, just over five years before. She had not even corresponded with him since he had last turned down her request for a divorce, three years ago.

'Well, Anderson,' he said. 'Still dreaming, careless of the lives, eh? You should be locked up, for the public safety.'

Edward said nothing. He was not in the mood for words, at this moment.

'Are *you* not aiming for speed, Mr Driscoll?' Austin asked, quietly. 'Are you not proud to be the holder of the blue riband? Sailing a ship designed by Captain Anderson, here?'

'I hold the riband, Sir Charles,' Henry said. 'And I shall continue to do so, you may be sure of that. Of course I go for speed, properly controlled. My new ship, the *Spartan*, will cruise at eighteen knots. We shall do Cork Harbour to Ambrose Light in six days and twelve hours. Not a moment longer, and not a moment less. But my ships, sir, are tested for strength. I believe in advancing slowly, sir. One knot at a time. You may challenge me whenever you wish, sir. You and this...this renegade. You may be sure at least that *my* ships will never fall apart, no matter how fast they are driven. Good day to you, gentlemen.' He gazed at Penelope, raised his hat, and walked on.

'Do you still hate him?' Penelope asked. She sat on the side of the bed, watching Edward, stretched out with his eyes closed. He looked so tired. She, more than anyone else, knew what an ordeal the day had been.

Edward sighed, and shook his head. 'I do not hate anyone, any more,' he said. 'I will have too many shades chasing behind me, in any event, when I go down to hell.'

She held his hand, folded those immensely powerful fingers into their own palm and squeezed them. 'You must not think like that,

520

Edward. Do not generals have to send men to their deaths from time to time?'

'Soldiers. Not innocent women, and their children.' Another sigh. 'Did you see Robert, after the hearing?'

She shook her head. 'He'll come home, Edward. When he has the time to think.'

'Why should he? I killed his fiancée. My God, do you realise that he must just have proposed, when it happened? Why should he ever forgive me?'

'He'll forgive you when he realises that it was not your fault. That you were merely taking your pre-ordained place in the march of human progress. Man *will* cross the Atlantic at twenty knots. You told me once that it would be done. And that you were the man to do it. You *are* the man to do it, Edward. Everyone knows that. You have devoted your entire life to that ideal. Had you been in command of the *Charlotte Austin...*'

'I could have ordered Hargreaves,' he said. 'Whether I was in actual executive authority or not. I could have ordered Ransome, for that matter. I did not, because I did not wish to. Milne was right. I did want to cross the Atlantic in five days. I knew something was wrong with that shaft, but I allowed myself to believe that nothing would happen, that it could be weed. I allowed myself to think what I wanted to think, instead of obeying my instincts.'

'Every other man in the world would have

done the same,' she said, and bit her lip as he looked at her. 'But you are not every other man in the world. I know that, Edward. And when the new ship goes to sea, you will be in command, without question. You will have no one to hide behind, except yourself. That is how you have always wanted it, how you have always worked best. And then you *will* break the record. And I will be there to see it.'

His head turned sharply. 'You? There is no way I can allow that. Not after last time.'

She blew him a kiss. 'You cannot forbid me, Edward Anderson. I am not your wife, you know. You cannot give me any orders. I have already booked my passage, and I have booked passages, at their requests, for Mother, and for Jimmy and Yvonne as well.'

'You...are you mad? Suppose...'

'Suppose what? Do you think this new ship will sink as well?'

'Of course not.'

'Well, neither do I. And thus I shall sail in her. Perhaps some time you will tell me what you propose to call her.'

He gazed at her, and then raised her fingers to his lips to kiss them. 'She will be called the *Penelope Anderson*.'

'The *Penelope Anderson*? But...there's no such person.'

'There is now, a ship. Besides,' he took her in his arms. 'There will be such a person, one day, my own dear love.'

Sir Charles Austin entered the office and threw the newspaper on the desk in front of Edward. 'Read all about it,' he said. 'As they say.'

Edward scanned the headlines:

"*SPARTAN* CROSSES ATLANTIC IN SIX DAYS AND TWELVE HOURS AND FIFTEEN MINUTES.

ANOTHER TRIUMPH FOR THE DRISCOLL LINE. BLUE RIBAND FIRMLY IN KEEPING OF AMERICAN COMPANY."

'Just what he said he would do,' Edward remarked.

'Oh, indeed.' Austin sat down. 'When do we launch?'

'On schedule,' Edward said. 'August fifteenth. The *Penelope Anderson* will be completed by the end of September. That will give us a fortnight to work her up, and she will sail from Southampton for New York on the night of October fourteenth. Exactly one year after the *Charlotte Austin*. We must prove to the world that we've no superstitions about it.'

'Correction,' Austin said. 'She will sail from Southampton to Cork, on the night of October thirteenth.'

'Eh?'

'I'm afraid we're going to have to prove more than that we're just not superstitious, Edward. We're going to have to match Driscoll exactly, minute for minute, mile for mile, only get there quicker. We have to catch the public's imagination in a big way. God knows I don't like the idea of racing across the Atlantic any more than you do. But the public sees it that way, and we have to give them what they want, if we're going to get them to sail with us at all. Besides...' he gave a grim smile. 'Cork is where the main emigration trade is from. And we're not going to have much else on board.'

'No first class takers?' Edward asked.

'Half a dozen, so far. It'll pick up, I'm sure, after she's launched. But right now they're mainly of the "we'll risk anything" variety, which is not the image I really wish to project. I've decided to sail on her myself.'

Edward frowned at him. 'If we go, we all go together, is that it?'

Austin grinned. 'Maybe a little of that. But principally to smooth over any difficulties we may have with the crew. The Board of Trade have refused to give you a British Master's ticket.'

Edward leaned back in his chair slowly.

Austin shrugged. 'You can't altogether blame them. Their laws are quite rigid on this. You have to be at least a naturalised British subject. I don't suppose...' he saw Edward's expression, and sighed. 'I did not really think you would. But the fact is that you cannot legally command a British ship on an American ticket. The fact of your vast experience means nothing, and of course there will have been Milne's report on the Inquiry. That's secret,

524

and has not been released as yet. It is still officially under scrutiny by the Board of Trade. I doubt it will ever be released, unless we come a cropper again. But there can be no doubt it's fairly hostile to you.'

'Then I guess the best thing would be for me not to come along at all,' Edward said. 'I'll only be the ghost at the feast.'

'Like hell you will,' Austin declared. 'We'll be sailing under sealed orders. And the moment we drop Cork behind us, those orders will be read, in my presence. They will appoint you Executive Commodore of the Line, with instructions to take over the ship until we pass the Ambrose Light.'

'You'll wind up in gaol,' Edward said.

Austin winked. 'Only if we fail, Edward. Only if we fail. And if we fail this time, I think the best thing for us both will be to go down with the ship.'

'Captain Hardisty,' Sir Charles said.

Edward shook hands. The captain was bluff and hearty in appearance, but there was a suitable amount of steel in his eyes. Edward wondered how he would react to being superseded.

'First Officer Parkinson.'

Tall and thin, with weatherbeaten features.

'Second Officer Martin.'

'Welcome back, ' Edward said. 'I thought maybe you'd had enough of sailing on my ships.'

'I wouldn't miss this one for the world, Captain Anderson,' the young man said.

'Third Officer Graham,' Austin said. 'Mr Graham is a nephew of Mr George Graham, my partner.'

Edward shook hands.

'And Chief Engineer Smith.'

Short, inclined to stoutness, and red-faced. Edward smiled at them. 'Well, gentlemen. Welcome aboard. What do you think of her?'

The *Penelope Anderson* lay quietly at anchor, a blaze of lights in Southampton Water. She was the fourth ship Edward had personally launched, and the third to bear the name *Penelope*, as she was the second to be named by Penelope herself. The two previous Penelopes had both been lucky ships, up to a point. But he could not rid himself of the lurking apprehensions which seemed to fill the recesses of his mind. Apprehensions these men must never suspect to exist.

And Austin? But he sometimes thought that Charles Austin knew him better than he knew himself.

'She's a fine looking vessel, Captain Anderson,' Hardisty said. 'Oh, a fine looking vessel.'

'I've never sailed on board an all steel hull before,' Parkinson confessed.

'Neither have any of us,' Austin told him. 'There aren't too many of them about. How do you rate your engines, Mr Smith?'

'Best I've ever seen, Sir Charles. The very best.'

'Good. You'll understand what our purpose is?'

'To beat Driscoll,' young Graham said.

Austin looked at Edward.

'It is to cross the Atlantic Ocean in six days or less,' Edward said. 'One hundred and forty-four hours from Cork to the Ambrose Light. A minute longer than that and we have failed.'

'Regardless of the weather, sir?' Hardisty asked.

'No man can tell what the weather will do, Mr Hardisty. But we must maintain our *attempt*, regardless of the weather.'

'What of Fortune?' the captain asked.

Austin frowned at him. 'I'm not sure I understand you, Captain.'

The Captain hesitated, then squared his shoulders. 'Well, sir, there's those that say this is an unlucky ship, because she's sister to the *Charlotte Austin*. And there's those that say she's dangerous to sail in, both because she has too much power in her engine room, and because she's built in steel. I don't hold with either of those points of view, sir, or I wouldn't be here. But I'm a seaman, sir, and I know it's bad luck to put to sea on the thirteenth of the month. But this is what I understand you're planning to do.'

'That is correct, Captain Hardisty.'

'May I ask why, sir?'

'Because our original schedule called for us to begin our voyage on October fourteenth, the same day as the *Charlotte Austin* last year. That date has been advertised and publicised. But since then it has become necessary to call at Cork first, so we have to leave Southampton a day early. That it happens to be the thirteenth of the month is neither here nor there. I do not subscribe to that superstition myself, and I do not expect my officers to, either. When we are in regular service we shall sail from either Southampton or New York every other Tuesday, regardless of the date of the month. I hope you understand this.'

The captain looked from Edward to Austin, and then at Parkinson, with whom he had obviously sailed before. 'Well, gentlemen, you may be sure that we shall do our best.'

'If we had not been sure of that,' Austin said. 'We would not have offered you berths. Thank you, gentlemen. You'd best be about your duties. Our first class passengers board at dawn.' He watched them file out of the executive suite, situated just behind the bridge. 'What do you think?'

'They'll do,' Edward said, and thought of Cas Malewski and Mark Trethowan and Jehu.

'They'd better. Well, Edward, happy?'

Edward raised his head.

Austin flushed. 'I meant, content with the ship.'

'Oh, content with the ship, certainly.'

528

'And no doubts about pushing her, now?'

Austin had only ever crossed the Atlantic once before. He had never known the bite of a hurricane, the feeling of a ship sliding away beneath him into the ocean. He did not have the shrieks of the passengers in the First Class Ballroom ringing in his ears, the vision of those floating bodies whenever he closed his eyes. Edward got up, went to the window, looked out at the night. Penelope and the children, and Priscilla Meigs, were already on board. Because they trusted him. Everyone trusted him, even Charles Austin. The only person who didn't have absolute faith in Edward Anderson was Edward Anderson himself.

Yet no one must suspect that, either. 'No doubts, Charles,' he said. 'We'll have that bit of blue bunting, this time next week.'

'That's what I wanted you to say,' Austin said, and looked at the doorway, which was opening, to admit Penelope Driscoll, and at her side, Robert Anderson.

With a blaring of sirens the *Penelope Anderson* slid past the village of Crosshaven and into the broad waters of the lough beyond, preparatory to dropping her anchor off the town of Cobh, the seaport for Cork. It was still early in the morning, but her decks were lined with first class passengers who had made the overnight journey from Southampton, all thirty-one of them, barely a sixth of her intended cabin class

529

complement. Yet they were excited. Perhaps too excited, Edward thought. They felt they were dicing with death, for all that the passage from England had been both slow and uneventful—but then, the *Penelope Anderson* had developed nothing more than twelve knots on this first leg of the voyage. Yet had they sailed on October thirteenth, transgressing one of the oldest superstitions of the sea; no doubt each felt they had survived a thousand hazards already.

And was *he* excited? He stood on the bridge wing as Captain Hardisty issued the quiet orders preparatory to stopping the ship. Hardisty was a good man. This much Edward could tell even on so short a voyage; he was less sanguine than Ransome had been, more inclined to interest himself in details. A man he would regret having to replace. More excitement?

Because he *was* excited. He was excited to be at sea again, after a year. The blue water always made him excited. He was excited to be having another chance to attempt the goal he had devoted his life to achieving. He was excited because this was not merely a faster and more efficient version of any steamship ever built—in her all steel construction she was unique, a completely new concept, a portent of the future. If she was successful, the time would come when every ship would be built in steel.

And he was excited because he could allow

himself to be excited, at last. Robert stood at his side now, with him gazing at the opening anchorage in front of them. They had said little. There had been little needed saying. The mere fact that he had returned had been sufficient. Amazing to think that in many ways Robert, at twenty-one years of age, was at least his father's equal in experience. He too had had a loved-one die, and he had had *two* ships slide away from beneath his feet into the measureless depths of the ocean. In his brief life he had crammed enough incident and adventure to last most men a lifetime. Yet he was here again, at his father's side, to make this bold challenge of the sea.

And to take part in the race of the century. Because there, as they had anticipated, was the *Spartan*, riding at anchor, but with launches and pinnaces plying back and forth, laden with Irish immigrants for the New World. She had obviously been here for at least twenty-four hours, Edward estimated, and was almost ready to sail. He studied her through his binoculars, realised that she was an exact sister to the *Amanda*, even to the additional three masts and the furled sails. She flew the Stars and Stripes at her stern, the Driscoll house colours of maroon and gold from her bow, and the long, waving blue pennant from her masthead which told the world that she was the fastest ship that had ever sailed. To this moment.

The anchor plunged into the pale green

531

water, and the *Penelope Anderson* came to a halt. Captain Hardisty stood beside them. 'I have informed the cabin passengers that they may go ashore if they wish, Captain Anderson,' he said. 'It will take us until dusk to load our seven hundred wild Irish.' He allowed himself a grim smile. 'No doubt they're all at this moment in church, having a last prayer.'

Because he too, Edward thought, had never known the agony of being *aware* that six hundred people, who had devoted all of their savings to a passage on board his ship in their search for a better life were helplessly battering at the hatches which confined them in their inferior quarters while the waves rose around their nostrils. He could still joke about them.

'No, Captain Hardisty,' he said. 'I do not wish to go ashore.' He pointed. 'No doubt anyone who wishes to communicate with me, will come to me.'

For a barge, a gleam of highly polished mahogany timbers and flying the Driscoll flag, was leaving the side of the *Spartan* and approaching them, oars glistening in the morning sunlight.

'Ahoy there, the *Penelope Anderson*,' came the hail. 'When do you sail?'

'At midnight,' Hardisty replied, studying the passengers through his glass, as were Edward and Robert through theirs. 'By God,' he said. 'That's Driscoll himself.'

'Good morning, Henry,' Edward called. 'I

was not aware you made this crossing regularly. Would you care to come on board?'

'I shall see you in New York, Anderson,' Henry said. 'If you ever get there. We sail at noon. I would delay to spend some of the time in your company, should you require assistance, but my schedule requires us to be docked in New York at midnight on Monday.'

Austin had come on deck. 'That is our estimated time of arrival also, Driscoll,' he said, 'So we shall have to spend our last few minutes in company, to be sure, even if we are leaving twelve hours after you.'

'Would you care to wager on that, Sir Charles?' Henry asked.

Austin hesitated, glanced at Hardisty and then Edward. Then he looked back at Henry. 'I am not here to race, Mr Driscoll,' he said. 'Merely to reach New York on schedule. Good day to you, sir.'

'Do you suppose I should have taken his beastly wager?' Austin stared after the *Spartan*, slowly disappearing down the channel towards the open sea. Her orchestra was playing, and she was still flying all her flags, while her sails were already being unfurled, despite the puffs of black smoke issuing from her funnel. There was no question but that she meant to hurry. 'After all, everyone, including Driscoll, knows that we *are* meaning to race him. Or he wouldn't have made the trip.'

'I am sure you did the right thing,' Edward muttered, also staring after his rival. Of course, it would be like Henry to wish personally to enjoy the triumph he anticipated. But there could be another reason for his presence. *He* had been so bound up in the excitement of the ship and the coming voyage he had not given his rival any thought in recent months, but undoubtedly Henry would know that Penelope and her children were also travelling by the *Penelope Anderson*. He could complete his triumph by meeting them in New York with a sheriff and a writ.

'But you'll catch him up, Edward. Promise me that,' Austin said.

'If it can be done, Charles,' Edward said. 'Without endangering the lives of the passengers or crew, at least wilfully. Then it will be done.'

Robert Anderson moved away from them, went down the ladders to the first class promenade deck, stood at the rail to look down at the launches arriving in a steady stream from the shore, each containing twenty or thirty people, whole families, ranging from white-haired grand-dads to babes at the breast, clad in a variety of garments, mostly their Sunday bests, staring up at the sides of the ship as they came into her shadow, gazing at the open entry port, gaping at them like a gigantic mouth, waiting to suck them into its embrace, quite literally. Once they were taken down to their steerage quarters, they would not again see the sky until they were disgorged in New York Harbour.

If they ever got there. Because he had watched a similar crowd of people boarding the *Charlotte Austin* in Southampton. Once *they* had gone below they had never seen the sky again, at all. He shuddered, as he thought of them, a huge coagulated mass of dead bodies, still pressing against the ship's hatches, at the bottom of the sea.

So why was he here? Because he *had* to support his father, when the chips were down—he had no one else? Or because, like Father, the sea, the lust to conquer the sea, or if that was beyond the ability of mortal man, at least to do battle with it, had entered his veins?

The amazing thing was that, unlike Father, he was sure, he *feared* the monster which had ruled his life. He had twice been held in its icy embrace, and twice had survived. He would not be so lucky a third time.

'Hey, mister,' a voice called. 'Is this ship *safe*?'

There were several peals of laughter, and he turned his head to search for the questioner, located her in one of the launches waiting its turn to get alongside. There were five girls standing in a group in the stern, holding their woollen shawls close about their shoulders as the October afternoon breeze was already cool. But he easily spotted the one who had spoken, and shuddered again. Because there was flowing red hair, and a freckled face, and entrancingly pert features...of course she was not the least like Charlotte. She had none of Charlotte's elegance, and she was tall where Charlotte had been below-average height, and thin where Charlotte had been inclined to plumpness. Nor would she smell of perfume or rustle delightfully as she walked. It was just the smile and the twirl of red hair...he turned away, hurried for the ladder up, followed by another peal of laughter.

'What d'ye think of that, Kathleen,' someone shouted. 'He's seasick already, the toff.'

'Ahoy, the *Penelope Anderson*,' came another call, and Robert checked and looked down again, this time at a steam pinnace carrying but two people apart from its crew. The man stood in the bow, his cape flowing in the breeze, and his moustaches too, for he had tremendous handlebars. The woman, presumably his wife, was huddled further aft; she wore no shawl, but rather a pure white, full-length coat made from the fur of the mink, Robert estimated, while even at this distance the sunlight glinted from the diamond rings on her fingers. 'You got a decent suite on that ship?' the man shouted.

'We have several suites, sir,' Edward answered, from the deck above. 'Would you be seeking a passage?'

'Looks like I'll have to,' the man said. 'Where's the *Spartan* gone?'

'To sea, sir.'

'God dammit. I'm in a hurry to get home. How fast does this tub go?'

'Faster than the *Spartan*,' Edward said.

'Without sails? Don't try to bull me, fellow. But I'll come aboard. Make way there,' he bellowed. 'Get those boats out of the way.'

The sailors hesitated, then pushed the immigrant boats to and fro to allow the pinnace alongside. Edward came down the ladder, Austin and Hardisty at his heels, in time to meet their latest passenger as he emerged on to the first class promenade.

'You'll get your pinnace out of there, sir,' Edward snapped. 'And wait your turn.'

The man stared at him for a moment, already red face seeming to turn purple. Then he gave a roar of laughter. 'You'll be Anderson. Seen your picture in the newspapers. You drown people.'

'I think you had better rephrase that, sir,' Charles Austin said. 'Or else take yourself off with your boat.'

'God damn, but you fellows are *tetchy*,' the man said, and held out his hand. 'Jay Christopher Smart, gentlemen. Pleased to make your acquaintance. This is the wife. Flo, meet these gentlemen. She don't like ships, and that's a fact.'

Florence Smart smiled wanly, while Edward and Austin stared at her husband in amazement.

'Jay Smart?' Austin asked at last. 'Not the
537

railroad man?'

'I own a few railroads back home, and that's a fact,' Smart said. 'Hell, you may as well get it straight. I own a whole hell of a lot of railroads. And I wanna get home, see. I had aimed to catch the *Spartan*, but if she's gone, then I guess it'll have to be you. You fellows drown me, and I'm gonna be right sore.' Another roar of laughter. 'I've a board meeting on Tuesday. See that I'm there.' He looked around him, at the other passengers, attracted by the noise, at the ship's officers, at Penelope and the children, gave them an embracing grin. 'Say,' he said. 'I'm on board now. Let's get to sea.'

'Slow ahead, Mr Parkinson,' said Captain Hardisty.

The telegraph jangled, and the *Penelope Anderson* slipped quietly through the still waters of the lough. Ashore, the church clock was striking exactly midnight—yet Cobh had not yet gone to sleep. There were no sirens, and no orchestras playing on board the ship, but everyone in the town, in company with everyone on board, was awake to watch her leave. Edward stood with Penelope on the bridge wing to look back at the land, and listen to the sudden song which arose from several thousand throats.

'They're singing *Oh God Our Help in Ages Past*,' Penelope whispered.

538

Edward said nothing. He wondered if his steerage passengers felt the same as the relatives they were leaving behind?

From the deck below there came Jay Smart's bellow of laughter. He had been a thorough nuisance all evening, calling constantly for them to up anchor right away, since he had joined. Now he was happy at last.

Edward looked forward at the slow moving Atlantic swell surging across the entrance to the channel and felt Penelope's fingers tight on his arm. It was utterly dark out there, save for the stars. There was no moon. But there had been no moon a year ago, either.

'Scared?' he asked.

'Yes,' she said. 'Aren't you?'

'About the next hour,' he said. 'You go to bed. When you wake up...'

'You'll be in command of the ship, or in the brig,' she said.

He kissed her on the cheek. 'This ship doesn't have a brig.'

She went to her suite, and he pulled his reefer jacket tighter and waited for Austin. Now the ship was outside the entrance, and Hardisty was ringing down for increased speed. The engine revolutions quickened, and were accompanied by a slight vibration. But this vibration had been present from the beginning, Edward reminded himself to quell the treacherous slivers of alarm which kept running through his mind. He had spent half the journey from

Southampton to Cork down in the engine room reassuring himself that all was well. And all was well.

The noise began to dwindle below him as the passengers left the deck. He doubted many of them would go to sleep tonight. But it was too cold to stay in the open air.

Too cold for him, as well. He opened the door, went into the enclosed warmth of the bridge. Both Hardisty and Parkinson were up here, as well as Graham and Martin, peering into the night, and already they could see the wink of the Fastnet Light House, low on the western horizon. That apart, the sea was empty.

'The *Spartan* will be more than a hundred miles ahead of us, Captain Anderson,' Hardisty said. 'I'm not promising we'll see her much before Sunday.'

'So long as we do,' Edward said.

The door opened and closed again, and Chief Engineer Smith came in. Hardisty turned, sharply. 'Something wrong?'

'Not a thing, Captain,' Smith said. 'They're just purring, down there. But I was told to report to the bridge.'

'I asked Mr Smith to join us, gentlemen,' Sir Charles Austin said, also entering the wheelhouse. 'I wish to have a word with the four senior officers. Will you step into the captain's cabin, please.'

Hardisty hesitated. Then he said. 'Take command, Mr Graham,' and went into his office, followed by Parkinson and Smart and Martin. Austin and Edward brought up the rear.

'It's a bit early for an officer's conference, Sir Charles,' Hardisty remarked. 'We're still within sight of land.'

'But we are more than three miles off, are we not?' Austin asked. 'In international waters?'

'Oh, indeed, sir.'

'Thank you.' Sir Charles sat down, gestured them all to chairs. 'What I have to say may surprise you, and even be disagreeable to some of you, but I would ask you to consider very carefully before you make any reply. You will know that this ship was designed and virtually built by Captain Anderson here. He is in fact the world's greatest living authority on the development of steamships, and has been sailing the most advanced of their types for more than twenty years. As you will also know, we lost the *Charlotte Austin*, because of a structural flaw no one could have foreseen.' He paused, to search their faces with his gaze. 'However, there is no doubt in my mind, or in the minds of my directors, that the *Charlotte Austin* would still have been afloat had Captain Anderson been in executive command.'

Hardisty's head came up and he looked at Martin; the Second Officer had instinctively nodded.

Edward could only wait. He felt neither apprehension nor exultation. He knew only that this was something which had to be done, and for his personal sake as much as any other.

'This is not intended as a reflection upon you, Captain Hardisty,' Austin went on. 'Or on Captain Ransome, may God rest his soul. It is simply that Captain Anderson has the experience to *feel* when a ship of this sort is performing as she should, and when she is not. Now, gentlemen, it is my fervent hope, and yours, I have no doubt, that we will proceed on this voyage in just such calm weather as we are enjoying now, with no mechanical breakdowns, and with no acts of God. And that we moor this ship in New York on the morning of Tuesday, October twenty-first, 1870 after having passed the Ambrose Light at one minute to midnight on Monday. But that is still six days away, and no one can tell what is going to happen during those six days. It is therefore my wish, and the wish of my directors, that Captain Anderson assume executive command of this vessel until the Ambrose Light is sighted.'

He paused, looked at Hardisty.

But it was Parkinson who spoke first. 'Does Captain Anderson hold a British Master's Certificate, Sir Charles?'

'I do not,' Edward answered. 'My Master's Certificate was issued by the United States Government.'

'Then, sir, what is proposed would be illegal.

Unless you intend to haul down the British flag and hoist the Stars and Stripes. And that, I doubt, would be acceptable to the crew.'

'I have no intention of changing flags,' Austin said. 'I am asking you to accept a private agreement, for the good of the ship, and of all those who are sailing in her, including yourselves. And for which I will take full responsibility.'

'You doubt my capability, sir, to take this ship across the ocean,' Hardisty said.

'No, sir. But both Captain Anderson and myself feel, in view of what happened to the *Charlotte Austin*, that the ultimate responsibility for what happens on this voyage, if anything does, should be ours. Or we are placed in an intolerable position.'

'Yet you are asking me to step down,' Hardisty said. 'After having left port. And you do not consider that is placing *me* in an intolerable position? That, sir, is an insult.'

'We are not asking you to do anything, Captain Hardisty,' Edward said. 'Which should be repugnant to you. This is your ship, and believe me, you will be given the credit for all the success that she is going to enjoy. Sir Charles wishes me to have, as I have in any event, the ultimate responsibility for any mishaps that may occur. My God, sir, do you suppose I could survive another disaster like the *Charlotte Austin*, unless I also knew the final decisions had been mine? We are being honest with you,

Captain Hardisty. Not insulting. Sir Charles has in his pocket a letter signed by the directors of his company, this company, sir, authorising him to place me in command whenever he thinks fit. It would be very simple for him to leave that letter where it is, and produce it only in an emergency, and require you then to surrender your command or be dismissed. But he is telling you now, long before there is any thought of an emergency, when we are all hoping and praying and expecting that there will be no emergency, and is asking for your co-operation. There is no question of asking you to step down, to cease being master of this vessel. We are requiring you merely to understand that there is a higher authority than yourself on board, from whom the ultimate decisions regarding the safety of the ship, should the occasion arise, will emanate.'

'I may say,' Austin added, 'that a copy of this letter, and a copy of my resolution to raise this point, and carry it, the moment we pass the three mile limit, is in safekeeping in London. Should any mishap arise, that letter will be used in evidence, and will absolve you from any blame, placing the responsibility squarely on the shoulders of Captain Anderson and myself. Nothing that can happen on this voyage can in any way affect your future career, except to boost it by our successful arrival in New York. On schedule.'

Hardisty gave a bitter smile. 'Save that if I

do *not* co-operate, I will be dismissed at the end of the voyage, is that it?' He got up, walked to the window, looked out at the night.

The others waited. The decision had to be his alone; they would obviously follow his lead.

At last he turned. 'You are my Managing Director, Sir Charles, and thus my employer. I think this is a fine ship, and I have no doubt that she will succeed, and that you will build many more like her. I hope to command some of those ships. Thus I am prepared to acquiesce in your wishes. But I wish to state before these gentlemen, and before yourselves...' he looked directly at Edward, 'that I think your actions are dictated by a horror of what happened to the *Charlotte Austin*. This is understandable, but to my mind it calls into question the effect that catastrophe has had on your nerves, Sir Charles, and also on the nerves of Captain Anderson. I am bound to express the opinion that I have serious doubts as to Captain Anderson's mental ability to command this ship in an emergency. But if it is still your wish to put him in overall command, then I am prepared to honour that wish, in view of everything that has happened these past twelve months.' He looked at his officers. 'I think I may speak for all of us.'

But they were all looking at Edward.

'Begging your pardon, sir, Captain Anderson,

but Captain Hardisty asks to see you, sir, on the bridge.'

The steward stood to attention beside the Commodore's table. Like so many of the crew, who had sailed with Hardisty before, they were mystified by the way their old man constantly referred decisions to Edward. But they were content. The ship was a dream, and handling like a dream, as she drove at twenty knots through the calm waters of the North Atlantic.

Even Smart seemed pleased, and now he gave a bellow of laughter, as Edward pushed back his chair and got up. 'Captain's conference, eh? Say, isn't tonight the anniversary of the loss of the *Charlotte Austin*?'

His voice, as usual, boomed across the dining room, which was nearly empty in any event, although all the first class passengers were at the meal. Now the hubbub of conversation fell away, as did the rattle of cutlery and crockery; the stewards had also heard the remark. Even the orchestra seemed to diminish its volume.

'No, sir, Mr Smart,' Edward said quietly. '*Tomorrow* is the anniversary of the sinking of the *Charlotte Austin*.' He looked at his watch. 'You have exactly twenty-four hours to wait.' But he glanced at Penelope as he left the room. She was as aware as he was—and as nobody else in this room was— how much he was on trial, how anxiously Hardisty and Parkinson, without malice, he was sure, but with a very human concern, were waiting for him to prove his inability to command, his loss of nerve—too many people remembered the tear he had shed in the courtroom.

And he could not even resent their attitudes. Hardisty had in fact behaved both like a gentleman and an utterly loyal servant of the Austin and Graham Line. No man could ask for anything more. And were not his fears entirely justified?

He squared his shoulders, climbed the ladder to the bridge. Both Hardisty and Parkinson were waiting for him. 'I thought you should consider these barometric entries in the Log, Captain Anderson,' Hardisty said.

Edward studied the page. As was customary, each officer on watch had entered the barometric pressure every hour. The general pressure pattern was low, hovering about sixteen inches, but hovering was an entirely accurate word, he realised, as he noted the small but continuous fluctuations. Memory took him back all of twenty-five years, to the cabin of the *Regina*, just before his first hurricane.

The officers waited. They would give no hint of what they feared. It was up to him to reveal his experience, or lack of it.

Edward straightened. 'We are entering the area of a tropical storm,' he said.

Hardisty and Parkinson exchanged glances.

'But it is still at least twenty-four hours away,' Edward went on, and moved to the windows to look out at the empty night sky. 'You'll

547

stop engines, Captain Hardisty, if you please.'

'Stop engines?'

'We are obtaining a false wind reading, Captain,' Edward said. 'Travelling at this speed. It is very necessary for us to know accurately the direction of the wind. It will only be for ten minutes.'

Hardisty glanced at Parkinson again, and then rang down for slow ahead, followed by stop. The *Penelope Anderson* slowly glided to a halt, rolling gently in the shallow swell, blowing off steam in great clouds of black smoke. From below there came raised voices. 'You'll send an officer down to tell the passengers that this is merely a meteoriligical check,' Edward said. 'There is no need to mention the likelihood of a storm. And I wish the steerage passengers also informed of it.' He went outside, where Austin was hurrying up the ladder. The ship had now quite lost way, and the light breeze was coming in over the port bow.

'Whatever is the matter, Edward?' Austin asked.

'There is a tropical storm, out there.' Edward turned ninety degrees away from the wind and pointed over the starboard bow, into the darkness.

'A tropical storm? You mean a hurricane? I had no idea they came this far north.'

'They do, from time to time. We have no means of knowing, at this moment, how intense it will be, but it could well have hurricane-force winds near its centre, Charles, yes. This is the tail end of the storm season.'

'What do you mean to do?'

'Fortunately,' Hardisty said, having joined them, 'we have been doing so well that we have approximately a day in hand already. If we were to alter course now and steam due south, we should probably skirt the storm.'

'And for how long will we have to steam south?' Austin inquired.

Hardisty shrugged. 'As Captain Anderson has said, it is impossible to tell the size or the intensity of the storm at this distance. But the moment the glass settles down and begins to rise steadily, why, then we may resume our proper course.'

'And no doubt miss our schedule,' Austin said. 'Do we have to do that, Edward? It will make us the laughing stock of the shipping world, and just about ruin us into the bargain.'

'We do not have to alter course,' Edward said. 'Not yet, at any rate. This ship has been designed to cross the Atlantic every fortnight from January to December. She cannot always turn away from every depression that may cross her path.'

'With respect, Captain Anderson,' Hardisty said, 'there is some difference between a depression and a hurricane.'

'I will grant you that, Captain Hardisty, and remind you that we do not yet know for certain that it is a hurricane out there. But even

549

if there is, as you no doubt know, there are two semi-circles in a hurricane, one dangerous, the other navigable. In this case, if we presume that this storm has originated in the West Indies, which seems certain, it is therefore travelling in a north-easterly direction, which means that the southern semi-circle will be the navigable one. By holding our course, and with the centre of the storm where it is indicated to be, we should pass through that less dangerous area. If the storm changes direction, then we shall change our plans. But for the time being, we shall hold our course and our speed. Every moment we gain may be vital later on. There is no need to take any other action tonight. However, first thing tomorrow morning, should we still be closing the storm, I wish the ship prepared. I wish deadlights screwed over every port, and the lifeboats double lashed. I wish all the passengers issued with lifejackets, and I wish all water tight doors cleared and prepared for closing. It would be best if you made up the necessary list this evening.' He gazed at Hardisty, and then at Parkinson. 'You may get under way, Captain. And I shall resume my dinner.'

CHAPTER 15

'Say, look here, Anderson, what's all this talk I'm hearing about a hurricane?'

It was just on midnight, and the orchestra had ceased playing. The first class passengers were beginning to drift away to their cabins. But now they halted as Smart's bull-like bellow roared across the evening. 'My steward tells me it's coming straight for us.'

'On the contrary, Mr Smart,' Edward said. 'There happens to be a tropical storm out there, and *we* are heading straight for *it*.'

'Eh? But if you know it's there, man, can't you go round it?' His huge forefinger jabbed the air. 'Flo don't like storms at sea. Like I told you, she don't even like the sea.'

'The voyage to Europe was the first time I'd ever been more than three miles from land.' Florence Smart confided, clutching her mink coat tightly around herself. 'It was terrible. I should die if anything happened on this one.'

Probably a very accurate forecast, Edward thought, but he decided against saying it.

Priscilla Meigs, however, was apparently even more irritated by the millionaire and his wife than he was. 'But, my dear Mrs Smart,' she said, in her most reassuring tone. 'There is nothing to worry about. You're well within three miles of land, now.'

'Are we?' Florence Smart squeaked in delight. 'Oh, that makes me so happy.' She ran to the rail. 'Where is it?'

'Straight down,' Priscilla said, brutally.

Penelope squeezed Edward's hand, but she was having difficulty in stopping herself from laughing.

'Oh,' Florence Smart said. 'Oh, that was a terrible thing to say, Mrs Meigs. Wasn't that a terrible thing to say, Jay?'

But Smart, perhaps for the first time in his life, was speechless.

Robert left them, went down the ladder to the welldeck, where he could be sure of being alone, to stare at the sea. The still calm sea. Would it still be calm this time tomorrow night?

Was he afraid? He supposed he was. He had seen the sea in all its moods, but never at hurricane force. That was outside even his experience. And that was the sea at its ultimate. The sea which had snatched at him twice already.

But thoughts like that, fears like that, simply had to be overcome. Or he should have remained on land for the rest of his life.

Was Father not afraid? Father had done battle with the wind and the sea often enough before. And had all but come to grief on more than one occasion. It was impossible to suppose that he did not feel at least a tremor running up and down his spine at the thought of again facing a hurricane. But he never showed it. Therefore his son could not show it, either.

'Hey, mister,' a voice said. 'Do you think we could come on deck? Just for a breath of air.'

His head turned, to look at the stairs leading down to the steerage accommodation. The actual bulkhead door was open and from down the steps there came the sound of an accordion and the clapping of hands, but at the top were the girls who had shouted to him from the launch, led by the tall redhead. They could not come any further because the doorway was barred by a steel gate, which was bolted on the outside.

He looked left and right. The welldeck was deserted, and very nearly completely dark, as it was sheltered from the promenade decks by the overhang of the bridge.

'I don't see why not,' he agreed. 'For five minutes, mind. You promise to go back, after five minutes?'

'Sure we promise,' the girl, whose name he now recalled was Kathleen, said. 'We'd not take advantage, mister. But those weeds the lads are smoking down there, why, they're like to turn our stomachs, that they are.' She stepped past him, followed by her friends, to stand at the rail and draw long breaths of sea air. 'Holy Mother, but that smells good.'

'Hey, mister,' said one of the other girls. 'Is it true there's going to be a storm, and we'll all be drowned?'

He stared at her.

'Well,' said another girl. 'That's what the steward man says. He says that by this time tomorrow we'll all be feeding the fishes.'

'He's having a joke on you,' Robert said 'There's going to be a little wind, and we may roll a bit. But nothing more than that.'

'Oh, I'm scared,' said the fourth girl. 'I think we should go back down now. I'm scared.'

They filed past Robert, and back down the stairs. But the girl Kathleen hesitated. 'You're awful kind, mister,' she said. 'I'm sorry I was rude, back in Cobh.'

'Like the steward, I guess, you're entitled to your little joke.'

She gazed at him and he discovered that her eyes were green, and the biggest he had ever seen. 'Say,' she said. 'You wouldn't let me have a look upstairs? The steward man says its real plush up there. I'd love to look at it.' He hesitated, and she pressed her point. 'They've all gone to bed, haven't they? I'd just like a look. A quick one.'

'Why not,' he said. 'Quiet now.'

'Like a mouse,' she promised.

He led her up the ladder, and on to the First Class Promenade. This was deserted, although the lights still glowed; but the lights would glow all night.

'Oh,' she said. 'Ain't it grand? Such a view...'

He opened the huge double doors into the Main Saloon. Here the lights had been turned down, but the fire still glowed in the grate. Kathleen stared at the leather upholstery, the great bar, the rows of bottles, then tiptoed across the carpeted floor to look through the archway into the dining saloon.

'I ain't *never* seen anything so grand,' she said. And glanced at him. 'Say, you an officer or something?'

He shook his head. 'Just a passenger.'

'And you live up here? It must cost a fortune.'

He hesitated, tempted to tell her who he was, but decided against it. She was an incredibly attractive girl. Not pretty, in any way, he supposed, with her snub nose and curiously rounded features, while her body was so slender it would have been difficult to decide whether she was a man or a woman, had she not been dressed as a woman—and had it not been for the hair—but she exuded an intense vitality which was irresistible.

Now she was flushing. 'Do you think...we could look in a bedroom?' she asked.

'They call them "staterooms",' he said, aware that his heart was suddenly pounding. 'You can look in mine, if you like.'

'Aren't there any empty ones?'

'Well, yes,' he said. 'But I don't know which

555

ones are empty and which are occupied.'

'But what about the people you're sharing with?' she asked.

He led her along the corridor, between the walnut panelled doors. 'I don't share with anyone,' he said. 'Quiet now.'

'You don't share with *anyone?*' Her voice rose to a squeak, but she was endeavouring to whisper, and a moment later she was in the cabin, where the steward had already lit the gas lamps, staring around herself at the bed, and the washbasin, and the comfortable chairs... 'It's like a palace,' she said. 'Just like a palace.'

Robert closed the door. But she did not seem to be aware that she was alone in a bedroom with a strange man, as she hunted about, and even knelt on the bed to look out of the porthole, her booted feet slipping from beneath her gown. 'It's wonderful,' she said.

'But you have portholes, down in steerage,' he said. Did he *want* to take advantage of her? He was not even sure what "taking advantage" might mean. He and Charlotte Austin had done no more that hold hands, until that last dreadful night, when he had kissed her, and she had promised to be his...but suddenly he did want to hold this girl in his arms. And do more than that. Because he was afraid. Because this might be his last night on earth.

He would not be lucky a third time. How that thought haunted him.

She turned her head, and her body, sat on

the bed. 'We're not allowed to open ours, at sea,' she explained. 'Or the water would come in. Say, isn't this bed soft? I'd love to sleep on a bed like this.'

'Would you really like to?' he asked, his heart now sounding like a bass drum.

'That'd be grand,' she said sadly, and got up. 'But it'd be against the rules, I guess.'

Robert drew a long breath. 'You could stay here,' he said. 'If you wanted to. No one would know.'

This time she looked at him with genuine interest. 'With you?' she asked.

'Well...'

She gave a curious little laugh. 'That'd be fun,' she said. 'That'd be real nice. But after, why, you'd have to marry me.'

'Marry you?'

'You hadn't thought of that,' she said. 'Men never do. But me father and me brothers, they'd make you. Come to think of it, they'd make you anyway, if they even knew I was here. You're a toff. You couldn't be expected to put up with the likes of Kathleen O'Reilly from Tipperary. You wouldn't like that at all.' She went to the door. 'But you know what,' she said. '*I'd* like that very much. Pity you're a toff. I'd like that *very* much.'

'There it is,' said Captain Hardisty.

Edward stood beside him on the bridge staring at the seemingly solid black mass rising over the horizon, appearing even darker and more menacing than it actually was because of the afternoon sun still hovered above it, as if afraid to sink any lower and be engulfed. The wind had dropped away completely, and the *Penelope Anderson* raced across a flat calm sea. Towards a raging maelstrom.

He checked the barometer, glanced into the Log. The glass had now commenced to fall, and would gather pace as the afternoon drew on.

'There's still time to turn away,' Hardisty remarked. 'With this speed, we can outrun her easily. There's no proper hurricane travels at more than fifteen knots over the sea.'

'Yes,' Edward agreed. 'We could run all the way back to England, Captain Hardisty.'

'But you mean to stand on.'

'Have you carried out all storm preparations?'

'I have done that, Captain Anderson.'

'Then we shall stand on.'

Hardisty hesitated. 'I should like to record my opinion in the Log, that we are taking an unnecessary risk,' he said at last.

'You may make such an entry, Mr Hardisty,' Edward said. 'But may I ask if, as captain of this ship, you intend to maintain your schedules in the future?'

'In so far as I can, Captain Anderson.'

'Then you must realise that the object of a ship such as the *Penelope Anderson*, Mr Hardisty,' Edward said, speaking very evenly, 'is that she should maintain a fortnightly service to and fro across the Atlantic, regardless of the weather. Our passengers must know the dates on which they will depart and the dates on which they will arrive, and they must be quite sure that nothing short of an Act of God will prevent them from arriving or departing on those dates.'

'You would not call a hurricane an Act of God?' Hardisty inquired.

'It is an act of nature, sir. That is not the same thing.' Edward left the bridge, went down the ladder to the next deck. Here the first class passengers were all gathered, to stare at the approaching storm.

'Say, Anderson, we really going right through that?' Smart wanted to know.

'There's blue sky, and your board meeting, on the other side, Mr Smart,' Edward said, and walked on, to where Austin and Penelope were waiting.

'You're sure about this, Edward?' Austin asked.

'Hardisty is recording his objections in the Log,' Edward said. 'You're welcome to put yours beside his.'

'Now don't get annoyed,' Austin said. 'It's just that I've never been in a blow like this promises to be. Suppose, well...'

'There's another perished bolt in the engine room? Then we've had it anyway. You want to remember that the *Charlotte Austin* went down in the most perfect weather I've ever experienced at sea. And that if one supposed retaining bolts or rivets would part, one would never put to sea at all.'

'Yes,' Austin said. 'Yes, I suppose you're right.' But he was clearly worried. And not least, Edward understood, by the evidence of some uneasiness on *his* part. As Penelope recognised. She joined him in their cabin, where the deadlight had already been screwed into place and the gas lamps already glowed, even at four in the afternoon.

'Will she do it, Edward?'

'Of course she will do it,' he said. 'If she's capable of crossing the Atlantic at all, she has to do it.'

'But you still have doubts.'

He raised his head to look at her. 'Yes,' he said. 'I have doubts. Of myself, as much as the ship, as much as of freak disasters.' He squeezed her hand. 'But if I can't overcome those doubts, my darling, then am I wasting my time in being here at all,' He grinned. 'You reckon the *Spartan* is still ahead of us? If she is, she's in it already.'

'I never thought of that,' she said. 'Do you think Henry would?'

'I think he might, on an occasion like this. Besides, if he had turned away, I think we'd have sighted at least his smoke. He can't be more than fifty miles ahead of us now. So we'll

560

have company. Now let me sleep. I think it's going to be a long night.'

He awoke at six that evening. By then the wind was rising; he could hear its howl and he could feel the pitch of the ship and the slap of the waves. But by then, too, Penelope and Martin had prepared the wreath and were waiting for him. He put on his thick reefer and added an oilskin jacket as they had done, and went on deck. The entire sky was prematurely dark and there were no stars visible, while every so often a rain squall swept across the evening, splattering on to the deck with loud plops.

Hardisty had been instructed and reduced speed; the motion became easier. The other first class passengers gathered in a group in the shelter of the Saloon, watched the five of them—they had been joined by Robert and Austin—stand at the rail. Edward spoke a short prayer, and then the wreath was thrown over the side, to float down into the choppy sea and almost immediately disintegrate.

'I think I'm going to cry,' Florence Smart said, and burst into tears. Penelope was already weeping, silently. While the four men looked at each other. There would be no surviving, in this sea, and even less as it would become in a few hours time—not even if the *China* or the *Java* were actually cruising in company.

And five thousand feet below them was the no doubt still-intact hull of the *Charlotte Austin*,

561

with weed growing out of her engine room, with fishes swimming through the main saloon —and with fleshless skulls grinning at her ports.

Waiting for them.

'Time,' Edward said. 'You may resume cruising revolutions, Captain Hardisty.' He addressed the passengers. 'Dinner will be served early, tonight,' he told them. 'Starting now, as a matter of fact. After dinner, you may of course remain in the Saloon, if you wish, although we would recommend that you retire to your staterooms, as there may be some considerable rolling. At all times you should have your lifebelts to hand. There is absolutely no danger, but this is a simple and necessary precaution.' He gave Penelope a squeeze. 'I think you should put the children to bed in our stateroom, and stay with them. To the bridge, Mr Martin. I'll join you in a moment.'

'What about me, Father?' Robert asked.

'I reckon you'd best come up to the bridge as well. Wait for me, there.' He went down the ladders, into the bowels of the ship. Down here he couldn't hear the whistle of the wind, and there was much less movement. It was easy to get a false sense of total security. But the engine room *was* reassuring. The lights glowed, the pistons thumped back and forth, the gauges held steady readings, the stokers gleamed with sweat as they shovelled, and every officer was at his post.

'Freshening up, eh, Captain Anderson?' Smith inquired.

'Just a little,' Edward said. 'I'm going to need everything you have, Mr Smith.'

'You shall have it, sir. These lads know what they're about.'

'And you'll watch the telegraph,' Edward said. 'We can't just steam through what's coming. We have to *drive* her through. You understand me?'

'Aye-aye,' Smith said. 'You send the orders down, Captain Anderson, and we'll carry them out. You may rely on that, sir.'

'This whole ship is relying on that, Mr Smith,' Edward said. 'And every soul on board.'

The seas were breaking now, racing in from the north-west, striking the bows of the steamer and causing her to shudder, while they leapt high into the air as spray, to fall with a splatter on the welldeck, foam around the bulkhead door leading down to steerage and the base of the ladders leading up, scatter across the windshield of the bridge as a fine mist. And the wind was starting to howl. But it was still only gale force.

Edward stood beside Hardisty. 'What do you reckon is the greatest danger from a hurricane, Captain Hardisty?' he asked.

'I would say too great a windforce for the ship to withstand,' Hardisty said. 'Resulting

563

in a knockdown or a broach.'

'That applies to a sailing ship, Mr Hardisty,' Edward said. 'But we're a steamer. The wind can't hurt us. It is the seas we have to worry about. And the seas can't hurt us either, while they are battering at our hull, and throwing spray. It's the solid water which comes on board that will damage us, if anything does. The longer a drop of water remains on deck, the longer the ship is in danger. That's our business for the next twelve hours; making sure we are under water for the least possible period in each wave. I'm going to take the helm, now...'

'You?' Hardisty was amazed.

'Yes, sir,' Edward said. 'And I want you beside me, to work the engine room telegraph.'

'Me?' Hardisty asked, even more astonished. He looked at his junior officers.

'You and me, Mr Hardisty,' Edward said. 'If we can't do this thing, nobody else can.'

But his confidence was growing. The barometer had fallen with colossal speed in the past two hours. Too fast for a prolonged storm to be in front of them. If the ship was everything she was supposed to be, everything she *had* to be, then he would drive her through it. The old exhilaration began to surge through his veins as he took the helm from the scandalised coxswain, wrapped his powerful fingers around the spokes, felt the ship answering to his touch. That had been what had gone wrong with the

564

Charlotte Austin. There had been no challenge. The ship had just died. When the sky in front of him suddenly opened up in a jagged flash of forked lightning, followed almost immediately by a mind-numbing peal of thunder, he laughed aloud.

The electrical storm was accompanied by a tremendous downpour. Rainwater cascaded in such solid sheets that he could not see past the windscreen, much less make out the bows of the ship; but the rain had the temporary effect of deadening the breaking seas, gave him time to reflect how much more comfortable it was in this sheltered wheelhouse than on the poop deck of a clipper—but also how much more insidious it was, because he could not feel either the force or the direction of the wind.

The rain stopped, the *Penelope Anderson* plunged forward, slid down the side of the biggest trough they had so far entered, and suddenly they saw an immense wall of water rising immediately in front of them looming through the darkness, high as a two-storied house and looking every bit as solid.

'Christalmighty!' Parkinson gasped.

'Full speed ahead,' Edward snapped, and swung the helm to plunge straight into the wave.

Hardisty hesitated.

'Gun it,' Edward shouted, and the wave broke. Green water poured twelve feet high over the bows, forcing them downwards, while the wave kept on coming, smashing against the front of the superstructure, obliterating the bridge windows with a force it hardly seemed possible for the glass to withstand. The ship seemed to check and began to fall away. Edward's heart came all the way up into his throat as he felt her roll. He watched the clinometer slide across to twenty degrees of list and keep on going—she would not recover if she went over more than thirty five degrees—and heard the shattering of crockery from below decks and the screams of those passengers who had not yet gone to bed. But Hardisty had at last obeyed, and thrust the lever on the telegraph full forward. The ship roared back into life and the foaming water, which had even scorched along the promenade deck, poured back over the sides, and the men on the bridge could see the night sky again and an even more frightening gap into which the bows of the vessel were now dropping.

'Throttle down,' Edward commanded, as the propellers came out of the sea and the engines started to race. This time Hardisty was more ready to respond, dragged the lever back; the roar of the engines died, and the ship lost some of her dizzy speed, although she was still falling into what seemed to be a bottomless pit. Her bows dipped, and there, rising above them again, was another huge mountain of foaming water.

'Full speed,' Edward roared. Now Hardisty

responded immediately, and the *Penelope Anderson* hurled herself at the sea, bursting through the wave in less than half the time she had taken previously. 'Throttle back,' Edward yelled, and once again the ship slid down the trough, while the decks cleared of water. 'Damage report, Mr Parkinson,' Edward snapped, without turning his head. 'Full speed, Mr Hardisty.'

Parkinson returned in a few moments. 'Three boats carried away,' he said. 'And a length of rail. I can't say for below.'

'Send someone down to check the engine room,' Edward said. 'And the steerage.'

'I'll go,' Robert volunteered, and ran for the internal ladder.

'And for God's sake, take care,' Edward said. 'Full speed, Mr Hardisty.'

The ship drove into another wave, and this time Hardisty did not have to be told what to do. He brought the lever back the moment the bows broke through.

'Good man,' Edward said. 'We've got it now.'

'How long do we keep this up?' Hardisty gasped. 'All night, did you say?'

'Until we're through the storm, Mr Hardisty,' Edward said. 'Until we're through.'

Robert reached the first class deck and looked into the Saloon which was a shambles. The passengers had now all retired to the safety of their staterooms, but the stewards were trying to cope with the huge leatherbound armchairs, several of which had been torn from the bolts which held them to the floor, just as in the dining saloon half a dozen of the tables had been thrown over and lay in tangled wreckage. Pieces of potted palm were strewn in every direction, together with shattered crockery and scattered cutlery. In the main bar there was a mind-dizzying smell of mixed liquor from the broken bottles. And there, alone, sat Sir Charles Austin, not drinking, but merely staring at the bulkhead opposite, sharing the agony of his ship, willing it to survive, and conquer.

Robert decided against interrupting his reverie, went along the main corridor to Penelope's suite, knocked, and looked inside. The gas had been turned off and the only light in here was from a swinging lantern. Remarkably, both children were fast asleep, although the motion of the ship had rolled them together in the centre of the bed normally occupied by Edward and Penelope. Penelope herself sat in a chair, a book on her lap, but obviously not reading. She kept looking at the porthole; she could not see out because of the deadlight but she could hear the rattle of the spray on the glass and the huge rumbles of thunder, feel the jar as the ship hit the waves. Now she turned her head in quick apprehension.

'All's well, so far,' Robert said. 'Father just

asked me to check on how things are with you.'

'We're as good as the ship,' she said.

'I don't think he really doubted that.' He blew her a kiss and closed the door, going to the next set of ladders. These led straight down to the engine room, a distance of some thirty feet, and he was through the well and actually emerging into the roof of the boiler room when the *Penelope Anderson* was struck by another huge wave. The force of the blow and the angle of the immediate heel seemed much more severe down here; he clung to the steel ladder as he found himself hanging out into space, immediately above the boilers themselves, listening to the shouts from below him, imagining the ship sliding sideways down the trough and wondering if there might be another huge green monster about to overwhelm her before she could again come upright. But up she came, and he listened to the telegraph jangling to reduce speed once more, showing that all was at least still well on the bridge.

Smith was there to welcome him at the foot of the ladder. 'My God, but you had me scared,' the engineer said. 'Thought you were going to drop, I did. What's it like up top?'

'Boisterous,' Robert said. 'But we'll manage. So long as we have sufficient steam.'

'You'll have steam,' Smith said. 'You'll have steam.'

Together they went aft to look at the shafts, spinning round with smooth precision, and then to check the bilges—but there were only a few inches of water. The steel hull remained as tight as a drum, although the noise down here was enormous, even the booming roar of the engines being almost drowned by the thuds and crashes of the water against the sides, the scream of the propellers as they came too near the surface, the constant jangling, to and fro, of the telegraphs.

'They'll wear themselves out,' Smith grunted. 'Or they'll wear the lever out.'

'I'd like to go through into steerage,' Robert said.

Smith glanced at the bolted bulkhead door. 'You can't open that, Mr Anderson. You'll have those passengers coming into here. And that I can do without.'

'Not if we're quick about it,' Robert said. 'I'll be through before anyone knows it's open. And you can bolt it behind me. But mind you're there to open it again if I call.'

'They'll tear you apart,' Smith warned, but he unbolted the door. Robert stepped through, into the third class storerooms, and the door clanged shut behind him. Here was utter darkness, save for the pale glow of his lantern, but here too there were new noises, the concentrated *moan* of several hundred people in terror. He climbed the ladder into the Dining Saloon, where most of the passengers seemed to have huddled, men and women and children, many being seasick, others clinging together, one or two brave souls attempting to sing a hymn, and more than one of the men very obviously drunk. But they were sufficiently alert to notice the newcomer, and swarmed forward, staggering as the ship rose and fell, tumbling to their hands and knees as they surrounded him in the doorway.

'What's happening up there, mister?'

'Say, mister, we drowning?'

'We going to die, mister? Tell me, please. We going to die?'

'How much longer, mister?'

'I can't stand it, mister.'

'It's me wife, mister. She's proper poorly.'

'Not much longer,' Robert bellowed. 'We'll soon be through. Everything's fine up top. There's no danger. Everything's fine. I just came down here to make sure everybody's okay. Captain's orders.'

They subsided, staring at him, at least partly reassured, and he could begin to walk amongst them, asking a question here, rubbing a youthful head there, searching, always searching. But she was not in this crowd, and he made his way along the narrow corridors between the tiny cabins, heart thumping as he was sent lurching from bulkhead to bulkhead. He had escorted her back down to the well-deck, and let her in the door down to this floating hell, was it only twenty-four hours ago? And then had gone to bed, but hardly to sleep. Excited fear over the coming storm had been overlaid with a remarkable excitement over the girl herself. It was an absurdity, of course, he had told himself. She was an Irish immigrant, fleeing the poverty and injustice of her homeland in search of a better life in the United States, while he was the son of Captain Edward Anderson, the conqueror of the Atlantic. Any sort of union between them would be unthinkable. But why? Had his great-grandfather not been an immigrant himself? Had his very famous father not once been a ferry-minder?

She was neither beautiful nor elegant. She was just a girl who excited him as no human being had ever done before. And with whom he was again sharing the worst the sea had to offer.

He opened door after door, careless of manners, looking in at huddled families, who stared at him with blank terror in their eyes, but did not seem to mind the intrusion. And then came upon the four girls, all in one bunk, holding on to each other.

Kathleen, who had her arms around all of them, it seemed, looked up in surprise. 'Why, mister,' she said. 'Don't tell me we're going to die?'

Robert sat beside her, put his arm around her waist. Almost instinctively her head of red hair came to rest on his shoulder. 'No,' he said. 'No, Kathleen. We're not going to die. We're going to live, you and me. For ever and ever.'

Edward became aware that he could see, an endless vista of white spume streaked sea, of hills and valleys, starting to gleam in the first rays of the sun. It was only with the dawn that he realised the electrical storm had ended some time before and he had been steering into darkness for the past hour.

Just as it was only with the dawn that the night began to take shape in his mind. He remembered the huge, foam-crested waves, the stomach-churning troughs, the terrifying rolls, just as he remembered entering the eye of the storm, when the wind had suddenly dropped to nothing, and it had even been possible to see the stars immediately above the ship, while the seas had remained as mountainous as ever, with the added danger of now being confused rather than regular, of seeming to boil about the vessel instead of coming in over the starboard bow in a series of battering rams. Then the wind had started again, perhaps even stronger than before. But now it had been behind them, and although holding the ship and keeping her before the waves had been even more difficult, they had known that instead of closing the storm they were at last steaming away from it. They were through, and their survival, and their triumph, was now certain.

At some time during those final, tumultuous hours Martin had come to help him on the helm, just as at some time Hardisty had collapsed from exhaustion, and his place been taken by Parkinson. And now that the dawn had come, and he could see that the ocean if still running high, was no longer dangerous, Edward became aware of his own total exhaustion. Great rivers of pain seemed to run from his hands up his arms into his shoulders, and then all the way down his back again and through his thighs into his legs. His brain was a banging drum of agony, and his eyes seemed to have screwed themselves into permanent pinpoints of tortured vision with the hours of attempting to peer into the darkness.

But for all the physical pain, his heart and his mind were singing. The *Penelope Anderson* had proved herself. The North Atlantic Ocean was her servant, and not her master.

'You look done in, Captain,' Parkinson said.

'I wouldn't say no to a cup of coffee,' Edward said. 'Take the helm, coxswain. Steady as she goes.' He opened the engine room voice tube. 'How are things down there, Mr Smith?'

'Hot, Captain. But under control.'

'Very good, Mr Smith. My thanks for a grand job. Assume full cruising revolutions, and stand down your emergency watch.'

'We're through the storm, Captain?' Smith sounded as if he didn't really wish to believe it.

'We're through the storm, Mr Smith,' Edward said. 'Your watch, Mr Parkinson.'

He went down the ladder, slowly and painfully. The stewards, still busy cleaning up, stared at him. He walked past the bar, gazed at Charles Austin.

'By God,' Austin said. 'You did it.'

Edward shook his head. 'The ship did it, Charles. The ship.'

He went into his stateroom. His knees buckled as he closed the door, and Penelope had to catch him and lay him on the bed alongside the now wideawake children. Their questions flowed around his head though he didn't actually hear any of them. He was aware that a steward had brought in coffee and breakfast, but he was too exhausted to eat and fell asleep while Penelope was actually holding the coffee cup to his lips. Hardly had he seemed to have closed his eyes when he became aware that there was a whispered conference going on in the cabin.

He sat up, suddenly anxious. 'Robert!' he said. 'Robert went down at midnight, to check the steerage. He never came back.'

'He's here now,' Penelope said, and Edward gazed at his somewhat dishevelled son.

'Is all well down there?' Edward asked.

'All is well, Father,' Robert said.

Edward realised that Hardisty and Austin were also in the cabin.

'Is something wrong?' he asked.

'Not to us, sir,' Hardisty said. 'But we've sighted rockets, and they appear to be coming from a steamship in distress. She's dismasted and listing. I think she's the *Spartan*, sir.'

575

Edward forced his exhausted limbs once more to move, climbed to the bridge, accompanied now by Penelope and Robert, stared at the stricken vessel. The *Spartan* had lost both her forward masts, and a good deal of her rail, together, he estimated, with all of her boats. No smoke issued from her funnel, and she listed at about fifteen degrees, he thought. Her decks were crowded with exhausted and frightened people, waving at them, shouting and cheering as they saw help at hand.

'Close her, coxswain,' Edward said, and picked up a speaking trumpet before going on deck.

'What are you going to do?' Sir Charles asked him.

'Offer her assistance.'

'We cannot possibly take all her people on board.'

'I suppose we could, if she foundered,' Edward said. 'But I don't think she's about to do that.'

'You mean to offer her a tow?'

They looked at each other. There was no hope of a five day crossing, towing another ship.

'We must,' Edward said. He stood at the rail as they approached the other ship, could now see the officers on the bridge wing, watching them. 'Do you require assistance?' he bellowed.

'No,' Henry Driscoll shouted back.

'Yes,' shouted the captain of the ship.

'Yes,' shouted the passengers with one voice. Edward and Penelope, and Austin, watched an altercation taking place between the men on the bridge.

'You'll prepare to receive a line, Captain Hardisty,' Edward said, quietly. He levelled his glasses, watched Driscoll leave the bridge, shoulders bowed.

'Will you take our line?' shouted the captain of the *Spartan*.

'We will approach your lee,' Edward shouted. 'Stand by.'

He went inside, took the helm himself, manoeuvred the *Penelope Anderson* downwind of the *Spartan*, brought her as close as he dared, so close he could see the now terrified faces of the passengers, and could hear their cries of alarm, as well, as it seemed certain that the two ships must touch and hole each other as they rolled in the swell left by the storm. He could also hear the calls of his own people, amongst them the bull-like bellows of Jay Smart. But the light throwing line, made up with a monkey's fist in its end, a large ball of knotted cord with a lead weight in the centre to give the thrower additional impetus and accuracy, had come whistling over to be seized and secured by the eager sailors in the stern of the *Penelope Anderson*. The line was brought in, and then the huge hawser to which it was attached was slowly dragged across, dipping into the sea, but being steadily winched up until it could be made fast to the mooring bollards.

As soon as he saw the throwing line secured, Edward was able to increase revolutions and move away into safety. Then it was a matter of slowly taking up the strain before steaming ahead into the still big seas, the *Spartan* plunging behind her, the hawser slackening and then tightening again with snaps which seemed certain to part the rope but always holding, as Edward nursed the two ships forward.

'What do you think happened to her?' Penelope asked.

'She must have been knocked down, at least once,' Edward said. 'To be so badly dismasted. I reckon they left sail on her just a few minutes too long. And then when she went over her coal must have shifted in her bunkers. That's why she's listing.'

'Will you be able to take her in?'

'I don't see why not. Providing she's not actually making water now. And providing we don't hit another hurricane.' He grinned at her. 'At least we'll be first across the line.'

'But she'll still hold the blue riband.'

Edward gave her a hug. 'We've proved we have the finest and safest as well as the fastest ship on the sea. That's what we set out to do. Nothing more than that.'

The sun was high in the sky on the morning of Tuesday, October twenty-first, 1870, when

578

the *Penelope Anderson* steamed past the Ambrose Lighthouse. For the last thirty-six hours of her journey the seas had calmed right down, and she had been able to increase speed considerably, but her engines had been dragging nearly twice the weight for which they had been designed, and there could be no denying the fact that she was nearly twelve hours behind her original schedule.

Yet she was a happy ship. Her passengers no less than her crew had a sense of achievement, not only in beating the weather, but in bringing the *Spartan* safely home behind them, after forty-eight exhausting hours. And by the time they had taken on the pilots, word had been spread by fast sloops, and steam tugs were racing out of New York Harbour to take over the tow, and allow the *Penelope Anderson* to slip quietly towards her berth on the East River. Quietly, until she was close to the dock, when the entire morning, by now well-advanced, burst into sound. There were three brass bands, and nearly all of New York, it seemed, waiting to welcome them with flags flying and shouted cheers of congratulation.

Edward, almost too tired to speak, leaned on the rail, Penelope at his side, and waved to the throng below. Hardisty stood beside them.

'Well, Captain Hardisty,' Edward said. 'Take command of your ship.'

'Never my ship, Captain Anderson,' Hardisty said. 'Never my ship. I hold her in trust for

579

you, sir. And I am proud to have sailed with you.' He turned to Austin. 'You may tear up that letter, Sir Charles. I should like to add to my last entry in the Log that my officers and myself, as well as the crew of this ship, voluntarily accepted the command of Captain Anderson, and would do so again.'

'Letter?' Austin asked. 'What letter?'

Hardisty stared at him, and then looked at Edward. But he too was open-mouthed.

'You mean you did *not* have the authority of your board?' he asked.

'I would never have dared even mention the idea to them,' Austin said. 'That crowd of stuffed shirts? They'd have voted me off, I shouldn't wonder.'

Hardisty and Edward looked at each other again, and then burst out laughing together. 'Well, then, Charles,' Edward said. 'It is you must take the real credit for the success of the crossing.'

'Begging your pardon, sir,' said First Officer Parkinson. 'But the Mayor is here.'

They faced the Mayor of New York, top hat shining to match the beam on his face, gazed at the huge blue ribbon with the crest which he carried in front of him as he advanced on them. 'My congratulations. From what I've been hearing from your passengers, you've made the crossing of the century. You boys ready?' He looked over his shoulder at the crowd of reporters who had followed him up the ladder, three of them even armed with cameras, which they were hastily erecting on the deck.

'I beg your pardon, sir,' Austin said. 'We are very appreciative of your gesture, but we have broken no record, surely?'

'Ain't you?' asked the Mayor. 'Say, which one of you is the American?'

'I am,' Edward said.

'Well, sir, Captain Anderson, is it true you designed this ship?'

'It is,' Edward said.

'Then it's to you, as an American, I am presenting this riband, even if you are flying the British flag. Catch this one, boys.' He held the ribbon up, then draped it over Edward's head, while the flash bulbs exploded and the air became clouded with smoke.

'But...didn't you hear Sir Charles?' Edward asked. 'We're nearly twelve hours behind our scheduled arrival.'

'Sure you are, Captain Anderson,' said the Mayor. 'But the schedule you advertised was going to break the record by twelve hours anyway.'

'By God,' Austin said. 'I'd forgotten that.'

'You passed the Ambrose Light at five minutes past eight this morning,' the Mayor explained. 'That is six days and eight hours and five minutes after you dropped your mooring in Cork Harbour, as I understand it. The previous record, held by the ship you towed

581

in, the *Spartan*, was six days, twelve hours and fifteen minutes. Now, sir, Captain Anderson, you may have aimed at making the trip in six days. And you may still do that, one day. But you sure have broken the record at this moment in time. And I want you to know that we're all right proud of you.' He looked up at the ensign. 'If you'd take that red duster down now and hoist up the Stars and Stripes, we'd be even prouder.'

The noise, the cheers, the congratulations, flowed around Edward's head. Dimly he was aware of the hundreds of people who wanted to shake his hand, the women who wanted to kiss him. Even Florence Smart, it seemed, was trying to kiss him.

And then he realised he was facing a man wearing a master's uniform, like himself, also holding out his hand, his face a strange mixture of sadness and pleasure.

'John Holt, Captain Anderson, of the *Spartan*. I have not had the opportunity to thank you, sir, for saving my ship.'

'You would have done the same for us, sir,' Edward said.

'None the less, it was a gallant thing with so much at stake.' His mouth twisted. 'We'd not have been in that mess, but for the riband. I wished to heave to, but Mr Driscoll insisted on standing on. It's what Anderson will do, he kept saying. Ah, well…I'll support your claim for salvage against the owners, you may be sure of that. And I'm happy to congratulate you on taking the riband. It's yours for the rest of the century, I'd guess.'

'I doubt that,' Edward said. 'Driscoll will be building. He hates my guts too much to let me get away with licking him. And then rescuing him into the bargain.'

'I doubt Mr Driscoll hates your guts any longer, Captain Anderson,' Holt said, quietly.

'Then why isn't he man enough to come over here himself?' Edward asked. And felt Penelope's fingers closing on his arm. She had a woman's instincts.

'Because, sir, Mr Driscoll blew out his brains in his cabin at four o'clock this morning,' Holt said. 'The very moment we reported sighting the Ambrose Light. Good day to you, sir.'

He walked away, and, the crowd having receded, they were alone. To look at each other.

'He couldn't accept defeat,' Priscilla Meigs said. 'Oh, my God. Poor Henry.' She held the childrens' hands, led them away. Jimmy was twelve, Yvonne eleven. It was six years since they had last lived with their father, and perhaps they had always known that he felt little affection for them.

But he had been their father.

Edward had nothing to say. When had their rivalry started? The day the young soldier had returned from the war, and chosen to cross by the chain ferry? Or even before that, the day

583

he had elected to drive the *Regina* through that first hurricane? Certainly they had hated, from time to time. He had, anyway, when he thought of the years in a Nicaraguan prison. But he had overcome his hate. Henry had never learned to do that.

And now...he realised that Penelope was staring at him.

'Will you marry me, Penelope?' he asked.

'Just as soon as we can, Edward,' she answered.

'Say, lookee here,' bellowed Jay Christopher Smart, throwing his arms round both of their shoulders together. 'I've been thinking, and talking. And listening. I never reckoned this here blue riband was more than a gimmick. But I guess it's an important honour, eh? And it seems to me that it's all wrong, it's downright *un*patriotic, that it should be held by a British ship, when that ship was designed by an American. Sir, I cannot stand for that. I will not stand for it.'

'You'll have to take it up with Congress, Mr Smart,' Edward said.

'The hell with Congress. They don't like me, anyway. There's hotheads up in Washington say I'm a Monopolist. Well, hell, I guess I *am* a Monopolist. How the hell else could I have got my railroads built? And what does Congress have to do with it, anyway? They don't build ships.'

'But they pass the laws which say that an

American registered ship must be built by an American yard,' Edward said. 'And there is no American yard will accept my work.'

'Is that a fact. Well, I'll tell you, Anderson: how's about we buy one?'

'Eh?'

'Say, you do intend to build a faster ship than this one?' Smart demanded.

'Well...in time, I suppose.' Edward glanced at Austin.

'Mr Smart has made us an interesting proposition,' Austin said. 'That we form a new company, and go shares on two new ships. One to be built here in America, and one in England.'

'Only the one built here will be half-a-knot faster,' Smart said. 'That's going to be written into the Agreement. I have to get ashore now, Anderson. There's that board meeting waiting for me. Besides, Flo's feeling seasick now this ship has stopped heaving. But you join me at the Astoria Hotel for dinner tonight. Bring Sir Austin with you. And we'll chew this thing out. Like hell we'll chew it out. I want the keel of our ship laid by the end of the month. Oh, bring your lady as well,' he added magnanimously, and made for the ladder.

'Can we really do business with a man like that?' Edward asked.

'I don't see any reason why not,' Austin said. 'He has the financial backing. And the enthusiasm.'

'He'll build your ships for you, Edward,' Penelope said. 'We don't have to dine with him *every* night.'

He'd have his very own shipyard. And his very own ships. The fleet of fast steamers of which he had dreamed for so many years. It was unbelievable. It would make all the bitter years worthwhile. Almost. And it opened up the most fantastic future for Robert.

'Robert,' he said. 'Where is he?'

The boy had taken no part in any of the celebrations.

'I haven't seen him since just before we docked,' Penelope said.

'Look at the quay,' Austin suggested.

The steerage passengers were being allowed to land, and were streaming ashore, carrying their boxes and bundles, looking around themselves in wonderment at the city of which *they* had dreamed for so long. Robert, with his well-cut suit and his vast height was easily discernible in their midst, walking with his arm round the waist of an equally tall, redheaded girl. And as they walked, they talked, and smiled at each other.